# A PASSION

# SO DEADLY

Hilary Bonner is a former showbusiness editor of the *Mail on Sunday* and the *Daily Mirror*. She now lives in Somerset, and continues to work as a freelance journalist, covering film, television and theatre.

*Also by Hilary Bonner*

The Cruelty of Morning
A Fancy to Kill For
For Death Comes Softly
A Deep Deceit

# HILARY BONNER

# A PASSION
# SO DEADLY

ARROW

First published in the United Kingdom in 1998 by
Arrow Books

1 3 5 7 9 10 8 6 4 2

First published in the United Kingdom in 1998 by William Heinemann

Arrow Books
The Random House Group Ltd
20 Vauxhall Bridge Road, London SW1V 2SA

Random House Australia (Pty) Limited
20 Alfred Street, Milsons Point, Sydney,
New South Wales 2061, Australia

Random House New Zealand Limited
18 Poland Road, Glenfield
Auckland 10, New Zealand

Random House (Pty) Limited
Endulini, 5a Jubilee Road, Parktown 2193, South Africa

The Random House Group Limited Reg. No. 954009

www.randomhouse.co.uk

A CIP catalogue record for this book is available
from the British Library

Papers used by Random House are natural, recyclable
products made from wood grown in sustainable forests. The
manufacturing processes conform to the environmental regulations of
the country of origin

Typeset by SX Composing DTP, Rayleigh, Essex
Printed and bound in Great Britain by
Cox & Wyman Ltd, Reading, Berkshire

ISBN 0 09 943514 4

For Tony Peake

With special thanks to Detective Superintendent Steve Livings and Detective Sergeant Frank Waghorn of the Avon and Somerset Constabulary and to Home Office Pathologist Dr Hugh White.

# One

There was nothing unusual about the tall elegant woman who parked her car with neat efficiency, reversing it at the first attempt precisely into her chosen slot in the quiet avenue alongside the school playing field.

She emerged with athletic ease, swinging first one long shapely leg and then the other out through the driver's door, and reaching at the same time for the large leather briefcase on the back seat.

It was late afternoon on a pleasantly warm August day – the weather a welcome break in the unseasonably wet and unpleasant conditions which had plagued the Southwest of England throughout most of the month. The sun still shone bright in the sky but was casting deep shadows from the sycamore trees which lined either side of the road like giant leafy sentries. A distant view of Bristol's famous Clifton Suspension Bridge, glowing orange, could just be glimpsed in a gap between the buildings and their surrounds of heavy foliage high above the city centre. In the playing field a noisy pre-season schoolboy football match was in progress.

The woman locked her car, carefully checking that each door and the boot were all secure. She glanced around her with similar care, as if making sure there was nothing that might be disturbing to her in her surroundings, before setting off at a brisk walk.

Clifton, stretching up to the Downs on the Northwest side of Bristol, was built in the late eighteenth and nineteenth centuries to provide homes for the city's wealthy merchants and seafarers, well away from what was then a dirty bawdy port below. It remains an exclusive area, and the tall elegant woman, stepping out before a backdrop of grandly imposing dwellings left over from another age, looked as if she belonged there absolutely.

She was wearing an unmistakably expensive cream linen jacket over a black silk shirt and tailored cream trousers. Her high-heeled black suede boots clicked rhythmically as she walked, each foot hitting the concrete slabs of the pavement with a purposeful tread.

Suddenly there was a yell from the playing field and a football, spinning out of control over the high wirenetting fence, landed right in front of her, almost causing her to trip. The woman looked down, momentarily startled, and then across at the teenage footballers, several of whom were running towards the fence.

She put the briefcase she was carrying on the ground, took three steps backwards, loped easily forwards and struck the ball precisely with the toe of her left foot so that it lifted and soared over the fence back on to the pitch. Her action was rewarded by a spontaneous outbreak of applause and several wolf whistles.

The woman, one of the kind who was probably even more attractive in early middle age than she had been in her younger days, treated her teenage admirers to a broad smile and continued on her way.

She was still smiling as she strode through the gateway of the Crescent Hotel, a small but not unattractive establishment set in its own pleasant and secluded gardens. She entered the main building, one of the Victorian villas so typical of Clifton, and approached reception. Standing there holding her briefcase, make-up discreet but immaculate, glossy blonde hair beautifully cut and shaped, her smile radiating confidence and self-assurance, she looked every inch a businesswoman of the nineties.

The receptionist greeted her by name, welcoming, respectful.

'Your usual room is ready, Mrs Pattinson.'

The woman merely nodded in response, a regular guest being treated just as she would expect.

'I shall be leaving very early in the morning, Janet, so I'd like to pay in advance as usual.'

Janet, an eighteen-year-old Bristolian still young and coltish enough to feel awkward in the presence of such self-assured elegance, produced a pre-prepared bill at once. And she showed no surprise when she was offered cash, rare in the hotel trade, in full payment.

Mrs Pattinson put her receipt in her jacket pocket, thanked Janet profusely for her efficiency – causing the girl's rather overly plump cheeks to flush slightly – and walked out again into the garden.

Several of the rooms at the Crescent took the form of individual chalets surrounded by shrubs, trees and bushes which served the double purpose of providing privacy for those within and also camouflage for those without. In stark contrast to the stylish grandeur of the main building, these rooms were nonentities – small neat cream-painted boxes, each identical to the other, with imitation oak front doors and double-glazed plastic-framed windows. They were, however,

3

clean and comfortable. And although the lay-out could be confusing to a first-time visitor, Mrs Pattinson strode through the grounds towards chalet ten with the purposeful certainty of someone who knew exactly where she was going and was rather looking forward to getting there.

Within the privacy of the room – painted cream inside as well as out, unimaginatively furnished, totally characterless, quite anonymous – she tore the receipt into little pieces which she dropped into the wastepaper basket. Then she lay her briefcase on the chintz-covered double divan bed, unlocked it and opened it. The case somehow looked as if it should carry business papers, but there did not appear to be any. Instead Mrs Pattinson removed a large carrier bag from Bristol's John Lewis department store which contained a dark brown woven-silk designer suit. She had been shopping, and like most women who have just bought something new, gave the impression that she could not wait to try on her purchases. Swiftly she took off her jacket and trousers and tried on the suit, posing in front of the mirror which ran the full length of the wall next to the wardrobe. The suit flattered her figure and complemented her glossy blonde hair, and Mrs Pattinson looked as if she were well aware of that. There could be little doubt that she was a woman of both taste and means.

Eventually she took off the suit, delved once more into the briefcase and this time removed a much smaller plain paper bag, a package conspicuously lacking any indication of its place of origin. Mrs Pattinson stroked the bag with one hand, lightly, almost caressing it, her face suddenly a picture of anticipation. As if dragging herself away from some unexplained pleasure, she wandered into the adjoining bathroom and ran a bath, pouring in a generous slug of sweetly scented oil. As she lowered herself into the warm suds everything about her seemed sensuous, and her obvious enjoyment of the bath was even accompanied by small murmurs of pleasure.

After a lengthy soak she wrapped herself in a big bath towel and turned her attention to the plain paper bag, emptying its contents on to the bed. Out spilled a selection of exotic underwear of the kind most usually associated with Soho sex shops. Smiling to herself, Mrs Pattinson picked up a bright red lace G-string and rubbed it against her face. There was also a skimpy red suspender belt and fine black stockings with seams.

She discarded the towel and, in a series of slow and sensual movements, rubbed moisturising cream into her body before putting on the skimpy garments. There was also a matching lace brassiere which uplifted her already ample breasts. Her nipples, which were firmly erected, protruded through strategically positioned holes in the flimsy material. Mrs Pattinson played with her own breasts for a few seconds – glancing approvingly at her reflection in the wardrobe mirror – before covering herself this time with the towelling bath robe provided by the hotel. She seemed quite relaxed, almost peaceful – yet expectant.

From the briefcase she also took a bottle of whisky and three paper cups which she set on the dressing table. She poured herself a small measure, adding water from the bathroom tap. Then she removed the final package, two tall black candles, which, in a manner suggesting the ease of regular habit, she inserted carefully into the necks of the pair of small Chinese vases standing on the tables set on either side of the big bed. She lit the candles, fussed for a moment over their exact position, drew the heavy dark curtains across the window, and sat down to wait.

Her hands were clasped lightly in her lap. Her eyes were closed. An indecipherable smile danced on her lips.

After just a few minutes there was a knock on the door, which she answered at once.

Two rather good-looking young men stood on her doorstep. She looked them up and down, rather in the manner a farmer might appraise his livestock.

She seemed to know only the shorter one – a well-made young West Indian wearing tight black jeans, a bright white T-shirt, and a leather jacket – addressing him as Charlie.

'Good to see you again,' she said. Her voice was softer than before, almost husky. Her eyes, strikingly deep green, were very bright.

She reached out and touched Charlie's cheek fleetingly. He pushed her gently back into the room, gesturing to his companion to shut the door behind them, took hold of her by both shoulders and kissed her briefly but firmly full on the lips.

She drew apart from him, running her tongue over her teeth as she did so.

'This is Bob,' said Charlie.

Mrs Pattinson turned to the second young man. He was tall and blond-haired, with curls which framed a full-featured face, making him look vaguely cherubic.

'OK,' said Mrs Pattinson. 'Let's see what you're made of, Bob, shall we?'

She did not sit down, choosing instead to lean against the wardrobe.

Bob looked uncertainly towards Charlie. 'Well get on with it mate, get your kit off,' ordered Charlie.

Bob looked as if he were about to say something, but didn't. Instead he silently complied, removing his cotton bomber jacket first and then his shirt. He had a fine body. Mrs Pattinson gave a small appreciative gasp, but said nothing.

Instead she waited patiently.

'Get on with it, Bob,' said Charlie again.

Just a little self-consciously Bob peeled off his trousers and paused only briefly before, with an almost imperceptible shrug of his shoulders, also removing his underpants. Without warning Mrs Pattinson stepped forwards, reached out, and put a hand briefly on his crotch. Bob did not yet have an erection but the contact seemed to exert a certain knee-jerk reaction. Mrs Pattinson smiled. It did not seem that Bob would need much encouragement to perform.

'Not bad, Charlie,' she said, lifting her whisky glass in his direction. 'Would you like to join me in a drink?'

She gestured to the whisky bottle and began to walk across the room towards it. Charlie moved swiftly behind her and, without warning, pulled the bathrobe apart and off. She stood in the silly underwear, still with her back to him. She was visibly trembling. In seconds his hands were everywhere. Then he pushed her, not so gently this time, face down on to the bed, holding her there with one hand while he casually undid the zip of his jeans with the other.

Mrs Pattinson's breath was coming in short sharp gasps. Charlie pushed her stockinged legs carelessly apart.

Bob watched closely, as if entranced, anticipating perhaps whatever part he was to play. The atmosphere in the room was heavy with excitement.

# Two

Freddie Lange roared the big four-wheel drive into the farmyard, tyres squealing on wet cobbles. As he skidded to a halt he began to shout so loudly and in such a state of panic that his voice came out in a kind of squeak.

'Constance, Constance!' His voice strengthened somewhat as he steadied his breath, forcing the power from his lungs. 'It's Harley Phillips, he's under the tractor. His arm . . . he's losing blood . . . Constance . . .'

Freddie was close to hysteria. The words tumbled out. Inarticulate in his haste and distress, he began to run towards the big old farmhouse. He was a tall handsome man, complexion tanned and made ruddy by years of outdoor work, his abundant shock of longish hair – yellow fading into silver-grey – plastered to his skull by the rain which had been falling steadily all morning. It was a particularly dreadful day for the end of August and Freddie had already had a good soaking. His physical discomfort – he had not expected to be exposed to the elements, he'd forgotten his cap and was wearing just a tweed jacket, now sodden, over equally wet overalls – was quite possibly increasing his panic.

The kitchen door opened just as he reached the back steps.

There stood Constance, a handsome woman in her

9

forties, short bouncy dark hair framing a well-boned intelligent face. Her pale hazel eyes were calm and kind. The very sight of her was soothing to Freddie. She must have heard him from inside the house. Already she had in her hand the emergency medical kit which she kept in the kitchen cupboard and on her feet a pair of sturdy boots. She took her Barbour jacket from the hook by the door, slung it over her shoulders, and then placed her free hand firmly on her husband's arm.

Her skin was almost ageless in appearance, creamy in texture and remarkably unlined, her mouth a full, strong line.

'It's all right, Freddie,' she said. Her voice was well-modulated and calm as her eyes. She spoke English with the perfectly enunciated care usually applied only by those who have had to learn it as a second language. 'Just take me there.'

'Right.'

Freddie wiped his face with one hand, brushing away a mixture of rainwater and sweat. He found he was breathing more easily already and realised as he spoke that much of the panic had gone from his voice.

Nonetheless he ran to the vehicle, a Land Rover, fumbling with the door catch in his haste to be behind the wheel again. His wife merely walked purposefully, ignoring the rain, and yet she somehow managed to be installed in the passenger seat before he had hoisted himself into the car.

This time she lay a hand on his knee.

'Don't drive like a maniac. We won't help Harley if we end up in a ditch.'

He nodded, struggling for control. He grated the gears trying to find reverse but ultimately managed to manoeuvre his way out of the yard with a little more aplomb than the manner in which he had entered it.

'Now talk to me,' Constance instructed when they were safely on their way. 'First, someone has called for an ambulance, I hope?'

Freddie nodded again. He was peering anxiously ahead, windscreen wipers on full speed to give him the best possible vision in appalling conditions. 'Bill did it on my mobile, but they could take ages, you know what they're like . . .'

Constant interrupted him. He knew he was starting to babble again. 'Don't worry about that,' she said. 'Just tell me what happened and what condition Harley is in. The more I know before I get there, the better prepared I'll be.'

She could hear the boy's screams from inside the Land Rover as Freddie roared it across Brook Meadow. The scene ahead was not a pretty one.

Young Harley's tractor had somehow tipped itself off the edge of the steeply angled expanse of land which he had been ploughing, its weight carrying it through the bushes and scrubland lining the edge of a steep drop leading down to the little stream at the bottom. The tractor had left a deep furrow in the red earth and already a stream of water was pouring down it.

Constance knew Harley well, and his family had worked for the Langes for generations. The lad was a good worker but inclined to be reckless. She guessed he would have been driving the tractor as fast as possible. This was not his first accident on the farm, but it looked like it might be his worst to date. The tractor had rolled down the steep-sided ditch and eventually come to a precarious upside-down halt, trapping Harley beneath it. The machine was fitted with a safety cage, but, as Constance knew well, these were worse than useless unless the workers wore their safety harnesses – and she doubted that any of them did.

Harley had been thrown out of the tractor but his left arm had somehow become caught in the tangled metal and was trapped beneath the six-ton machine. His problems were not helped by the awkward spot in which he and his tractor had ultimately landed. Most worryingly of all, the tractor looked as if it could fall further on top of Harley, causing him even greater injury. And the weather conditions naturally made matters worse. Two other Chalmpton farmworkers were already trying to free the injured young man. One of them, Harley's father, Norton, whose obvious distress and blind panic were not helping the situation, was attempting to tow off the wreckage and free Harley, while herdsman Bill Macintyre frantically pulled and pushed at bits of twisted machinery with his bare hands.

Constance jumped quickly out of the Land Rover and summed up the scene at once. Harley's arm looked as if it had been nearly severed just above the elbow and the buckled tractor crushing it was, in fact, also probably holding the artery together. Every time the tractor moved, a fraction the blood from the terrible injury gushed out and young Harley's screams of agony grew more frantic. If Norton Phillips actually succeeded in towing off the crashed machine it looked likely his son would bleed to death.

'Stop!' commanded Constance.

The engine of the second tractor was howling, its wheels cutting great muddy gouges in the soft earth,

Harley's screams of pain were ear-piercing, his father and Bill Macintyre were shouting misguided instructions at each other, the engine of the Land Rover was still running. The combined noise was deafening. Yet, although Constance barely raised her voice, the response was immediate.

Norton Phillips at once ceased his rescue attempt, and pushed the tractor gear shift into neutral. Bill Macintyre, who had been crouched alongside Harley, stood up and faced Constance, quiet now, waiting for further instructions. Freddie switched off the Land Rover engine. Even Harley's frenzied screams subsided into muffled sobs.

The attention of all four men was now focused on Constance. There was no longer any question about who was in charge. Even poor injured Harley was calmer. Part of this effect, which Constance knew very well she so often seemed to have on people although she could not explain how or why, might have been due to her early training as a nurse. But it was more than that. There was something within Constance which set her aside from others on occasions like this. In a crisis, almost any crisis, there could be few people in the world better to have on your side than Constance Lange.

She moved forward carefully towards the edge of the deep ditch, taking into account every aspect of the situation. Harley remained in danger of further injury if the tractor remained where it was. But if it was pulled away the result could be just as disastrous for him.

'Lock on the brakes, Norton, make sure that tractor is not going to move one centimetre and then cut the engine,' Constance instructed.

13

She slithered down the slope towards Harley. Naturally agile, she made it look easy, and she crouched beside him, ignoring the six tons of finely balanced machinery looming above.

'You know, young Harley, sometimes I don't think you should be let out at all,' she said. And the gentle smile and the warmth in her voice belied the possible harshness of her words.

Almost casually she lay her hands on Harley's forehead, soothing him and at the same time ascertaining to her relief that the blood on his face, at least, came only from superficial scratches.

She began to open her medical bag. She had the makings of a tourniquet, a bandage and a metal ruler, which she had always carried since having to improvise desperately when called to the scene of a similar injury some years earlier. The very idea of deliberately cutting off someone's blood supply thoroughly frightened her actually – although she would never show it. But during the brief journey in the Land Rover her husband's frantic description of the accident had left her in little doubt of what would be required.

Her steady gaze never left Harley's face. The boy's bulging blue eyes, racked with pain and fear, cleared, just slightly. He even stopped sobbing.

'I'm sorry, Mrs Lange,' he said. An automatic response.

'So you jolly well should be – that's a tractor, not a scrambling bike you've got there.'

'It's a lot bleddy 'eavier too,' muttered Harley through clenched teeth. Seconds ago, although conscious throughout his dreadful ordeal, he had been incapable of coherent speech. Now he was almost making a joke.

'You've always been a brave lad, Harley,' said Constance. 'Daft as a brush, but brave.'

She glanced at the sky. Thankfully the rain seemed to be easing but Harley was already wet through and lying in an unpleasant bed of wet mud. The tractor creaked and shifted slightly of its own accord. Harley winced, but made no sound.

Constance turned to her husband, at her side in close attendance as usual.

'When I say twist, twist,' she ordered.

The tourniquet was already in place around the top of Harley's arm. All the time Constance had been indulging in apparent light banter with the boy, her hands had been busily at work.

When the job was completed she rocked back on her heels. 'I think we can get that tractor off you safely now Harley. It's going to hurt. Are you ready?'

Harley looked at her with wide trusting eyes. 'If you say so, Mrs Lange,' he replied.

'Right then,' said Constance. With one arm she cradled the young man's head, his mud-streaked ginger curls spread over her jacket sleeve, and with her free hand she took his uninjured one.

'Hang on to me,' she commanded, and glancing at her patient's father, 'Forward as smooth as you can, Norton.'

The wheels screeched again, sending great showers of wet mud flying across the field, spraying the rescuers. Eventually the tractor lurched forward, dragging the mangled wreckage off the injured boy's arm.

Constance knew that the pain must be terrible for Harley as his mangled hand and lower arm were freed and, even allowing for the tourniquet, the life flowed back into the partially numbed area. But this time, lying within the calming influence of her cradling arm, Harley did not even cry out. There were no more screams, but the boy gripped Constance's hand so tightly that his fingernails dug into her flesh. She did not flinch. She could see that his teeth were clenched and he had bitten the side of his lip. A trickle of fresh blood ran down his chin. His eyes spoke volumes.

'I've got you, Harley, the worst is over now,' she said softly.

Norton had parked the tractor again and was by her side, looking anxiously at his son.

'What do us do now, Missus? Shall us get 'ee up the bank?'

Constance shook her head. But she was aware that Harley was starting to shiver violently. The rain had slowed to just a light drizzle now, but the damp chill in the air remained. It was hard to believe it was still August. Harley, half-buried in the thick wet mud, was beginning to be severely affected both by shock and cold.

He was also now clutching his side with his uninjured hand and Constance suspected that he had broken ribs at the very least and, judging from the awkward angle in which he was lying, he could have a damaged back as well.

'We'd be best not to move him till the ambulance arrives,' she said. 'We don't want to risk any change of position that might cause him to lose more blood, and I'd like him properly checked out for any other injuries. We need to keep him as warm and dry as possible, though, so fetch me the rug from the back of the Land Rover.'

As she spoke she slipped out of her Barbour jacket

and wrapped it around Harley as best she could without further disturbing his broken body.

'I'll have your coats too, you guys,' she ordered. 'Just pile them on him.'

It was only fifteen minutes later when they heard the ambulance siren wailing in the distance on the road through the village, but it seemed for ever.

'I'll go to the lane gate,' said Freddie as, able to think properly again now, he climbed behind the wheel of the Land Rover. 'They'll never get an ambulance across a ploughed field in the state of this.'

Minutes later he was back with two paramedics – a tall young man, boyish-faced but prematurely balding, and his woman partner, small, slight, possibly even younger, but somehow clearly the senior – laden down with equipment.

'Jesus,' said the female paramedic peering down the precipice-sided ditch. 'How did you get yourself in this mess then, mate?'

'That's just what I've been asking him,' said Constance.

Harley managed a wan smile.

The paramedics were in control within minutes. They did not touch the tourniquet. Harley was quickly checked from head to toe before being given a powerful pain-killing injection, wrapped in warm life-restoring foil and carefully loaded on to a stretcher. Acting on instructions from the paramedics the farm workers and Freddie helped carry Harley on the stretcher up to the field and then load him into the back of the Land Rover.

'Who did the tourniquet?' asked the woman paramedic.

'She did,' said Freddie, glowing with pride as usual

17

and gesturing towards his wife who was standing quietly to one side now, gratefully wrapped in her Barbour jacket once more.

'Good job,' said the paramedic. 'He's got a lot to thank you for, that young man.'

Constance smiled but did not speak.

'He'll be all right, you can save his arm, can't you . . . can't you?' she heard Norton Phillips ask over and over again as he clambered into the Land Rover alongside his son.

There was no answer from the medical team.

Constance sighed. She was the practical one, the doer. She had attended so many emergencies locally. Always it was her they called for. And, although with the passage of time she considered herself to be no more than a competent first aider, her long-ago learned medical skills – she had been an SRN at Bristol Infirmary – were rarely allowed to go rusty for long. Nonetheless, when the moment of crisis was over she almost always experienced a kind of emptiness.

You could never do enough, she felt. Constance didn't believe in miracles. She certainly knew enough to appreciate the extent of the damage to Harley's arm - and it was his right arm too, unfortunately. The boy was a manual labourer, a farmworker, and never likely to be anything else. He needed that arm in full order.

The ambulance was belting off down the lane now, its siren wailing again. In the distance Constance heard her husband's voice.

'Come on, old girl. Let's go home and put the kettle on. You've done a wonderful job, again.'

Constance inclined her head, smiling just a little.

She was so used to holding everything together in an emergency, it was second nature to her. Perhaps it wasn't that strange that she was inclined to suffer a reaction when it was all over. She wanted to be on her own for a bit, to regain her strength. It was also second nature to Constance never to show signs of weakness.

'You know, I think I'll walk back, if you don't mind Freddie,' she said lightly. 'Stretch my legs. I could check that fence down by Marsh Wood where the cattle broke through yesterday, too.'

Freddie hesitated just a moment.

Constance glanced up at the sky. 'It's brightening up, I think we could have a lovely evening. The walk'll do me good . . .'

Freddie smiled at her. 'Of course,' he said finally. 'If that's what you want.'

'See you later then,' said Connie, already setting off at a good pace.

'Right.' Freddie hesitated again. 'And, thank you, love. I don't know what we'd do without you . . .'

She waved her acknowledgement over her shoulder. He was a good man. She was a lucky woman and she knew it.

Before her stretched all the splendour of Somerset. The beautiful English oak in the top corner of Brook Meadow spread its lushly foliaged arms wide over the rolling field. Beyond it was a huge American oak, the second biggest in England, so Constance believed, which barely changed colour at all in the autumn and was always the last deciduous tree to drop its leaves – sometimes not until the new year.

The English oak would turn golden-red early this year, she suspected. September was still almost a week away and yet the weather had felt autumnal for days. But this particular day, that had earlier offered only more of the heavy rain which had been drenching the countryside for so long, was in the process of transforming itself. The skies had lightened almost simultaneously with the moment young Harley had been made safe in the ambulance.

Constance skirted around the edge of the ploughed field, meadow in name only nowadays. All was quiet at last. She relished the silence and the solitude. At the bottom end of the ploughed meadow, she turned off left through the little hunting gate and on through the woodland which had been partially cleared and replanted with saplings the previous spring.

There were enough big trees left to make it dark already within the wood. But a weak late-afternoon sun was now shining wetly – she could just see its glint in dappled patches through the foliage.

She could have walked home from Brook Meadow in half an hour across country had she taken the most direct route through the woods, crossing the footbridge over Chalmpton Water and along the lane behind the school. Instead she had chosen to detour, on the pretext of checking the fence down by Marsh Wood. In spite of the damp chill still in the air and the shock of the afternoon's events, she was beginning, very slightly, to enjoy herself. Being alone in the country always did this to her. It was rejuvenation.

The cattle, one of the last remaining herds of pedigree Red Devon in the country, were grazing contentedly exactly where they should be. Constance spent longer than she needed counting their number, checking them out. Then she carefully inspected the hastily mended fence which would have to be properly rebuilt before winter set in, she reckoned.

There was a footpath that led from the site of the suspect fence alongside Chalmpton Water – little more than a stream but running swiftly now after the consistently heavy rainfall – through Marsh Wood, beneath Church Rise, and all the way back to Chalmpton Village Farm.

Constance liked this route, and set off almost eagerly along the path. At one point she noticed two flashes of brilliant blue over the water and stopped at once, peering through the bushes which partially masked the brook from her gaze. She had glimpsed, she knew, a pair of kingfishers in darting flight and the sight never failed to make her heart soar. She leaned against a tree trunk and remained there for several minutes, quite still, watching, almost trance-like.

Even after almost twenty-five years of marriage to a major landowner, Constance found it hard to believe that this beautiful place belonged to her and her husband. In fact they owned almost nine hundred acres of prime Somerset land. And unlike Freddie, who was the nearest thing Chalmpton Peverill had to a lord of the manor and whose family had farmed in the village for generations, Constance had not been born to the kind of world into which she had, however, so splendidly fitted. In fact, very far from it.

Constance had been brought up in children's homes and a string of foster homes. Her Irish mother, whom Constance could barely remember, died when she was a toddler. She knew of no father.

There were things she could remember that she would rather forget – like the foster mother who had strapped her daily into a pushchair and then ignored her, and much later, the male helper at the children's home who had tried to fondle her at every opportunity. She had borne any misuse silently and stoically, always remaining a bright, friendly, and hard-working child. And perhaps because of this, apart from a few unfortunate incidents, had been by and large treated as well as was possible within the framework in which she was brought up. There was never any bitterness about her. She blossomed into a pretty and intelligent teenager and seemed to rise easily above the hardships and loneliness of her early life.

Indeed Constance always appeared to want to help people. It seemed natural that upon leaving school she should train to be a nurse, helping to pay her way by working as a waitress in a local night-club – a lucrative and entertaining sideline she continued when possible even after qualifying. And Constance had never seemed to have any problem reconciling the two different sides to her life. In the hospital she was one person, in clubland another.

It was at the club that, at the age of twenty-one, she had met Freddie Lange, making, at a close friend's stag do, a rare excursion into any kind of night life.

Constance sighed at the memory, no longer watching for the vivid flash of the kingfishers, but instead rolling back the years inside her head until it felt as if she were once again in the smoky club, the music bluesy jazz, the clientele just blurs through the haze. Except Freddie. Freddie had turned to thank her politely when she had brought drinks to his table, and she had realised at once how out of place he was in this environment.

'Can I get you anything else?' she had asked,

uncomfortably aware that her voice might have sounded simpering.

He had looked into her eyes, deep and long, and made a remark that was quite out of character.

'You can't get me out of here, can you?' he had asked, then blushed crimson. It was only much later that she learned how unlike him it was to be so forward or so rash.

The heir to Chalmpton Village Farm was good-looking – his shaggy mane of then bright-blond hair framing a narrow sensitive face – charming, ten years her senior and extraordinarily innocent.

'Come this way,' she had said with complete disregard to the employment which had so far served her so well.

She led him without ceremony to the door and then walked with him several blocks to her little bedsit behind the cemetery. It had all seemed so natural. Looking back she could hardly believe it. They had talked until the early hours, drinking coffee, and he had told her, for no particular reason as far as she could recall, that he was still a virgin. She had been astonished, not so much because he remained so at his age, as because of the straightforward trusting way in which he had imparted the information. The thought had crossed her mind that he was a closet gay, but somehow she had known instinctively that was not it, either. She suspected instead that Freddie, who also confessed in the beginning how awkward and ill at ease he had always felt previously in the company of women, had been damn near asexual before her.

They did not go to bed together that night nor for several weeks to come, although they immediately

23

formed what seemed to her at least to be a very special relationship, with him driving to Bristol as frequently as he could after his day's work on the family farm. She had been careful not to push him. She allowed him to take the lead. And when they finally slept together for the first time, on a balmy late-spring night after she had cooked him supper and served it outside on the little terrace she shared with the occupant of the room next door who fortuitously was hardly ever there, he had had no idea that she was not a virgin too.

He had made love with a passion born of genuinely deep feelings rather than knowledge or experience and she had been deeply moved by him. Afterwards he had held her so tightly she had thought that he might crush her ribs but she gave no complaint, not wanting to do or say anything that might spoil the precious moment.

'You're an angel,' he told her again and again.

'Hardly,' she had replied. But she revealed very little about herself to him and he asked few questions. Certainly he never asked her about any other men there may have been.

Constance knew that in some ways her husband had seen in her in those days the woman he wanted her to be rather more than the woman she really had been. That was something that had never changed, but Constance hoped now that she had actually become the woman he had seen her to be. And she knew that, in most ways, she had.

Offered on a plate a life beyond her wildest dreams, she had somehow known instinctively how to behave and had become, to all appearances, she hoped, the perfect country wife.

Their marriage did seem to be blessed. Almost everything had gone right for them from the beginning. Three splendid children had been born just when desired and after remarkably trouble-free pregnancies. Elder daughter Charlotte was married, a mother herself now, and lived nearby in the village. Son William, destined to take over the farm one day, to continue the Lange tradition, was at agricultural college, and seventeen-year-old Helen, academically the brightest of the bunch, was at boarding-school studying for her A-levels and talking about becoming a doctor.

All three of their children, each of whom had inherited their father's blond hair and their mother's hazel eyes, had grown into fine young people, Constance reflected with some satisfaction. Naturally both she and Freddie were proud of their children. Their marriage and their family life was often envied, she knew, and was indeed just about as happy as it seemed. Constance made sure of that. It wasn't exactly hard work. She loved Freddie Lange and she knew that he loved her too.

She smiled to herself. The reverie into the past was over now. Today, after the experience with Harley, after coping with the strain and tension she had so effectively kept to herself, she had really needed the breathing space of her walk. She had felt exhausted, drained. Already she was revived, the solid soil of Somerset beneath her feet, the glowing sky surrounding her, the peace of the grazing cattle, the sound of the rushing water and the flash of the kingfishers had all combined to soothe her.

She continued on her journey, but it was somehow nearly an hour and a half – and almost 5.30 p.m. –

before she reached the farm, leaving the footpath which led on to the village to cross the paddock behind the farmhouse. From there she had a picture-book view of Chalmpton Peverill, the squat tower of its little Norman church rising above clustered cottages, many of them thatched, a row of council houses and a smattering of modern bungalows running in a straggly line off towards the main road. Unusually nowadays, Chalmpton still managed to retain not only a village pub but also its own shop and sub post office, outside which three women were gathered in animated conversation.

Constance smiled to herself. News travelled fast in a country village. She knew the women would be discussing Harley Phillips' tractor accident. As she drew closer she could see that one of them was Marcia Spry, queen of the local gossips, a small elderly woman with tightly permed iron-grey hair framing a pinched and equally tight-lipped face. Constance did not want to get involved. She turned smartly away to her left, before Marcia's laser-beam eyes locked in on her, and hurried into the garden of Chalmpton Village Farm through the gate in the far corner by the chicken coop.

The early evening sun, dropping now in the sky, bathed the old farmhouse in ochre light. It was actually an eighteenth-century Devon longhouse – there were several of them in this part of Somerset not far from the Devon border – with six bedrooms, three facing due west, three due east. The big square kitchen was on the east side, facing the sunrise, and the sitting room on the west, facing the sunset.

Her black Labrador, Josh, came tearing around the house from the back door and flung his not inconsiderable bulk at her legs. He rubbed against her, oozing affection but there was also reproach in his eyes as he looked up at her, as if well aware that she had been for a walk and not taken him with her. The ultimate betrayal.

Constance talked to the dog soothingly as she made her way around to the kitchen door. The Virginia creeper which covered most of that side of the house was already heralding autumn with its annual vibrant red-orange blaze, and every time her eyes fell upon it Constance never failed to appreciate its glory.

Inside it was quickly apparent that Freddie had abandoned the working day immediately after Harley had been taken to hospital. He was sitting at the kitchen table with his herdsman, Bill Macintyre. There was a teapot on the table and also a bottle of whisky. Freddie looked slightly flushed and the bottle was nearly empty. Constance didn't blame him for having had a good drink.

'Con, I was just beginning to worry about you,' he greeted her. 'Mac and I have been toasting young Harley's health. Will you join us?'

He waved the whisky bottle. Constance glanced at it – a litre bottle of a cheap supermarket brand.

'No fear,' she said. 'I don't know how you can drink that stuff.'

She reached into the kitchen cupboard which housed the family's alcohol supplies and found the remains of a bottle of Glenmorangie.

'Some people have got no taste,' she said lightly.

She poured herself a generous glass, which almost emptied the bottle, and drank deeply.

'Here's to you, my old darling,' said Freddie, expansively raising his own glass in her direction.

'You've done us proud again today, just like always.'

Later, when Mac the herdsman had departed, Constance and Freddie opened a second bottle of Glenmorangie and polished the bulk of it off after supper – unusual for them, but then, it had been an unusual day. The news from the hospital, when Constance called to check on Harley, was cautiously optimistic – certainly cheering after the drama of the day. At last they were able to relax, two people who loved each other and were content in each other's company over-indulging somewhat following the satisfaction of a job well done.

In bed that night, and although just a little drunk, Freddie reached out for her. Their love-making was just how it always was, warm and tender, but perhaps, particularly on Freddie's side, curiously polite. Constance enjoyed making love with Freddie, but she found it reassuring rather than erotic. She regarded it as a kind of ultimate cuddle and her enjoyment came from their mutual expression of deep affection more than from passionate sexual arousal.

As for Freddie – she knew that her husband's entire sexuality, such as it was, had been awakened by her, and by her alone. She did find that erotic. She also knew that her husband was completely satisfied with his sex life with her, and that it never occurred to him that anyone, least of all Constance, could possibly ask for more.

The next morning Constance and Freddie were awakened by a persistent hammering on the front door. Constance sat up in bed quickly and a sharp pain shot across her forehead. She had quite a hangover.

28

She looked at her watch: 6.25 a.m. Whoever it was banging on the door had beaten the alarm clock by only five minutes. Beside her Freddie groaned slightly as he started to climb out of bed. A farmer through and through, he was an early riser by nature and was usually up and about a good half hour at least before the alarm woke Constance. Not today though. Freddie was suffering too.

She pulled on her dressing gown and followed him out on to the landing, watching from the top of the stairs, as, wearing only his pyjama trousers, he went downstairs and unlocked and opened the front door.

Norton Phillips stood there, unshaven, his face showing the strain, bags under his eyes, obviously still tense and wound up. He was, however, smiling broadly.

''E's out of danger, 'e is, an' they reckon they've saved 'is arm,' he blurted out. ''T'won't be good as new, but not far off with a bit of luck. 'E's been in surgery most of the night. I had to tell 'ee soon as I knew for certain – and I wanted to do it face to face, like. I 'ope yer don't mind . . .'

The words poured out, so eager was the farmhand to share his good news.

Constance called down to him from the upstairs landing. 'Of course not, Norton, we're absolutely delighted.'

She was telling no more than the truth. Both Constance and Freddie had a big soft spot for Norton, a true English eccentric whose whole personality radiated simple good nature. He was a motorcycling nut who had actually been christened Norman, but had unofficially changed his name to Norton in honour of his favourite British motorbike.

29

Also, overcoming the mild protests of his wife, although he usually deferred to her in everything, he had even insisted on naming all of his seven children after motorbikes. As well as Harley there were sons, Davidson and Maxim, and four daughters, Triumph and Daytona, Aprilia and Suzuki. Iris Phillips had given in to him because she truly loved him – as did all who were close to him – but remained the only person in family or village who still resolutely called her husband Norman. And she had indignantly drawn the line at changing the family surname to Kawasaki.

Norton peered up the stairs at Constance. 'There's summat else, Mrs Lange, they said he might not even be alive at all if you hadn't done what you did.'

The big brawny farm worker, bright ginger-headed like Harley and all his children, shuffled his feet, unused to expressing emotion. But his voice cracked as he spoke and there were tears in his eyes.

'You didn't just save the boy's arm, missus, you saved 'is life, and us'll never forget it.'

'Oh, come on now, Norton,' responded Constance, typically making light of it. 'It'll take more than some old tractor to do for that boy of yours.'

Norton continued as if she had not spoken. 'The wife'll be round, 'er's still at the hospital. 'Er says you'm a saint. You know, like, what's 'er name, Florrie . . . thigee nurse . . .'

Florence Nightingale,' responded Freddie solemnly, shutting the door behind a swiftly departing Norton Phillips who had the rest of the village to relay the news to and probably before breakfast at that.

Constance, half-way down the stairs now, smiled

30

but remained silent.

'Right then, Florence, get the kettle on,' ordered Freddie.

Arriving at his side, his wife responded with a playful punch and hoots of laughter.

After a few seconds of horseplay Freddie caught her by the shoulders and held her by the arms.

'The luckiest day in my life was the day I met you,' he told her.

It was something he quite frequently said and she never failed to be moved. There was a lump in her throat. But it was not Constance's style to be too serious.

'Get on, you great softy,' she said. 'If you want to show how much you care don't just talk about it, fetch the Alka-Seltzer.'

# Three

Charlie left the Crescent Hotel with a smile on his face. Mrs Pattinson was a very imaginative woman. Charlie had seen a lot of life in an action-packed twenty-four years, but he had never met anyone quite like Mrs Pattinson before.

He and his companion, the lad he knew only as Bob and had worked with just once before, had arrived separately for their assignment. Charlie had parked his nearly new BMW 325i convertible a couple of streets away from the hotel. Mrs Pattinson insisted on discretion. Bob's seven-year-old Mini was coincidentally just a few cars along the road – he had yet to aspire to Charlie's lifestyle.

Charlie waved Bob a cheery farewell, clicked off his car's alarm system and sank contentedly back into the driver's seat. Involuntarily he checked the pocket of his leather jacket, fingering the thick wodge of twenty-pound notes which nestled there.

Charlie was a male prostitute, a rent boy – although the term more usually referred to the gay trade and that was not Charlie's game. He preferred to be called an escort and, after all, he worked for a rather up-market agency – Bristol's Avon Escorts, which still operated under the vague pretence that it provided escorts and nothing more. He was also undeniably straight – well, more or less. A few times in the past, when the price had been right, Charlie had serviced wealthy businessmen. But he didn't enjoy gay sex. He didn't feel demeaned by it or anything like that. It was just doing a job after all and there were aspects of every job that didn't appeal to you much, Charlie reckoned. But he liked to enjoy his work. He took a pride in it. He looked after his body. Worked out. Kept himself clean. Never had unprotected sex with anyone. Charlie knew what he was doing.

Charlie had a smart flat in a recently redeveloped part of the old Bristol city docks. The three-roomed apartment in Spike Island Court, a red-brick residential complex of strikingly contemporary design, overlooked a marina full of satisfyingly expensive yachts – and Charlie had read all the home and design magazines he could lay his hands on before he had furnished and decorated his home.

A series of lively nights with an extremely well-preserved and very wealthy widow at her big country house had all but paid for the fashionable pale oak flooring he had laid throughout. Charlie remembered her with pleasure and affection as he did all his best clients. He suspected she had been in her early sixties, although she didn't look it, but Charlie wasn't ageist. By and large he actually preferred mature women, albeit with a few flaws. He certainly had little time for girls his own age. Compared with him, he felt, they knew so little about life and even less about sex.

Charlie pushed the button which lowered the roof of his car. It was still warm. He was playing Beethoven loudly on his state-of-the-art CD player. He had discovered Beethoven when he watched a pirate version of *A Clockwork Orange* – the 1971 Stanley Kubrick film which he had been surprised to learn was still banned from British cinemas and television. *A Clockwork Orange* was about mindless violence and Charlie had no violent tendencies at all that he knew about. The one thing he wouldn't have anything to do with was sado-masochism – the very thought of it made him sick and they knew that at the agency. Nonetheless the excitement generated by Beethoven's Ninth Symphony in the film had got to him and it was because of it that he had begun seriously to listen to classical music.

He parked the BMW in his allotted place in the covered area beneath Spike Island Court and erected the electrically operated roof again. He couldn't be bothered to wait for the lift. Instead he bounded up the concrete stairs to his third-floor flat, with Beethoven's Ninth still reverberating within his head.

Inside the front door he allowed himself a small sigh of satisfaction. He slipped off his highly polished Gucci loafers and removed his socks as well. He liked to feel the coolness of the polished wood on his bare feet. And, as he often did, he thought about the floor's provider. That arrangement had ended abruptly when the woman's daughter had returned home uninvited after a broken marriage, naturally expecting that her widowed mother would be lonely and therefore grateful for her company. The woman was neither of those things and had been extremely irritated by an untimely interruption to an immensely well-ordered and satisfying life. She had her garden, her bridge parties, her dog, her books and Charlie. And she once told Charlie that she was much happier than she had ever been when her dull and rather grumpy husband had been alive.

She had never really enjoyed sex before either, she confessed. And, as Charlie had run a finger tantalisingly across her naked belly, she had gasped in pleasurable anticipation, then said crossly: 'This is going to have to be the last time, damn it. We will have to end our little arrangement.' Adding in a rather more amused understatement: 'My daughter would never understand . . .'

Charlie smiled at the memory. He often knew more about his clients, their hopes and their fears, their true feelings, than their closest family and friends. But, he thought to himself, his mind switching to his most recent client, that certainly was not true of Mrs Pattinson.

Lost in thought, Charlie padded across the floor into his bedroom. The big double bed with its deep cream linen bedspread and black silk scatter cushions looked inviting. Charlie hated to admit it to himself, but he was a bit tired. That woman was demanding. He gave in, stretched out on the bed and lay gazing at the pale cream painted ceiling. The whole flat was painted in pale cream, but while in the unimaginative little rooms at the Crescent Hotel such choice of decor was simply utilitarian, here the effect was striking.

Charlie did not like the new trend for garishly bright colours. He didn't think they were stylish. He also couldn't quite get over the feeling that it was exactly what would be expected in the home of a young black man. Therefore he didn't want to know. He never dressed in bright colours either. His clothes were mostly black, white or various shades of beige and cream. Even his car, although in every sense dashing, was an understated dark grey, and not even the metallic kind.

Charlie's clothes lived in a fitted wardrobe at one

end of his long narrow bedroom. His bed was at the other end. The wardrobe doors were made of a fine pale oak that matched the floor. The only other furniture in the room was a bedside table, also of pale oak – upon which stood a large cream ceramic table lamp – and a big squashy black leather armchair. There was no mirror visible. Charlie had spent too much time with people who liked to watch their own sexual activities strategically reflected.

The long side of the room opposite the door was almost entirely window and the view from it was a sweeping one out over the marina in the foreground and across the stretch of water branching off the River Avon known as the Floating Harbour, with Bristol Cathedral in the background. The window was framed by pale cream muslin curtains which almost blended with the walls.

The light was fading now although it was still a beautiful evening. Charlie always found his bedroom so relaxing. He wasn't sure that he wanted to sleep, just to rest. He was still thinking about Mrs Pattinson and the sensational few hours he had spent with her. Apart from her sexual preferences – upon which he was something of an expert – Charlie knew nothing at all about Mrs Pattinson, even though he had been her regular for almost two years.

That was unusual. Charlie had begun to understand what women prostitutes had known for centuries. Their clients often treated them as therapists. Charlie had looked after a number of clients, some regulars, some just one-offs who kept their identity secret. In fact they almost all did and he automatically assumed that most of them used false names. The widow who had entertained him in her own home had been one of just a handful of exceptions to this rule. But even those who hid behind some fictitious personae were inclined to confide in him – this stranger who had brought them whatever release it was that they so eagerly sought.

Not so Mrs Pattinson. Mrs Pattinson occasionally liked Charlie to talk about himself. He had told her all about his new apartment when he acquired it and she had applauded his plan to keep it simple and minimalist.

She had listened to his description and then told him: 'I like the sound of it, Charlie. Very dramatic. Don't clutter the walls either. Just one or two good paintings. Better one decent original, if you can afford it, than a dozen prints.'

He had remembered that. In his bedroom now hung a pastel original, in the kind of muted colours Charlie favoured, by a local Bristol painter not yet celebrated enough to be out of his price range. And on a specially purchased round white table in one corner of the living room stood an abstract bronze by West Country sculptor Clive Gunnell. Charlie had saved up for his two original pieces of art only out of money given him by Mrs Pattinson. It seemed appropriate.

Charlie glanced around him with quiet satisfaction. He had achieved something here and he knew it. Mrs Pattinson and all the rest of them were part of it. The painting and the bronze were from her, that was how he thought of it. The floor was his widow's. The muslin curtains had been bought through six months of regular Wednesday afternoon sessions with an overly thin woman who called herself Angela and seemed to live on nervous energy and nothing else.

She would remove her sensible low-heeled shoes, strip off her formal business suits and with them discard the last vestige of her tight-lipped, tension-filled respectability. She had been rampant that one, Charlie remembered.

Mrs Pattinson was rampant too. But, even though she was paying him, Mrs Pattinson gave as well as took. Charlie's body still glowed pleasurably. He always looked forward to the times spent with her at the Crescent Hotel. Every time was different, you see, every time a new experience. What a way to earn a living, he thought to himself smugly. And what a good living it was too.

Charlie took a winter holiday in his native West Indies every year, and this February planned to take his mother with him. His family were very proud of him. He was bright, likeable, self-assured, fun to have around. But Charlie's family had no idea what Charlie really did for a living – something in computers, never too precisely explained, was his cover – and neither did most of his friends. It wasn't that he was ashamed, it was just that, in common with the Merry Widow's daughter, he didn't think they would understand. In fact he knew his mother would throw a fit. There were three older brothers and two sisters, one older than him and one younger; the elder, Mary Anne, married to a decent enough but unexceptional man. His younger sister, Daisy, strikingly pretty, looked set to escape to a better life than might be expected, as Charlie considered that he had done. Daisy had caught the eye of a clever young black man who had recently graduated in Law from Bristol University. He had landed a job in London and they were soon to be married. Charlie was ecstatically

38

happy for Daisy. He wanted the best for all his family, but for the others it was probably not to be.

Charlie and his brothers and sisters had been brought up in the St Paul's area of Bristol which had improved greatly since the terrible days of the notorious race riots, but remained a rough and tough place. Many of the boys and girls he had gone to school with already seemed to have wrecked their lives. Some were in jail or just out. Drugs figured heavily in the day-to-day life of St Paul's, and Charlie knew that one of his elder brothers, Bart, who had always liked dope a bit too much, was now into crack. That frightened Charlie, but he didn't blame Bart. Life was hard and you took your pleasures where you could in St Paul's. The dangers rarely presented themselves until it was too late. Charlie knew that about drugs and always had done – but never even considered that the same premise could be applied to his chosen way of life in which he saw no hidden dangers at all.

Both the older brothers, Jack and Winston, were married and held down steady labouring jobs with the council. They earned little for hard dirty work and Charlie thought they both deserved better. His family was not like many in the St Paul's area. They had been brought up by a mother who had sacrificed everything for them – his father, who had come to Bristol because of the docks and never got over their closure, had died suddenly of a heart attack when Charlie had been seven years old – to be well behaved, honest and hard working. It seemed to Charlie, though, that these qualities did not necessarily help you get on in life. He knew that up in Clifton, all around the Crescent Hotel where he had spent half the afternoon and evening with Mrs Pattinson, a host of privileged white kids without half his intelligence were being handed opportunities on a plate that his brothers and sisters would have crawled over beds of nails for.

Charlie had determined that he was going to have a future, whatever he had to do in order to build one. His real work was conducted with great discretion. Unlike most of his kind Charlie did not fall into male prostitution by accident. He had made a conscious decision that this was what he would do. After all, sex was what he was best at, what he had always been best at. It was no different really, he told himself, from being good at football, and a hell of a lot better, he reckoned, than being good at boxing – and those were the other two great working-class means of escape.

Charlie first realised how good he was at sex when, aged only thirteen, he had been seduced by the Sunday-school teacher who was supposed to be giving him confirmation class – Mrs Collins believed in religious education above all else. The young woman – although being around thirty she had seemed quite old to him then – had, in between outbursts of self-flagellating guilt, set about giving him a superb sexual education over a period of several months.

At around this time Charlie remembered one of the few things his daddy had told him. If you have a talent you should make the most of it, his father had said. He had been thinking, Charlie had known all too well, of his own abandoned talent as a jazz trombonist. Charlie's father had even sold his treasured trombone, passed on to him by his own father, in order to provide for his family. Ranwell Collins' talent died years before he did, and before Charlie had even been born, and Ranwell never stopped mourning it.

Charlie knew what his talent was all right. He also knew his father would not have approved any more than would his mother – but he didn't think about that. Charlie was a natural sexual athlete whom nature had equipped particularly well for the job. He had been told by veterans in his trade, mostly women, that one day it would destroy him. Some had advised him to get out while he could. It was advice Charlie had no intention of taking. In fact, he couldn't quite comprehend what they were talking about.

Charlie reckoned he was totally in control of his own life. And he was particularly happy that day. He always was after being with Mrs P. Happy, if exhausted. Invariably exhausted. Charlie chuckled. He liked Mrs Pattinson. Charlie didn't understand why women were still not supposed to reveal the same kinds of appetites men had quite freely exhibited for years. He didn't see anything wrong with Mrs Pattinson's behaviour. And he thought it was sad that she had to be quite so secretive. She was a complete mystery to him, that one. Even the occasions when she would talk to him about his life were few and far between. Mostly she only wanted to talk about sex. That seemed quite reasonable to Charlie. He saw nothing wrong with sex. If you were sensible and used your head, sex was simply about pleasure and nobody need get hurt. Charlie had no time for double standards. Nonetheless, it was largely thanks to double standards that business was so good for him. His market was a growing one. There were quite a lot of Mrs Pattinsons around looking for no-risk sexual adventure, Charlie had discovered, and he was very grateful for it.

He gave Mrs Pattinson a good time, no questions asked, no emotional ties, pure sex – and she paid him handsomely. That seemed like a perfect arrangement to Charlie. And there was the added bonus, of course. As Charlie had yet to become jaded by his work, Mrs Pattinson gave him a pretty good time too.

But this was an adventurous and imaginative woman. She also liked to try new young men from time to time and sometimes she liked to have two of them together. Charlie didn't mind that. He quite liked watching as well as doing, come to that. And, in any case, there wasn't a lot that Charlie minded. Life was good.

He smiled languorously, stretching his limbs out across the bed, reliving the afternoon and evening. He could feel her naked body pressed against his, see her face close to his face as she whispered into his ear the erotic details of her most intimate needs and desires, as she dreamed up some new sexual adventure, each more exotic than any that had gone before.

Recently she had come up with a particularly novel idea, a sex game Charlie had never heard of before. It was amazing really, Charlie thought, that any woman could still do that. Charlie was quite impressed.

# Four

On the second Tuesday of every month Constance Lange's family were accustomed to her absence when she travelled to Bristol to visit her one surviving relative, a great aunt who had been kind to her throughout her lonely childhood. Aunt Ada was now a very old lady living in a nursing home on the outskirts of the city. She had suffered for some years from Alzheimer's disease. In the early stages of her illness she had spent occasional weekends at Chalmpton Village Farm with Freddie and her great niece. But for more than five years now that had been impossible due to the deterioration in her condition. Constance would describe to Freddie how the old woman now lived in some other world, a strange and frightening fantasy place where the past moulded with the present, what had gone before with what could never be, and where there was no future. Sometimes Aunt Ada knew her, sometimes she did not. And when she was well enough Constance would take her great aunt for an afternoon drive in the country.

'I'm not sure how much she understands, even whether or not she knows she is in a car, but driving through the countryside seems to have a soothing affect on her, Alzheimer's sufferers get so agitated, you see,' she explained to her husband who made sympathetic noises but always had too much else on his mind to listen properly.

Usually Constance stayed until the evening and had supper with the old lady - a service in the nursing home provided at a small charge to visiting relatives – and then drove back to Chalmpton Peverill. The journey took just over an hour and on occasions she did not arrive home until between 10.00 and 11.00 p.m.

But Freddie Lange never minded these absences – if the truth be known, he was usually so engrossed in his farm that he barely noticed. Constance frequently took the opportunity to make a day of it, shopping in Bristol, having lunch with a girlfriend, and Freddie thought it was important that his wife escaped from the village occasionally. Too many people depended on Constance and took her for granted. Freddie was honest enough to admit that he came into that category himself. She was so calm and steadfast, so bright, clever and positive – and at the same time such fun to have around. It was a heady combination. He could also never quite get over how beautiful his wife was.

He really did not know what he would ever do without her. In fact he hoped beyond hope that he would never have to do without her. Losing her was the biggest dread of his life. Freddie was a practical sensible man and he did not dwell on the ultimate prospect of death. There was no point. He was a farmer. He understood there could be no beginnings without endings. He was fatalistic and not overly imaginative. Therefore he did not fear his own death. But he feared his wife dying more than anything else in the world.

Every Sunday morning he and Constance went to church. Freddie wasn't sure whether or not he had

44

any religious convictions – men like him didn't think about things like that. He went to church on Sunday mornings because that was what he had done since he was a boy, that was what his family had always done and they had always sat in the same pew. Naturally when he married he assumed that he and his new wife would continue the tradition and so would their children. Constance had never questioned it. Neither had he asked her if she believed in this God they both went through the weekly ritual of worshipping. It would not have occurred to him to pry in that way.

Nonetheless, and he never told a soul, there was not a Sunday, sitting in the stony chill of that little Norman church, that he didn't pray that he would die before Constance. That was how much she meant to him.

Any man lucky enough to have her would feel the same, he told himself with simple certainty as Constance cheerily left the house on the morning of Tuesday, September 8th.

Freddie stood by the back porch as she reversed the Volvo into the barn, swinging the car around so that she could drive forwards into the village street. It was yet another miserably wet day. He could barely see his wife within the car until she switched on the windscreen wipers as she reversed. She handled the big estate so easily, with so much more aplomb than he ever did. He always found the Volvo cumbersome and much preferred to drive his little MGB roadster – a beautifully preserved concourse job in British racing green – although he didn't really like taking it out of the garage in the rain.

He waved when Constance pipped her horn as the

Volvo's back end slipped smoothly forwards through the gateway.

He knew Constance remained fond of her aunt regardless of the old lady's sorry condition. And although he doubted he would ever see Aunt Ada again – in spite of her visits to the farm he had never known her well and really couldn't see the point when she almost certainly wouldn't have the faintest idea who he was – Freddie was glad that his wife still took the trouble. Freddie had a strong sense of family. The Lange family tree could be traced back to the time of William the Conqueror. Freddie took that kind of family history for granted, but it was very important to him. He thoroughly approved of Constance caring for her one elderly relative. That was how things should be, in Freddie's opinion. His own parents had died a few years ago, both in their mid-seventies, within six months of each other, and he wished they were still alive for him to look after. Freddie liked looking after people. His family. His workers. The villagers whom he knew relied on him, as they had done on his father before him, for advice and support in a way outsiders would probably consider unhealthily feudal. It seemed perfectly natural to Freddie.

He still missed his parents dreadfully, but he could not really imagine either one of them having survived long without the other. And that was how he felt about himself and Constance. They were a team. Together they were indomitable. Apart they were nothing.

That night Constance arrived home in high spirits.

'Aunt Ada was bright as a button today,' she told Freddie. 'I said you sent your love and I don't think

46

she had a clue who I was talking about, but she chattered away all the time. Nonsense it may have been, but she seemed content enough, and at least she didn't fall asleep on me like the last time.'

It had been just on ten o'clock when Freddie had heard the Volvo purr into the yard.

'Do you want a night cap?' he asked now, reaching, without waiting for his wife to reply, for the bottle of Glenmorangie in the kitchen cupboard.

Constance, carrying two large carrier bags, was in the hallway, heading for the stairs, and trying to avoid falling over Josh whose excitement at her return caused him to run in circles around her legs.

'You bet,' she called. 'Just let me sort out my stuff.'

She was down within a couple of minutes, in her hand a small paper bag which she gave to her husband, brushing his weathered cheek with her lips as she did so.

He thought how fresh she smelt after a whole day out, almost as if she had just bathed. But then, Constance invariably seemed so cool and fresh, sometimes appearing to be made of different stuff from other poor mortals.

'You don't always have to buy me a present when you go out, you know,' he remarked.

'Right, I'll have it back then,' she said quickly, reaching out as if to snatch the package away from him.

He swung his body backwards, laughing, avoiding her.

The bag contained a rare early edition of *The Trumpet Major*, probably Freddie's favourite Thomas Hardy, beautifully bound in leather with gold embossing. Freddie, although a well-educated man, was no intellectual and not a great reader either, but he had a passion for the famous Wessex writer, perhaps because Hardy wrote about things that Freddie instinctively understood and that did not seem to him to have changed fundamentally since Hardy's day.

Freddie's face lit up. He put down the book and took Constance in his arms.

'Where on earth did you find this?' he asked, his delight bubbling over.

'I've been on the case for months,' she said. 'I take it you like it.'

'Not as much as I like you, but it'll do,' he said.

She poked out her tongue at him.

'You know, I think if my mother had ever done that to my father he would probably have collapsed in shock,' remarked Freddie. He couldn't stop smiling.

'Easily shocked, your family,' said Constance. 'Forgetful too. Where's that drink?'

He reached behind him for a glass already half filled with fine whisky.

'Just waiting for you, you impatient woman,' he told her.

He picked up the book again, handling it carefully, appreciatively turning the pages. 'Thank you for this,' he said. 'It is so beautiful – really the most wonderful present.'

'You're welcome,' she replied. 'You deserve it, and more actually – only don't get too big-headed.'

She raised her glass, taking a long appreciative swallow. He turned around to pour himself a drink.

When he faced her again it seemed that she had changed slightly, as if slotting back into a different mould. And indeed when she spoke again her thoughts were obviously no longer on her day away, the shopping and lunch she had told him she had enjoyed in Bristol, her visit to her aunt, or indeed on him. She had switched her attentions to the village she was so much a part of, with its almost daily round of rural drama. Drama was how it seemed to Freddie. Connie took things much more calmly.

'Did Harley Phillips come out of hospital today as planned?' Constance asked.

'Uh huh.' Freddie grunted. He didn't really want to talk about Harley because the boy was now yet another problem that had to be dealt with. Harley's arm had been saved but nobody knew yet how much it would return to full use. And certainly, at best, it would be a long time before he could work properly on the farm again. Freddie had no wish to lay Harley off and in any case knew his wife would not allow it – but, although his was a rich farm, Freddie had relatively little disposable cash. Like most farmers, his wealth was in his assets and he could not afford to carry passengers.

As if reading his mind, Constance spoke. 'I'll visit Harley tomorrow, then,' she said. 'And we'll have to think of some gainful employment for him as soon as he is able. Knowing Harley, he'll try like mad. You know how eager and energetic he is.'

Yes, thought Freddie, with a mixture of affection and irritation. And that was what had probably caused the boy's accident in the first place. More brawn than brains, like the rest of his family.

Out loud he merely said, 'Yes, he's a good lad. If he does his best for us, and I'm sure he will, we'll just have to do our best for him.'

'I knew that's what you'd say, Freddie,' replied

Constance, smiling broadly at him. 'That's what you always say.'

It was too. And it was what his father used to say before him. Indeed if that wasn't the way of his family they might all be multi-millionaires by now, he reflected. But Freddie had never sought to make a fortune, any more than had his father. It was his wish only to keep Chalmpton Village Farm at the very least in the fine fettle in which it had been handed to him, and perhaps, if possible, hand it on to his own son in even better shape.

His own son. William. Oh God. The news from William, received that morning only minutes after Constance had left, had put a blight on his entire day. It was quite extraordinary. The elation he always felt when he was reunited with his wife, even after such a brief parting, and the joy of her wonderful gift, had put the whole sorry episode right out of his mind.

He must tell her, he supposed. He opened his mouth to speak, but before he had quite found the words, she began to talk first.

'You know, I'm really quite worn out,' she said, as she emptied the whisky glass with a second big swallow. 'It's been a long day. And I don't like driving as much as I used to. I think I'll have an early night. Do you mind?'

'Of course not,' said Freddie. He decided the news of their son could wait till morning before he shared it with her. He knew she would be upset. She idolised the boy and sometimes, Freddie felt, put him on a pedestal he did not deserve.

Freddie was up at six as usual. He pottered in the kitchen making tea and then laid up the fire in the sitting-room which this year they were already light-ing in the evenings even though it was still only early September, because the weather remained unseason-ably cold and damp. He contemplated how best to break the bad news to his wife. He could come up with no easy way.

He took tea up to Constance at a quarter to seven as he always did.

'By the way, William will probably be home today,' he told her conversationally as, sipping from her favourite mug, she propped herself up on the pillows. And not until he had finished speaking did he realise what a clumsy approach that had been.

Momentarily her face lit up. Then the clouds came.

'Freddie, the new term has only just started, what is going on?'

Her voice was sharp. But he knew her so well, knew she was not really angry, only anxious.

'Things aren't too good, apparently . . .' Freddie stumbled over his words, wanting so desperately not to hurt her, knowing he could not avoid it.

'For goodness sake, Freddie!' she said.

He sighed. 'He's been given his marching orders.'

'Oh no!' she exclaimed. First she looked merely distressed, then puzzled. 'I knew he wasn't doing very well, but surely not that bad, and why now, at the beginning of term?'

'There's more to it than that. They've only been back a week and he's already turned up drunk for afternoon lectures at least twice and missed one morning session. He was warned last term, apparently.' Freddie sighed. 'Yesterday he actually threw up in the lecture room, the idiot. And that was his lot!'

Constance now seemed to be both upset and exasperated.

'But why, Freddie? I know he likes a pint, but I'd no idea his drinking was getting out of hand. The boy's got everything, why does he need to get drunk like that?'

Freddie sighed again, he understood that if you hero-worshipped somebody, especially your own son, the blow was all the greater when you realised that maybe he wasn't quite such a hero after all.

'I think he's just going through a bit of a wild patch . . .'

'God, Freddie, with all he has to look forward to, he is so lucky . . .'

Freddie knew she was thinking of her own childhood and how hard she had had to fight in order to make anything of her life before meeting him.

He spoke to her very gently. 'You know, it is not always so easy when you see your life mapped out before you, either. Not at twenty. He's rebelling, that's all. He'll grow out of it.'

Freddie turned away slightly. He was, after all, trying to reassure her. He didn't want her to see how worried he also was. But he guessed that she saw all right. She never missed much, not Constance. Particularly not about how people were feeling. She had such wonderful natural sensitivity. He thought it was that, more than anything, that had made him fall in love with her. She had understood all his doubts and insecurities and given him a belief in himself, both emotionally and physically, that he would not as a young man have thought possible.

'Freddie, just tell me everything,' she demanded, but in a tone of voice just as gentle as that he had used to her. 'That's far from all, isn't it?'

He gave in then, explaining that after William had called telling him rather sulkily that he had been chucked out, would be home tomorrow, refusing to give reasons bar a brief admission of having had a few drinks too many, he had telephoned Ted Parish, a lecturer at William's agricultural college. Ted, an old schoolfriend whose elder brother worked the family farm fifty miles or so away in Devon's South Hams, explained that the real problem was that it seemed likely that William was involved in the drug scene – and not just marijuana either, but cocaine and maybe even harder stuff as well. Ted's boss, the principal, would probably not send a man down for drunkenness unless it became totally out of control, but he wouldn't tolerate drugs for a second.

Freddie, ever sensible, understood that. But – after ascertaining that while his son admitted to the allegations of being drunk on college premises (it seemed he could do little else) he hotly denied using drugs – he had asked his friend to push for William to be merely suspended unless the drug allegation could be substantiated. The old-school tie works as well in the farming community as any other and Freddie would always use any means available to protect his family.

'But that was the best I could do,' he told Constance. 'Ted agreed that he would speak up for William, although he sounded as if he was pretty fed up with the lad himself. It seems this has been going on for some time, although we knew nothing about it.'

Constance was horrified. 'Oh, not drugs, Freddie, surely not that,' she said.

Freddie shrugged. 'Let's hope not. William says

no, so all we can do is accept that. Ted said he'll call as soon as he has an answer from the boss. But even if it's just a suspension, and even if William is prepared to mend his ways pretty sharpish, the college will take some convincing that he's turned over a new leaf before they let him back in, I reckon.'

Constance put her mug of tea down carefully on the bedside table. She reached out and touched Freddie's hand.

'I can't believe William would do this to us,' she said.

'Con, whatever it is he's doing it isn't *to* us,' responded Freddie patiently. 'He's just a young man kicking over the traces a bit, I'm sure that's all . . .'

'You never kicked anything over when you were a young man,' said Constance, forcing a strained smile.

'I never felt the need, and then I met you and I've never wanted to kick anything since, not really,' he said.

She smiled again. This time rather more naturally.

'I was the odd one out though, particularly in that generation, in the sixties,' he continued.

She was holding his hand now, his big capable farmer's hand, and she leaned forward and kissed his calloused fingers. Absurdly he hoped they were clean from carrying the firewood.

'Whatever you say, I'll ring his bloody neck if he hurts you, Freddie Lange,' she said. 'And anyway, at what time do we expect the little bugger?'

Her voice had its usual sparkle back in it now. She spoke determinedly, facing up to a problem while at the same time making as light of it as possible. Typical Constance.

That was better. Freddie could cope with almost

anything as long as he had Constance in the trenches with him. Without her strength and her compassion, without her leadership, her calming presence, he was, in his own opinion, nothing.

William was due to arrive some time during the afternoon or early evening, it seemed. He had not been precise. His mother supposed it would be too much to ask for any consideration from him at the moment.

It was still only just after 8.00 a.m. Freddie had a problem in the piggery to sort out. Constance was sitting at the kitchen table drinking coffee. She had far too much to do to sit around moping all morning, but she had to sort out her thoughts.

It was probably wicked, she considered, for a mother to admit to having a favourite among her children, but William had always been extra special to her. She supposed it was partly because of how much she had known Freddie had wanted a son, an heir to take over and work the land that had been in his family for so long. But also, as William had grown, he had come to resemble his father so much physically it almost made her heart leap when she looked at him.

Freddie Lange had been thirty-one when Constance first met him and William was only twenty. Sometimes she was not sure if she looked forward to her son reaching thirty or not. She was quite sure he would by then be almost a carbon copy of the father he was already so like.

And yet in personality the two were completely different. William was much more like her. He had her drive and ambition – or at least she had thought that he had. Maybe Freddie was right. Maybe it was hard to be ambitious when plans had already been made for your life before you were born, when there was nothing to strive for. But William had never indicated that he wanted any other kind of existence. Never said that he dreamed of being a writer or a painter or a soldier. Not even anything mundane. 'What I really want in all the world is to be an accountant, mother.' She let her imagination run riot for a moment, playing games now. And she smiled in spite of herself.

No, William had no dreams beyond Chalmpton Peverill and the nine hundred acres of prime Somerset farmland he would one day inherit – she was sure of it.

He had always seemed so well-adjusted. Certainly so personable, so charming. He had been both articulate and at ease among adults much earlier than most children. He shared his mother's sense of fun and she thought that perhaps she had never laughed with anyone as much in her entire life – not even with Freddie – as she had with her son.

Indeed, she supposed she had so far had the kind of relationship with all her children that many mothers would envy. All three of them, probably particularly William, always seemed to have regarded her as much as a friend as their mother – amusing and entertaining to be with and certainly so much more fun than the mothers of any of their contemporaries. That's what they told her anyway. And William, in particularly, always stressed the fun. All three eagerly sought out her company rather than avoiding it, she knew that, sometimes almost competing for her attentions.

She was also aware that when there was such a competition, however subtly mounted, it was always William who won. She felt guilty about that, but did not seem able to fight it somehow and just hoped that her daughters, whom she also adored, were not as starkly aware of it as she was.

It was just that they did not have William's charisma. Nobody did. It was quite a package for a mother to have a son whose appearance was a mirror image of his father and whose personality was a mirror image of her own. She and William did not clash either as they might have done. They complemented each other perfectly. They thought the same way, liked the same people, laughed at the same jokes before they were even completed.

Only a couple of weeks before William had returned to college, they had danced together most of the night at the hop staged in the village hall in order to raise cash for a new roof. Unlike most young men nowadays, William could dance properly. Constance always thought of traditional ballroom dancing as dancing properly, although she knew that would seem old-fashioned to many, and indeed, she had had to learn herself when she wed Freddie and realised the kind of life she would be leading in a village community. There had not been much opportunity in her childhood for the foxtrot, she reflected wryly.

Freddie had not minded his wife and his son monopolising each other, she knew that. He was so proud of both her and of William and he always remarked on how well they danced together and how splendid they looked. They did too, Constance was well aware.

She had been, however, more distressed than she admitted to either her son or her husband when she spotted the look in Marcia Spry's eye as the notoriously malicious old woman studied her having such a wonderful time with her only son.

God, that woman is disgusting, Constance had thought, but she said nothing aloud. She had been aware that her body had tensed involuntarily and William, holding her lightly in his arms, noticed at once.

'What's wrong, mother?' he asked.

She had made a physical effort to shake off the tension. 'Nothing, darling,' she replied. 'It's just that there are some really quite monstrous people living in this village, that's all.'

William had shrieked with laughter, causing even Freddie, standing on the edge of the dance floor talking to the vicar, to look mildly askance.

'You mean it's taken you all these years to realise that, mother,' he said. 'I didn't know you were so innocent.'

And, outrageously, he had swung her across the dance floor towards the table Marcia Spry was sharing with the vicar's wife – a sweet woman although without a brain in her head in Constance's opinion – and called to the old gossip over Constance's shoulder. 'Don't forget I must have a dance with you before the night is out, Miss Spry,' he said, and Constance knew his features would be composed into the most charming of expressions.

She had heard Marcia Spry mutter something stiffly and could imagine how set her face would now be, flushed slightly probably, having been confronted so blatantly.

Constance had not dared turned around. Secretly revelling in her son's behaviour, she had difficulty in preventing herself from laughing out loud. Only now did she wonder if William's sparkling high spirits had been artificially induced – and perhaps even by something more potent than alcohol. She shuddered at the thought. Then she had had no such doubts.

'You are appalling, William,' she had whispered in his ear, in such a way that he was made well aware that his mother was actually quite delighted with him.

'Maybe,' he had responded. 'But I'll have a long way to go before I'm as appalling as that twisted old bat. I don't know why you and dad ever have anything to do with her.'

But he did know, of course. William was steeped in village life, like all of them. Marcia came from a family established in the village for almost as long as the Langes. Whatever you thought of her, she was a force to be reckoned with in Chalmpton Peverill. And it was an absolute certainty that within minutes of William arriving home so early in the term the dreadful Marcia would be sure to know that he was back – and God knows what she would make of that.

Constance knew she shouldn't care. And in her heart she didn't. She also know that the main cause of Marcia Spry's behaviour was envy, because her own life was such an empty one.

But Constance's family and the part it played in the village were at the very core of her existence – she had somehow slipped on that mantle as naturally as Freddie had been born to it. And if you accepted that kind of place in village life, you also had to accept that appearances mattered. They mattered terribly. If you wanted the uncaring anonymity of city life, which provided in many ways so much more freedom, then you should go to live in London. Even Bristol was big enough to give you a slice of that.

Here in Chalmpton Peverill everyone knew everyone else's business. The other slant to it was that if you needed help, in times of sickness or any kind of trouble, it was always there. You were never lonely in a village. Even those living without any near neighbours in cottages and on farms in the more remote parts of the parish, miles away from the village itself, experienced none of the isolation endured by so many living alone in a city tenement.

There was good and bad about village life and, perhaps because she had not been born to it, by and large Constance knew and had learned to live with both sides of that. She was quite realistic about it, and now dreaded not only having to cope with what looked like being a considerable family crisis but also having to deal with the reaction of a load of interfering busybodies. It was one of those times when, fleetingly, she was in fact finding it hard to remember the good things about village life.

Then she glimpsed movement out of the kitchen window. Dawn had arrived with yet more rain, but this had ceased at last, and she looked up and out into what was swiftly becoming a glorious morning, the sun rising spectacularly above the Quantock Hills in the distance. And in the foreground, silhouetted against an orange and crimson background, bustled Harley Phillips' mother.

The woman's plump face was an animated picture. She was excited, happy, couldn't stop herself hurrying. Her anxiety about her son's injury still showed, but the woman was bursting with good news. You could see it written all over her. Constance smiled easily through the window, slightly cheered already. She couldn't help it. She liked Iris Phillips every bit as much as she liked Iris's husband Norton. Iris was exactly the way village people were supposed to be, warm-hearted, kindly, the best of neighbours, a truly good sort. If only they were all like her, Constance thought wearily as she pulled open the kitchen door.

''E's 'ome, 'e's 'ome and 'e's that grateful to you, Missus Lange.'

Iris's voice was a sing-song. Her chestnut-brown hair, permed tightly, framed rosy cheeks. She wore a floral-patterned crossover overall which did not entirely conceal a contrasting floral-patterned dress beneath. No stockings. Lace-up shoes. No coat or jacket either. But if she was cold running around the village like that so early on a still chilly morning, she gave no sign of it. Constance always thought Iris looked just the way farmers' wives do in children's books.

''E wants to see 'ee. Says 'e was too dopey to thank 'ee properly when 'ee came to thigee hospital. I said you'd sure to be over. You will, won't 'ee?'

There was just a tinge of uncertainty in the last questioning sentence.

'Of course I will, Iris, of course. Tell him, later this morning. I do hope he gets well soon.'

'Oh 'e's on mend all right. Daft bugger. Talking 'bout going out shooting with 'is dad this very weekend – just for the walk, 'e says. I told 'im what for, don't you worry.'

Iris stepped forward and thrust the basket she was carrying into Constance's hands. It contained six perfect goose eggs nestling in tissue paper.

'My Gert's laying a treat,' said Irish. 'There's nought like a goose egg, flavour all of its own I always says . . .'

She was beaming. A woman who accepted all that life threw at her and just got on with it. She had so

61

much less than Constance and yet no aspirations for more, let alone any envy, would ever enter her head. There was such splendid simplicity in her.

Constance rather wished she could be more like Iris Phillips.

William arrived in his little Renault, a present from his father, naturally, soon after 5.00 p.m.

Constance, although she would never admit it, had been waiting by the upstairs window which gave the best view of the yard. As always now when she saw him after they had been apart she was struck all over again by his resemblance to his father. She watched him slam shut the door of his car and walk quite jauntily towards the house.

Instinctively she knew that he was going to play the whole thing down. Of course she knew. That was exactly what she would do in his situation. Exactly. But she could not let him get away with it, and she wasn't going to. It was time for William Lange to grow up. The strength of her feelings for him increased her sense of having been let down, made her angrier than she might otherwise have been.

In addition to that, she was afraid. Constance Lange was a woman who had lived a bit. But she knew nothing about drugs except that they frightened the life out of her. Even the suggestion that her only son might be a drug user, and the hard stuff at that, was enough to send her into totally uncharacteristic panic.

Just before William reached the kitchen door Constance saw him pause and drop the cigarette he was smoking on to the ground, stamp on it and then kick the remains into the edge of the flower bed. He knew that she hated smoking and at the last moment had decided not to antagonise her by smoking in the house, she realised. Grudgingly she judged that to be a fairly good sign. At least it indicated that he might not mean to totally disregard his parents' wishes. She could still feel a nervous flutter in her heart, though, and an unfamiliar sense of foreboding.

As soon as he was inside the kitchen William called out for her. But she let him wait a minute or two before going downstairs.

He beamed at her and, as he always did, strode towards her and took her in a big bear hug. She did not respond. He stepped back, eyebrows raised quizzically, a small smile playing on his lips. She knew only too well that he was quite convinced he could always get around his mother.

'It's not going to work, William, not this time.' She spoke firmly and she was not smiling.

'Oh, come on mother, it's not as bad as all that, everything'll be all right, you'll see.'

The small smile stretched into that big cheek-splitting grin which she already knew had set the hearts of half the girls in the neighbourhood fluttering. He was laying on all the charm, with which, with some justification, he thought he could overcome anything and certainly his poor besotted mother.

Indeed she could feel a part of her melting, as always. But she was not going to have it. No way. Her fear would not allow him to succeed in soft-soaping her. Not this time.

'William, it isn't going to be all right. Nothing is going to be all right until you start behaving like a man and not a child.'

Her voice was hard and cold. She had made it so.

63

She knew that he had never heard her speak to him quite like that. It was, in fact, a long time since Constance had spoken to anyone like that. The words were not so awful, but the message she had managed to put into them was designed to be quite chilling – especially so when you considered the tremendous warmth there normally was between her and her son.

William flinched and coloured slightly.

She made her voice just a little gentler. Before going any further she must make sure she knew the truth.

'You'd better tell me all about it, William,' she said. 'And I mean all.'

'Just a few drinks, mum, honestly.' He spoke quite casually, still trying to make light of things.

'That's not what we've been told,' she said bluntly.

He shrugged. Lowered his eyes. His body language said believe what you like. Constance felt herself growing angrier and struggled to maintain control.

'I want to know if you have been taking cocaine, or even something stronger, William.'

William raised his eyes to meet hers. His face was a picture of wounded astonishment. 'I'd never touch hard drugs, mum, honest.' He managed to sound quite hurt.

'Honest?'

He nodded vigorously. 'I promise you, mum.'

She so wanted to believe him. She eyed him up and down, wishing she could read his mind, hoping fervently that he was telling the truth.

'OK,' she said eventually. 'OK. Let's say I accept it's nothing other than alcohol. It's still a fact that the college is investigating the drug thing. You're in big trouble. I love you very much, William, but I'm not putting up with this kind of behaviour. I won't have you letting this family down. And I certainly won't stand by and watch you destroy yourself. Your father sees you as his future. I will not allow you to break his heart.'

William tried one more time to smooth things over. 'Oh, come on mum, you're over-reacting, just like they did at college . . .'

'I am what?' She raised her voice this time, trying to make herself as cold as she could ever be with this son she idolised. She needed to shock him, to frighten him a bit, she reckoned. After all she was frightened enough. He had to be made to realise that this marvellous life of his really could disappear unless he played his part too. The world might be full of sons of the privileged who idled and wasted their lives away, who allowed themselves to become zombies, but she was not going to let that happen to her boy. And if that meant being hard and tough – well, she could do that. She knew how to. She had, after all, seen the other side of life.

She caught hold of him by the shoulders.

'William, you're a highly privileged young man. Don't you understand that privilege brings responsibility too? I've always known you could be self-willed, but I didn't realise you could also be stupid. You've no idea what it is like to fight for anything and I don't wish you ever to have to. But I do know what it is like to have nothing, no family, no joy, no future . . .'

She paused, but not for long enough to give him a chance to respond. It was because she loved him so much that she was so hurt, because she was afraid that she was so furious. There was contempt in her voice when she continued. 'God, you are a fool!'

He flinched again. She did not grasp for a moment quite the effect her attack was having on him. She should have known. After all, she knew that he loved her every bit as much as she did him. And she knew she had rarely spoken harshly to him in his life, and certainly never slammed into him like this.

His eyes narrowed. 'You've not had any problems since you married dad though, have you,' he remarked. His voice had a nasty edge to it, a peevishness she had never noticed before. 'That was a pretty good move for you really, wasn't it?'

She didn't hesitate. She had, after all, been only barely in control of her emotions ever since William had arrived home. And that was a state of mind so rare for her that she had little concept of how dangerous it can be.

She slapped him hard on the cheek. He raised one hand to his face and took a step forward. For one awful moment she thought he was going to hit her back. Then he stopped and looked at her, the shock all too apparent in him.

She realised too late how badly she was handling the whole thing. But before she had time to say anything he spoke again.

'Well, I'll just go to the pub and get drunk then, shall I? Might as well behave the way you expect me to. Might as well finish the job.'

He slammed the kitchen door behind him when he left.

Constance sat down at the table, poured a large scotch, cursed herself roundly and gave up the fight against the tears which had been threatening to overwhelm her for some minutes. It was not like her to mishandle things like that. Then again, although she was quite used to dealing with other people's crises, she had perhaps grown accustomed to her own family not having any worth mentioning, she thought wryly.

Freddie turned up just minutes later. For once she did not welcome even his arrival.

'Seen his car, where's the prodigal son then?' he called from the hall.

'Gone out,' replied Constance in a flat tone.

Her husband came into the kitchen and looked at her questioningly. Her face was tear-stained. A pile of damp paper tissues was on the table before her. It was obvious that she had been crying.

Constance sniffed and blew her nose, attempting to regain the control she so wished she had never lost.

'I gave him a bollocking and then he said something really unpleasant and so I slapped his face and then he stomped off to the pub.'

'Good God!' said Freddie. 'You've had a row with William. I never thought I'd live to see the day.' His voice was light. He did not sound worried.

'I'm afraid I've made a right mess of it,' said Constance.

'Well, it's nice to know you're human.'

'What do you mean by that, for goodness sake?'

'Constance, you're jolly near perfect, don't you realise? Mothers are allowed to lose their tempers with their sons, you know, especially when their sons have been behaving like prats. You'll never love him any the less whatever he does in life, will you? And he feels the same about you. So what's the great tragedy? I thought somebody had died.'

She managed a watery smile.

'Freddie, sometimes you are just wonderful,' she said.

'It's my turn,' he replied affectionately. 'And now I think it would be a good idea if I went to join my son for a pint, don't you?'

William was in the back bar of the Dog and Duck when his father joined him. The boy's face was pale and his eyes red-rimmed. Freddie wondered for a moment if he had been crying too. A pint of bitter stood on the table in front of William. He had hardly touched it.

'Thought you had a drink problem,' said Freddie, by way of a rather obscure greeting.

'It's not a problem, dad, honest.' William sounded subdued, nonetheless.

Freddie smiled, leaned across the table and embraced his son. 'Fine. Then let's not make it one.'

'I'm sorry, dad.'

Freddie leaned his head to one side, mildly surprised, and studied his only son carefully. Certainly William looked sorry. Those handsome features seemed quite morose. His shoulders were slumped and he sat almost hunched over the virtually untouched beer. Perhaps Constance had done more good than she realised. She'd given the little blighter a shock, that was for sure.

Freddie was ever an optimist. Unlike Constance, he could not bring himself even to mention drugs. The boy couldn't be that daft, he told himself. He's gone a bit off the rails. He's had a shock, he'll be fine now. He'll not let anybody down.

'I'm glad of that, son, pity you couldn't have told your mother so, though,' he said quietly.

William winced. 'Did she tell you what I said to her?'

'No. What did you say to her?'

'If I told you, you'd kill me.'

'Best not, then.' Freddie looked him up and down again. 'So let's just try and straighten this mess out, shall we?'

Ultimately William stayed at home for little more than a week. Eventually he assured his father, as he had his mother, that he had not been taking drugs. Neither did he have a drink problem, he insisted, he just liked to party. He promised to control his partying and to work hard at college were he given the opportunity to do so again. And he apologised to Constance who accepted his apology warmly. But there remained a certain edge to relations between mother and son.

Some things that are said, particularly within families, can never be quite unsaid. Constance had been very deeply hurt. She couldn't help wondering if her only son had always harboured the thoughts about her that he had expressed, the awful idea that she had been some kind of gold digger. She knew better really, but sometimes in temper people do say what they really mean.

Certainly she realised that it would take her a while to get over it and she was delighted in more ways than one when the family was told that William could return to college after all. In addition to continuing to want the very best for her son, she felt that a time apart would do them both good.

Ted Parish called with the good news. He also made it clear that the college principal was still suspicious about William's possible involvement with drugs, but had accepted that nothing could be proved and agreed therefore to allow William to return – provided he pledged that there would be no further complaints about his behaviour.

William, by now apparently eager only to please, did so most earnestly. He also received a letter sternly informing him that the decision to allow him to continue with his studies had been made primarily in deference to the standing of his family and that should he fall by the wayside again he would not be given another chance.

Predictably there was plenty of talk in the village. Constance had quite rightly foreseen that the local scandal-mongers would somehow learn of each development in the saga of her son almost as quickly as did the Lange family.

'I hope for 'is poor father's sake that boy don't turn out to be a black sheep,' commented Marcia Spry to Mrs Walters in the village shop. Like a lot of dedicated gossips, Marcia had a penchant for speaking in clichés and using hackneyed expressions. 'Of course, there's always been a question mark 'anging over that mother of 'is. 'Er was never in Freddie Lange's class. They was wed in no time, too. Marry in haste, regret at leisure, that's what I always say . . .'

Mrs Walters had heard it all before from Marcia Spry and didn't particularly wish to hear it again. There was always bound to be gossip about someone of Constance Lange's standing in a rural area and Mrs Walters was not above enjoying a certain amount of idle tittle-tattle – you could hardly run a village shop and not indulge in a little gossip now and again. But that Marcia Spry always went too far, Mrs Walters thought, and she really was a rather unpleasant old busy-body.

Mrs Walters didn't say any of that, of course. After all, she had a business to run and Marcia Spry was a customer who visited her shop far more frequently, and therefore spent considerably more money, than anybody would have thought necessary for an elderly spinster living alone. But Mrs Walters understood perfectly well that buying her groceries was only the secondary reason for Marcia's frequent shopping expeditions. First and foremost Marcia Spry always wanted a good natter. And if Mrs Walters wished to make a living she had to accept that she had another function in Chalmpton Peverill in addition to selling stamps, newspapers, sugar, soap and bread, and generally considered equally important. The village shopkeeper and post-mistress was also widely regarded as both an audience and a sorting house for all the latest and juiciest gossip.

A meeting of the committee set up to arrange the village's annual Christmas festival, which Constance was chairing and upon which both Freddie and Marcia Spry served, was held a fortnight after William Lange returned to college. The Langes had publicly made light of the whole incident and, on the surface at least, life seemed to be pretty much back to normal.

Miraculously perhaps – based on his initial response to the trouble he had got himself into, Constance had to admit to herself – William seemed to be settling down. Ted Parish had reported privately to Freddie that his son's work already showed signs of improvement and certainly there had so far been no more unexplained absences nor bouts of public drunkenness. William appeared to be behaving responsibly again – much more like a Lange, Ted had told Freddie.

The meeting went as well as these things ever can, taking into account the various rival factions competing to gain maximum credit while at the same time putting in minimum work. The only unexpected moment came when the proceedings were virtually over and the discussions had more or less become small talk.

Without warning, a neighbouring farmer jokingly referred to having recently spotted Constance somewhere she should not, indeed, unless she hadn't been telling her family the truth about her various movements, could not, have been. Her husband glanced at her inquiringly.

Constance studied the neighbour with interest. She assumed that the man thought he was making some kind of joke. Certainly he had spoken without any appearance of deliberate malice – but in village life you could never be sure of these things. Nonetheless Constance decided to give him the benefit of the doubt.

'I think you must have made a mistake, Joe,' she said casually and with an easy smile.

'Oh no I 'aven't, Missus,' insisted the man. 'Come on then, tell us what you was up to?' And he proceeded to tease her mercilessly.

Finally Constance flashed him her most challenging look. 'Actually, I was visiting my toyboy lover,' she remarked, grinning broadly, and causing an outbreak of laughter around the table. After all, Constance was known for her wickedly dry sense of humour.

'God, not him *again*,' said Freddie, quite untroubled.

And Constance knew that she had passed the whole thing off beautifully, but she did sometimes wish that she did not have to put up with quite so much small-minded silliness.

Marcia Spry, however, was captivated. It didn't take much to get Marcia going and this was the kind of exchange upon which she thrived. In her capable hands even a smattering of intrigue could be almost instantly transformed into a full-blown mystery.

The next day Marcia found herself actually standing on the doorstep of Mrs Walter's shop when the other woman opened up at 8.00 am. She hadn't been able to wait to pass on her latest bit of news.

'You mark my words,' she remarked sagely, after treating Mrs Walters to a full account of the events of the previous night, 'there be things about thigee Constance Lange that just don't add up.'

Several days later, on a cool but bright autumn afternoon, the weather having apparently settled at last, Charlie was driving through Clifton on his way to see Mrs Pattinson. That always put him in a good mood. He had with him a young partner, a rangy fair-haired young man called Sandy, rather less experienced in the work than was Charlie.

Charlie had met Sandy in the Brasserie as arranged and was giving him a lift in his BMW. Charlie liked showing off his car. The sunshine glinted on the bonnet and reflected against the windscreen. Charlie was wearing his new pale grey Armani jacket and had his Ray Ban shades on. He felt cool. Beethoven blared from the CD player. Charlie hummed along with the music.

Sandy did not seem to be very interested in music,

and if he was surprised by Charlie's choice he gave no sign. Neither did he seem impressed by the car, which was a shame. Perhaps he was just too busy thinking about the job ahead.

It was the first time that Charlie had teamed up with Sandy – and Sandy told him that he had only done three jobs so far for Avon Escorts. He liked the work, though, he said with a broad grin. Certainly Sandy seemed sure enough of himself, relaxed, excited even. And he reacted with gleeful enthusiasm when Charlie explained to him the details of Mrs Pattinson's latest sex game.

'A lot of them like games,' remarked Charlie knowingly, as he explained to his partner exactly what would happen to him and what he would be required to do.

'Wow!' said Sandy eventually.

'Think you can manage it?'

'I'm horny already . . .'

# Five

On the second Tuesday in October Constance travelled to Bristol to visit her aunt as usual. But this time she arrived back at Chalmpton Peverill much later than ever before. It was nearly 1.00 a.m. Freddie was distraught.

He had been unable to raise her on her mobile phone and had spent the final hour before her eventual arrival wondering whether or not he should call the police. Ultimately he had set himself a 1.00 a.m. deadline before doing so – his wife just made it.

'I'm so sorry, darling, I let the batteries on the phone go flat. Forgot to charge it last night. Stupid of me.'

Freddie was quivering with anxiety.

'But where on earth were you? And why didn't you use a pay phone to call? You must have known I'd be worried sick.' Freddie spoke loudly, a rare edge to his voice. He could not help being angry, as people are when they have worried unnecessarily. It wasn't like Constance to be so inconsiderate.

'I had a break-down on the motorway, that's all,' his wife replied quietly. 'Something to do with the carburettor, they said. And you can only phone the emergency services from those motorway phones.'

'But they'll pass on messages, for goodness sake.' Freddie snapped at her, something he hardly ever did. 'Why didn't you ask them to call?'

'I didn't think it would take so long. They promised to be quick and I know women on their own on motorways have priority nowadays. Especially after dark. But everything seemed to take longer than I'd thought, including fixing the car. And when I got going again I didn't want to stop. I just wanted to get home.'

'Well, I can understand that, I suppose,' said Freddie, a little doubtful nonetheless. He was already not so angry, but still concerned.

He had gone out to meet her in the yard as soon as he had seen the headlights of the Volvo swing in through the gateway. Now they were standing together in the kitchen. She was still clutching the usual carrier bags.

Suddenly she swayed slightly, almost as if she were feeling giddy, dropped the bags without ceremony and clutched the edge of the kitchen table.

'I'm going to have to sit down,' she said in rather a weak voice, slumping quickly into a chair.

Josh was by her side of course, his tail frantically indicating his joy at the homecoming of his mistress. She had ignored him from the start and, as if desperate to attract her attention, the dog began to bark.

Freddie irritably ordered the Labrador to shut up and lie down – and only later reflected on how out of character it was for Constance not to make a huge fuss of the creature. The farmer had not really noticed before how tired and drawn his wife looked. He took in the pinched features and the wan paleness of her cheeks. He was even more alarmed now.

'Are you all right?' he asked, his voice suddenly full of concern, his irritation reserved for Josh who had stopped barking but was now running agitatedly around the kitchen.

Constance nodded, although her appearance made the gesture a lie.

'It's just that it's been a long day – and I think I've eaten something that disagreed with me,' she said. Even her voice sounded strange.

Freddie had a sudden, disquieting thought. He sat down next to her and took her hand in his.

'Nothing happened, did it? You know, out there on the motorway . . . while you were waiting?'

Constance managed a weak smile.

'Oh no, Freddie, nothing like that. No, I was fine. I just don't feel all that good, that's all.'

'Oh, darling, I'm sorry I was ratty,' he responded. 'I was just worried, that's all. Why don't you go up to bed. Maybe a good night's sleep will put you right.'

She kissed him good night in a rather abstracted way, he thought, and he wondered if she was in pain. A little later he heard her retching in the bathroom.

'I expect I'll be better now,' she said, as if by way of explanation when he went upstairs and joined her in the bedroom.

Freddie was almost as worried as he had been earlier when he had sat in the kitchen waiting for so long for her to return. Constance was always so capable, so in control. About the only time he could ever remember her losing control was when she had that row with William. He suspected that had upset her more than she had let on. Neither of them had ever told him exactly what had been said, but Constance did not have a monopoly on sensitivity in the Lange household and he was aware of the tension remaining between them. Rows like that were commonplace in many families, he supposed, but rare indeed for the Langes.

This, though, was much more than that. He wondered, the dread burning hot within him, if she were really ill. What if she had something seriously wrong with her and had not told him? He tried to get his imagination under control as his mind ran swiftly through a list of dreadful illnesses which could cause someone to be physically sick.

He continued to fret as he climbed into the big double bed beside her. Moonlight shone through the window on to them. Being careful to move as little as possible he studied her drawn face, the parchment skin, the slight furrow in her brow. God, he loved her. She was lying quite still, her features passive, as if she were asleep, but Freddie suspected somehow, he could not have explained why, that she was not really sleeping.

He lay like that, watching her for at least an hour. Constance was an icon to Freddie. She was his rock. He knew he had handled the problem with William well, better than his wife for once, but he wasn't sure if he could ever give Constance the kind of support she had always given him, wasn't sure if he was capable of that. She was the one who listened to his problems. And if she ever had any of her own she never let on. She was certainly never ill.

Eventually, fitfully, Freddie drifted into troubled sleep.

By his side Constance stirred. She studied Freddie closely, as if making sure that he was truly asleep, and then slipped carefully out of bed. She spent most of the rest of the night sitting in the armchair in the spare bedroom gazing at the moon.

Josh heard her moving, trotted tentatively upstairs and nosed his way into the room. The bedrooms were normally out of bounds to Josh. But the dog knew this was not a normal night. Not only did Constance make no effort to order him downstairs, yet again she seemed virtually unaware of his presence.

Josh wrapped his warm furry body around her legs and rubbed his moist nuzzle into the palm of her hand. There was no response. The Labrador moved away, tail down, and lay on the rug by the window, whimpering his hurt.

Josh did not sleep either. The dog's every nerve was twitching. The hair on the back of his neck bristled. There was something happening that he did not understand. All night long his soft brown eyes remained fixed on his mistress's face, lit by the white gleam of the moon.

In the morning Freddie woke to find an empty space next to him in the bed. He started into a sitting position. Where was she now? This was another break in his treasured routine. He always got up first. Then he always brought Constance her mug of tea in bed.

He pulled on his dressing gown and, anxiety gnawing at him like a hungry mosquito, set off downstairs, in search of his wife.

He found her in the kitchen, teapot in the hand.

'Good morning,' she said. 'Thought I'd give you a treat and bring you a cuppa in bed for once. You beat me to it.'

She smiled at him warmly, but Freddie thought he could still see lines of tension around her mouth which were not usually there.

He went to her and kissed her. Was it his imagination that she was not quite as responsive as he had grown to expect?

He took the tea she offered him and sat down at the table to drink it.

'Do you feel all right this morning?' he asked. 'I was worried about you last night. I wondered what had made you sick.'

'Something I ate, I'm sure of it, I told you.' She was all reassurance. 'I feel absolutely fine today, I promise you.'

He nodded, hoping with all his heart that she was telling him the truth.

'I suppose I'd better get the Volvo into the garage so that Bert can check it out,' he remarked casually. 'We don't want the same thing happening again, do we?'

She spoke quickly. 'I don't think there's any need. The AA fixed it properly, I'm sure, that's why it took so long. They said the car was fine now.'

Her voice was back to normal. She was busying herself with everyday tasks, already preparing a load of washing for the machine.

'Are you sure nobody . . .' he paused, seeking the right words and not really finding them, '. . . bothered you out there?'

'Darling, I've told you. It wasn't very nice sitting alone in the dark with ten-ton trucks hurtling by, but I was perfectly OK. Really.'

Still Freddie remained uneasy.

'Do you think you ought to go and see Jim Forbes? I'll take you to the surgery, if you like. Have a check up, just to make sure you're all right?'

'Freddie, I've told you, I feel fine. I don't need a

doctor. Look, it's market day, that bloody man from the ministry is coming to check out the piggery again, and we've both got a busy day ahead. Stop fussing, will you?'

He held up both hands as if in resigned apology. Constance, it seemed, was her brisk businesslike self again.

# Six

Mrs Pattinson was a creature of habit. She had a regular booking with Avon Escorts from which it was highly unusual for her to deviate. She was also quite meticulous about her arrangements. She routinely called Paolo at Avon to confirm her appointment as soon as she arrived at the Crescent Hotel, even though she must always know that the agency would already have her in the diary.

It was therefore a surprise to hear from her at any other time than her usual day. She wanted Charlie – fast, she said.

'I'll do my best, Mrs Pattinson,' said Paolo in his broad Bristol drawl – he was of Italian descent but West Country born and bred.

As he spoke he consulted the computer. Avon Escorts was a business just like any other and kept proper records – when it suited, of course. The situation was just as Paolo had thought.

'Thing is, Mrs Pattinson, Charlie's on a day off today. Wouldn't you like a nice change? I've got this new lad on the books, lovely boy 'e is, only nineteen, but you should see the build on 'im . . .' Paolo paused as if making it clear that his last remark was open to all kinds of interpretation.

Mrs Pattinson's voice on the other end of the line was cool and firm.

'It's Charlie I want,' she said, and it may have been

Paolo's imagination but he reckoned there was already a slight sexy huskiness in the way she spoke. 'I'm sure he will come to me.'

Paolo wasn't so sure, but he knew that Charlie regarded Mrs Pattinson as a very special customer, as did he. She regularly coughed up £200 – an extra £150 if she asked for a second boy – without a murmur. The agency took half the fee, that was the arrangement, and half of that went through the business for the tax man. After all, this was a reputable escort agency. The other half went into the back pockets of Paolo and his partner – the man who had put up the money to start Avon in the first place, although he had little direct involvement nowadays.

Paolo also suspected that Mrs Pattinson tipped Charlie generously. The handsome West Indian was a favourite with a lot of the ladies. He was also considerably brighter than most of the lads and lasses who ended up in this game, Paolo thought. On reflection he reckoned there was a good chance that Charlie would break into his day off for Mrs Pattinson. Charlie understood about business, about looking after the customers.

'I'll try and track Charlie down,' he said.

'I'll be waiting,' said Mrs Pattinson. And now Paolo was quite sure of the note of sexiness in her voice.

He quickly dialled Charlie's home number.

Charlie answered cheerily and then lowered his voice to a conspiratorial whisper.

'I've got me mum here,' he hissed down the line. 'It was me little sister's wedding this afternoon. There's no way I can get away.'

83

'She asked for you special, Charlie, like she always does,' said Paolo. 'I don't want to let her down.'

He could have been talking about a regular customer in a restaurant who wanted a favourite table that wasn't available.

'Neither do I,' said Charlie, his voice still low. 'She's all right is Mrs P. Look, we've just sent 'em off on their honeymoon and tonight we're having a family knees-up down at The Abbey Arms. I can't get out of that, Paolo. Me mum would know there was something up, and I'm not having her upset.'

Charlie was a very loving son. Paolo knew that.

'You'll just have to send someone else this time, mate,' said Charlie. 'You know these middle-class honky bitches. One black arse is the same as any other. Send Marty.'

Charlie put the phone down quickly. He knew that his last remark wasn't true, not of Mrs Pattinson. She had not taken a particular interest in Charlie because he was black – colour genuinely meant little to her one way or the other, Charlie was sure – but because of what he could provide. Charlie knew he was the best she had ever had. She had told him so, hadn't she – and at times when he had been damn sure she hadn't been fibbing. But at least Charlie had got himself off the hook. Nonetheless he found his thoughts turning towards Mrs Pattinson, as they did quite often nowadays. Of all his clients over the years she was the only one who had got under his skin.

He was still standing in the hallway by the phone – he kept it there, a black one hanging on the wall almost like a piece of sculpture, so that he could take calls in some privacy even when he had guests. There was something so honestly responsive about Mrs Pattinson. Charlie had never known a woman quite like her and, goodness knows, there had been enough of them in his life already.

The voice of his mother calling from among the hubbub in the living-room brought him abruptly back to the present.

'Charlie, son, what are you doing out there? Are we going to have this party tonight or not?'

Miriam Collins still had the sing-song voice of her native Jamaica. She had been born and raised there until she was ten years old when her parents, along with so many in the years following the war, had emigrated to the UK, to the land of promise.

Through most of her life that promise had never been fulfilled. Her parents had died young, of disappointment and cold, Miriam always said, and it had not been far from the truth probably. Miriam had made a wonderfully happy marriage, but that had been cut short by the premature death of Charlie's father. Home throughout Miriam's entire life in England had been a slum of some kind or other in St Paul's. She still lived in the same terraced house in a little street off the Ashley Road in which Charlie had been brought up, but much of that area of St Paul's had been given a face-lift recently, and Charlie did his best to make sure that his mother was not short of home comforts nowadays. She had had a hard life and he adored her. It was his greatest wish that he could make the rest of her days happy and comfortable.

Certainly he loved giving his family treats and he loved entertaining them in his flat, showing off a home of a style and quality that none of them had so

85

far aspired to – nor, with the exception of his kid sister Daisy, were ever likely to.

Smiling broadly, he walked down the passageway over the beautiful wooden flooring and into the living-room. His mother, slim and somehow elegant still, a far cry from the stereotype of a middle-aged black woman, stood by the big picture window with his elder brothers, Jack and Winston, whose wives were sitting close together at one end of the big sofa. They were firm friends, those two. Elder sister Mary Anne and her husband Lewis were somehow managing to share an armchair, giggling over the champagne Charlie had provided. Only brother Bart was missing – he had been at the church earlier, looking, thankfully, in reasonable shape, and had promised to meet them later at the Abbey. Charlie hoped for his mother's sake that Bart would keep his promise.

Children seemed to be everywhere. Lewis and Mary Anne's twin two-year-old boys were mercifully asleep in their double pushchair, but two of Jack's three girls were waltzing each other around the room, their shoes making disturbing squeaking noises on Charlie's immaculate floor, while the third competed with Winston's little boy and girl to see who could bounce highest on the springy sofa. Their mothers, deep in conversation at the other end, were oblivious. And nobody but Charlie noticed when Winston's son decided to toss one of the cushions at his father, missing him by several feet.

Not for the first time, Charlie congratulated himself on having decided against his original choice of yet more cream and going for black leather furniture in his living room. He would allow nobody but his family to behave so cavalierly in his home, but family was different. That was what Charlie had been brought up to believe and he did so, with all his heart.

Charlie had never had a girlfriend, really. He didn't want one. He couldn't quite face the idea of more sex on a regular basis at the end of a stint of being paid for it. And he felt no need for any emotional ties other than his family. Charlie's family were everything to him.

'Oh, there you are,' said his mother as he picked up the last bottle of Moet. The words were nothing, but her voice was warm with pride and affection. It always was when she spoke to Charlie. She had been laughing when he entered the room, a great belly-shaking laugh which was stereotyped West Indian and which totally belied her size. She was wearing a royal-blue linen suit, the skirt just short enough to show off her still shapely legs but not too short for her years, Charlie thought. The hat of matching colour which she had earlier worn at a rakish angle for the church service was on the glass coffee table in the middle of the room. Miriam Collins had several nice outfits now, and Charlie had insisted on buying something new for her to wear on this special day. He thought his mother – and all his family come to that, they were a good looking bunch, the Collinses, dressed in their best for the occasion – looked absolutely splendid.

Charlie's eyes were admiring as he put an arm around his mother and attempted to refill her glass. The bottle was almost empty.

'That's it then, the end of the champagne,' he said. 'Let's go down the Abbey and show 'em how the Collinses can party.'

*

Paolo put the phone down, resigned to having to find Mrs Pattinson an acceptable alternative after all. He wondered whether he should try to call her at the Crescent Hotel. But he had never done so before. She might not like it. In any case, Charlie was probably right, he reasoned. When the crunch came, one black arse might well be just the same to her as another. And he really didn't want to lose the booking. Two hundred quid was a lot of dosh to turn your back on for no good reason.

He took Charlie's advice. Charlie would know better than anyone, surely.

Paolo sent Marty Morris – another young West Indian from St Paul's, slightly shorter than Charlie but around the same build.

Marty arrived by cab, alighting a hundred yards or so before the hotel. Be discreet, Paolo had reminded him. He approached chalet ten through the garden, also according to instructions.

It was 7.00 p.m. by the time Marty got there, wet and dark on a particularly nasty October evening. The rain was back with a vengeance again, turning the little-used path he had to follow into something of a hazard. But Marty had been to the Crescent Hotel before and he was able to find his way to chalet ten easily enough, even though the gardens were only poorly lit away from the central buildings.

He entered the hotel's grounds through the small pedestrian gate set in the brick wall which backed on to a lane off the main street around the corner from the principal entrance. Then he followed the path until he reached a stone fountain, which, even in the bad light, he could see was covered in moss and looked as if it had not operated in years. He remembered that he must turn right there.

The path was quite overgrown after that. Rhododendron bushes lined it on either side, their tips virtually touching above his head, forming a kind of tunnel. Marty had the collar of his leather jacket turned up against the rain, although it was now little more than a light drizzle, and was walking with his head slightly bowed. Within the rhododendron tunnel water fell steadily from the glossy leaves of the big bushes and several icy droplets trickled down his neck, inside his shirt, causing him to shiver. His feet, shod in unsuitable leather-soled loafers, slipped occasionally on the path's muddy surface. Once he nearly fell.

Straight ahead he could see a brighter light. That should be chalet ten, he reckoned, unless he had turned the wrong way in the dark. And he would be quite glad to be inside out of the cold and wet, there was no doubt about that, whatever might lie in store for him.

There was a rustling in the bushes to his left, which he registered to be moving closer to him, but automatically assumed it must be a cat out on a spot of nocturnal hunting. Marty didn't have a nervous disposition nor a vivid imagination. It didn't go with the territory really, for people in his line of work. And he never did find out what was causing the rustling noise.

Neither did Marty ever reach chalet ten.

The knife slid easily between his shoulder blades. It was driven straight into the soft fleshy core of his body, the point scoring a direct hit on his spinal cord.

The shock was total. The blow lethal. Marty did

not even have time to scream. One searing flash of unspeakable agony. One tearing burst of pure white-hot pain. Then nothing.

He died virtually at once. And even had he lived he would have been of no use to the police who were to investigate his murder. The attack on Marty Morris was swift and efficient. Marty did not even see his assailant.

# Seven

The investigating officer assigned to the murder of Marty Morris was Detective Chief Inspector Rose Piper of the Avon and Somerset Constabulary. She arrived at the scene of the crime wearing a big black overcoat buttoned up around the neck. Only she knew what she was wearing underneath. Rose Piper had been at her husband Simon's fortieth birthday party when she got the call. Nonetheless, she hadn't wasted a moment getting to the Crescent Hotel.

Rose, young for her rank at only thirty-three, particularly young for a woman at that rank, was a career policewoman and she relished the idea of a juicy murder. Not for the first time, her marriage had to take second place, even on such a special night. She had merely told Simon she had to go to work, whispered a brief apology giving him little or no chance to reply, and slipped quickly away. She had been aware though, of his hurt angry stare following her as she left the restaurant, abandoning him to their friends.

But she certainly wasn't going to allow anyone else to muscle in on a murder like this one. It had been given to her, and she wasn't going to let it go. Rose was based at Southmead Police Station, conveniently placed for Southmead Hospital which housed the city mortuary, and Marty Morris had been murdered in Clifton, an area squarely in her Southmead patch. Rose was rather glad about that.

In fact she could hardly wait to get stuck in. She had asked for a pair of Wellington boots to be ready at the scene but hadn't even considered taking the time to change her clothes for more suitable apparel. She had just thanked God for the big black coat as she walked out into the street and over to the patrol car which had been sent to pick her up – not only did it completely cover the unsuitable party attire she was wearing underneath, it would also keep her warm and dry on a cold drizzly evening. She also thanked God that the bash, in the stylish private room at the back of Bristol's fashionable San Carlo restaurant, hadn't been going long enough for her to have had more than one drink and a few sips of a second before her mobile phone had called her into action.

She liked a drink when she had the chance, did Rose. She liked a good party. And she had been looking forward to this celebration with her husband as much as she knew he had. But nothing was more important to her than the chance to show what she was made of on a really big case. However it might seem to the public reading the newspapers, you still didn't get a nice juicy murder all that often in the UK. Most of them, Rose was well aware, turned out to be boring domestics, and called for no real policing skills at all.

Rose had always secretly been sorry to have missed out on the Fred West affair which, as it had centred around Gloucester, a mere thirty miles from Bristol, had fallen into the domain of the Gloucestershire Constabulary. In Bristol alone there were six police stations, all with strictly defined territories, all with detectives of sufficient rank to be put in charge of a murder inquiry. You had to get lucky to land a juicy one, that was the way Rose saw it. There was nothing like solving a good murder to give your career a quick hoist up the ladder. And she wasn't going to put herself in a position where it would be her own fault if she missed out on this one, that was for certain. So if that meant upsetting Simon, well, it wouldn't be for the first time. He'd get over it. He always did. She could get around him. She always could.

Rose hunched her shoulders against the weather, shoved her hands deep into her pockets and made her way briskly along the path through the overgrown gardens of the Crescent Hotel towards the crime scene which was already cordoned off and brightly lit by portable floodlights. A duck-boarded route had been laid down away from the murder victim's path, now part of the protected crime scene – but the drizzly rain continued and the boards were treacherous, particularly for a woman wearing absurdly high-heeled bright orange shoes. To her annoyance the boots she had requested had been forgotten and eventually the inevitable happened. Looking ahead at what awaited her instead of watching her step she slipped off the greasy wood and landed in a particularly unpleasant puddle – that was the end of her extravagant shoes, Rose suspected. She realised that the young uniformed police constable escorting her had noticed what she had done and was studying her closely waiting for a reaction. She gave none.

Rose was the most feminine looking of women, small, slight, fluffy blonde hair fairly obviously owing most of its colour to a good hairdresser, and lots of make-up. She also dressed like an extremely feminine woman and not like the usual conception of a police-woman at all. Certainly most people who might be confronted by her in the street, even if she was dressed for work and not for her social life, would never dream that she were a police officer, and definitely not a Detective Chief Inspector.

Rose Piper's looks were very deceptive. She was about as tough and ruthlessly ambitious as they came. She was also clever.

She stopped outside the tent which had been constructed around the body of the murder victim, and stood silently for a moment studying the situation.

The SOCOs – scenes of crime officers – were already at work within the patch of ground now surrounded by a tape fence and were combing the cordoned-off area for evidence. It was down to Rose, as Senior Investigating Officer, to eventually decide the extent of the area to be sealed, but the SOCOs had got there first this time and they were an experienced bunch who knew well enough what had to be done. All wore white paper suits, overshoes and surgical gloves.

A similarly clad character, smaller and slighter than any of the others, crouched on the ground, bending over the body. Rose presumed at once that this was Dr Carmen Brown, even though the doctor had her back to the policewoman and the hood of her paper suit was pulled up over her head concealing her distinctive auburn hair. The stature and attitude of the Bristol-based Home Office pathologist, whose territory included the entire area policed by the Avon and Somerset Constabulary, made her virtually unmistakable.

Rose was always pleased to see Carmen Brown. There were only forty or so Home Office pathologists in the country, of whom just a handful were women, and Rose knew that, just like her, Carmen always felt under pressure to do a better job than the men.

The DCI made no attempt to step within the crime scene. She was not yet suitably clad. But as she stood, taking it all in for a moment, the biggest and burliest of the white suits inside the cordon spotted her and called out to her in greeting.

'Evening boss,' said a strong male voice.

It was Rose's sergeant, Peter Mellor, and she was relieved that he was there before her. She had assumed he would be as, unlike her, Sergeant Mellor had been on duty that evening. Mellor was a graduate entrant to the force, a big man physically and mentally, black, just twenty-five, married and a father already. He had a strong sense of morality and was a high achiever with little time for those who did not share his capabilities or his ideals. But even if he was sometimes just a little too unbending for Rose's taste, he was a top-class copper and having him there already would speed things up no end for her, she knew that. Mellor was every bit as clever as she was, she suspected, and considerably more methodical. He had an incisive brain and an ability quickly to gather and sift information. He would already have learned all that was so far possible, she was quite sure of that.

Indeed, without waiting to be asked, the sergeant stepped outside the hastily erected tape fencing and began to brief her.

The victim was a young black male, he told Rose. And even Carmen Brown – who continued to examine the corpse without acknowledging Rose's arrival, if indeed the thoroughly engrossed doctor had even noticed it – was not prevaricating about the cause of death on this one, said Mellor. It seemed the young man had been stabbed in the back. Just once.

'Murder weapon?' asked Rose briskly.

'No sign, boss. There's a couple of good footprints in the mud though. Very distinctive. Big size. I'm pretty sure they're Timberlands actually – got a pair myself.'

Rose nodded. In that case it was a pity Timberland boots were as popular as she knew them to be, she thought.

'Time of death?'

'The doctor's hedging her bets on that one like they always do,' replied Sergeant Mellor. 'But she's prepared to speculate that it was around twenty-four hours ago.'

'Was the body moved here after death, then?'

Peter Mellor shook his head. 'They don't think so, boss. No sign of that.'

'So a body has been lying here undetected all this time, right through the day? In a hotel garden in the middle of Clifton?'

Sergeant Mellor shrugged. 'Apparently nobody uses the gardens at this time of year. You can see how overgrown it is around here. This path leads to a gate in the wall back there, but you can drive right up to the main entrance and there's a car park at the front too. Visitors all go in that way and the staff use the tradesman's entrance which is also round the front.'

Rose nodded. 'Do we know who the victim is?'

'We think we know his name. We found a wallet on the ground beside him which looked as if it had fallen from his jacket pocket. Not much in it, about £30 in cash, a couple of photographs, no credit cards. But there was a membership card to the Riverside Health and Fitness Club, in the name of Marty J. Morris.'

Rose nodded again. She knew the Riverside, it had a gymnasium which specialised in body building and was particularly popular with the gay community.

'Is he known at the hotel?' she asked. 'Has anybody interviewed the management or staff yet?'

'No boss. We were waiting for you. But the whole area has been secured. Staff and guests all know that nobody leaves the premises until we say so.'

'Good. OK. I'd better have a closer look, I suppose. Where can I get kitted up?'

Rose looked around her without much enthusiasm. The rain which seemed to have been falling intermittently for days had mercifully stopped while she and Sergeant Mellor had been talking. But drops of water were still showering from the trees and shrubs above her head and the ground around the scene of crime, including the path, had been turned into a bog by tramping feet, although tarpaulin sheets had been laid down in the immediate vicinity of the body.

'They've given us a couple of chalets – there are some suits in room nine over there,' said Peter Mellor, pointing vaguely through the undergrowth.

Rose picked her way further along the muddy path, aware that the care she was taking was really a lost cause as her shoes were definitely already history. There was a police constable in the room brewing tea with the kettle provided for the hotel's guests. Unceremoniously Rose turfed him out. She removed her black overcoat, exposing a bright orange velvet suit with a plunging neckline and a short straight skirt, its hemline several inches above her knees. She had bought it at vast expense especially for her husband's birthday party because she had known Simon

97

would adore it – ironic in the circumstances. Although he was a man disinterested in his own clothing, he loved to see Rose in stylishly sexy clothes, particularly in bright colours – the kind of clothes she would never normally wear to work, which was undoubtedly part of their attraction because he considered that she wore them especially for him, as indeed she did. Certainly she hadn't wanted to reveal the undoubtedly provocative little orange number to Somerset's finest and she hadn't wanted to ruin it in all the muck out there, either.

Hesitating only for a moment she removed her skirt, wrapping it in her black coat and placing the bundle carefully on the bed, and pulled on the paper overalls on top of her suit jacket. Sighing resignedly, she yanked plastic galoshes over her spoiled shoes, hoping that the sharp heels wouldn't break through them.

When she was ready she took a few deep breaths before entering the fray. She had wanted a juicy murder and it looked like she had got one. But, paradoxically, Rose could never quite get over the initial shock she experienced each time she was confronted with a dead body. She had lost count of the number she had seen now. In her earlier uniformed days there had been the usual mix of road-accident victims and other incidental deaths. Once she had had to break into an old man's house and had found him lying dead on his kitchen floor. She could still remember the stench which had greeted her. He had died of a stroke, it turned out, several days earlier.

This would be only the second murder enquiry she had headed, although it already looked as if it might be the most interesting she had ever worked on, but she had assisted on many more. Bristol was a tough city. Domestics and gang fights might not make a detective's reputation, but they still counted.

Nonetheless she had to steel herself. She certainly knew better than to show any sign of weakness. She had learned that a long time ago, she thought to herself, as she ducked under the tape fence and approached her city's latest victim of violent crime.

Carmen Brown was now standing up and this time she turned around at once as Rose approached. The doctor was a youngish woman, even smaller and more slight of build than Rose, with intelligent eyes and, although so young, already a permanent somewhat world-weary expression which detracted from her natural prettiness.

'Oh, it's you, is it?' said the pathologist, by way of greeting.

'And good evening to you, too, Dr Brown,' responded Rose.

They were two women in jobs which remained predominantly male territory. They liked and respected each other, understood each other even. They both knew how hard each had had to work to achieve the success that they had so far attained. There was never any need to articulate their mutual respect.

Rose's gaze was drawn to the ground at Carmen Brown's feet. The body was spread-eagled there, lying awkwardly on its front, one arm thrust out as if in a bizarre fist-clenched salute, the other tucked beneath the torso, legs apart. The leather jacket the victim was still wearing concealed the fatal wound Rose already knew was somewhere on his back. Bending a little closer she could see the rip through which the blade of the weapon must have passed. It

99

was a surprisingly small abrasion, the damage to the jacket only slight.

The victim's head was to one side and Rose could see his face clearly in the bright lights which so starkly illuminated the scene. He was lying partly in the shallow ditch running alongside the path, and his head and upper body were at a lower level than his legs and feet, explaining probably why the contents of his pockets seemed to have dropped out as he fell forwards and slightly downwards. His entire body was covered in splashes of gooey mud. The rain which had been falling so steadily throughout most of the previous twenty-four hours had washed the mud into rivulets and the corpse was soaking wet, although Rose reasoned that it would have been protected from much of the earlier downpour by the arc of rhododendron. The victim's eyes were wide open as if frozen in fright. Obliquely Rose found herself trying to imagine what it would be like to know you were about to die a violent death, and then, remembering that this young man had been stabbed just once from behind, wondered if he had even known. The mouth of the corpse was stretched open in a skeletal grin, made all the more startling by the even whiteness of his teeth contrasting with the deep ebony of his skin.

Rose forced herself to bend further over in order to take a closer look. There was very little blood and no smell. It is a myth that sudden death causes victims to urinate or to defecate. Carmen Brown, who attended between forty and fifty deaths a year, once told Rose that she had only seen that on one occasion when she had been called to examine a young woman who had hanged herself. Hanging was the only exception and even then not always, but the sudden snapping of the spinal cord in a vertical position sometimes caused pressure on the bladder, forcing it to open. Rose shuddered. The amount of macabre information she had stashed away over the years was quite frightening.

In this case there was very little external indication of violent death – although as Rose leaned closer to that distorted face, to those staring eyes, she suffered her usual chronic reaction. The shock of death never failed to hit her.

She gagged, putting her hand to her mouth, somehow retaining the presence of mind to pretend she was having a coughing fit. Men could show human frailty occasionally and get away with it, even be applauded for it – women could not, certainly not if they wanted to reach the top in the police force, Rose believed.

She stepped back, forced herself to recover quickly, and spoke to the pathologist.

'Died twenty-four hours ago, I gather?' she said.

'Time of death is an inexact science as you well know, Chief Inspector,' replied Carmen Brown coolly.

'And I also know you're never far out, doctor,' Rose responded, continuing in the formality the other had begun, although the two women frequently called each other by their Christian names and certainly did if they met off duty.

Rose looked around her carefully. 'What do you reckon did for our boy, then?' she asked.

'A knife of some kind with an extremely long blade,' answered the pathologist. 'It could have been just an ordinary carving knife but it would have had to have been razor sharp. Probably a butcher's knife of some kind, but then, loads of people have those in their kitchens nowadays. You can clearly see the incisory wound in the small of his back.'

Deftly, Dr Brown lifted the victim's jacket and shirt so that Rose could see the deceptively small entry wound centrally placed just below his shoulder blades. Even on the skin immediately surrounding the stab wound there was little blood.

'And there's very little tearing either to the victim's clothes or skin,' Carmen Brown continued. 'With a wound like this the bleeding would be almost entirely internal. That knife slipped straight in. Easy. And deadly. You're hard-pressed to miss a vital organ of some kind if you stab somebody in the middle of their back.' The doctor looked thoughtful. 'Probably hit the spinal cord, must have sliced through at least one major artery – could even have ruptured a lung. Depends on the angle . . .'

Carmen Brown might have been giving the prognosis on a broken-down car. All pathologists were like that, able to discuss and investigate the most gruesome detail with absolute professional detachment. Rose assumed that was the only way they could work. She suppressed another shudder and had to fight back a second threatening attack of nausea.

'So, what can you tell me about the victim?'

No longer in close contact with the body, the pathologist pushed off the hood of her white suit with the back of one hand, releasing a cascade of auburn curls somehow quite incongruous amid the sterile austerity of the crime scene. She glanced down at the body lying at her feet as she spoke.

'He was a fit young man in his early twenties or perhaps even a little younger. About five foot seven inches, stockily built. Good teeth. An old bruise on his right temple. Wore contact lenses. And he died at once.'

Rose's attention was momentarily diverted by the noisy banter of a familiar double-act behind her. The Cataldi brothers, the coroner's pick-up men, had arrived.

Carmen Brown followed the policewoman's gaze. 'There's nothing more I can do at the scene in conditions like this,' said the pathologist, waving a hand vaguely at the sodden ground and dripping foliage. 'We may as well get him bagged up,' she continued.

Ron Cataldi, the elder and slightly larger of the brothers, passed a folded stretcher over the tape-fence.

'So when are you two ladies going to find us a body in a nice warm sitting-room somewhere?' he asked, an easy grin spreading across his broad face. Another of Bristol's small Italian community, his voice still bore just the faintest hint of Mediterranean lilt.

'What, and leave you guys with nothing to grumble about?' responded Rose.

She liked the Cataldis, everybody did. Their job was to collect bodies whenever a post-mortem examination was required – not just the victims of violent crimes, but all accident and sudden death cases – and deliver the corpses to the nearest mortuary. All coroners' offices employ a full-time team like Ron and Tommy Cataldi. In the Avon and Somerset constabulary, with the blunt graveyard humour common in the police force, they were invariably known as The Body-snatchers.

The Cataldis, who covered the entire Bristol area and probably collected a dozen or so bodies a week in their blue Ford Transit van with its blacked-out rear windows, got through their work by assuming an attitude of relaxed joviality. Their way of dealing with death was to lighten the moment whenever possible, and their manner was such that not only did they get away with it, to the other professionals involved they were always a welcome arrival, however grim the occurrence requiring them. Ron and Tommy wore neat dark suits at all times and at first glance, Rose always thought, they looked and sounded like Mafiosi a long way from home. Then you learned how surprisingly gentle they could be. They had a natural sensitivity about them. Rose had many times witnessed these two big and apparently bluff men coming into a situation where they had to deal with shocked members of the public and sometimes grieving relatives, and do so with a sympathetic deftness she only wished she could emulate.

Tonight, though, there were only professionals about. No public in attendance who might not in such circumstances appreciate the finer points of Tommy and Ron's almost obligatory repartee – which therefore continued fluently as the SOCOs began to carefully lift the body on to the open body bag.

'Oooh, careful with that zip, lads,' said Tommy. 'Good job he's still got his trousers on . . .'

'Yeah, it's 'is lucky day, really, only he don't know it,' interspersed Ron.

Rose raised her eyes heavenwards. Carmen Brown did not even seem to hear. She continued to study the victim intently as he was being zipped into the grey plastic body bag, almost as if she were asking him to tell her more. Eventually she bent down and reached into her medical bag lying on a tarpaulin sheet by her side and produced three transparent evidence bags which she passed to Rose.

'When I took his temperature I found these little items almost hidden by his leg, close to where we found his wallet,' she said matter-of-factly.

One of the plastic bags contained three packets of condoms. The second a small quantity of cannabis resin and the third a scrap of paper on which was scribbled a telephone number.

It was Peter Mellor, back in the Major Incident Room already set up at Southmead Police Station, who dialled the number. His call was answered quite quickly in spite of being just past midnight and in a manner which indicated that calls at all hours were commonplace.

'Avon Escorts,' said a voice with a strong Bristol accent.

Sergeant Mellor replaced the receiver.

'You must have heard of Avon Escorts, boss,' he told Rose a few minutes later. 'They're little better than a mobile knocking shop, and they provide boys as well as girls. A male Tom, that's what our lad is.' Mellor could barely keep the contempt from his voice. 'I'd stake a month's pay on it . . .'

Rose had started to feel very tired. She was, sitting at her desk, legs stretched before her, resigned now to revealing her sexy orange suit which looked just as out of place and attracted just the same sort of raised-eyebrow half-appreciative, half-amused glances in the station as she had known it would at the scene of the crime. But at least it stood less chance of being ruined at the nick than at a muddy crime scene, with a bit of luck anyway, she had been idly thinking to herself as yet another of her colleagues, called back on duty, did a double-take at the sight of her as he entered the already buzzing Incident Room.

Sergeant Mellor's words banished all such trivia from her weary brain. The news jerked her into full alertness. She was instantly excited. Rose had quite a lot of imagination for a copper. She immediately found herself thinking about the Yorkshire Ripper and the other cases throughout history of serial murders of prostitutes. Had she possibly got a similar case on her hands with a new twist – the victims being male prostitutes? She accepted that she was probably being fanciful. The murder was more than likely a one-off. But a little guiltily she also realised she was half hoping that would not prove to be the case.

Avon Escorts had a proper office in a small prefabricated-looking building on the outskirts of the city centre alongside the A38, the main road which links Bristol with Bridgwater, Taunton, and then runs into Devon. It operated as a bona fide business, VAT rated and paying tax. The front was quite simply that it was an escort service, a perfectly legal enterprise, and if any of its employees were involved in additional activities, that was nothing to do with Avon. Rose learned that the vice boys had been keeping an eye on the outfit for years, but Avon Escorts was efficiently run and had never been involved in any kind of scandal. It and its operatives had always kept out of trouble – until now.

The agency apparently tried to run a full twenty-four-hour service. The office number Peter Mellor had called had had a divert on it, but that didn't take long, with modern telecommunications technology, to trace. On this occasion the calls were being referred to the home of one Paolo Constantino, of 16 Clarence Terrace.

Rose knew that the correct procedure for a Senior Investigating Officer was to send a team round. But she could rarely resist taking a first-hand look at anyone she reckoned was likely to become a key figure in a case. It didn't always make her popular.

'Right,' she said. 'Let's go.'

It was 1.00 a.m. when Paolo – who liked his sleep and had been fitfully dozing between telephone interruptions – was summarily awakened by the hammering on his front door. Like Charlie, he had a nice home – a small Victorian terraced house which had been attractively renovated – in a nice area. He was horrified to discover the police on his doorstep. He didn't need that, he really didn't.

There were four of them. A small blonde woman in a big overcoat, a tall black man wearing a grey suit and two uniformed constables. Quite a turn-out. Who did they think he was, for goodness sake? Bristol's Al Capone for the millennium?

It was the small blonde woman, just a slip of a thing really, who almost pushed him back into the hallway.

'Paolo Constantino? I'd like a word with you.'

She managed to make the simple remark sound quite ominous.

'I am Detective Chief Inspector Piper of the Avon and Somerset Constabulary and I have some news for you,' she continued, her voice quietly controlled yet somehow extremely menacing. 'Marty Morris is dead. He's been murdered.'

If it had been her intention to shock Paolo, she certainly succeeded. But he did his best to look non-committal, disinterested even.

'Marty who?' he heard himself say.

'Don't give me that shit!'

Paolo started. Paolo was as streetwise as they came, but he was confused by the contrast between the way the blonde woman looked, feminine almost to the point of frailty in his opinion, and the way she spoke and behaved.

Paolo didn't speak. If he could stay silent for long enough, he might be all right, he reasoned. He sincerely wished that he didn't have to deal with this in the middle of the night. Paolo, perhaps curiously in his chosen trade, was not at his best at night and did not function well at all if his sleeping pattern was disturbed. The agency phone had only been switched over to him because the old man who normally handled the night-time referrals – answering the late phone for Avon Escorts was, after all, a good all-cash pension-boosting number which involved no travelling expenses – was ill. Paolo played for time, trying desperately to gather his thoughts.

After a brief pause the woman chief inspector continued.

'The evening before last Marty Morris was stabbed in the back in the grounds of the Crescent Hotel in Clifton and it's my belief that he was on a job for you when he was attacked. Now, are you going to tell me about it here or would you rather come down to the station?'

Paolo was waking up now, beginning to think a little more clearly. The evening before last at the Crescent Hotel. Christ, he thought. Mrs Pattinson!

He reminded himself that Avon Escorts had never had any trouble with the filth before. Paolo himself had no police record, he had always managed to remain a step ahead. The police turned a blind eye to discreet prostitution unless there was trouble, that was his philosophy, and had been the secret of the success of Avon Escorts. Problem was, there was trouble now. You couldn't get much bigger trouble than a murder. His partner, of whom Paolo was actually a little afraid, would have to be informed pretty smartish too – and he wasn't going to be best pleased. Still, one problem at a time.

Resignedly, Paolo led the intimidating party of police officers into his sitting-room.

The truth was that he had already been mildly anxious about Marty. The lad should have been round the office in the morning to hand over half his fee and he'd never turned up. But Paolo hadn't thought about him being hurt. He'd more or less assumed that the boy had gone on a binge of some sort. Marty liked his blow, Paolo knew that much about him, and his kind were inclined to go missing from time to time when they got a bundle of money thrust at them. Paolo had been concerned only because he had thought he was going to have to sort Marty out. Remind him to behave himself. Help him recollect where his loyalties lay.

'Yeah, OK, Marty was on a job for us,' said Paolo eventually. 'A straight escort job, you understand. We're a respectable agency.'

'Spare me the commercial,' snapped the women inspector whom Paolo, rendered unusually observant by a combination of native cunning, grim realism and long experience, thought might be inclined to sometimes over-compensate for her extremely feminine appearance.

'I want to know exactly where Marty was supposed to be going,' she continued relentlessly. 'I want the time of everything. I want every detail. I need to know whether he reached his destination before he was killed and who he was going to meet.'

So Paolo told her. Everything he knew. He didn't have any choice.

'Marty was booked for Mrs Pattinson . . .' he began.

'Yes, I am absolutely sure,' said the manager of the Crescent Hotel an hour or so later. 'Mrs Pattinson didn't check in here yesterday. It would be on the records and anyway Janet, the receptionist, knew her well by sight.'

Rose did not like the man. Henry Bannerman was plump with greasy skin, his bald head shining almost unnaturally, and exuded a smug self-confidence which his appearance certainly did nothing to merit. His face was fleshy and his somewhat beady eyes blinked incessantly within deeply folded layers of skin.

Rose thought she wouldn't trust him as far as you could roll his unpleasantly rotund form downhill. Nonetheless, she was fairly sure that he was telling the truth.

And it was somehow no surprise also to learn from Henry Bannerman how thoroughly Mrs Pattinson had protected her anonymity.

'Didn't you think it was strange in this day and age that this Mrs Pattinson always paid in cash?' Rose asked the hotel manager, with only a slight edge to her voice.

Bannerman shrugged. 'We do still take real money here,' he said.

His voice had a patronising whine to it. Rose made a mental note to pay more attention to the supercilious bastard at a later date. However, Janet the receptionist indeed confirmed the Chief Inspector's belief that the man had not been lying to her – not so far, at any rate.

'Oh no, I haven't seen Mrs Pattinson at the motel for more than two weeks now,' Janet sleepily assured the two detective constables, sent around at once by Rose, who unceremoniously raised her from her bed just before 4.00 a.m.

The girl – her plump cheeks which coloured so easily glowing increasingly redder as she became more awake and more aware of what was happening – also confirmed that Mrs Pattinson paid cash in advance. Always.

It was about an hour later, at around 5.00 a.m., that Rose decided she could continue no longer without sleep. She had already appointed an office manager she was sure she could work well with, a woman inspector, Phyllis Jordan – whom she had known for many years and considered to be a first-rate organizer. Fortuitously Phyllis had come on night duty just as the murder investigation had been swinging into operation, and, yes, she had assured Rose, she would stay at her post until the Chief Inspector returned to the station as soon as possible after grabbing a few hours sleep.

A police driver took Rose home to the spacious bungalow, 1970s' vintage, which had been home for her and Simon for almost five years now. She wasn't quite sure how she had ended up in a bungalow. She hated bungalows. But this one, on the outskirts of Bristol, did have spectacular views to the southwest out over the Mendip hills.

Simon seemed to be sound asleep, but had somehow contrived to be sprawled across almost the entire breadth of the double bed. That was going to make it very difficult to creep into bed without waking him. And she didn't want to do that unless she had to. It had been planned that the party last night would be very special indeed. Toni, the manager of San Carlo, had produced a customised menu for the occasion and festivities had been expected to continue into the early hours.

Rose had left Simon surrounded by his closest friends, but she knew that the whole thing would have ceased to be special at all for him once she had gone. Although so little had been said she was well aware of how upset he must have been, and how angry. And she didn't want to have to deal with all that now. She was too tired.

She undressed quietly without putting on the bedroom light, draping the prized orange suit carefully over a chair, and then tried to find a corner of the bed into which she could slot herself without disturbing him. It was a lost cause. As she gently attempted to move one of his arms, just a few inches, he woke up with a start, peering at her through the half-darkness. The curtains were open and the street-lamp a few yards down the road outside gave the room a certain pale illumination.

Simon's silky brown hair had fallen across his eyes. He brushed it away in one of those gestures that had been part of his attraction for her when they had met nine years earlier. Simon had just left college after deciding relatively late in life that he wanted a career change. He had been a school teacher. Now he was a social worker. And he was dedicated. She liked that in him. Although she was pretty sure he didn't much like her dedication to her chosen career. In fact she suspected that he would prefer her to be almost anything other than a police officer – mercifully the only thing he had in common with her mother with whom Rose had a distinctly strained relationship – although he had yet to tell her so. Indeed, often she thought he did not want her to be dedicated to any career. Simon badly wanted children, had done for some time. He was seven years older than her, he reminded her frequently, and he didn't want his kids to have the oldest father in town. Rose was still not ready, and sometimes wondered if she ever would be, although she did not admit that to her husband.

Simon had known, of course, both what her job was and her attitude to it, from the start. She had been a keen and newly promoted sergeant at the beginning of their love affair. But nothing would have made any difference then. When Rose met Simon the world had, for a time, stopped revolving for both of them.

They had fallen in love swiftly, deeply and irrevocably, after bumping into each other – literally – on a train from the West Country to London. As Rose, somewhat precariously clutching a plastic beaker of coffee, had been manoeuvring her way back from the buffet car to her seat at the rear of the train, Simon had been manoeuvring his way towards it. And just as they were attempting to squeeze past each other in the middle of a carriage the train had lurched dramatically. Both were sideways on in the passageway between the rows of seats, trying to give each other as much room as possible, and not, at that point, looking at each other at all. The sudden movement of the train propelled Rose forwards, pushing Simon backwards on to the table behind him, their two alarmed faces suddenly pressed close together. Then Simon had smiled – he still had such a wonderful gentle smile – and Rose had melted. It had been difficult for her to find her feet again because her legs had felt like jelly. Simon had started to laugh. He told her later it was because she was gaping at him, as if in some kind of shock, her mouth wide open.

It had been shock. A shock wave. Amazement that it was possible to feel whatever was coursing through her whole being – just like that. She had become aware that the coffee, squeezed out of the plastic beaker past the lid when her grip on it had involuntarily tightened as she fell, was dripping down one of his trouser legs on to his shoe. She had started muttering apologies. He had continued to laugh, he hadn't been able to stop, and it had been the laughter of great joy, he had explained many times when they had relived the encounter. Without meaning to she had started to laugh with him, and it seemed perfectly natural that when they eventually managed to disentangle themselves, he had escorted her back to her seat, forgetting whatever it was that he had been going to the buffet car to buy.

They had spent the rest of the journey together. He had been going on a course at the LSE, she to take a few days leave with her sister, who lived in Islington with her civil servant husband. Simon had telephoned within minutes of her arriving at her sister's home and Rose had been waiting for the call, while at the same time telling herself resolutely that she would never hear from him again. They had spent the next evening together, and the evening after that, and the evening after that. Indeed they had not really been apart since.

Rose had always felt that their meeting sounded like something out of a bad Mills and Boon novel. Nonetheless it never ceased to give her warm glow to remember it. And she quite enjoyed telling new acquaintances, who asked the inevitable question of how she and her husband had met, that she had jumped on him aboard an Inter City express train.

Simon propped himself on one elbow and used the hand with which he had been attempting to brush his hair out of his face to rub his eyes. Rose smiled at him warmly, still locked in the memory of their splendid beginning and forgetting for a moment all the tensions which had latterly entered their relationship.

But there was small chance, it seemed, of Simon, whose smile she still so enjoyed, smiling back at her. His lips were set in that sulky line she had become increasingly more familiar with.

'For God's sake,' he said irritably. 'First you bloody wreck my party and then you wreck my night's sleep. Couldn't you have gone into the spare room?'

She flinched away from him. For a brief moment, she had been thinking, in spite of her extreme tiredness, how nice it would be to make love to him, to cuddle up to his warm body and let him sleepily explore hers. Their love-making was still good, although not as frequent as it used to be. It could be sometimes earthy and urgent and sometimes gentle and sweet and undemanding. The latter was what she would have liked then – but she patently wasn't going to get it.

She did understand his irritation. Simon was disappointed. He felt let down. The party had been important to him. And she had undoubtedly jerked him awake into that uncomfortable limbo when you were still a bit drunk but the hangover was beginning too.

'I'm sorry,' she murmured. And she meant it, although not enough to actually regret what she had done. To her it had been the only possible course of action.

He did not reply, but merely turned his back and seemed to fall almost immediately asleep once more. Again in spite of her exhaustion, she lay awake for a few minutes.

It would be all right in the morning, she assured herself, it usually was. Simon would forgive her, he usually did. He still loved her, she had no doubt about that. And she still loved him. It was just that they were so different. They didn't seem to want the same things or even want to do the same things. She loved almost all sports, both playing and watching. He hated sport. They appreciated different kinds of music, read different sorts of books, enjoyed different films and TV programmes. And, perhaps most devastatingly, they rarely even liked the same people. But you don't think about things like that when you fall in love. Not the way she and Simon had fallen in love.

Fleetingly she wondered if Simon had ever strayed. Goodness knows, he was attractive enough not to be short of opportunity, and sometimes she thought she wouldn't altogether blame him. He was a modern, liberal-minded man, but he still wanted a wife. And she was only barely that. She had at least been faithful to him – so far. But occasionally – particularly after solving a difficult case – she had to admit that she had been tempted. She had always enjoyed sex, yet, perhaps curiously even though she had been only twenty-four, had not had a single serious relationship with a man before Simon. Her ambition in her career had, of course been part of the reason for that – she had never seemed to have the time. But that wasn't all of it.

As a young single woman Rose had relished the thrill of sex without ties and of quite casual one-night stands too. She had often been told that was unusual in a woman – but that, of course, had always been by a man.

Even thinking that way made her feel disloyal, as if she was betraying the man she loved. She resolved that she would make it all up to him. That she would show him how much she loved him. Maybe even try for the child Simon so wanted.

But all of that, naturally, would have to wait until her current big case was over. When you were heading a murder enquiry you could not let yourself worry about anything else. You had to clear your mind and your desk of all except the case in hand. You could not carry baggage.

Rose Piper's last conscious thoughts before she sank into much-needed oblivion were not of her husband, but of the murder investigation she had been placed in charge of. Who *was* Mrs Pattinson, she wondered? Almost certainly that was not her real name. And where was she? Was Mrs Pattinson really the killer? And would she strike again?

One thing Rose knew for certain. She had to find her.

# Eight

Constance and Freddie were sitting at the kitchen table together drinking coffee and watching breakfast television. The discovery of the body of a young man in the grounds of a Bristol hotel was just a brief item. Few details were given but the bulletin identified the Crescent Hotel and showed a quick shot of it. The young man was not named. Next of kin had yet to be informed.

'God, Bristol's getting like Chicago nowadays,' remarked Freddie cheerily.

Constance put her coffee mug down carefully on the table.

'Right, I must get on,' said Freddie in a determined voice. 'We've got the milk tester again. Blasted EEC. If it's not one regulation it's another nowadays.' He looked out of the window. Another wet day. 'Wish they could regulate the weather. We couldn't half have done with some of this rain in the spring. Weeks of drought when there's crops coming up and now this downpour right through the autumn.'

He rose from his chair, kissed Constance absent-mindedly on the top of her head, pulled on boots and coat and departed through the kitchen door, still grumbling contentedly.

'Global warming, my aunt Fanny,' he muttered. 'There's somebody up there determined to put us poor bloody farmers out of business, that's what I think . . .'

For Freddie this was just another day. Business as usual. He was not unhappy, nor unduly concerned. Farmers enjoy a good grumble. It goes with the territory. And the truth was that he took the attitude that Chalmpton Village Farm had suffered lousy weather conditions and an assortment of stupid rules and regulations throughout its long history and still survived. Freddie Lange did not really believe he had anything in the world to worry about. Farming had its problems like any other way of life. And what you did was cope. That was the way Freddie had been brought up.

He was, however, perhaps a little more preoccupied than usual this morning. He did have a heavy day ahead. He certainly had not noticed his wife react at all to the news item about the Bristol murder. And if her hand had been trembling when she placed her coffee cup on the table, Freddie hadn't noticed that either.

Charlie also saw the report of his colleague's death on breakfast news. He kept a small portable television in his bedroom, inside his wardrobe and concealed behind the wardrobe doors when not in use, so it didn't spoil his decor. It was his habit when at home to make himself a pot of tea in the mornings and then go back to bed and drink it while idly watching television. He had quite a cosy side to his nature, did Charlie.

When the shots of the Crescent Hotel were shown Charlie's blood turned to ice. Marty Morris had been sent to Mrs Pattinson in Charlie's place, and now he was dead.

'That should have been me,' Charlie muttered to himself.

He felt slightly sick. Charlie did not often consider the grim realities of his trade. He had it all worked out in his head. He never thought about the dangers, so many different sorts of dangers, which would be so obvious to almost anyone else. Prostitutes were more likely to be the victims of violent crime than any other sector of the community. But Charlie did not think of himself as a prostitute. He regarded himself as a professional, just like any other. And he was a man. He was fit and strong. He could handle himself. In almost ten years on the game now, Charlie had never been hurt once. There'd been that weirdo at the Portway Towers Hotel who'd been heavily into S and M. That wasn't Charlie's game. No way! When he'd found out what he was being required to indulge in he'd headed straight for the door. The mark had turned nasty. There'd been a struggle, but Charlie had coped easily. He wasn't sure, but at the time he thought he'd broken the mark's arm. No problem. Charlie had no crisis of conscience about that. It was however, the last time he'd been with a man. He was getting established by then, had a good clientele, didn't need the gay trade any more. So he'd told Paolo there'd be no more of that for him.

Paolo. That was it. He must call Paolo, find out what was going on.

'Don't panic,' said Paolo in his broad Bristol drawl. 'Looks like we've got a nutter out there. But young Marty was never careful. It'll all be sorted . . .'

Charlie's brain, however, was starting to function again.

'Paolo, Mrs Pattinson called you and she asked for me,' he said as calmly as he could. 'Not just any lad, and certainly not Marty.'

Chillingly it occurred to him that the murderer could actually have mistaken Marty for himself. After all, it should have been him walking through those gardens. And he knew what the grounds of that place were like after dark. The lighting was worse than useless. Marty was black and more or less the same size as Charlie.

'I reckon the whole thing was a set-up,' Charlie blurted out, his voice trembling a little.

'Naw,' said Paolo. 'Just a coincidence, mate.'

Charlie could hear the tension as he spoke and knew exactly where Paolo was coming from. He was trying to cover his tracks. Paolo had a good thing going with Avon Escorts. Everybody got their cut, including the tax man, the police had never before been involved – Paolo had a partner who saw to that, Charlie had always been told – and the boys and girls earned good money without the risks and stigma of going on the street. They were also often able to maintain some kind of perfectly respectable front, if they wished, as Charlie had always done. Everybody had been happy. Paolo ran a happy ship. He was another professional. Charlie knew that Paolo would be just as dismayed to hear himself described as a pimp as Charlie would to be described as a male prostitute. But suddenly the facts of his way of life were beginning to penetrate the fragile veil of pretence which Charlie had created.

'Oh yeah,' he said. 'I know those gardens, somebody must have been waiting there for Marty.'

'What's the matter with you, Charlie? Marty could have been followed. A nutter, like I told you.'

'They said on the TV he was killed in the early evening. He must have been on his way to see Mrs

Pattinson. Did she call to ask where "her Charlie" was?'

'No,' said Paolo.

'Oh shit!' said Charlie. 'I don't like this. It breaks a habit of a lifetime, but I reckon I should go to the filth.'

'They'll eat you alive,' said Paolo.

'As long as I am still alive, man!'

Charlie heard Paolo sigh at the other end of the phone. 'Look they've been to see me already. In the middle of the fucking night, as it happens. They already knew who Marty was and that he was one of ours. I don't know how.'

'Oh shit!' said Charlie again. 'What did you tell 'em?'

'As much as I had to, and no more.'

'Did you tell them about Mrs P?'

'Yep. More than anything else they wanted to know who Marty was going to see.'

'Well, of course they damn well did. Mrs P's got to be the number one suspect, hasn't she? And if it was her, it was me she thought she was topping, not Marty Morris, that's for certain.'

Charlie could feel rivulets of sweat running down his back. He was frightened and he was also confused. Why on earth would Mrs Pattinson want to harm him? It didn't add up.

Paolo started to speak again. 'Look, the filth'll catch up with her in no time. I wouldn't get in a state. It could still be a nutter. A one-off. If you go to the police now that'll be the end of that wonderful double life of yours, mate. Finito. Think about it.'

Charlie knew that Paolo had his own reasons for wanting to keep everything as quiet as possible. When the word got out that one Avon boy had been topped and the Old Bill were running around all over the shop, that would be bad enough. The prospect of it being anything more than a random killing would be even worse. Nonetheless Paolo had come up with the most persuasive argument of all for Charlie to keep quiet.

Charlie thought about the wedding two days earlier and entertaining his family in his beautiful apartment. He could see his mother's smiling face inside his head, her pride in her youngest son tangible enough to touch. He had to keep what he did a secret. He really did.

'Oh shit!' he said for a third time. 'OK, I'll stay stum, at least for now, hope it all gets sorted. But I'm taking a holiday, Paolo, starting this minute. I'm not bloody working again until we know what's going on.'

After hanging up the telephone Charlie hurried to the only window in his flat which was on the street side of Spike Island Court and checked to see if anyone seemed to be watching. All was quiet. And he stepped back from the window feeling vaguely silly. Maybe Paolo was right. Maybe he was over-reacting. Maybe his imagination was running riot. He had always had plenty of imagination. However, Charlie could not help having really bad vibes about everything.

He decided to take no chances. He thought for a moment and then called his mother.

'How'd you like me to come home to stay for a few days, ma?' he asked.

'Now why on earth would my rich son want to leave that fancy new apartment of his to slum it with his old ma?'

He knew his mother was pleased, but there was amusement in her voice too. Already he felt reassured by the familiar sound of her lilting West Indian accent.

Charlie had the lie ready. 'Fancy it might be, but the whole block has got to be re-wired. There's been a major cock-up. Building regulations job. They're coming to do my place tomorrow. The builders have to re-decorate and all that, but it's going to be mayhem.'

His mother's lovely warm rolling laugh seemed to make the telephone receiver shake in Charlie's hand.

'So, no sooner have they finished building that fine apartment block than they have to knock half of it down and start again, is that what you're telling me, boy?'

'Kind of.' Charlie supposed he'd asked for this. 'So, if you don't find the whole thing just too funny, have I got a bed for a few days or not?'

Miriam Collins stopped laughing. 'Son, do you really have to ask me? As long as I'm living and there's a roof over my head, it's your roof too.'

Charlie felt a lump in his throat. What on earth was he getting emotional about? His mother was always saying things like that. He knew that he was tensed up, likely to be easily upset or moved. Nonetheless he realised he had made the only decision. He really couldn't do anything that would hurt his mum.

Decisively he went into his bedroom and removed his prized painting from the wall, revealing a state-of-the-art wall safe. He punched the combination number into the control panel and swung open the steel door. The interior of the safe was divided into a series of drawers and each drawer had a label. Among them were 'Alice', 'Angela', 'Joanna', 'The Merry Widow', 'The Weepy One', 'Mrs Pattinson', of course, and 'Miscellaneous'.

The names were all of Charlie's regular clients. He didn't really know why, but often he was more comfortable using nicknames than the names the women gave him, perhaps it was because it kept his business more impersonal. In any case he knew that most of the names were made up anyway and sometimes he was not given one at all.

'Miscellaneous' was his collective label for his more casual clients, one-off or very occasional customers.

Each drawer contained money, some more than others. Charlie kept careful records and knew that in total the safe contained almost £20,000 in fifty, twenty, ten and five-pound notes.

He liked to know exactly how much he earned from each of his clients and that was why he stored the cash they gave him separately in the fashion that he did. That way he could indulge his habit of attributing the purchase of his various possessions to specific women.

Joanna, whom Charlie still met regularly in her room at the Holiday Inn where she stayed while on business trips, was responsible for his lavish wardrobe. She dressed beautifully and always passed comment on Charlie's appearance. He felt sure she must be something big in the rag trade. And although she never actually told him what she did it seemed appropriate that his earnings from Joanna should pay for his clothes.

He began putting the contents of each drawer into envelopes which he labelled in the same manner that the drawers were labelled – he wanted to keep his system intact and he reassured himself that everything would be back to normal in no time – before packing them into a small suitcase.

'Miscellaneous' had paid, among other things, for his bedroom furnishings and decoration. He did not like the idea of sleeping in sheets provided solely by one client. That would seem wrong, somehow. Charlie had always slept soundly when alone in his own apartment – until now at any rate – and he did not want any specific images disrupting his rest.

'Alice' was an extremely large woman who liked her food. And she was equally enthusiastic about sex. She had been making use of Charlie's services for even longer than Mrs Pattinson – almost three years now. Charlie attended to her needs at her home – she lived in a big house with a discreet back entrance – whenever her husband was away on business, which seemed to be frequently. Sometimes Charlie was called there as often as four or five times a month. He couldn't imagine that Alice's husband really had no inkling of what his wife got up to during his absences, and assumed that the man probably didn't care. More than likely he had his own diversions. And although willing, in fact eager, to try anything, 'Alice' was by far the least attractive of his regulars, and so fat that when she got excited he sometimes feared that either he was going to be squashed or bounced across the room. Nonetheless he liked Alice. She was jolly and accommodating and, after they had completed the serious business of the day, always insisted on cooking him a lavish meal. At first he had demurred. Eating with them was a waste of time really, Charlie thought. Time was money, and anyway he preferred to eat alone or with company of his choice.

Sometimes, though, he had no choice except to go through the motions. And Alice had turned out to be an extraordinarily good cook. The meals and his genuine appreciation of them were all part of the routine now.

It therefore had seemed appropriate that Alice should pay for his superb stainless-steel kitchen. Even the doors of the kitchen units were faced in stainless steel. It looked more like the interior of a spaceship than a kitchen, Charlie reckoned. He was very proud of it, and it was rare for him to cook a meal there – although his efforts were humble compared with hers and usually relied principally on the freezer and the microwave – without thinking of Alice.

He wrote Alice on an envelope stuffed full of ten pound notes and put it in the suitcase.

There was not much money left in the drawer labelled 'The Weepy One'. After all, incredible though it might seem, she had paid single-handedly for his £30,000-plus motor car. 'The Weepy One' had been abandoned in middle age by her husband who had left her for a younger woman. For six months she had been Charlie's most frequent client, summoning him as often as two or three times a week to a suite in the Portway Towers, probably the most expensive hotel in the city. There was always champagne in a bucket, and something light but delicious to eat like caviar or *foie gras*. She explained to Charlie that it was her ambition to spend every penny of her husband's money before the divorce she had never wanted was finalised. She spent most of his visits to her in copious floods of tears which did not prevent her demanding increasingly more fervent sex from him, during which she would frequently cry out that she wished her husband could see her now. Charlie had realised from the start that she was just using him for revenge, and that when she screamed in orgasm it was her errant husband's face that she saw and not his. Afterwards she would ply him with vast quantities of cash – much much more than the £200 which was all he was obliged to split with Avon Escorts. Once, and even more hysterically tearful than usual, she had tipped him £1,000 in fifty-pound notes. He had been so taken aback that he had actually been moved to murmur a mild protest – after all, Charlie saw himself as a professional. All he wanted was to be properly paid for services rendered. Anything more than that was not really satisfactory to either side in any business transaction, he reckoned. But 'The Weepy One' had insisted, telling him she didn't want her husband's money any more, and she could think of nothing better to spend it on than being fucked by Charlie.

Charlie winced at the memory. The word 'fuck' always made Charlie wince, except when used actually during sex. He had been brought up that way, and it was strange how that sensitivity had remained with him throughout his bizarre working life. It particularly made him flinch when used by a woman obviously of a certain educational standard and social position in whose vocabulary such language really should not, in his opinion, figure. Charlie thought such things were important. He was sure that 'The Weepy One' would not normally use that kind of language and he realised that she must be a deeply disturbed woman. Nonetheless he swallowed his lurking feelings of guilt and took the money. £31,000 in all, over the six-month period.

Five weeks ago 'The Weepy One's' calls to Avon

Escorts had ceased abruptly and Charlie thought he had a fair idea why. There had been yet another suicide jump from the suspension bridge, which had a long history of fatal leaps into the Avon Gorge below, at about the same time. Of course Charlie didn't know for certain that the woman who died had been 'The Weepy One' – after all, he didn't even know her real name – and he certainly made no attempt to find out. To tell the truth he didn't even like to think about it.

He packed the last of the envelopes into the suitcase and wondered again if he was over-reacting. Better safe than sorry, though. He wasn't going to risk losing all that hard-earned cash.

More hastily he packed some clothes in a second, slightly larger suitcase, then he left the flat, locking it carefully behind him and setting the burglar alarm. He ran down the stairs to the car park just as he always did, in spite of holding a suitcase in each hand. Even the prospect of driving his BMW did not improve his doom-laden mood. But he roared out of the car park confident at least that he was doing the right thing.

And it would only be for a few days, a week or so at most, he told himself yet again. The whole thing would blow over in no time.

At about the same time that Charlie was shutting up his flat, the Reverend Roland Morris, accompanied by Sergeant Peter Mellor, arrived in a patrol car at Southmead Hospital in Monks Park.

Southmead is an old army hospital which has grown in a straggly kind of fashion into a major medical complex spread over several acres. The

Reverend Morris was driven straight past the main reception area to the detached single-storey pathology block which houses the city mortuary.

Investigations undergone throughout the night had ascertained that Marty Morris was the only son of the popular Baptist minister. The Reverend Morris had duly been contacted at his home in one of the toughest parts of St Paul's and told, as gently as possible, that Bristol's latest murder victim might well be his son. And the minister had agreed to submit to the necessary ordeal of identifying the body.

Rose Piper had somehow wanted to be there even though there seemed little doubt that the identification would be merely a formality. But when Mellor brought the Revd Morris into the waiting room and introduced him to Rose, she felt quite ashamed of half wishing, the previous night, for a serial killer. Once again she was confronted with the awful aftermath of violent crime. She suspected she would never get used to it and indeed rather hoped she wouldn't.

Roland Morris was a small man with a big presence. His hair was almost white, his skin deep ebony – exactly the same colour as the body of the young man they believed to be his son, it quite suddenly dawned on Rose. The Reverend's eyes were bright with pain, yet warm and gentle. She thought he had about the kindest face she had ever seen. There was about him the sadness of one who has seen pretty much the worst life can throw at the world, and the patient resilience of one who still carries on trying to make the best of it, trying to help. He looked to be in a state of total shock. Hardly surprising, she thought.

Peter Mellor, all six foot four inches of him, bent almost double by his side, leaning towards the older man as if trying by his mere physical closeness to give comfort and support, more considerate in manner than Rose had ever seen him before. The sergeant, a practising Baptist, had already told her that he knew the Reverend Morris and had explained that the older man was regarded, with justification in Peter's view, as some kind of saint in St Paul's, which alongside the drug pushers and pimps for which it was famous, boasted a big devoutly religious community. Mellor had asked to break the news to the minister himself, and to be the one to take him to the mortuary for the identification.

Rose accompanied the two men into the chapel of rest, inside the pathology department, where Marty Morris lay, his body having been cleaned up and made to look presentable before any relative would be called upon to identify him. Rose knew that most people who have been fortunate enough not to have to undergo this experience imagine the B-movie concept of mortuary drawers being pulled open to display the body, which doesn't actually happen in the UK. At Southmead, with its tastefully decorated little chapel, everything possible is always done to diminish the unpleasantness. Nonetheless, as Rose was well aware, formal identification remained a terrible ordeal.

As the little party walked through the door Peter Mellor had a hand under Revd Morris's left elbow, ready. The older man obviously at once recognised the body, discreetly covered by an ornamental cloth, which lay before him. He seemed to slump against the policeman. He did not speak at first, just nodded his head. Rose saw that tears were starting to roll down his cheeks.

'I have to formally ask you now, Reverend, is that your son?' said Peter Mellor.

'Yes. Yes. That's Marty.'

Roland Morris seemed even smaller when he left the mortuary than when he had arrived. They sent him home in a patrol car again, but this time Peter Mellor did not accompany him.

'Forgive me, Reverend, I have a murderer to catch,' he said quietly.

Although patently deeply distressed, the elder man still had great dignity about him. But he seemed to have no further words. He merely patted the sergeant's hand.

There was nothing more for anybody to say. The two police officers stood silently together watching the car drive him away. Neither spoke nor moved until several seconds after it had disappeared around a corner out of sight. Then quite suddenly Sergeant Morris smashed a clenched fist against the wall of the pathology unit. Rose, engrossed in her own thoughts, was shocked. Mellor was normally icily controlled.

'Why the hell did it have to be the Reverend's boy?' he half shouted. 'Can you imagine how he's going to feel when he finds out what his blessed son did for a living?'

'Ah,' said Rose. 'You didn't tell him, I gather.'

'Didn't see the point in making it even worse for him. I know he has to know. And I know we have to talk to him about it. But I reckoned the shock of his son dying was enough for one day.

'Fair enough,' said Rose, who was not used to this degree of sensitivity from the sergeant. 'You don't suppose then that he might know already?'

'No way!' Mellor spoke quite angrily.

'All right, all right,' said Rose, holding up both hands, palms towards him, in a gesture of conciliation. She eyed him with interest.

'So tell me,' she continued. 'Just what's so special about the Reverend Roland Morris, anyway?'

Peter Mellor turned to look at her. 'He's about the most decent man in the history of St Paul's, that's all,' he said. His voice was still clipped and angry. 'Now he's going to have to live with knowing that his worthless shit of a son was a male Tom who got himself murdered. Marty Morris hasn't just let down his family, he's let down his race. I resent his kind. He had a good father and a good upbringing yet he still turned out rotten – and that's exactly what the majority of people in this country still expect from a black. Pity the sick little bastard was ever born, if you ask me.'

Rose was again startled. Usually if she had any criticism at all of Peter Mellor it was that he was such a cold fish. Now she thought that might be preferable to this sudden explosion of pent-up emotion. Fleetingly she wondered what lay behind it. Something must, she was sure of it. But she didn't have the time to play psychiatrist.

'Peter, it's not your job to judge,' she reminded him sharply. 'We do the police work. That's all.'

He did not reply. His mouth was set in a thin hard line. For him there were no other standards, no other rules in life than his own, she knew that.

'Right,' she said. 'The PM's due to begin in ten minutes.'

They walked back into the pathology block just as the body of Marty Morris was being wheeled into the mortuary. It annoyed Rose that she could never quite get used to the sight of the line of fridges along one wall which provided storage space for over thirty corpses. The stench of formaldehyde was already heavy in the air. The other smells would come later. Rose shuddered.

She had watched enough post-mortem examinations to have become reasonably hardened, but her tendency towards a weak stomach still occasionally let her down.

Marty Morris had been naked beneath the cloth which had covered him in the chapel. All his clothing, so wet that it had to be dried first using the facilities at Southmead Police Station, and personal effects had already been removed, bagged up by an evidence officer and sent to the regional forensic laboratory at Chepstow.

Now the dead man was lifted on to a mortuary table, a marble slab with shallow gutters around the edges and a drain hole at one end. Post mortems are a messy business, as Rose knew only too well. It was the initial incision which always caused her the biggest problems. If she could get over that she would be all right.

Dr Carmen Brown, of course, had no such qualms. 'Morning, Rose, Peter,' she said cheerily, rather as if they had popped round for nothing more than a cup of rather good coffee.

The doctor asked for the corpse to be laid face down at first. Before opening up the body, she would of course conduct a thorough external examination, looking for anything she might have missed in the unsatisfactory surroundings of the murder scene, and paying particular attention to the wound in Marty Morris's back.

From that alone she could not really take things much further than she had at the scene of the crime, she said. Almost certainly a knife with a long, very sharp blade had delivered the death blow. There had only been one incision. That was all that had been needed.

'The blade penetrated several inches into the body,' said Dr Brown, in her usual matter-of-fact way. She was using a tape recorder to chronicle her findings as she worked. 'We'll see exactly what damage it did when we open him up.'

Even the thought of that made Rose feel vaguely nauseous. She pulled herself together with considerable concentration of will.

'How much actual physical strength would be required to push the blade of a knife that far into somebody's back, Carmen?' she asked.

'Not a great deal.'

'Even through a leather jacket?'

Carmen Brown shrugged.

'Finest Italian kid,' she remarked. 'Would have provided hardly any extra resistance to the kind of weapon used. If you want to kill somebody quickly and efficiently with a knife, some knowledge of human anatomy is a lot more useful than brute force. But in this case it needed to be only the most elementary. Small of the back, up behind the ribs. The heart's around there. Can't miss something vital . . .'

'So a woman could have done it?'

'Yes, no problem in that.' Carmen pushed and prodded the area around the wound. 'In fact, one blow like this is the way women do kill. Men are inclined not to be able to stop once they've started.

Gay killings are often the worst, really frenzied attacks – but then you know all this . . .'

Eventually Carmen and her assistant turned the body of Marty Morris over and began the nitty-gritty of the post-mortem examination. The first deep incision caused the corpse to emit a kind of whistling noise, as if air or gas were escaping. Rose had to struggle not to visibly flinch as the thorax was swiftly split from throat to pubis.

Carmen Brown, however, might have been slicing open a melon for all the reaction she showed as she parted flesh, exposed and sawed through bones and carved into organs.

'I was right,' she remarked conversationally. 'The killer scored a direct hit on the spinal cord. Caught the aorta too. Our victim had no chance. Would have died at once.'

Rose found the post-mortem examination as disturbing as ever but at least managed to hang on to the contents of her stomach. What there were of them. She'd had no time for breakfast, merely grabbing tea and biscuits on the run. This was always a mistake. Curiously perhaps, she found she was usually less queasy with a full stomach than an empty one.

On the way back to the station she asked her driver to stop for fish and chips. The diet of the average police officer is not often a health-conscious one, and Rose knew it was a miracle she remained as slim as she did. However, this was not a moment for worrying about such things. Some good British grease was what she needed both to settle any remaining stomach flutters and to get her through the rest of the day. The afternoon and evening would be taken up with pure admin, and Rose was still getting used to exactly how much of it was required from a senior investigating officer.

It was gone nine when Rose got home, the end of another long day, but Simon was still waiting to eat the meal he had prepared for both of them. Sometimes it seemed to her that he only cooked supper in the first place, knowing that she was in the middle of a big case, to put pressure on her – and she almost wished he wouldn't.

But she sat down at the dining table and did her best to attack rather dried-up lamb chops with a gusto she certainly didn't feel.

Simon had thawed out a little during the day, as Rose had known he would. He wasn't that unreasonable about her job, after all. And he did love her. But there was still an edge between them. And their early attempts at starting a conversation seemed to Rose to resemble a couple of wrestlers stalking each other around the ring, each waiting for the other to make the first move.

'So, you haven't caught your killer yet, then,' remarked Simon, who it transpired had at least been interested enough to watch the TV news bulletins of the murder case. 'I'd have thought a top-drawer cop like you would have had the whole thing sewn up by now.'

Rose realised that he was almost certainly being sarcastic, but decided to play the thing straight. She didn't need a quarrel right now.

'It'll be a while before we do that on this one, I'm afraid,' she said. 'We've found out one or two interesting things that wouldn't have been on the news yet, though. Our victim was a male prostitute.'

'What, a rent boy, you mean?'

'Well, yes. But he was on his way to see a woman client – not a man.'

'Good God!' said Simon.

Rose smiled. In spite of his determination to be a liberal new man, Simon was pretty conventional in his attitude to women.

'Why on earth would a woman want to pay for sex?' he asked.

'For exactly the same reasons men do, I should imagine. They're lonely. They want something they don't get at home. They find it exciting.'

Simon shuddered. 'Good God!' he said again.

Rose found that she was becoming irritated in spite of her good intentions.

'Male prostitution is no different from female prostitution, Simon,' she said coolly.

'That's as maybe, in theory,' he responded. 'But you have to admit that female prostitution is more normal.'

'Normal,' repeated Rose, almost sadly. 'No Simon, I don't have to admit any such thing. I'm sick to death of living in a man's world, as a matter of fact. I get it day in and day out at the nick, and I sometimes think you're just as bad in spite of your liberal pretensions. The truth is that the male attitude to women in this country hasn't really changed in centuries.'

'Rubbish,' said Simon. 'You can't possible believe that, Rose.'

And now even he sounded as if he was patronising her. Well, damn him, he'd asked for it and he was going to get it. The first forty-eight hours of a murder investigation are always considered the most important, and they are certainly the most pressurised. This is the vital time – after that the trail is likely to cool rapidly. Rose already feared that the case might slip away from her now. She was tired and fed up. She had no patience with him suddenly. She put down her knife and fork, giving up all attempts to do battle with the unappetising lamb chops, and let rip.

'Rubbish, is it?' she stormed. 'Have you never had a laugh with your mates about what they did in the knocking shops of Bangkok or Amsterdam? You wouldn't find that distasteful, would you, because you're steeped in double standards. All men are.

'Our Royal Family, the so-called upper classes, they have a full-scale tradition of using brothels. The Duchess of York's father was stupid enough to get caught out and there was a bit of a fuss, but you knew damn well that privately his male friends were probably clapping him on the back. That's the way it is. And if it's more or less socially acceptable for men to use prostitutes, almost lauded in some circles, then what is wrong with the situation being reversed? But how many men could accept that? I know bloody well, you can't. However, I see absolutely no difference.

'Come to that, I can understand totally why there are women, married to some missionary-position bore, who seek out no-strings fun with young lads. If the only price they have to pay is a few quid a time – then it's damn good value.'

Rose pushed back her chair and stood up. Already she regretted her outburst, but it was too late now. All that was left was to beat a fast retreat before she said even more that she would later regret.

Simon had not replied and she knew that was an ominous sign. She sighed.

'I'm going to bed,' she said, rather more quietly.

Simon sat at the table for several minutes more. He was shocked. Rose was quite right up to a point – he would maintain that he believed in sexual equality but, all the same, he had been appalled by much of what she had said.

He still loved Rose and had always been confident, even at their blackest moments, of her true feelings for him. Rows like this were not that unusual in their marriage and did not necessarily upset Simon that much. He accepted that he and his wife were both volatile independent people who were bound to clash occasionally. And, in fact, he had always taken the attitude that husbands and wives who proudly professed that they hadn't had a cross word in twenty years together were probably too boring to have a point of view worth having a cross word over.

This time, however, he had found Rose's outburst deeply disturbing. He wondered uneasily how much she had been expressing her own suppressed views on sex. And, not for the first time in their marriage, he found himself harbouring suspicions about her sexuality and where it might occasionally lead her.

# Nine

Simon had obviously slept in the spare room. Rose did not check whether or not he was still in bed. She just showered and dressed as quickly as possible, grabbed a quick cup of tea without which she really could not start the day, and left the house.

It was just before seven. There would be the usual team briefing in the murder incident room at 8.30 a.m. After that Rose planned another visit to the Crescent Hotel. She felt the key to it all must lie there somewhere. The only chance of tracing the mysterious Mrs Pattinson seemed to be through the Crescent. She had intended to blitz the place as soon as the identification of the body was over and she was actively looking forward to giving that slimy little manager a good going over.

The early briefing passed uneventfully. Certainly nobody had any kind of break-through to report. Rose gave the obligatory pep talk, stressed the importance of finding Mrs Pattinson, and then, accompanied by Peter Mellor, set off for the Crescent Hotel.

On the way out, two veteran detective constables were standing chatting by the coffee machine. Rose had particularly good hearing. Sometimes she was not sure whether this was a blessing or a curse.

'There she bloody goes again – and God knows when she last interviewed anyone before getting the big murder,' she overheard one remark sarcastically to the other when they presumed she was safely out of ear-shot.

She didn't know whether Peter Mellor had also heard, but she was aware of the old-fashioned look he gave her as they climbed into their car. Most rank-and-file policemen and women think that no officer over the level of sergeant ought to be on the road at all, let alone interviewing suspects. Certainly the place for a senior investigating officer is considered to be firmly behind his or her desk. Indeed, Rose knew she was going to have to watch it or she would face censure from above for doing too much running around and not enough organising. Perhaps it was because she was still new to the top job that she could not resist.

At the Crescent Hotel DS Mellor remained stiffly disapproving of everything - of a woman buying sex, of the hotel, of Avon Escorts, and of the murdered young man whose unsavoury way of life he seemed to regard almost as a personal slight. But Mellor's grim presence was almost a bonus when Rose gave the hotel manager the third degree she had been so looking forward to.

She had already discovered from the housekeeper that, as far as the woman knew, Mrs Pattinson had not once been still in residence when the maids had arrived to clean her room in the mornings. Rose suspected that the mysterious Mrs Pattinson slipped quietly away as soon as she finished doing whatever it was she did with the young men from Avon.

'She never stayed overnight, that's the truth, isn't it?' Rose was quite openly aggressive with Henry Bannerman now.

'I wouldn't know,' Bannerman replied, but he was not nearly as smugly superior as he had been on the night that Marty Morris's body was discovered. Rose wondered exactly what he was hiding. She was quite sure there was something.

'You must have known what Mrs Pattinson was using your hotel for, it was quite obvious, surely?'

'Certainly not,' said Bannerman, attempting to bristle, but not succeeding very well.

The interview was conducted in the hotel manager's office, Bannerman sitting behind his desk, DCI Piper sitting on the upright chair opposite him and DS Mellor standing by her side. The sergeant moved menacingly forwards and leaned on Henry Bannerman's desk so that his face was only inches away from that of the other man.

'This place is little more than a knocking shop, that's what I think,' he said. 'And personally I'm not going to be happy until I've closed it down.'

The sergeant's voice was cold and quiet. Rose found him quite frightening when he was like this, so the effect on Henry Bannerman came as no surprise.

The pompous little man cringed in his seat. There was no sign at all now of the patronising attitude which had previously so irritated Rose. That gave her considerable satisfaction. But nothing much else was gained by the confrontation. If Henry Bannerman knew anything more about Mrs Pattinson, Avon Escorts, or Marty Morris and his violent death, then he certainly wasn't telling.

As the Detective Chief Inspector and her sergeant left the hotel, Peter Mellor's mobile phone rang. He listened in silence for a couple of minutes and it seemed to Rose that his face hardened as he did so.

'It seems that our young friend batted for both sides,' he said grimly. 'He had a gay lover who didn't like what his boy did for a living one little bit. Obsessively jealous, he's been described as apparently.'

'We might be getting somewhere at last, then,' commented Rose. 'Do we have a name?'

'Yep. Smoothie called Jonathon Lee. We know him apparently. Given to outbursts of violence, particularly if he's been on the crack. Into that too and deals in the stuff, so it's more than likely young Marty was as well. They've picked him up, by the way. Taking him into the nick now.'

'What are we waiting for?' asked Rose.

Mellor regarded her without a deal of enthusiasm.

'Shouldn't we get a couple of DCs to talk to him, boss?' he said.

Rose knew that was what she should do. Mellor wasn't often wrong. That was why she liked to work so closely with him. She also knew what the lads had started to call him too. And if she knew, she assumed that so did he. 'Her ladyship's bum boy.' Rose was the wrong sex, too young and had the wrong colour hair. Whether or not she was a good police officer was not always a factor in the Avon and Somerset Constabulary.

No matter. Other people's opinions were something else she couldn't worry about. She could only do things her way.

In Chalmpton Peverill that morning, Constance could not concentrate on everyday farm routine, however hard she tried. She went through the

144

motions, of course, but her mind kept wandering. She had so much to think about.

Midway through the morning she gave in to temptation, poured herself a whisky and sat down at the kitchen table with the telephone. Her call was not successful and was in any case interrupted by Freddie in search of coffee.

'Who was that?' he asked in an automatic sort of way as she replaced the receiver in its cradle.

'Nobody,' she said.

Freddie glanced at her inquiringly.

She realised she had sounded short.

'I was trying to phone William,' she said. 'He wasn't there.'

Freddie's glance switched to the large whisky before her. It was unlike Constance to drink so early in the day. She realised another explanation was called for.

'My tummy's a bit dicky again and I thought a drop of Scotch might settle it,' she said, and, seeing the instant panic this simple remark aroused in Freddie, immediately wished she hadn't.

'What do you mean?' he asked anxiously. 'You're not still being sick, are you?'

She shook her head. 'It's nothing, honestly.'

'I wish you'd go to the doctor, you look so tired.' He took her chin in one hand, raising her face slightly towards him.

'I'm all right, really,' she protested.

'Have a lie down anyway, I do wish you would.'

'This afternoon,' she promised, and made herself flash him a cheery smile.

★

145

Jonathon Lee, Marty Morris's lover, was every bit as smooth as Sergeant Mellor had promised. He was a white man in his late thirties, of average height, slimly built, beautifully dressed, meticulously courteous and, on first acquaintance, appeared deceptively pleasant in manner. His pupils were dilated, Rose noticed, a sure sign of drug abuse, but she could appreciate what young Marty Morris had seen in the older man. Jonathon Lee possessed considerable charm, and it was only as the interview progressed and he became slightly agitated that he displayed the other side to his nature. His mouth tightened and turned downwards, his voice dropped almost to a hoarse whisper, and everything about him led Rose to suspect that he was capable of great cruelty. He was wearing a heavy gold ring on the little finger of his right hand which he twirled continually with the thin bony fingers of the left.

Rose found the mannerism inexplicably disconcerting. It was definitely easy for her to believe that Lee had beaten up young Marty whenever he felt like it, and Marty could well have been afraid to leave him even if he had wanted to. But if their information so far was correct he may not have wanted to. Because if the lad had been hooked on crack cocaine and Lee was a dealer with almost unlimited access to supplies of the drug, that would have made Lee the most attractive man in the world to Marty Morris, regardless of his tendencies towards violence.

Lee was an obvious suspect. Not only did he have a history of mental instability and drug abuse, neither could he account satisfactorily for his movements on the evening of Marty's death.

'I'd been on the crack, you know how it is,' he muttered.

146

'No,' Rose retorted sharply. 'I don't. Tell me.'

'Well, when I've scored I don't know where I am or what's going on, sometimes, you see . . .' Lee paused, as if realising what he had said. 'No, no, I'd never hurt Marty. It wasn't me. I didn't kill him. I wouldn't do anything like that . . .'

'Mr Lee, Marty Morris had a rather nasty bruise, just beginning to fade, on his right temple. Were you responsible for that, by any chance?'

''Course not.'

'We know you can be violent, Mr Lee. Particularly when you are under the influence of drugs. You had a lover whom you knew was a male prostitute and you hated that. Do you seriously expect me to believe that you never hit Marty during your relationship?'

'Well, I may have given him a slap once or twice, but that's all, honest.'

Lee tried one of his most charming smiles, a little late in the day, but Rose could not get any further.

'Bound to be him, guv,' said Peter Mellor over a lunch-time drink in the Compton Arms. 'Motive, opportunity, everything. And out of his mind.'

'What about Mrs Pattinson then?' asked Rose. 'If Lee is our killer, where does she fit in?'

'We've only got Paolo's evidence that she called at all.'

'OK. But he is so sure of himself and has no reason that I can think of to lie. Let's assume for the moment that Mrs Pattinson did call.'

'Well, maybe she waited for Marty, then saw Lee attack him and did a runner.'

'Peter, we believe that she pays young men to have sex with her in a hotel room. This time it seems that she phoned Avon Escorts yet she hadn't even checked in to the Crescent,' said Rose. 'It just doesn't add up.'

'At least Lee's got more or less the right-sized feet,' said Mellor. 'We've now checked that those were Timberland bootprints, and they've been measured. Size ten. Lee says he takes a nine. All that calls for is a thick pair of socks.'

Rose sighed. 'I know what you're getting at, Peter. You wouldn't expect a woman to be wearing a pair of boots that big. But you see, I actually reckon that smoothie Lee would be no more likely to be wearing a bloody great pair of Timberland boots than a woman.'

Mellor was making an effort to concentrate on analysing the facts, Rose knew that, but he still looked grim. She suspected that he was thinking about the effect this latest bit of juicy news about Marty Morris's sexuality would have on the victim's father, the man Mellor seemed to have such regard for. The Reverend Morris's little boy was about to be revealed to be not only a male prostitute but also gay, and possibly a junkie. She could understand why Peter Mellor would like the case buttoned up fast, even more than she would. At least the Reverend Morris's agony would not then be prolonged.

Rose watched her sergeant take a swig of his pint, his face screwed up almost as if the drink were poisoning him. He certainly wasn't enjoying it, but then he didn't seem likely to be able to enjoy anything much at the moment.

'Why don't you tell me about it, Peter?' she invited.

The sergeant put down his glass and wiped his mouth with the back of his left hand. 'Don't know what you mean, boss.'

'Peter, this case is really getting to you. It's unlike you, that's all.'

Mellor managed a wry smile and took another drink of his beer, this time without quite as much apparent distaste. When he spoke again his voice was quiet, his manner pensive.

'I grew up in St Paul's, you know that. In one of those tower blocks down the Stapleton Road – and you don't get much rougher than that. I had no father – well, none that I ever knew. My mother was too busy trying to scrape a living to take much notice of me. She wasn't too fussy how, either . . .'

Mellor paused. Rose studied him enquiringly. Was he suggesting that his mother had been on the game? If he was, it seemed he did not intend to spell it out.

'When she wasn't working all she wanted to do was party,' he went on. 'She was pissed or stoned half the time, and I ran wild as a kid. One way and another it's a miracle I'm sitting here with you, boss. I was destined to end up in and out of prison myself rather than putting villains behind bars, no doubt about it.

'The Reverend ran a youth club. He saw it as a kind of mission in life to try and give a chance to youngsters who didn't have any. He always had time. For a bit he was like a kind of father to me. Nearest I ever had. More than anything else he taught me that I had a brain, and how to use it.'

The sergeant had a faraway look in his eye. Rose realised that until this moment she had known absolutely nothing about his background beyond the fact that he had been a graduate entrant to the force.

'So, if you were so wild, how did the Reverend Morris tame you the way he did?' she asked. 'He must be a very persuasive man.'

Peter Mellor smiled again. 'He is. He makes you trust him and he makes you want to please him. But there was more to it than that. I was just ten years old when I was caught trying to break into a car to nick the radio.

'There used to be this policeman then who patrolled St Paul's, an old-fashioned copper. A big man, in every sense of the word. He wasn't put off by the riots either. He was like the Reverend, he believed that kids like me should always be given just one chance to make good. And he ran his patch by his own rules. So he didn't take me in, didn't put me through juvenile court or any of that crap. Instead he gave me a deal. I had to join Reverend Morris's youth club, I had to do exactly what the Reverend told me, and if I didn't keep my nose clean, the next time he caught me he'd lock me up and throw away the key. I believed him. I understood deals. I was streetwise.

'That was the beginning of it. The Reverend made me feel as if I was worth something. Nobody had done that before. I started working at school instead of fooling around all the time. The rest is history.'

He paused again, then, as if remembering that he was supposed to be a coolly cynical police detective, added: 'Sorry, all a bit cliché-ridden really, isn't it?'

Rose leaned back in her chair. 'And that's why the Marty Morris thing makes you so angry?'

'Of course. He was born with more chances than any black kid in Bristol, with a father like that. Look what he became. A rent boy, a poof and a druggie. It makes me sick.'

Rose could see the sergeant's brow furrowing again. She still didn't like to hear him talking like that, although maybe she understood his motivation a little more. And she remained much less convinced than most of her colleagues seemed to be, not just Peter Mellor, that Jonathon Lee would eventually be proven guilty of murder. But then, neither was she as prejudiced, either racially or sexually, as most of them. She decided to try to lighten the moment.

'Speaking of clichés, don't tell me it was because of that one good policeman that the poor little underprivileged black kid grew up to join the honkie police force?' she asked, her affectionately bantering tone taking the edge from her words.

'No way,' said Mellor. 'I wanted to go to university and I didn't want to survive on a grant. It was either the police or the army and I reckoned I stood marginally less chance of getting shot if I became a cop.'

'Thank Christ for that,' responded Rose with a grin. 'I've always had you down as a cold calculating bastard, Mellor. I'd hate to have to change my opinion . . .'

The sergeant gave a little snort which may have been the beginning of a laugh.

'And you, boss? So what about you? Why did you become a cop?'

Rose looked away. It was so long since she had even thought about it.

She had been born and brought up in the Somerset seaside town of Weston-super-Mare. Her father, whom she adored, had held down a stupefyingly boring job as a clerk with the local council. And he worked ceaselessly in order to satisfy the unquenchable desires of Rose's mother to keep up appearances. In latter years Rose had regarded her mother as a kind of slimmer Hyacinth Bucket without any of the humour.

Rose's father, still only in his early forties, died of cancer when she was thirteen and Rose had blamed her mother entirely for this on the grounds that it was she who had forced him into mindless soul-destroying daily drudgery and therefore destroyed his will to live. Only much later did Rose accept that this arbitrary judgement was completely unfair. But at the time she was going through a stage when she blamed her posturing and rather unintelligent mother – not always so unfairly – for almost everything.

From that moment on Rose had only two great aims in her young life. She wanted to escape from her mother, whose small-minded attitudes she came increasingly to resent and dislike, and at the same time she wanted to shock the woman.

Failing dismally to find a dreadlocked Rasta or any-one else suitably disreputable enough with whom to run away from the lace-curtained terraced house, Rose decided to go to the opposite extreme. She announced that she was going to join the army, ironically the same alternative Mellor had considered to a police career. This also had the required effect. Her mother was horrified – but so, when she began to find out more about her allegedly chosen profession, was Rose. She didn't like the idea of square bashing one little bit and she certainly was not going to join any outfit which didn't treat women as equals.

This made her eventual decision to switch her alle-giance to the police force even more baffling, Rose reflected wryly. Even now she could recall no positive reasoning behind it. Often, and only half jokingly, she would remark that she could merely assume that she had been going through a stage of having a uniform fetish. However, joining the police also produced the required result of both winning the disapproval of, if not actually shocking, her mother who certainly did not think it a suitable career for a young lady, and efficiently securing Rose's escape from home.

Something else, quite unexpected, happened. From the moment the nineteen-year-old Rose was taken on as a probationary constable by the Avon and Somerset Constabulary and installed in a Bristol section house, she had known at once that she was in the right place – that she had chanced upon the only job she would ever want. And she knew also that she was going to do everything within her power to get to the very top of her trade. Her determination disturbed her sometimes. Even she sometimes found her habit of getting what she wanted rather disconcerting.

She glanced back at Sergeant Mellor. Oh no, she thought. Oh no, you don't. This is not going to turn into a mutual therapy session.

'Why did I become a cop?' she repeated, smiling. 'You've just given the answer to that, Peter.'

'Sorry, boss?'

'Exactly – to hear a man call me boss!'

That night Peter Mellor carried on drinking, which was totally out of character. Normally he rushed straight home to his wife and child at the first opportunity. He was that kind of man.

On this day, though, he was depressed, which was also unusual, and angry with himself. He had lost control on more than one occasion lately. Now he also considered that he had made a fool of himself. He sincerely wished he hadn't told Rose Piper the story of his life. He'd even come precariously close to telling her his mother had been a Tom, and the only person in the whole world he had ever revealed that to was his wife. He somehow couldn't have married Rebecca without confiding in her and the complete lack of concern she had demonstrated had made him love her more than ever. The truth about his mother remained Peter Mellor's deepest, and in his opinion, darkest secret. He could never quite get over the idea that he had in some way been to blame for what his mother had been, or at the very least that he shared what he saw as her shame. He had cut the woman out of his life as soon as he'd become old enough to stand on his own two feet and for some years had succeeded in hardly even thinking about her. Not until this damn case. The DCI was right. It was having quite an effect on him. Certainly it wasn't like him to open up the way he had. And his lapse had been made all the more apparent, he felt, because the guv'nor had so starkly refused to share the same kind of confidence. Something of a betrayal that, he reckoned. She'd coaxed all that stuff out of him and then backed right off, just making that silly crack about being called boss which had been guaranteed to make him feel even more of a prat.

Sitting alone on a bar stool in a pub which he hoped nobody he knew ever frequented, Mellor ordered a second large whisky chaser for his third pint of bitter. He could feel his head beginning to swim and this was an unfamiliar and disconcerting sensation for him.

Mellor was really fed up. He had considerable respect for Rose, particularly for her flair and intuition – never his strongest qualities, he knew – but she often operated on such a disconcertingly emotional level. Sometimes he longed for a more regulated working life, and rather wished he worked for a straight-down-the-middle old-fashioned sort of copper. Preferably a man too.

He also thought that if Rose Piper didn't start spending a lot more time at her desk instead of running around trying to do everyone else's job for them she was going to find herself in big trouble. All he wanted was for this case to be wound up as quickly and efficiently as possible. It was stirring up far too many forbidden memories for him.

# Ten

It was the second Tuesday in November and Freddie expected his wife to be going to visit Aunt Ada as usual. It was only over breakfast that morning that she told him, without at first offering any explanation, that she would not be doing so.

It was unlike Constance to break her routine, to alter the established pattern of her life – just as it was for Freddie. He was surprised and also mildly curious. He asked why she had abandoned her regular monthly trip.

'I've just got so much on in the village,' his wife replied. 'And there's a lot to do here on the farm, goodness knows.'

She sounded distracted. Not for the first time recently, Freddie thought that perhaps Constance was finding it more difficult to cope with all her many roles than she used to. They all expected so much of her.

He rested his hand lightly on hers. 'There's always a lot to do here, and you usually manage to run the entire village as well,' he said. 'In the past I've just assumed you were superwoman.'

Constance smiled, but he could see the tension in her face.

'I can't imagine why,' she said.

'Because, my darling, through most of our marriage you have continually behaved as if that is what you are.'

Constance manoeuvred her hand so that she was able to wrap her fingers around his, and her grip was tight and somehow urgent.

'I do love you, Freddie, you know that, don't you? Whatever happens, you know that?'

'Of course I do, my darling.' She seemed to need the kind of reassurance that it had never before been necessary for either of them to give each other. And what did she mean by 'whatever happens'? What on earth did she think was going to happen? They had always been happy, hadn't they? And they had such a good secure life together – he had never had any doubts about that before. He leaned forward and touched her cheek with his free hand.

'Of course I know you love me, Constance. And I love you. Don't I always say the best day of my life was the day I met you?'

She turned her head so that her lips brushed against his fingers.

'I just hope you never change your mind about that, Freddie.'

'No chance.'

He spoke easily but he was beginning to worry more and more about his wife. She seemed nervy and even perhaps unhappy, both of which were quite unlike her. He remembered again the aftermath of her last visit to Aunt Ada when the car had broken down on the motorway and she had been so violently sick when she arrived home. And she had admitted to feeling poorly since then. Again he felt that now familiar chilly tremor run up and down his spine. Could she be ill? Was she keeping some horrible illness a secret from him? Now that would be just like her. He thought about it for a moment. She had not been physically sick since that one occasion a month ago, as far as he knew. But he realised that she could easily have been ill when he was not around, he spent so much time out and about on the farm. And she was definitely looking increasingly tired and drawn. It also occurred to him that she might have lost weight. Anxiously he studied her face, she was so pale, the high cheekbones more prominent than ever and now giving an almost gaunt appearance to those finely sculptured features.

Her gaze was riveted on their entwined hands, as if she didn't want to meet his eye. His words of reassurance had provoked a wan smile again, but he was sure he could see tears beginning to form.

Several times in the last four weeks he had expressed his anxiety about her health, and asked her bluntly if she were quite sure she was well. She had remained adamant that she was perfectly fit. Nonetheless Freddie was moved to try again.

'Constance, if you were ill, you would tell me, wouldn't you?' he said.

'Of course.'

She replied quickly, automatically almost. He continued to stare at her. Eventually she spoke again, as if accepting that he needed, even deserved, a little more than that.

'Things have been getting a bit on top of me lately, that's all, Freddie. I can't believe it's less than two months before Christmas. I'm supposed to be putting on the village pantomime again and we've barely started . . .'

Freddie interrupted. 'Bugger the village pantomime!'

He rarely swore, but he wanted his wife back the way she used to be, he wanted everything the way it was. He didn't know quite what had changed and he certainly didn't know why – but he knew something had.

'You're overdoing it, that's what this is all about, isn't it? It's about time the rest of this village pulled its weight. Let somebody else stage the damn panto . . .'

Constance squeezed his hand even more tightly. 'I'll be all right, Freddie, honestly,' she said. 'Everything will be fine, you'll see . . .'

There was a faraway look in her eye now, and Freddie had the feeling she was assuring herself of that as much as him. He could think of nothing else to say. He sighed heavily. There was a load of over-due paperwork in the farm office that he really must turn his attention to today. Constance had always done most of it in the past and invariably had been bang up-to-date, but every time he had mentioned the backlog to her over the last couple of weeks, she had murmured vaguely that she would try to get around to it tomorrow – and never had. That wasn't like her, either. She was normally so efficient. Now Freddie had no choice but to attend to the paperwork himself. He didn't really mind that, although he would have preferred a heavy stint of manual labour to take his mind off things, but it was yet another indi-cation that, however much she protested, all was really not well with Constance.

Freddie had never felt so uneasy in the whole of his life.

Later that morning Freddie and Constance's elder daughter Charlotte popped into the farm. She lived on the edge of Chalmpton Peverill in Honeysuckle Cottage, which Freddie had given her and her husband as a wedding present.

Charlotte, a tall, slim, long-limbed, and strikingly attractive twenty-four-year-old, had been born with a sunny disposition which a near-perfect childhood and a so far happy marriage to a local man, Michael Lawson an architect with Somerset County Council whom she had fallen in love with while still at school, had only enhanced.

She was, however, unusually anxious. On her way to the village shop a little earlier she had encountered her father who had told her that her mother had cancelled her usual monthly trip to Bristol and would probably appreciate a visit. He had said no more than that, but Charlotte could read between the lines. She suspected that he was as concerned about her mother as she had become, and was hoping she might be able to find out what was wrong – although neither father nor daughter had actually expressed their feelings of anxiety to the other yet, perhaps not wanting to fully admit them even to themselves.

Charlotte, her long fair hair tied carelessly back in a rather ragged ponytail, entered, as all the family did, through the kitchen door, which was hardly ever locked during daylight hours. She was clutching her two-year-old son by the hand and, as soon as little Alex spotted his grandmother seated at the kitchen table, he tugged himself free of his mother and toddled his way eagerly across the room to her. Alex was used to his doting gran making a huge fuss of him.

Absent-mindedly, it seemed to Charlotte, Constance picked her grandson up and smiled a greeting at her daughter. Her mother seemed pre-occupied and rather disorientated, just as she had done for some weeks now.

'Hi mum, no visit to Aunt Ada today then?' Charlotte tried to sound casual, just as she knew her father had earlier.

'No dear, too much to do here and in the village,' replied her mother rather listlessly.

The younger woman took in the scene around her. It didn't appear as if her mother had done anything all morning. And that in itself was cause for concern.

Constance was still wearing her dressing gown. It was part of the usual farm routine for her to come downstairs in the big pink towelling gown, right after drinking the tea Freddie brought her just before seven, to share an early breakfast with her husband. They had always liked to start the day together in that way, Charlotte knew. But the breakfast things still littered the table. It was now well gone ten and it looked as if her mother had been sitting there for three hours. That was unheard of. Charlotte could feel alarm bells clanging, but decided not to show it. Not yet, any way.

'I suppose you'd like me to make coffee now you've got that lump on your knee,' she said, gesturing to a chortling Alex, happily ensconced with the grannie he loved, and blissfully unaware of any lurking tensions.

'That would be lovely, dear,' said Constance. The words were all right, thought Charlotte, but the way her mother said them was so distant she could have been speaking to a visiting cattle-feed salesman, not to her elder daughter.

Charlotte put freshly ground coffee into the filter machine – she'd just as soon have drunk instant but she knew how her mother hated it – and then sat down to wait for it to drip through.

She studied her mother. Perhaps they were all fretting too much, surely everyone was entitled to have a down patch occasionally – even Constance. That was the trouble, she expected, much as her father had said earlier, they probably all expected too much of her. Constance had always seemed to sail through the kind of schedule few others could cope with, but maybe the years of pressure and responsibility were at last taking their toll. Constance had not only lavished love and attention on her own three children, but had always been there for every family in the village.

With affection and admiration, Charlotte remembered the times Constance so willingly helped nurse the chronically sick, comforted the bereaved, listened with endless patience to the ramblings of the elderly, coaxed good behaviour out of seemingly impossibly wayward sons and daughters, sorted out financial problems for those totally clueless in such matters and generally behaved as if any problem faced by her family and neighbours was automatically hers to solve. At the same time she was a parish councillor, a stalwart of the WI and the Mother's Union, as well as chairman of the Village Fête Committee, the Village Hall Committee, the Christmas Festival Committee, of course, and a member of just about every other committee going.

In everything that she did Constance was meticulous and competent. When the village primary school was threatened with closure it was Constance who confronted the County Council with an argument for its continuation so forceful and well-constructed that even that famously high-handed body had given in. It was Constance who had launched the campaign, still going on – an uphill struggle, but not lost yet – to save the local cottage hospital, Constance who always seemed to spot first, and then lead the fight against, any threat to the community of Chalmpton Peverill.

Nothing had ever seemed beyond her, no crisis too big or too small for her to deal with. She had once safely delivered a villager's twins as if it were something she did every day – although the doctor who eventually arrived remarked that, without the resources of a hospital, it would have been a monumental achievement even for a practising nurse, let alone one whose nursing skills had been learned years before and used on a regular basis only for a short time after that.

At the other end of the scale Charlotte remembered the time when little Betsie Ambrose had cried ceaselessly for two days after her pet guinea pig went missing. It was Constance who organised half the village into a search party which she then orchestrated with military precision, resulting in the small creature being eventually discovered cowering in a remote corner of the churchyard and safely returned to its ecstatic owner.

Charlotte also recalled the occasion when she, not much older than young Alex was now, had ineffectually wielded a paint brush after her mother decreed that dear old Mrs Hewitt – whose only son had moved to London and gave no signs of caring a toss about his mother – was not going to live in slum conditions a minute longer. With little or no fuss, Constance redecorated Mrs Hewitt's cottage herself, scrubbed and polished the old lady's floors and furnishings, and replaced anything beyond rescue with bits and pieces from her own home which she always described as 'something I was going to take to the jumble sale, anyway, Mrs H.' Mrs Hewitt had thought her mother a saint, Charlotte knew, and sometimes during her childhood that judgement had seemed hard to argue with.

But Constance could be tough as well as compassionate. And she had never had any patience with the small-mindedness which so often played a part in village life. When the son of a particularly simple village couple had returned on a visit to Chalmpton Peverill flamboyantly showing off his overtly camp male lover and announcing that he was gay and proud of it, Marcia Spry, with her unpleasantly inverted sense of morality, had predictably proceeded to make his family's life a misery. Discovering how upset the family were, Constance had unceremoniously taken Marcia to one side and read her the riot act. Her message, although rather more tactfully delivered, had been that Marcia was a malicious old biddy who should know better than to torment a family who had never done anyone any harm – and that included their gay son. He was a consenting adult consorting with another consenting adult and minding his own business, which was exactly what Marcia Spry should try doing for a change.

The memory of her mother telling her that story and remarking with complete lack of concern that Marcia Spry would doubtless dislike her more than ever from then on, was still one which Charlotte relished. Of course, the dreadful Marcia never knew that Constance also took to one side the 'proud to be gay' young man on his next visit to the village and told him in no uncertain terms that she couldn't care less about his sex life and neither, she reckoned, could anybody else in Chalmpton Peverill. It would therefore be far better, wouldn't it, if he didn't flaunt a way of life which he must know would be sure to cause problems – albeit wrongly in her opinion – for his elderly parents.

Nothing daunted Constance. Unlike so many in a small community, Constance could invariably see both sides of most issues. And, in her daughter's opinion, her mother's lack of fear of involving herself in the trickiest of matters was just one of the many characteristics which made her remarkable – along with her ability to turn her hand to almost anything and her skill in coping with just about every situation life threw at her.

It was difficult to reconcile those memories with the woman Charlotte saw before her on that bleak November morning – a woman who had previously displayed more spirit than anyone her daughter had ever known, and who now seemed to have none at all.

Watching the automatic way in which Constance was cradling her beloved grandson, as if she was only half aware that he was in her arms, Charlotte could not help wondering what could have happened to cause this change in her mother, to make it seem as if this extraordinarily capable woman could no longer cope with anything.

Charlotte decided to continue the cheery approach. She thought she knew of something guaranteed to put her mother in a better frame of mind.

'So, have you bought yourself a new outfit for the eighteenth yet?' she asked. 'I think you should, after all it's going to be pretty special.'

November 18th was the day of Freddie and

Constance's silver wedding anniversary. The family had decided months ago that this merited a major celebration, and Charlotte had been landed with the job of organising a big party at the family's favourite hotel in the area, the Mount Somerset at Henlade, a beautifully renovated old manor house with sweeping views across half the country.

To tell the truth, Charlotte hadn't minded the task at all. She had inherited her mother's organisational skills and wouldn't really have trusted anyone else to plan the party properly. In any case, Charlotte loved to please her parents. They were the kind of people who brought out that desire in others, and rightly so, she considered.

But as she spoke, Charlotte realised to her astonishment that her mother looked completely blank. She can't have forgotten that of all days, Charlotte thought to herself. Then she saw the cloud pass across Constance's face. It was a cloud of despair, of desperation even. There was panic in her mother's eyes, pure panic. Charlotte was instantly overwhelmed by a wave of distress and confusion.

'Mum, whatever *is* wrong?' She blurted it out, and that wasn't what she'd intended at all, but she couldn't help carrying on. 'Surely you are looking forward to it, aren't you, mum? We're going to have a fabulous party. Helen's got special leave from school, remember. All the family, most of the village, will be there. It'll be wonderful . . .'

She knew that she was burbling and forced herself to stop. She wasn't going to help her mother by losing control.

There was a short silence. Charlotte could see Constance making an almost physical effort to com-

166

pose herself. The older woman even managed a big smile, and at a glance it seemed to be the same winning smile that had been so familiar and warming to Charlotte since the very beginning of her life. The smile was not in her mother's eyes, though, Charlotte could see that clearly. There was still panic in her eyes.

'Of course I'm looking forward to the party, darling,' said Constance eventually. 'I'm just a little tired, that's all. I'm looking forward to it immensely.'

But Charlotte was not convinced. She was more anxious about her mother than ever. And, like her father, Charlotte was beginning to have grave fears about Constance's health.


'She is human after all,' Charlotte remarked to her father when they had finally got around to properly discussing their worries. 'I sometimes think we forget that. Mother is so amazing it's quite easy to forget that she's only human, like all the rest of us.'

Since the end of October and the first ten days or so of November, which both father and daughter agreed had been her worst time of all, Constance had seemed to recover slightly from whatever it was that had been ailing her. She still looked thin and rather weary, but she seemed to be functioning again, if not with her usual level of energy. And she was beginning to muster a passable show of enthusiasm for the silver wedding celebrations which were now only three days away.

'You're right,' said Freddie. 'She just needs a bit more nurturing than usual, that's all. I'm trying to keep her away from all the farm business and I wish she would pull back a bit on everything else.

Somebody or other from the village has been on to her every day this week about the blasted pantomime. I wish she'd just tell them she can't do it this year, I really do, but some chance of that, I suppose.'

He had popped around to his daughter's cottage to show her the beautiful diamond and sapphire eternity ring he had bought for Constance as an anniversary present. The stones were set in a band of white gold.

'Well, it should traditionally be silver, but I wanted something better than a silver ring – so I thought platinum would be the perfect compromise . . .'

'It's truly beautiful, dad.' Charlotte enthused. And she slipped the ring on to her own finger in order best to admire it. As she did so the telephone rang. It was her brother William.

Charlotte, who knew all about William's near-dismissal from his college, greeted him jovially. She was a firm believer in the jovial approach to life whenever possible, something else she had inherited from her mother although it had not lately been much in evidence in Constance.

'William! I hope you're behaving yourself, you villain,' she scolded affectionately. 'Or I may have to drive over and sort you out. Then you'd be sorry.'

William, however, appeared to be in no mood for banter. 'Look, Charlie, I've got a problem with the party. I don't think I can make it.'

Charlotte was astonished. 'What!' she yelled into the telephone receiver. 'Why ever not?'

William mumbled something rather incoherent about having so much work to do, and trying to catch up, and not wanting to make a mess of things again.

Charlotte was furious. She was acutely conscious of

her father standing anxiously behind her, aware that there was obviously some new difficulty with his son but not knowing what. That made her all the more furious.

'So why are you telling me this?' she snapped. 'Why didn't you ring the farm?'

'Well,' William hesitated, '. . . I thought it might be better coming from you, I was afraid mother might answer the telephone . . .'

Charlotte completely lost her temper. 'I bet you were, you coward!' she shouted. 'Well, I'm not doing your dirty work for you. Dad's here. You can damn well tell him yourself.'

She thrust the receiver at her bewildered father, and she could feel tears pricking at the back of her eyes. What was her brother playing at? Without him, their parents' party could not possibly be a proper celebration and he must be aware of that.

'William, what's going on, son?' she heard her father ask. And then, when he got his answer, she saw his shoulders slump.

'Your mother will be dreadfully disappointed,' said Freddie. That was typical of the man, thought his daughter, he wouldn't admit to his own hurt.

She listened to a few more minutes of desultory conversation. Apart from the one mild remark about Constance's disappointment, Freddie, again typically, did not try to persuade his son. But when he hung up the phone and turned to her she could see just how upset he was.

'I don't understand it,' he said. 'The boy knows his mother idolises him. I can't believe he would let her down like this. She was worried enough when he was sent home. In fact I think it was all that bother with

William which sparked off her depression or whatever it is. You don't think he's up to those tricks again, do you, Charlie?'

His daughter replied that she hadn't the faintest idea, but if she could get her hands on him right now she would teach her little brother a few tricks he hadn't thought of.

It took Freddie a full day before he plucked up the courage to break the news of their son's proposed absence to his wife. He had expected Constance to be devastated. But to his surprise she took the news quite calmly.

'Boys of that age don't want to be with their old parents, really, do they?' she remarked with only the merest touch of edge. 'I expect it's perfectly natural for him not to want to come.'

Freddie could not believe she was expressing her true feelings. 'But it's our silver wedding anniversary,' he said. 'Not just any old night out with your mum and dad.'

'Well, he said he was trying to catch up with his studies. We both want that, don't we?'

'Yes,' said Freddie. 'Of course we do. It was just that I didn't really believe him. You know how I could always tell when William was fibbing when he was a boy – well, I think I still can, up to a point. He didn't convince me that was the true reason at all. I'm afraid he's in trouble, again, to be honest. That's what's bugging me. I mean, if the college was right before and he *was* taking drugs as well as hitting the bottle – that's not going to go away just like that, is it?'

Constance took his hand, still giving the impression

of being remarkably untroubled. 'Oh, I wouldn't go thinking the worst, Freddie. Not without any evidence. Perhaps he's found himself a girlfriend.'

Freddie hadn't thought of that. And the idea lifted his spirits a little, as he was sure had been his wife's intention.

'Well, yes, perhaps he has,' he murmured thoughtfully.

'I'm sure it's something like that, nothing to worry about at all, just a new girlfriend,' said Constance.

Freddie did not notice the catch in her voice or the way she contrived to turn her back towards him as she spoke.

On the day of the party, however, William unexpectedly turned up. At least he was unexpected by his parents but not entirely by his elder sister, who had called him back, told him how dreadfully he had upset his father, and generally given him a grade A roasting.

'Well done,' Charlotte whispered to her brother shortly after his arrival and gave him a warm hug.

William even managed a grin. That was pretty rare for him too, nowadays, as it wasn't just their mother who had been acting out of character lately, Charlotte reflected. Like her father, her thoughts automatically turned to drugs but, being the kind of person she was, she swiftly dismissed the idea as too awful even to contemplate. In any case William looked well enough. Charlotte had trained as a nurse just like her mother, given it up when Alex was born but hoped to go back to it one day, and had met a few junkies in her time. Her life had not been entirely as sheltered as it appeared. Although the problem might be worse in the urban jungles of Britain's inner cities, rural Somerset was not without its drug culture. No, she was somehow pretty sure just from looking at him that her brother, although he might well have experimented with strange substances, did not have a serious drug problem.

She personally thought it was more likely that he had been sulking. He had always had a sulky side to his nature, had William, even when he had been a little lad. And God knows who he got it from, either, she thought to herself. But, although he had appeared to ultimately take it well and had certainly agreed to knuckle down and go back to college when given the opportunity, Charlotte suspected that William had been far more put out by the tongue-lashing his mother had given him than he had let on – certainly to her.

Although she was unaware of the details of the exchange between mother and son, it had obviously been pretty serious, and Charlotte couldn't remember her mother ever having spoken a cross word to William before that. Her only son could never do any wrong in Constance Lange's eyes, everybody knew that. But the thought that William might be about to really upset his father – and drag the family name through the mud into the bargain – Charlotte's mother had shown that other tough side of her nature. The side Charlotte had always known existed, but which had probably come as a shock to William who was inclined to live in his own cloud cuckoo land. As far as Charlotte could ascertain, her mother had merely given William a thorough bollocking and told him to grow up – and not before time in Charlotte's opinion.

She loved her brother dearly and appreciated his charm and humour in much the same way as her mother did. But she really thought it was time he stopped behaving like a sulky schoolboy when anything didn't suit him.

However she watched approvingly as William hugged his father, handed him a beautifully wrapped anniversary gift and remarked in his most disarming way, 'In the end I realised I just *had* to be here. I couldn't miss this day, could I?'

Charlotte waited in vain for her brother to show the same warm affection towards her mother. William kissed his mother in greeting when he arrived at the Mount Somerset, but Charlotte realised that it would have been unthinkable for him not to in front of his entire family and most of the village. His body language, however, left Charlotte in no doubt that he did not really wish to do so. In fact, William showed no desire to be close to his mother throughout the entire evening, and barely spoke to her again. Instead he allowed himself to be monopolised by their younger sister, Helen, who hero-worshipped him – again rather too much for his own good, in Charlotte's opinion.

She couldn't help recalling the last village function when her mother and brother had so outraged that old busybody Marcia Spry by dancing together virtually the whole night long. Things had changed, that was for certain. Yet if her mother had noticed William's distant behaviour to her, she gave no sign of it, and that was unusual too because Constance had always been the most sensitive of women.

Charlotte considered giving her brother another lecture, but this was neither the time nor place, and in any case she did not really know what she would say. 'Why aren't you nice to Mother any more?' sounded fairly pathetic and was hardly likely to get her very far. Charlotte decided that all she could do was pretend she hadn't noticed and be thankful, at least, that apart from her, nobody else was likely to detect the strange chill between mother and son.

Charlotte had, of course, overlooked the acute observational powers of Marcia Spry, whom she had not wanted to invite to the party in the first place. It had been Freddie, ever the diplomat, who had insisted. And if he had been able to read old Marcia's mind as she had diligently studied his family throughout the evening, even the generous and easy-going Freddie might have wished that he'd thrown village protocol to the winds and denied her an invitation.

The shameless Marcia watched William's curiously distant behaviour towards his mother almost gleefully, and became increasingly more excited by the prospect of some kind of split between mother and son as the evening progressed. She too remembered the way William and his mother had danced the night away together only a few months before.

'Unnatural the way those two carry on, that's what it is,' she had sniffed to her cronies then. 'Tied to her apron strings, that boy's always been . . .'

Now Marcia was intrigued. The contrast between that evening and this one was fascinating to her. She began to wonder just how serious William's troubles at college were, and to speculate on what he might have been up to that could cause such a rift with his doting mother.

Even Marcia Spry could barely launch into

malicious gossip about her hosts while the party was actually in progress – and she had just about enough common sense to realise that this might not exactly be welcomed by her fellow guests at such a generous do, either. But she left the Mount Somerset shortly after midnight a very happy woman, barely able to contain herself until morning when she could begin to create mischief.

The postman, who called at her cottage even before Mrs Walters opened the village shop, was her first target.

'I don't know what's going on with that family, but something's rocked the apple cart, you mark my words,' she told him sagely, as if imparting some mighty slice of wisdom rather than as nasty a piece of tittle-tattle as she was able to create from the little knowledge she actually had.

Charlotte didn't know what was going on either – but she intended to keep her resolution not to confront her brother. Indeed she was given little opportunity to do so. William had left to drive back to the agricultural college even before she popped around to the farm at breakfast time on the morning after the party.

Constance appeared to be genuinely effusive in her appreciation of the party, which pleased Charlotte enormously, although she remained irritated by William's behaviour towards their mother during the previous evening.

'That brother of mine didn't stop long this morning then,' she eventually remarked casually to her mother.

'He had to get back for lectures, dear,' replied Constance levelly. And that was, of course, probably the simple truth. They'd all made enough fuss when he hadn't been pulling his weight at college, after all.

Charlotte, however, couldn't help pushing the subject.

'You two didn't have much to say to each other last night,' she said in what she hoped was a light tone of voice.

Constance was standing at the sink with her back to her daughter. She said nothing, but Charlotte thought her shoulders stiffened. Perhaps she was imagining things.

'I mean you've always been such great friends . . .' Charlotte hoped her voice was still light when she continued, 'Everything is all right between you two now, isn't it?'

Constance turned swiftly around to face her daughter. 'Why is everyone fussing about me so much?' she asked with a smile which was as warm and almost as reassuring as her smiles had always been.

Charlotte shrugged. She didn't know quite what to say.

'Don't fret,' said her mother. 'Your brother has his moods like all the rest of us. I thought I might pop over to the college and visit him as soon as I can find the time, actually. Maybe take him out for a spot of supper . . .'

'Oh, that would be a lovely idea, mother,' said Charlotte.

And now she really did feel happier.

There was even better to come. Within minutes of Charlotte arriving back at Honeysuckle Cottage the phone rang. It was William.

'Watcher, sis,' he said. 'I just called to tell you what

a great job you did last night putting on that bash for mum and dad. You couldn't fault it.'

Charlotte was still a bit angry with him, but in spite of herself she glowed.

'I'm just glad you turned up,' she said, with only the slightest edge.

William laughed. 'I never had any choice, did I?' he asked. 'You might have known I wouldn't let the family down.'

She warmed to him. 'Of course I know,' she said. But he'd made the first approach, so she thought she dared risk at least touching on her various anxieties.

'You know, if mum was a bit hard on you when you got sent home from college it was only because she was so worried,' she said.

'Of course.'

'Even I wondered if you'd become a druggie or something.'

William laughed again. 'Is this the girl who once dragged me off to the bottom of Brook Meadow and demanded that I roll her an extremely large spliff?' he asked teasingly.

'Which made me feel so peculiar that I never smoked dope again – but you did, William.' She was not to be that easily swayed.

'Yes,' he said. 'Dope and only dope. I am not, and never have been, into anything stronger. And I wouldn't put up with this kind of cross-examination from anyone but you, either, Charlotte.'

She knew that was probably true. They had always been close.

'I only rang up to say well done,' continued William almost plaintively.

Charlotte relented. 'I know, thank you.' She paused. 'Have you called Mother?'

'Not yet,' he said. He sounded quite relaxed.

She took advantage of the moment. 'Mum noticed, you know, that you didn't have a lot of time for her last night, and so did I.'

'You're a fusspot,' he chided her gently. 'You know I can be a moody sod, you've told me off for it enough over the years.'

'That's true,' she responded. 'I wish you'd grow up, that's all.'

'You don't half push your luck,' he informed her. 'All right. Tell mother I'm sorry if I seemed a bit off. Tell her I'll make up for it.'

'Why don't you tell her yourself? She said she'd drive over to see you some time soon.'

He did not reply for a moment.

'William, are you still there?'

'Yes. Sorry, I'm not supposed to be using this phone. I thought there was someone coming.'

'I said mother's planning to visit you.'

'That would be great,' responded William with evident enthusiasm.

'I'm so glad you said that,' said Charlotte.

And when she put the phone down she scolded herself for having made a problem out of something and nothing. Her mother was right. Her brother was right. She fussed too much.

# Eleven

Colin Parker considered himself to be a veteran at the game. His twenty-first birthday was still several weeks away but he had been working for Avon Escorts for almost three years.

It was the last Saturday in November, the 28th of the month, and this was just another job for Colin. He was sitting in a corner of the bar of the Portway Towers, which was generally regarded by Colin and his kind as little more than a super-posh knocking shop. The head porter had been on Avon's payroll for years, and any lonely businessmen or women staying at the Portway Towers had only to make discreet inquiries in order not to remain lonely for long.

Colin looked idly around the bar. Often, although not tonight, there were faces that he recognised at the Portway. Several of the local Toms sat around there regularly on spec, unbothered by the bar staff in return for a bit of commission occasionally. If you worked for Avon, though, you didn't have to hang around anywhere on the off-chance. You were almost always pre-booked, and the rates demanded meant your customers were likely to be pretty classy. Colin reckoned he was already firmly established at the top end of his trade.

A glass of Diet Coke was growing warm and flat on the table in front of him. It was a pretty boring drink in which he had lost all interest after the first couple of sips, but Colin wasn't going to risk spoiling anything by going on the booze. He was on duty, after all.

Colin had blow-dried his silky brown hair meticulously, shaved extra carefully – grateful that he was showing no signs of the adolescent acne which still occasionally troubled him – and was wearing his smartest suit, as instructed.

The woman Colin was waiting for had told Paolo exactly what she wanted. And she had indicated that if she were pleased with her escort's services, if he turned out to be fully satisfactory in every way, there would be a big bonus for him.

Colin smiled to himself. The murder of Marty Morris did not worry him one bit. Marty had been heavily into the gay scene, and Colin wasn't. Colin had convinced himself long ago that the only dangers in his game lay with the gay trade – after all, how could a woman hurt him? He was young, fit and strong, wasn't he? And he did kick boxing down the gym every Friday. It would take some tart to do him any damage. Colin really did not consider himself to be at risk. You weren't if you were sensible, he reckoned.

In any case Colin had already heard that the police suspected Marty's boyfriend. Dead right too, in Colin's opinion. Colin knew Jonathon Lee, they all did. He'd even bought some dope from him once. Colin didn't touch crack - too dangerous, he'd seen what it did to people – but he liked to smoke the odd joint. Colin reckoned that Jonathon Lee was a nasty piece of work beneath all that smarmy smoothness. And, sharing Rose Piper's opinion although he didn't know it, he considered Lee to be well capable of murder.

Colin checked his watch. The woman was almost a

quarter of an hour late. He glanced around the bar again. He had been told to look out for a tall red-head. Her name was Rachel – but don't approach her, she'll come to you, Paolo had instructed. There were only two women in the bar, neither was a red-head, and they were both with men.

Colin began to fidget with his shirt collar. He was a smart dresser, but he liked casual gear best. He didn't wear a tie very often and he had feared his collar would prove too tight. Seems he had been right. He was sweating. The bar was hot and stuffy, and that added to his discomfort. He looked around him. Bored now. Impatient. He ate a lot of peanuts, for something to do.

Eventually he became aware of the barman looking at him. The man had just answered the telephone and was nodding into the receiver. When the call was over he ducked under the bar and walked briskly across the room.

'Are you Colin?' he asked without much interest. 'Rachel says she's been delayed. She'll pick you up by the back door to the car park in five minutes.'

'Right, thanks mate,' said Colin, thinking 'At last!'

He paid for his Coke – he hadn't done so before because he had assumed Rachel would pick up the tab. You had to watch the pennies in this game just like any other business. He made his way through the hotel foyer and opened the door at the rear which led into the car park.

Outside the change in temperature was dramatic. He shivered as the cold of the damp November night engulfed him. He wished he'd brought an overcoat. He peered around him. The car park was ill lit, shadowy.

A female voice called his name. Where was she, for goodness sake? He couldn't see her. Then he spotted a dark saloon car with its side lights on, the motor running and the passenger door open. His name was called again. Yes, the voice came from the car, he was sure of it. He walked over to the motor and bent down to look inside. As he did so he felt a vicious punch in the small of his back. His knees buckled. His vision began to cloud. And his last coherent thought was the surprisingly clear realisation that he hadn't been punched at all. He had been stabbed.

Within less than a minute Colin Parker was dead.

Colin's body was found shortly after his death by a porter who nipped out into the car park for a quick smoke. No attempt had been made to conceal the body which lay, almost certainly as it had fallen, spread-eagled on the ground only a few yards to the left of the door into the hotel.

'I know I shouldn't have touched it, but I didn't realise he was a goner, you see. I went to help like. And he was still warm, I mean, it was a second or two before I realised he'd snuffed it.'

Young Micky Peters, a skinny undersized lad who didn't look strong enough to be employed to lug suitcases around, gave the impression that he was enjoying every moment of being the centre of attention when Rose Piper and DS Mellor questioned him. Indeed, thought Rose, it seemed as if finding the body was the most exciting thing that had happened to him in his entire nineteen years.

Once more the scenes-of-crime boys were already at work by the time Rose arrived. By unhappy coincidence she had again been forced to interrupt an evening with Simon at San Carlo. She had been in the process of buying him dinner in a bid to make amends for having walked out of his birthday party when her mobile phone had rung and she had learned of the second murder.

Ironic really. History repeating itself. She winced at the memory of Simon's glum resignation and made herself concentrate on the task in hand.

For once the internal communications of the Avon and Somerset force seemed to have worked pretty smoothly. DI Pearson from Bridewell nick had been the first senior officer called to the scene – the Portway Towers was squarely in Bridewell territory – but had made contact with Rose's murder unit as soon as he saw what had happened. Pearson, a very experienced officer, realised at once that the circumstances and manner of death were similar to the case already being investigated. And as he was nearing retirement, and as the city centre Bridewell was always considered ill-equipped and badly situated for major crime inquiries, there had been none of the behind-the-scenes power struggle which might have occurred with a different investigating officer from a different station.

DI Pearson had been quite happy to hand the case on. Relieved almost. He had priorities other than battling to make his name on a big murder case. Those kind of ambitions were long buried in DI Pearson, if indeed he had ever experienced them. It was his pub quiz night, he explained to an amused Rose, when he eventually excused himself from the scene.

Carmen Brown was crouched by the corpse, her

bag of tricks at her side. And there was really only one question Rose wanted answered right now.

'So come on Carmen, is it the same killer? Do we have a serial or what?'

Dr Brown leaned back on her heels and looked up at the Detective Chief Inspector. Her face was pinched with the cold.

'It's the same method, that's for sure,' she said. 'He's been stabbed through the small of the back – almost certainly by a knife with a long sharp blade. See?'

The victim was lying on his front, the ragged hole in the back of his jacket clearly apparent. As before, there was not a great deal of blood, but the light material of the jacket had not trapped and stemmed what bleeding there was in the way that Marty Morris's heavy leather jacket had done. An ominous dark bloodstain had spread over the pale tan of the suit jacket.

Rose struggled to control her breathing. Steeling herself, she focused her gaze on the man's face. Again the victim was lying with his head to one side. His eyes were locked open and in them Rose could still see terror. It may only have been a fleeting thing, but it was there all right, and remained frozen with death. She was beginning to get used to it. Once more this was a good-looking young man. His hair was clean and shiny, his skin unseasonably tanned as if he had either recently been on a sunshine holiday or had been using a sunbed.

Rose looked around her. 'No sign of a murder weapon again, then?' she inquired of a passing SOCO.

The white-suited officer shook his head mournfully. A team of four SOCOs were already at work examining the entire area, three of them on hands and knees. It was going to be a long night.

The Cataldi brothers arrived around 2.00 a.m. and were quite quickly authorised to take the body away.

'You know, I've not been able to look at a bin liner since I started this job,' remarked Ron Cataldi conversationally as he and his brother loaded the corpse in its body bag into their van.

At Southmead Hospital an exhibit officer as usual supervised the removal of the dead man's clothes and other effects which were all bagged and labelled ready for forensic examination.

Rose Piper and Sergeant Mellor arrived soon afterwards, just as the body was being fingerprinted. Rose had given up on sleep for that night. In any case her adrenalin was pumping. She doubted she could sleep and she was quite happy to delay going home to Simon. She suspected that Mellor would have been glad to escape for a few hours – but he had apparently not dared to suggest it.

Without comment, the exhibit officer handed Rose an evidence bag containing the contents of the dead man's pockets. She peered at the various items through the transparent plastic. There was a handkerchief, a pack of Marlboro, a small quantity of marijuana, a packet of Rizla cigarette papers, some loose change and a wallet containing fifty pounds, a Barclays Visa card and a driving licence. The latter two items identified their holder to be Colin Parker, of 1 Park Terrace, Bristol West.

Rose had a small silent bet with herself that Parker would turn out to have been another Avon Escorts boy. For more reasons than one she rather hoped it would prove to be so. A connection like that would be further indication that they were dealing with a serial killer. Rose could not help being excited by the thought of heading such an investigation.

'Right Peter, check Avon out,' she instructed. 'Get a team on to Paolo right away.'

The tall sergeant began to dial into his mobile phone and retreated into the corridor.

Rose stayed in the mortuary a little longer, watching as impassively as she could while the victim was cleaned up ready for identification. There would be a post-mortem examination later that day. Rose didn't know what more that could tell her. She was desperate for anything to link the two crimes.

Peter Mellor reappeared. He looked animated. He had obviously already got some kind of result. Rose felt a shiver run down her spine. She struggled to remain composed and professional.

'Paolo's running scared now,' said the sergeant. 'He admitted it right away. Colin Parker was on his books.'

'Yes!' Rose half shouted the word and, aware of appraising glances from both Sergeant Mellor and the mortuary attendant, immediately wished she hadn't. At least she had refrained from punching the air, that was something, she supposed. But she couldn't hide her satisfaction.

When she spoke again, however, her voice was calm and controlled. 'I reckon we've definitely got a serial, Peter, what do you think?'

Mellor nodded his agreement. That pleased Rose too.

She sensed the makings of a very big case. And she

found herself immediately focusing on the Mrs Pattinson connection again.

Mrs Pattinson had already missed one regular appointment with Avon Escorts, Rose learned. Paolo, damn him, had not previously revealed that the woman always used the agency on the same day every month. 'Well, you never asked that,' he muttered sullenly when confronted.

However it had not turned out to be such an important miss as it might have been because Mrs Pattinson had failed to surface on that day or any other. And in any case Rose had had a team monitoring Avon Escorts' telephones since the first murder, ready to spin into action should Mrs Pattinson ever be heard from again.

With the second murder, the disappearance of Mrs Pattinson from the vice scene in which she had apparently revelled gained additional significance. There had always been the possibility that Mrs Pattinson had backed off merely out of fear – of her true identity being revealed as public and police attention focused on Avon Escorts, and perhaps even fear of possibly facing violence herself – and that the evidence which pointed toward her was merely coincidental. Another murder, and still no word from the mysterious Mrs P was yet another coincidence. As was the evidence of the barman who had taken the telephone message from a woman called Rachel that Colin should meet her in the car park. Surely it must be almost certain therefore that his killer was a woman. Everything seemed to be leading to Mrs Pattinson.

Rose felt vindicated in her own judgement. After

all, she had always considered the gay killing theory to be stereotyped thinking – and investigations into the life and times of the latest victim indicated that Colin Parker did not have a gay bone in his body.

'So – are we still after a gay killer, then, Peter?' she asked DS Mellor somewhat smugly.

She should have known better than to exhibit any degree of smugness. Peter Mellor, who, having so unusually lost his cool already on this case was obviously determined not to do so again, studied her appraisingly.

'Could be camouflage, boss,' he remarked. 'If it was Jonathon Lee who topped Marty Morris, he could have killed again just to take the heat off.'

Rose didn't really want to be diverted from her pet theory.

'And Mrs Pattinson's voice on the phone to Paolo, the woman Rachel on the phone to the barman, was that all Jonathon Lee?' she asked irritably.

Mellor did not rise to her. 'Sometimes people hear or see what they think they should,' he commented evenly. 'And Lee could have an accomplice.'

'Peter, I think you're being stubborn,' said Rose. Secretly, though, she knew the bloody man had a point.

Soon after Charlie heard the news of Colin Parker's death he decided to contact the police. Enough was enough. Charlie was really afraid now.

'Colin was another of Mrs Pattinson's favourites, you see,' he told a fascinated Rose Piper. 'I've worked with him. We've serviced her together, she likes that . . .'

Rose thought the young West Indian sounded as if

he regarded himself as some sort of prize bull. Presumably he did. And there was an air of bouncy self-confidence about him, in spite of his loudly expressed fears for his safety.

'I want police protection, that's what I came here for,' he demanded.

Rose was sitting across the table from him in an interview room at Staple Hill Police Station endeavouring to appear stern, solemn and unmoved by events – whereas the reality was that she was bubbling over with excitement.

The murder enquiry team had been moved to Staple Hill that morning, as soon as Rose's superiors accepted her prognosis that there was a possible serial killer on the loose and certainly a link between the murders of Marty Morris and Colin Parker. In Rose's opinion, Staple Hill – being several miles out of the city centre, the station itself covering the South Gloucestershire area – was not perfectly situated to be the incident room of a Bristol murder. Neither did she have a high opinion of the building housing the Investigation Centre, which was an old portacabin originally constructed as temporary accommodation for the local magistrates' court. But the rather decrepit cabin remained permanently set up and ready to house a major crime unit such as Rose was heading. State-of-the-art computer equipment in the form of HOLMES TWO, the latest version of the Home Office Large Major Enquiry Systems, an advanced computer system on-line to other stations throughout the country, sat incongruously on cheap wooden tables stained with the rings of a million tea mugs in prefabricated rooms lined with wood-chip paper.

None of Staple Hill's shortcomings daunted Rose however. She was used to police stations with substandard conditions. In addition, to her immense satisfaction, she had now been officially appointed Senior Investigation Officer of both murders and would expect to be SIO of any possibly linked murders in the future. Rose had more than eighty officers on her team who between them, she could see from a glance at the computer on her desk, had so far made 6047 house calls, completed almost 4000 PDFs (Personal Description Forms) and taken 490 statements. Rose's further direct involvement with either possible witnesses or suspects had been minimal. Charlie Collins, however, fell firmly into the small category of those she was not prepared to hand on to anyone.

Charlie had turned up unannounced less than an hour earlier at Trinity Road – the St Paul's police station not far from his mother's home with which he was most familiar. Fortunately it had not taken the front office clerk at Trinity long to realise Charlie's importance to the current murder investigation and arrange for him to be driven straight to Staple Hill.

Rose studied the handsome young man. She had not met anyone like Charlie Collins before. She'd been involved in her share of vice cases. She'd met and had to deal with prostitutes and pimps often enough. Avon Escorts and this character were different. Charlie talked about his trade in the way any self-employed businessman might, bemoaning his loss of income in the present crisis.

'I mean, I can't work, can I? Too dangerous. And I can't even sleep under my own roof. That's not right, is it? You guys are going to have to sort this out. And

I gotta 'ave protection, haven't I?'

'Just tell me all you know, Charlie,' instructed Rose, still battling to suppress her excitement. She had a feeling the lad might provide the key to it all if she handled him right. 'Everything. You help us and we'll help you.'

Charlie did so. It took a long time. At one point Rose had to ask him to stop while a new pair of tapes were slotted into the recording machine. Charlie was a good talker. He told them all about Avon Escorts, his years working for them, the kind of clients he had, and how good it had always been for him. He even explained how the system worked. The money he earned and how he split it with Avon. He told them over and over about the lifestyle he had enjoyed and about how threatened he now felt.

And, of course, he told them everything he knew about Mrs Pattinson, her likes and dislikes, how she always asked for him, the games she liked to play. And repeatedly he told them how sure he had been from the start that Marty Morris had been killed by mistake instead of him.

'It should have been me there, you see. I was her special. Not Marty.'

Charlie's hands on the table before him were trembling. He was obviously in shock. The thought occurred to Rose that this rather extraordinary young man really had seen no special dangers in his way of life before and had genuinely considered his trade not to be so different to any other. Only now, for the first time, was he experiencing any doubts or fears.

'Where do Avon find all these young men they have on their books?' she asked, genuinely curious as much as anything else.

Charlie shrugged. 'We get all sorts,' he said. 'Not many are full-time pros like me. A lot of them work at something else during the day.' He managed a wry smile. 'It can be quite fashionable in certain quarters, you know. Something you dare your mates to do. You'd be surprised at some of the lads we get. Down the uni they reckon it's a great lark.' He affected what he considered to be a posh accent for the last few words.

Rose was getting a fresh insight into an old world. She didn't think there was much left that life could throw at her that would cause her too many surprises. But Charlie Collins was dead right, she reckoned. She would probably be surprised by a great number of the employees of Avon Escorts, as indeed she had been by Charlie. Charlie, with his mobile phone, his Armani suit and his Gucci brogues, was breaking the mould. Rose didn't reckon she would have guessed what he did for a living in a million years. He gave the impression of being quite sophisticated and very successful. He had a winning smile and an easy manner which even his obvious stress did not totally conceal. He was of a whole new breed, and so were the rest of them, it appeared. Students out to make what they obviously regarded as easy money and have fun into the bargain with a bit of luck. Charlie had apparently had fun with Mrs Pattinson, you could tell by his body language alone when he talked about her. Mrs Pattinson. Her shadow was everywhere.

Rose leaned back in her seat. 'Why do you think Mrs Pattinson would want to kill you?' she asked.

Charlie shrugged. 'That's the big problem, I just can't think of a reason.'

He had intelligent eyes, thought Rose. He was

192

streetwise. Probably nobody could give her a better insight into the mysterious Mrs P than Charlie Collins.

'We had good times together, over more than two years, don't forget,' he continued.

He had no problems talking about his business. He might have been discussing a business associate with whom he occasionally had lunch. Rose was beginning to gain the impression that that was in any case much the way Charlie Collins saw his relationships with his clients.

'You lot'll probably 'ave a laugh, but I always thought she liked me,' Charlie went on. 'Not just for sex. And certainly nothing to do with paying for it. I can't imagine her wanting to hurt me or any of the lads, but it's got to be her, hasn't it? It really has to be her.'

Rose wished it was even that straightforward. There was even still a small chance that Peter Mellor's theory about Jonathon Lee might yet prove correct. She wasn't convinced. Nonetheless, while she had no intention of answering Charlie's question directly, she did have more questions for him concerning Mrs Pattinson.

'What if Mrs Pattinson killed because she was being blackmailed?' she asked obliquely. 'What if she killed because she was being threatened with having her secret life exposed?'

Charlie grasped what she was getting at immediately. He looked quite indignant.

'No way!' he said. 'Don't even think about it. Not me. Not any of the lads. Working boys and girls don't do blackmail. It would be cutting off your nose to spite your face.'

The interview lasted almost two hours and at the end of it Rose felt she had learned more about the murky world in which both her two victims and her prime suspect had moved than throughout the entire murder investigation so far.

Thanks to Charlie, Rose now believed she was beginning to build up some kind of picture of Mrs Pattinson. But the one thing she had not learned was anything which could help her find the woman. Charlie could give her absolutely no information which could in any way lead to revealing the true identity of Mrs Pattinson. He had had sex with her once a month for over two years and yet she had never at any time said anything which had given him the smallest clue.

'Of course, I wasn't trying to find out who she was or anything, but usually they can't help talking about themselves in the end,' he told Rose. 'It's amazing what they tell you, sometimes. Things they never tell the old man, if they got one, that's for sure. But she never said a word about herself. Never.'

It was a blow, but Rose had to accept it. Ultimately Charlie Collins seemed to be no more help in unveiling the real Mrs Pattinson than anyone else.

Avon Escorts continued to insist, although increasingly ineffectually as more and more evidence began to present itself concerning the true activities of its employees, that it was both 'reputable and respectable'. Certainly it kept surprisingly businesslike records, although Rose had little doubt that not all transactions were recorded and she also assumed, quite rightly, that the sums of money listed were not always the full amounts paid.

The more Avon Escorts was investigated, the more Rose came to realise that this was big, big business. Certainly a real money spinner. Even the figures which went through the books alone indicated a healthy turnover and Rose reckoned that was just the tip of the iceberg. Avon supplied both male and female escorts, but specialised in young men.

'Well, you gotta move with the times,' Paolo told her honestly. 'There's a whole new market out there, you know. Women want what men want, nowadays.'

Rose murmured something noncommittal and thought to herself that women had probably always wanted what men wanted. They had just never dared to act out their fantasies before, even if they had them. And, certainly until confronted so explicitly with the extensive activities of Avon, Rose would have assumed that was still so. As in the majority of cases it almost certainly was, she thought.

Nonetheless, Rose was learning that this was a complex game and she wondered just how many Mrs Pattinsons there were out there, leading some kind of double life.

Paolo, who had plenty of practice at being economical with the truth, needed to be pushed to give more than he had already. But, under pressure, he provided a list of at least twelve young men who had escorted Mrs Pattinson. Unfortunately many of them were known to Avon simply by a Christian name which was often false. He also confirmed what Rose already knew about the wide catchment area for recruitment which Avon enjoyed, and how so many of their escorts had respectable day jobs and merely moonlighted with the agency occasionally.

'It's not just extra cash, it's kicks too for a lot of the

boys, the sort we have,' he told Rose. 'There's a lot to be said for a horny middle-aged woman when you're an eighteen-year-old bursting full of hormones, you see. Our boys have probably got girlfriends who wouldn't know some of the tricks our clients get up to had even been invented. And if they did they wouldn't take part in them . . .'

And that was about as voluble as Paolo got. Mostly he said as little as possible. He did however confirm that Mrs Pattinson's next regular appointment with Avon Escorts was just days away and was given strict instructions about what to do if she called. He should keep her on the line as long as possible, for a start, to give the police eavesdroppers time to act.

Unsurprisingly Mrs Pattinson did not resurface. Paolo was pleased about that if nothing else.

'Business is bad enough as it is,' he remarked to no one in particular as he lounged disconsolately about in the office one day, surrounded by silent telephones. 'Who's going to call an escort agency up to its eyeballs in a murder enquiry? The only hope we've got is for that bloody Mrs Pattinson never to be heard of again, then maybe, just maybe, the whole thing might go away.'

He didn't sound as if he believed that though.

Meanwhile Rose ploughed her way through the usual police procedure. As she had expected because of the clinically efficient way in which Marty Morris had been killed, there had been no forensic evidence other than the footprints in the mud, which might lead to his killer. All that forensic had been able to tell from the footprints had been that the Timberland boots which had made them were barely worn. There had been a brave attempt to trace and interview Timberland owners in the district, but no way of making this comprehensive.

Rose was still awaiting the full forensic report from the murder of Colin Parker, but again death had been caused by one lethal stab involving little or no human contact. She was not optimistic.

She contemplated possible murder motives. There was still no concrete evidence to indicate whether the killer was a man or a woman, only circumstantial stuff and conjecture. And if the killer was indeed a female client of Avon Escorts, Mrs Pattinson or somebody else, was she killing out of self-disgust, she wondered? It was all heavy psychological stuff.

'God, I could do with a Cracker,' she said to Peter Mellor. 'If only it wasn't such a lot of unmitigated crap.'

'What're you talking about, boss?' asked the sergeant.

'You know, Robbie Coltrane, *Cracker* – the man who can see inside other people's heads, allegedly,' responded his Chief Inspector wearily.

'Who, boss?'

Rose shook her head, half-exasperated, half-amused. 'Television, Peter, television – don't you have *any* vices?'

'I don't think so,' replied Sergeant Mellor seriously.

Charlie's fear increased as every day passed. He was unused to fear, unused even to being unsure of himself.

He had talked through the idea of police protection

with the woman Detective Chief Inspector whom he had rather taken a shine to in spite of his instinctive suspicion of and usual dislike for cops. He wasn't sure what kind of protection the police would really have been prepared to give him in any case, he supposed they didn't much like his kind, but in the end he had withdrawn his request.

The lady cop had suggested that he should be pretty safe staying with his mother, maybe even safer than at the centre of a more high-profile protection operation. But it had been thinking about his mother that had decided him not to insist. It was difficult enough coming up with some new tale of woe every day to explain to her why he had been unable to return to his flat for so long. The extent of rewiring, and therefore redecoration, required, grew greater every time and he was pretty sure his mother was beginning to find it hard to believe. She was not a stupid woman and he had noticed a funny look in her eye lately that was both sceptical and a little anxious. He certainly could not imagine a story he could come up with to explain away any kind of police presence at or around her home. No. He preferred to allow the Detective Chief Inspector to convince him that he was unlikely to be in any real danger as long as he continued to lie low.

He could not risk his mother finding out the truth about his lavish lifestyle. He found himself breaking into a sweat at the very thought. There were times when he wondered if he wouldn't rather be killed than have that happen. His mother must never know. That was more important than anything in the world to Charlie Collins.

# Twelve

When the second Tuesday in December arrived, Constance Lange again showed no particular inclination to make her usual visit to her aunt.

Freddie didn't like it. Constance's mood changes were really disturbing him. Briefly she had seemed almost to have returned to her old self until the last few days when he had become worried about her all over again.

He studied her over breakfast. She seemed nervy, distracted and forgetful, and she didn't look well – although she still continued to insist that she was perfectly fit.

'Look, if you're not ill, why are you pulling out of your Bristol trip again?'

Freddie supposed he should be getting used by now to the disruption of routine all around him, it had been going on for two months now, but it still made him uneasy, as did the way in which the wife upon whom he so depended continued to behave in a disturbingly out-of-character fashion.

'Have a really good lunch, do some Christmas shopping, buy yourself something nice, it'll cheer you up,' Freddie continued in spite of getting no response at all from his wife. 'I don't like it when you are out of sorts.'

Eventually Constance managed the wan smile

which seemed to be the best she could come up with nowadays.

'I'm sorry,' she said, although in a voice more resigned than apologetic. 'I expect you're right, of course I'll go.'

And so she dressed in one of her smartest suits and set off for Bristol, but there was an air of resignation about her, as if she had merely given in to her husband's wishes because she did not have the energy to do anything other. Certainly there was no sign of the energetic cheeriness which had always been so much a part of her.

Constance had been gone only a couple of hours when the phone rang at Chalmpton Village Farm. Freddie, in the milking shed with his dairy man, reacted quickly when he heard the loud ring of the amplified bell in the yard. Whenever the phone rang when Constance was not at home, Freddie's first thought was always that it might be his wife calling. Now, with the more or less permanent anxiety he was feeling about her, he immediately thought that she must need him, that she might be in some kind of trouble.

He dashed into the dairy to pick up the extension there. It was not Constance, but there was an emergency. The headmistress of Portland School, where their youngest daughter, Helen, was a boarder, was on the line. Helen Lange had been suddenly taken very ill and it was feared that she had meningitis. Her condition could be critical. A doctor and an ambulance were already at the school and Helen was about to be taken to the Musgrove Park Hospital in Taunton.

Freddie felt his knees turn to jelly. Although both Langes were careful to treat all their children equally, if Constance had always had a soft spot for William – until recently anyway – then Helen was Freddie's favourite.

Without giving his dairyman any explanation – he did not really trust himself with the words – Freddie hurried into the house, trying not to panic. At least he knew exactly what he had to do next. He used the kitchen phone to call his wife's mobile and waited impatiently for her to answer. Why was she taking so long? If she were in a bad reception area the phone wouldn't even be ringing. Oh, come on, Constance.

Then, in a moment of horrified clarity, Freddie realised that the ringing sound he could hear was something other than the ringing tone through the earpiece of the kitchen phone. He could actually hear Constance's mobile ringing somewhere in the house. Unable to contain his panic now, he began to run from room to room, ultimately discovering that Constance had left her mobile plugged into the charger in the farm office. Somehow, even in the stress of the moment, the earlier incident when she had told him that she had broken down on the motorway and been unable to phone because of flat batteries, flashed across his mind. Now she had left her phone behind. None of this was like Constance. And Helen was critically ill. Freddie felt as if everything were falling apart at once.

He forced himself to concentrate. He must go to the hospital at once – and the Musgrove, thankfully only two or three miles from his daughter's school, was a good thirty minutes drive from Chalmpton Peverill. But first he had to find Constance.

He needed her so badly, and so did their daughter, he could be sure of that. Constance had always been a wonderful mother. If anything happened to Helen without her being there she would never forgive herself.

Freddie struggled to clear his thoughts. All he could think of doing was to try to contact the nursing home where Constance was due to visit Aunt Ada as usual – but he could not even remember the name of the place. He had an idea that it was something or other Court. Damn! He wished fervently that he had taken more notice of what Constance had told him about Aunt Ada. He had only ever listened with half an ear to her reports of her visits. Then, in a flash of inspiration, he thought of the photograph of Aunt Ada which Constance kept on the hall table. It had been taken soon after the old lady had moved into the home five or six years previously.

Freddie rushed out into the hall. Yes, he had been right. Aunt Ada had been photographed in the garden of the home and its name was just visible on a board in one corner of the photo. However, peering desperately, straining his eyes, Freddie still could not quite read it. Hastily he dashed back into the office, found a magnifying glass and had another go.

This time he could just decipher the words on the sign, Firlands Residential Retirement Home. Strange, he didn't think that was the name Constance had mentioned at all. It just didn't seem familiar. Hastily he double-checked the photograph. He had made no mistake. He returned to the kitchen phone and dialled directory enquiries.

For once the system worked efficiently and Freddie was quickly given the number he sought.

'I wonder if my wife, Mrs Constance Lange, has arrived to visit her aunt yet, I need to get in touch with her urgently,' he told the female voice which cheerfully greeted him when he called Firlands Retirement Home.

Freddie did not really think Constance would be there yet, but he wanted to be absolutely sure she would be given a message as soon as she did arrive.

The response from the woman at the other end of the line was uncertain, confused even. Freddie did not have the time or patience for stupidity. His daughter was seriously ill. Impatiently he gave Constance's name for a second time, and repeated three times the name of her aunt.

'For goodness sake, woman, she's been with you for more than five years, surely you know who she is,' he snapped eventually, anxiety making him uncharacteristically brusque.

There was a pause, followed by a request that he hold on for a few seconds, during which Freddie could hear the murmurings of a muffled conversation. Finally a second, more authoritative, voice came on the line.

'Mr Lange, there must be some misunderstanding. I am afraid your wife's aunt died over three years ago . . .'

Freddie put the phone down very carefully. He could feel the remaining strength ebb from his body.

Freddie was sitting in the dark when Constance returned. The grandfather clock in the sitting-room had just struck ten times. This was her usual time. The sound of the car pulling to a halt in the yard, her footsteps on the gravel outside the kitchen door, the familiar creak as the door swung open – all this was the stuff of normality. This was how it had been so many times before. Yet this day, this night, was like no other in Freddie Lange's life. There was nothing normal about it. And he knew with devastating clarity that the last vestiges of normality had gone for ever out of his world.

The security light outside had come on as Constance drove into the yard. She stood, with the door still open, surprised perhaps by the darkness within, silhouetted in the blazing brightness from without. He was glad that he could not see her face.

'How was Aunt Ada?' he asked.

He had tried to make his voice sound the way it always did, but did not think he had succeeded very ably. His wife answered as if all was well, as if this were a perfectly ordinary enquiry on a perfectly ordinary day.

'Oh you know, much the same. Sends her love.'

She didn't ask why he was sitting in the dark. Maybe some dreadful premonition stopped her. Instead she reached out for the light switch with one hand while closing the kitchen door with the other.

The kitchen was lit by fluorescent strips, their light harsh and unforgiving. Freddie heard Constance give a small gasp as the harsh glare illuminated the room. He had been crying, for hours, it seemed. Helen was all right, thank God. Tests at the Musgrove had quickly ascertained that she did not have meningitis but a viral infection which gave rise to frighteningly similar symptoms. It would clear up in a couple of days with the help of a course of penicillin. Nonetheless since Freddie had got back from the hospital all he had done was weep. He could only imagine the sight he must be, sitting there at the kitchen table, red-eyed, puffy-faced.

Still Constance did not ask if anything was wrong. Instead she sat down on the chair opposite him, almost falling into it, as if her legs were no longer able to carry her. She looked shocked already. Freddie was glad of that.

'Your daughter might have died today,' he said in a matter-of-fact way.

'What?' Constance barked the word. It came out hoarsely, like the cry of a fox at night.

'It's all right. She's going to be OK. No thanks to you though.'

His voice was hard, cruel, he knew. It sounded distant and strange, even to him, as if it belonged to someone else.

'What happened, what on earth happened . . .'

Constance was distraught. Freddie silenced her with one hand raised like a policeman's at a road junction.

'Later,' he said. 'First, I have some questions for you. I know where you weren't today, Constance. Perhaps you had better tell me where you were.'

There was a notepad in front of him on the table and on it were written two phone numbers. One was for the Firlands nursing home.

Freddie saw his wife's gaze lock in on the second number. And when she eventually raised her eyes to meet his, he knew that her despair probably matched his own.

# Thirteen

Two days later there was a tragic accident near Chalmpton Peverill. Freddie Lange was killed outright at the wheel of his beloved old MG roadster. The Taunton police inspector, accompanied by a woman sergeant, who had landed the unenviable job of breaking the grim news to Freddie's widow, arrived at the Lange farm just before 2.00 a.m.

Constance had obviously not yet been to bed. She opened the door fully dressed, almost as soon as the police car swung into the yard. Inspector Barton was not surprised. She would have been waiting up for her husband, starting to worry because he was late, trying to assure herself that everything was fine, that he had just been delayed somewhere or had car trouble. Inspector Barton knew the drill. He had been through it all enough times before, after all. And the expression on Constance Lange's face told him quite clearly now that he hardly need speak. The very sight of him meant that she already knew.

'I'm so terribly sorry . . .' he began.

Wordlessly Constance Lange opened the door wider, stepped back, and let the two police officers into the house. In just a few seconds she seemed to have aged twenty years, the Inspector thought.

'Your husband died at once, that might be some comfort to you,' said Inspector Barton gently.

Constance Lange still did not speak. The Inspector

had hoped that learning her husband was unlikely to have suffered might soften the blow. He knew all about the Langes. They were a respected long-established Somerset family, good people. Why was it always the good ones who went young, he asked himself, not for the first time.

He went through the motions of explaining the details. The accident had happened shortly after midnight on an open stretch of the A38 just five miles from Chalmpton Peverill. There had been no other vehicle involved. Freddie's car appeared to have crashed into a stone wall at full speed. It concertinaed.

Mrs Lange seemed barely to be listening. She sat silently at the kitchen table. The woman sergeant set about making a pot of tea and then asked her if there was anyone else who should be informed, anyone who could be with her.

Constance at first shook her head. The woman didn't seem able to function at all.

'But you have a married daughter, don't you, Mrs Lange?' Inspector Barton asked in what he hoped was a soothing, coaxing sort of voice. 'Shouldn't she be told? She lives here in the village, doesn't she?'

Constance stared at him blankly for a few seconds, then nodded. As if she were being operated by some strange kind of remote control, she reached out for the kitchen phone, rejecting the inspector's offer that he or the sergeant would break the news if she preferred.

'Charlotte has a phone by the bed,' she remarked rather curiously, Inspector Barton thought, almost as if that made everything all right.

The phone seemed to be answered quite swiftly.

Mrs Lange did not waste any time or words, just told her daughter briefly and clearly, although in a small, very tired voice, what had happened.

Across the room the inspector could hear a shriek of despair and shock coming from the receiver. Mrs Lange's expression did not change. Distractedly she replaced the receiver in its cradle, walked back to the kitchen table, sat down again and continued to stare unseeingly into the distance.

Charlotte, her face already stained with tears, arrived within minutes, accompanied by her husband, Michael, a sensible, kind-looking young man who gave the impression, Inspector Barton thought with some relief, that he would be a solid fellow to have around in a crisis.

Certainly the inspector was very glad to see them both. It was not the first time he had broken the news of a sudden bereavement, and he knew from experience that it was often the ones who appeared to take it calmly and quietly who were actually taking it the worst.

Charlotte, sobbing quite openly, wrapped her arms around her mother, but seemed to get little more response from the older woman than had the policeman. Constance merely carried on staring straight ahead, her face drawn but her eyes dry – and blank to the point of being almost uncomprehending.

Inspector Barton thought there was something chillingly unreal about Mrs Lange's reaction. He had seen all sorts in his time, but this was different, no doubt about it, although he couldn't quite put his finger on how. He found it very disturbing indeed.

*

The Lange family withdrew into itself, closing ranks against outsiders. Helen was still in the Musgrove Hospital – kept there for observation although she had been recovering well and the original meningitis diagnosis had definitely been wrong – when her father died. It was Charlotte, thankful that she had married such a supportive man, who in the morning went to the hospital with Michael to break the news to her. And it was Charlotte who lavished her shocked and tearful sister with the comforting love she so needed. Constance, previously always so warm and so strong, this time did not seem to have the strength or the inclination to give solace to anyone – not even her seventeen-year-old daughter.

Constance appeared to be inconsolable and completely disinterested in anything other than her own misery. Michael and Charlotte brought Helen home from hospital straight away. She had in any case been due for release and they thought that the girl needed more than anything else to be with her family, particularly her mother. But Constance, although she went through the motions of taking Helen in her arms and uttering a few words of comfort, continued to act as if she were not really a part of all that was going on around her. She spent only a few curiously distant minutes with poor Helen before saying that she wanted to spend the rest of the day alone in her bedroom. She didn't want any food, she didn't want anything. She was unable, she said, to cope with people, even her own family.

Practical as ever, Charlotte did everything she could to help.

'I'll take Helen home with me tonight, mum,' she said, aware that her sobbing sister was now quite bewildered as well as distraught.

At first Charlotte saw nothing particularly amiss in her mother's reaction, accepting that she must be in deep shock – after all, everybody knew how close, how in love still, Constance and Freddie had been.

William returned from agricultural college later that day, and he seemed to be a completely different person from the wayward boy who had been temporarily suspended for bad behaviour three months earlier. He looked years older for a start, Charlotte thought, and it was William who provided the calming assurance the Lange family had always previously sought from Constance. Out of character, Charlotte rather disloyally considered, but welcome nonetheless.

William's grief was obvious in his strained and tense appearance. But there was also about him a grim determination. It was William who immediately took over the plans for the funeral and began checking at once that the farm was continuing to run as it should. This was indeed a greatly changed William.

He had been home for several hours – and had refused to allow his mother to be disturbed – when Constance finally emerged. She wandered into the kitchen looking almost as if she did not know quite where she was.

William was leaning against the Aga talking to Charlotte, who was standing alongside him making tea for the umpteenth time that day. Helen, exhausted by weeping, was asleep in the old armchair in the corner. Under other circumstances it would have been a cosy family scene.

As she walked aimlessly into the room Constance spotted William and her face broke into a big smile of welcome. She began to move more purposefully across the kitchen, arms outstretched as if she were about to embrace him. Charlotte felt instant relief. She had grown up knowing that her kid brother was her mother's favourite, in spite of Constance's valiant attempts to hide it, and had never minded. Her mother had always had more than enough love to go around. Perhaps William was going to be the tonic their mother needed. But then Charlotte saw Constance stop abruptly as she drew close to her son, the smile, which had perhaps been automatic, freezing across her face, her eyes, at first open and expectant, clouding over again. It was as if she had suddenly remembered something momentarily forgotten, Charlotte thought. She looked at her brother then. He was showing none of the warm response she would have expected. No compassion. No love. No emotion at all, in fact. His bearing was stiff and forbidding. He did not smile or stretch out a hand to Constance. Nothing. No wonder her mother pulled back.

Then Constance uttered a strange wailing sound and began to weep, the tears at last falling freely. And her previously detached, rather eerie calm, turned into a kind of hysteria. She cried out, her voice almost a scream, full of anguish.

'It's all my fault, it's all my fault . . .'

William spoke then, breaking the quite icy silence he had maintained since Constance had entered the room.

'Don't be ridiculous, mother,' he said. His eyes were very cold, his voice impersonal. Charlotte couldn't believe it, he sounded almost as if he were threatening his mother.

'For goodness sake, William, what on earth is wrong with you?' she shouted at him. 'Can't you see how upset Mother is?'

Charlotte rushed to her mother's side and took her in her arms. Constance continued to sob hysterically. At the same time Charlotte became aware that her sister had woken up, unsurprisingly in all the mayhem, and was no doubt confused and frightened by what was going on.

'At least look after Helen,' she snapped at her brother.

Obediently then, William went to his sister, muttered some desultory words of comfort and led her from the room.

'Come on, sis, let's leave Charlotte to it,' he said.

Charlotte returned her full attention to her mother who was still quite hysterical. She would never have thought Constance would react to anything like this, but then, her mother had been acting strangely even before her father's death. At least, thought Charlotte, she was weeping now – for the first time since they had heard the news, her face had not looked remotely as if she had been crying when she came down from her room. Maybe a good cry would release the demons for her.

But this was not to be. Constance remained inconsolable throughout the four-day period between Freddie's death and his funeral. All Charlotte's best efforts to console, comfort and even just to calm her, were to no avail. The doctor was called but Constance refused medication, demanding just to be left alone.

She spent most of the four days in her bedroom and often would not let either of her daughters in. She would not even let Josh in, and the dog spent hours at a time lying on the landing outside, his nose pressed against the small gap between the bottom of the door and the carpet, as if desperate to get as close as he could to his mistress.

Charlotte begged her mother to make an effort for Helen's sake, but to no avail. When she did see her daughters it was as if she were not really with them at all, her eyes were wild, her clothes crumpled as if she were sleeping in them, her hair unwashed. She was, it seemed, a completely broken woman.

'It's like . . .' an exhausted Charlotte anxiously confided to Michael on the eve of the funeral, '. . . It's like she's been driven out of her mind.'

The funeral was enormous, a typical country affair. Freddie Lange had been a pillar of the local community, farmer, parish councillor, joint master of the local hunt. In rural areas you still pay homage to your dead. Two thousand people turned up at Chalmpton Peverill Church and the service was broadcast on a sound system – set up outside the pretty little Norman building which held a maximum of only five hundred – to the mourners who braved the winter chill in the churchyard.

Early that morning William had visited his mother alone in her bedroom – only the second time he had seen her since his father's death. And whatever he had said to her seemed to have had some kind of effect.

To the surprise of all her family, if not to William, she arrived downstairs shortly before the funeral party was due to leave, looking, superficially at least, pretty much the old Constance. She was immaculately turned out in a well-tailored black coat and hat, her hair clean and tidy, perfectly made up.

William was quickly by her side. 'You and I will walk together, mother, of course,' he said. 'That is what is expected.'

Constance had flashed him a quick anxious glance and then nodded almost imperceptibly in agreement.

From that moment on William appeared to orchestrate his mother, telling her how to behave. Yet at no time did he seem to make any attempt to give her any comfort, to show her any affection.

Marcia Spry noticed this, of course. She'd noticed all of it. Somehow she had even learned how Constance had shut herself away from her family and how she had been virtually hysterical all week.

She didn't look hysterical, now, Marcia had to hand her that. She looked every bit the well-bred grieving widow, putting on a good front, keeping her tears for later, for private. But, sure as eggs is eggs, said Marcia to herself, there was something wrong between Constance Lange and that son of hers.

Fleetingly she wondered if William had turned out to be a wrong 'un like that other lad. Gay, they called it nowadays. Marcia sniffed her derision. In her day village fêtes and dances had been gay. Not men, if you could call 'em that.

The family party were walking away from the grave now and Marcia again watched William and Constance – close together, not touching, almost going out of their way not to touch. By golly, there was summat going on. But it couldn't be that gay thing. That wouldn't worry Constance Lange a bit, that wouldn't. Marcia sniffed again.

Her thoughts turned to a wider arena. There was

something fishy about that accident too, if you asked her. Smelt like a kettle of herrings, it did. Why should a careful driver like Freddie Lange end up smashed into a wall? He worshipped that silly old car of his, nursed the thing like a baby, never drove it at the sort of speed he must have been going the night he died, Marcia was sure of it. And there'd been no other vehicle involved either – so what had really happened, that was what she wanted to know. And she'd heard the police wanted to know, as well.

Marcia was quite right – Inspector Barton and his team were bewildered.

There was no obvious cause for Freddie's accident. The possibilities that Barton had initially considered included Freddie suddenly losing consciousness – a heart attack perhaps – his being drunk, or the car suffering mechanical failure. But there had been a post-mortem examination, routine in the case of sudden accidental death, and the autopsy had shown that Freddie was in perfect health when he died and that there had been no trace of alcohol in his blood - unsurprising to his family as Freddie had always been far too responsible to drink and drive.

And a thorough inspection of the wrecked MG revealed only that the car had been meticulously maintained. It appeared to have had no defects at all and indeed had been serviced and passed its MOT test only two weeks earlier.

Marcia Spry somehow contrived to know all of that well before it should have become public knowledge and saw it as vindicating her own theories concerning the accident.

'What did I tell 'ee?' she asked anybody who would listen. 'Summat mighty fishy going on, there be, I'm sure of it.'

Inspector Barton, although he would not have cared a jot for Marcia Spry's views had he been privy to them, was, however, becoming increasingly more inclined to a similar opinion himself.

He allowed the funeral to pass without further bothering the Langes. After all, they were an eminent Somerset family and Inspector Barton was the kind of man who was not quite able to ignore that sort of thing. Not that he would let his respect for the family stand in the way of any enquiries he thought were proper, but nonetheless he proceeded with perhaps a little more caution than he might otherwise have done.

Ultimately he decided that the grieving widow had to be confronted. Inspector Barton didn't like loose ends and the death of Freddie Lange was about as loose an end as he had ever had to deal with. And so, at around midday on December 17th, the second day after Freddie's funeral, the inspector called unannounced at Chalmpton Village Farm. Having made his decision to confront the grieving widow, he was quite blunt in his approach to her.

'Can you think of any reason, madam, why your husband might have taken his own life?' he asked Constance.

Mrs Lange had escorted him into the drawing-room, the first time he had been anywhere in the farmhouse except the kitchen. The room was beautifully furnished in traditional country style with big squashy chintz-covered chairs and sofa, the colours all gentle blues and golds, relaxing, easy on the eye. A log fire blazed in the big open fireplace and a weak wintery sun streamed through the windows, its pale light reflected in the gleaming pieces of brass and copper which stood on the mantelpiece and on either side of the grate. A fine grandfather clock dominated one corner of the room, and the silence between him and Mrs Lange was so intense that its ticking sounded as loud to the inspector as if a drum were being methodically beaten inside his head.

The newly widowed woman returned the policeman's gaze steadily. She certainly seemed to have recovered well enough now, on the surface at least, thought Inspector Barton. But then, he supposed that was only to be expected of a woman like her. She was, after all, Mrs Constance Lange. Whatever Mrs Lange was really feeling, now that the initial shock was over, she was unlikely to let it show to anyone and certainly not to a policeman. He was both impressed and a little unnerved. If Constance Lange was hiding anything, he didn't reckon she was going to give herself away yet. And the inspector proved to be dead right.

Constance was quite controlled. Only the tiniest tremor in her hands, folded neatly in her lap as she contrived to sit quite upright in an easy chair opposite the policeman, indicated that she might be suppressing any emotion. She regarded Barton coolly.

'No reason at all, inspector,' she replied eventually. And her voice was quite without expression.

# Fourteen

Wayne Thompson's back was aching. He reached behind him with one hand, exploring gingerly. Ouch! He resented his back ache. After all, it was only when he was forced to put in long hours on the day job that it played him up like this. Wayne Thompson was a big strong lad, but his height – he was well over six foot – did not help his tendency to suffer back trouble, and he didn't enjoy being a builder's labourer. He didn't like fetching and carrying in all weathers. And digging played his back up more than anything. But recently he hadn't had much choice. His other employment had more or less dried up.

It was Thursday, December 17th, the evening of the same day that Inspector Barton paid his fruitless visit to Constance at Chalmpton Peverill. Christmas was only just over a week away, thought Wayne, and that at least was good news. He got two days off on full pay then, and the boss had hinted there might be a bonus as well if he continued to pull his weight.

If his back could stand it, more like, grumbled Wayne to himself. He slicked down his abundant head of dark brown hair, pulled on his expensive knee-length fur-collared leather overcoat, bought in better times, admired his good looks – which he reckoned were not being put to any worthwhile use at all at the moment – for one last time in the hall mirror. Then he set briskly off along the towpath by the Feeder, the inland waterway which links the River Avon with the Floating Harbour, to his favourite pub down by Temple Mead Railway Station where he drowned his sorrows in eight pints of lager. At the end of that lot even his back ache didn't seem to be such a problem any more.

The journey home to his little bedsit in a ramshackle old Victorian house in Barton Hill always seemed to take longer. He prided himself that he could hold his beer, did Wayne, but he weaved a bit as he walked. He was in control though, and dark as it was along the towpath Wayne didn't feel in any danger. He wasn't likely to fall. He'd done this late night walk often enough after a few beers, hadn't he?

But on this occasion Wayne didn't make it home. He was only fifty yards or so from the lock and the footbridge where he usually crossed the Feeder when he seemed to lurch unnaturally to the left. Uttering not a sound, and with only a gentle splash, Wayne Thompson pitched sideways into the murky water.

They found him early the next morning. The corpse, floating face-down in the water, its feet tangled in weed sprouting from the bank, was spotted at first light by a woman out walking her dog.

She raised the lock-keeper who promptly dialled 999 and was told not to touch anything until the police arrived. But by the time the lock-keeper and the woman returned to the body, a couple of passing joggers had also spotted it and were in the process of clumsily dragging the sodden corpse on to the towpath.

A police patrol car, fortuitously close by when the driver was alerted on his radio, arrived on the scene just three or four minutes after the 999 call was made and its two occupants jumped from the car shouting to the joggers to leave the body alone and stand back.

One of the two officers did his best to keep the joggers, the lock-keeper and the dog-walker as far away as possible while his colleague checked that the man pulled from the water was indeed dead. There wasn't any doubt. Police Constable Smithers touched ice-cold flesh and found himself shivering inside his warm coat. This was his first body but he knew it would not be his last. He had to cope. With difficulty he maintained control of himself. He was nineteen years old and new to the job, but maybe it was partly the fact that he was a probationary constable still attending regular sessions at the National Police Training School in Cwmbran that made him so observant. PC Smithers took a good long look at the corpse and noticed that there was a small gash in the back of the dead man's coat. It was a good coat too, and the policeman was pretty sure somehow that it wouldn't have been put on with a tear in it. And PC Smithers was well aware of the two other recent stabbings of young men in the Bristol area.

He was unable to stop shaking, however much he fought against it, but he wasn't sure now if that were caused by the shock of being confronted by a dead body or by the feeling of excitement which was beginning to engulf him. He just hoped nobody else was aware of it. Swiftly he stepped back and used his police radio to contact his senior officer.

The SOCOs, in the truck which served as a mobile incident room, arrived within fifteen minutes with Rose herself only minutes behind them. She had already been in her office at Staple Hill when the call came through from the Chief Inspector at PC Smithers' station – she seemed to be getting in earlier every day – and had roared across town to the crime scene, this time beating Carmen Brown by a good twenty minutes.

It was raining yet again and the SOCOs were erecting a tent to protect the murder scene. The body lay awkwardly face-down along the side of the towpath. The ground was muddy. A number of assorted footprints were visible, none of them particularly clearly. Rose suspected that, if they had not been too distorted by the steady rain, one or two at least of the footprints would prove to come from a size ten Timberland boot. Thankfully the weather and the hour meant that only a handful of particularly resolute joggers and dog-walkers had passed by the towpath so far that morning. She gave instructions to seal off the crime scene, deciding quickly just how big an area she wanted fenced off.

'Nobody's been near since we got here, ma'am,' said PC Smithers.

Rose could see that the young PC was shaking. She knew he was trying desperately to hide his youthful inexperience beneath a thin but eager façade of efficiency. She had done it often enough, after all, she remembered.

The constable gestured to the joggers. 'They were dragging the body out of the water when we arrived. We just told them to drop it and come away.'

Rose nodded. She took in the little group of joggers, dog-walker and lock-keeper. You could almost see them bristling with self-importance. They weren't going anywhere, she thought, and in any case there was a second plod who seemed to be standing guard over them.

She went into the mobile incident room – at least it was dry there – removed her quilted raincoat and pulled the obligatory white paper suit over her indoor clothes. Fortunately she was wearing a trouser suit that day, which made things easier, and certainly she was considerably more suitably dressed than she had been when she was called to the first murder. By the time she stepped out of the truck the tent had been properly erected and the crime scene taped off according to her instructions. She stepped over the tape fence, shoulders hunched against the weather, glad of the shelter the tent gave, however inadequate.

The demands of modern forensic investigation did not pay much heed to climatic conditions. There was a limit to how many layers of clothing you could keep on beneath the requisite paper suits. Rose tried not to think about her own physical discomfort, although she did fleetingly wonder if it were actually a statistical fact that outdoors murders almost always happened in the winter or if it were just her imagination. Hers and the Cataldis'.

Taking a deep breath, she looked down at the body lying at her feet. Almost certainly the corpse was male. More than that, there was little she could be certain of and she wasn't going to touch anything until Carmen Brown arrived. But as she bent over the body she was almost sure the observant young constable – presumably the one who had greeted her at the scene – was about to be proven right. There was definitely a hole in the back of the leather coat the dead man was wearing. Everything pointed to a stabbing just like the other two.

Rose experienced the familiar frisson of excitement. She knew something PC Smithers had yet to discover. Cops were like racehorses. The more experienced they were, the more excited they got at the prospect of the big one.

She stepped back over the tape fence. The young policeman was standing rather stiffly a few yards back, still showing signs of the shakes.

'Was it you who spotted the slash in his coat?' she asked.

'Y-yes, ma'am,' replied PC Smithers.

Poor chap is stammering now, thought Rose.

'Well done, constable,' she said out loud.

Smithers turned slightly pink. Pride or embarrassment or a bit of both, wondered Rose.

While she waited for Carmen Brown to arrive there was little more she could do except talk to the witnesses. And here Rose Piper got lucky again. An observant plod and an observant witness, all in one day, she thought to herself.

The woman who found the body claimed she had recognised the corpse at once, in spite of agreeing that she had not been able to catch the merest glimpse of his face. It was actually his clothing that she had recognised.

'It's that Wayne Thompson. I live opposite his mother in the council houses round the corner – well, it's either him or someone's nicked 'is coat,' said Mrs Josephine Bird, with the self-righteous certainty of someone who was quite enjoying being the centre of attention although trying not to show it. 'I'd know that coat anywhere, I would. Nobody else round 'ere's got a coat like that. Great fur collar an' all . . .'

Mrs Bird was a small quick woman whose

appearance rather suited her name. And it soon became apparent that, while probably not in the same class as Marcia Spry and certainly not blessed with the advantages of a close village community in which to operate, Mrs Bird did have a certain penchant for immersing herself in other people's business. She admitted, rather grudgingly, that she hadn't known Wayne well, but yes, of course she could tell Rose what he did for a living.

'He's a builder's labourer, isn't he? Works darned hard, I should think. That coat must have cost a few bob and he's good to his mother. Always has been. This'll kill her, you know.'

Rose Piper recognised that Mrs Bird could be a very useful source of information, but reckoned she personally didn't wish to listen to any more from the woman. For once she was actually looking for a team to whom to delegate. With some relief she saw that not only had Carmen Brown just arrived, but also DS Mellor along with two of her murder enquiry detective constables. Rose gave instructions that Mrs Bird should be escorted to Staple Hill and a full statement taken from her.

On her own radio she called back to the Investigation Centre and asked DI Jordan to run every check possible on Wayne Thompson of Barton Hill.

'I want to know as much as we can about him as fast as we can, Phyllis,' Rose instructed. 'Most important of all, I want to know if he's not where he should be, if he's missing. Oh – and check out Avon.'

Carmen Brown went straight into the mobile incident room and like Rose quickly emerged fully kitted up in scene-of-crime apparel.

Rose stood for a while watching her crouched at work beside the corpse and silently bet herself another month's salary that Wayne Thompson would turn out to have had a night job with Avon Escorts. This was beginning to get scary. It really was turning into the big one. Rose just hoped she was big enough to handle it.

Eventually the pathologist stood up and beckoned Rose closer. The Detective Chief Inspector took her usual deep breath, banished her uncharacteristic feelings of self-doubt and composed her features into an expression of lack of concern.

The Feeder seemed to be smelling particularly ripe that morning, she thought, and its acrid aroma was not going to help the habitual nauseousness she experienced when forced to come close to death.

Although the body had already been moved once, having been dragged out of the canal by the joggers, Carmen Brown still intended to examine it closely where it lay before moving it again. The doctor gestured towards the hole centrally positioned in the back of the victim's leather coat. Once again it was surprisingly small and neat.

'Definitely another stabbing,' she said, with a small tight smile.

'Same weapon as before?' asked Rose, her excitement mounting again, making it easy now for her to forget the cold and even to overcome her usual nausea.

'Let's wait till we get him into the mortuary, shall we?'

Pathologists could be so damned pedantic, thought Rose. Carmen Brown wouldn't tell you the time unless she had a watch with a second hand.

The doctor called to two of the SOCOs standing chatting, waiting for her to finish her preliminary examination.

'OK, let's see what our boy looked like, shall we?'

The body was swiftly and efficiently turned over so that it was lying face-upwards now. Rose took another quick sharp, and she hoped silent, gulp of breath.

The victim had a nasty head injury which had turned his forehead into a concave shell, the white bone clearly exposed, and his lips were drawn back in a meaningless skeletal grin revealing even teeth. This time the eyes were mercifully closed, perhaps as an involuntary reaction to landing in icy water.

Neither of the other victims had suffered any injury except the one lethal stab wound. Rose said nothing, waiting for Dr Brown, who was once again crouched by the corpse, this time intently studying the head, to give her verdict.

Eventually the pathologist looked up at her. 'Can't be sure until I get him back to base, but I'd guess the head injury happened after he'd been stabbed, almost certainly when he fell in the canal,' she said.

She glanced over her shoulder. There was a broken supermarket trolley sticking out of the waterway just behind them and in the shallow water right by the bank you could make out the shape of some hostile-looking stones and boulders, one or two of which protruded out of the water.

'Could have hit his head on almost anything,' the doctor remarked.

She looked down at the body again. 'He can't have been in the water long judging from his condition, not more than eight or nine hours, I shouldn't think.'

'He was floating face-down when he was found, any significance in that?' asked Rose.

Carmen Brown shrugged. 'Only that he couldn't have drowned. A drowned man sinks as his lungs fill with water. Our man must have been dead when he hit the water – but there was never much doubt about that with the wound he's got in his back.'

'Why do bodies always seem to float face-down anyway?' Rose didn't really know why she asked that. She certainly hadn't expected to be taken very seriously. But Carmen Brown looked thoughtful.

'In this case a lot of air was trapped in that coat, I reckon. But you're right. With men anyway. It's all to do with the distribution of fatty tissues and the head and feet being the heaviest bits.'

She turned away then, not attempting to explain further. Very scientific, considered Rose. And she was still standing looking down at the body, contemplating the idiosyncrasies of the human form, when Phyllis Jordan called through with the news that Wayne Thompson had not turned up for work that morning. And his next-door neighbour, on the grounds that he was normally seriously disturbed by a noisy Wayne Thompson returning from the pub, was pretty certain he had not returned home that night either. A team was on the way to break the probable bad news to the young man's mother, and they hoped she would later be prepared to assist in identification.

Detective Inspector Jordan had one final bit of news to impart, and could not completely disguise a quiet note of triumph in her voice as she did so.

'It won't astonish you to learn, boss, that Wayne Thompson did a regular moonlight for Avon Escorts.

And our Mrs Pattinson was very fond of his services. That Paolo is getting to be quite cooperative. In quite a panic nowadays, he is. We don't need the thumbscrews at all any more.'

By midday the body of Wayne Thompson, delivered as usual to Southmead Hospital by the Cataldi brothers, had been formally identified by his distraught mother.

In the afternoon Rose – fortified by a particularly large and juicy hamburger, in deference to her perhaps strange tendency to be better able to control her nausea with a full stomach than an empty one – attended the post-mortem examination conducted by Carmen Brown. This was little more than another formality, although the pathologist was able to confirm her earlier prognosis that Thompson had suffered his head injury after death, presumably while falling into the canal. As in the two earlier murders there was no doubt that he had been killed by a single vicious stab wound made by a long and sharp-bladed knife of some kind.

Later, back at Staple Hill, and picking a moment when Peter Mellor was nowhere near to hear her make the call because she knew he would disapprove, Rose phoned Charlie Collins at his mother's home. She gave only her Christian name.

Rose had had several further meetings with Charlie, some officially at the station and some more informally. She was convinced that Charlie must know something, however inconsequential it might seem and quite possibly without realising it himself, which could just give her the start she needed to unravel the whole affair.

'I'll meet you in the bar of the Portway Towers at six o'clock,' she instructed, and added with a small smile, 'I'm sure you know it.'

Charlie was wearing a deep-tan jacket over a cream silk shirt and paler tan trousers. The clothes were well cut and classy. As Charlie joined her at a corner table Rose was aware of one or two curious glances from the barman. That wasn't surprising. It was quite likely that the barman knew exactly who Charlie was and what he did. Charlie, it seemed, had always been a very successful escort – a busy boy.

'Tell me again, Charlie,' she encouraged. The young man sighed. She could forgive him, this was after all the umpteenth time she had asked him to relive his meetings with Mrs Pattinson for her, and however much detail she demanded he go into, nothing new or revelatory had so far presented itself.

Mrs Pattinson had just never talked about herself, Charlie told her yet again, and certainly had never revealed to him anything of the other life Rose was sure that she must have.

Charlie was leaning quite close to her now, that silly drink he always ordered, Campari and orange – he wasn't really a drinker; apart from champagne, he only liked sweet drinks – almost forgotten on the table beside him, reliving his various meetings with Mrs Pattinson.

'. . . So that was the first time she asked for a second boy,' he said, his voice low and husky. 'And I told you before what she liked us to do, didn't I? The things she dreamed up . . .'

Rose had become aware that as their meetings had progressed Charlie's descriptions of his sexual adventures with Mrs Pattinson had become increasingly more explicit. She had reasoned with herself that any details at all of Charlie's relationship with the mysterious Mrs P were relevant, and might even be crucial. Nonetheless, listening to that resolutely sexy voice describing his carnal adventures could be quite mesmerising on occasions.

Swiftly Rose interrupted him. 'OK, I've heard enough of that,' she said as sternly as she could manage, although she was aware that her voice sounded almost squeaky in comparison with his.

Charlie smiled. He had a pleasing grin and the most beautifully white and even teeth she had ever seen.

'Have you?' he asked, and his eyes were locked on to hers.

'Behave yourself,' said Rose lightly.

She was well aware that Sergeant Mellor thought her relationship with Charlie had already become too close, and he might be right, she reflected. She knew she had already gone against procedure in her dealings with him. And certainly it had crossed her mind that were Charlie in a different line of work, and were she not investigating three murders in which he had an involvement, she might just find him rather attractive.

Wryly she considered that in her nick nobody would bat an eyelid if she were a bloke and Charlie were a call girl. Perk of the job, she'd once heard a Bristol vice cop describe a session with a prostitute. Not without some difficulty, she forced herself at least to behave as if she were the one in charge.

'Right then, young man,' she said, downing the remains of her half pint of bitter. 'I've got a husband waiting for me at home, and goodness knows who you've got.'

'Me mum,' responded Charlie with an even wider grin. 'But I won't have if she ever gets wind of any of this lot, that's for sure.'

It was only just after 8.00 p.m., quite early by her standards, when Rose got home. But unfortunately Simon had called Staple Hill soon after she had left at a few minutes before six, and had been told his wife was on her way home. On the strength of that he had begun cooking an early supper for them both, his own speciality pasta dish – penne with spinach, sun-dried tomatoes and slivers of fresh Parmesan.

The remains of it, dried-up and unappetising, just as the fateful lamp chops had been all those weeks earlier, were still in the oven. Simon was not in the best of moods – something she was having to get used to nowadays, she reflected.

'I've told you, I had a meeting with an informant,' she said for the third time.

'Well, why didn't they know at the station then? Why did they think you'd gone home?'

Rose realised she must have disappointed Simon yet again and sympathised with his obvious frustration, but she wished he didn't get so belligerent when he was upset.

'Because it was unofficial,' she said patiently. 'Like many of the most worthwhile interviews are. What is this, Simon? You're interrogating me, for goodness sake!'

'I just want to know where you've been for two hours. Is that so unreasonable? I am your husband, allegedly, aren't I? You've been drinking, I know that. And you had the car.'

Rose sighed. 'Two beers. I had a drink at the

Portway Towers with one of the Avon escorts who is particularly involved in the murder case, if you must know.'

'What?' Simon sounded outraged – again, thought Rose.

'You went to the biggest pick-up joint in town with a male hooker? Terrific! Great! What kind of bloody woman would do that?'

'A policewoman, perhaps, Simon.' Rose spoke more sarcastically than she had meant to, but that was too bad. It had been another long hard day. These almost nightly battles with Simon were becoming more than she could cope with.

Simon pushed his hair back from his eyes, and there was just the merest flash of the little-boy charm with which she had fallen so in love in the first place.

'Oh Rose, what's wrong with us?' He gestured almost plaintively at the table behind him, laid for dinner. There was a candle on it burned almost down to its polished brass holder and an opened bottle of red wine. 'I just wanted us to have a nice time together for a change, I was so pleased you were going to be home early, that's all.'

For a moment all Rose wanted to do was take him in her arms. But his petulance and, it seemed to her, his determination not to respect her job or her right to execute it how she and nobody else thought best, had really got to her.

'Look, Simon, I just don't have the energy for all of this right now – I'm trying to run a murder enquiry. I'm sorry about supper, but I'm not very hungry anyway. I'll just watch TV in the bedroom for a bit and have an early night, if you don't mind.'

She spoke with icy courtesy, no warmth at all in her

voice. She knew she was hurting him even more, and she didn't really understand why she was doing it. He had handed her the olive branch and she had turned away again. But somehow she couldn't help herself.

'What do I have to do, Rose . . . ?' she heard him begin, his voice raised and angry again, as she left the kitchen. She couldn't begin to tell him. Instead she shut the door firmly behind her, anxious at least to avoid further argument.

It was a bloody good job she'd grabbed that hamburger at lunch-time, she thought to herself wryly. These supperless nights were beginning to become a habit.

The next day Rose found that the pressure she was already under to charge Paolo with living off immoral earnings had been stepped up. Her day started with an unwelcome bout of verbal fisticuffs with her senior officer, Detective Chief Superintendent Titmuss.

Ironic at this stage really, she thought, as it seemed that the third murder had already put Avon Escorts almost entirely out of business. As Paolo had accurately predicted, the punters didn't want to know about an outfit at the centre of a murder enquiry. Even those who weren't frightened by possible physical danger were not going to risk getting caught up in the blaze of unwelcome publicity surrounding Avon.

Rose did not want to bring charges against Paolo and continued to fight against doing so.

'I need him free,' she told Titmuss. 'He and Charlie Collins are the only hope we've got of getting a lead on Mrs Pattinson. And we have to find that bloody woman.'

'You've got one last chance, Rose, to do it your

way, and I mean last chance,' responded the super-intendent, a dapper man, always immaculately dressed, whose priorities Rose thoroughly mistrusted. She considered that he was much more interested in his standing in the Bristol community than the nitty-gritty of police work.

However, she managed, just about, not to show how angry he had made her. The need to keep the Italian Bristolian on the streets was only half of the reason why she didn't want to charge Paolo. The official half. Unofficially she was irritated by the small-mindedness she was facing. She was hunting a serial killer and all around her people were wittering their outrage about an escort agency which catered for the latent sexual desires of women as well as of men. Not for the first time Rose wondered if either her colleagues or the general public would be so offended if Avon ran only female prostitutes.

Sitting at her desk later, the door to her office propped open, revealing the hubbub of the busy incident room working at full pace, Rose managed somehow to be lost in her own thoughts. The Feeder was still being dragged for clues but predictably nothing had been found so far and Rose had no expectations that anything would be. The murder weapon remained the property of the murderer, Rose assumed. Ready for the next time. She actively hoped not now. Things were beginning to run away from her, she feared. She really did not know quite where to go next. Yet at the same time she dreaded being replaced as SIO. This was her case. She suspected Titmuss would never have put her in charge of it in the first place, let alone kept her there as long as he had, were it not for the man's eternal desire – politically motivated, of course - to appear liberal and forward-thinking. And that was a joke for a start.

Her reverie was interrupted by Peter Mellor.

'Name of Terry Sharpe mean anything to you, boss?' he asked.

'What?' Rose was momentarily startled.

'Seems he's Wayne Thompson's landlord,' continued the sergeant.

Rose immediately found herself right back in the real world, absolutely alert. Terry Sharpe was a former Bristol vice cop who had been sacked from the force after getting too close to the trade he was supposed to be controlling. That had been around thirteen years ago, not long after Rose had joined the Avon and Somerset as a young uniformed probationary constable every bit as green as the boyish PC she had met by the side of the Feeder the previous day.

Sharpe had even been suspected of involvement in the murder of a young woman prostitute in Bristol. Nothing could ever be proved, but the case had never been solved. Rose had been assigned, as a woman officer, to accompany the detective teams investigating the murder as they moved among the city's vice community. Some of the girls they talked to were under age. They were all frightened. Rose had met Sharpe once back then, and known immediately that he was the kind of policeman she hated more than any other human being, the kind who believed they could make up the rules as they went along. Sharpe had seemed to her to be a thoroughly unpleasant character, well capable of everything he might ever be accused of, and Rose could still remember the mocking look in his eye. He had always contrived to give the impression that he was one jump ahead –

and most of the time he had indeed seemed to be just that.

There had been a smattering of press speculation and a lot of gossip. Ultimately Sharpe lost his job, which was something, in Rose's opinion, although not nearly enough. The feeling inside the force was that he had literally got away with murder. And it had all left a very nasty taste.

One way and another, the DCI was quite excited by the prospect of finally catching up with Terry Sharpe.

'Right,' she said. 'Let's see what the bastard's got to say for himself, shall we? Do we know where to find him?'

'He's got a big house up at Clifton and flash new offices in one of those old tobacco-bonding ware-houses they've just converted,' said Mellor. 'I got it checked. He's in his office even though it's Saturday.'

'Good.' Rose was already on her feet. And this time, if he thought that his SIO could be better employed than conducting an interview herself, the sergeant made no comment.

'Sounds as if he's made a packet then, since he left the job,' Rose remarked as she and Mellor headed for the car park. 'Do we know how, by any chance, as if I couldn't guess.'

'You'd guess right, boss, more'n likely. Property is the official line. But then there's what you use your property for. The vice boys reckon he just carried on the way he was going when he was in the force. He was running Toms then, everyone was sure of it. And he still is.'

The sergeant paused by the car and looked over the roof at the DCI.

236

'There's something else boss, I've got a team giving Paolo the third degree again. There's a suggestion that Sharpe has a connection with Avon Escorts.'

Terry Sharpe remained every bit as thoroughly unpleasant as Rose remembered him to have been. Now in his early fifties, he was smaller than average for a policeman. His skin was pale to the point of being pasty and his hair, which he wore quite long and combed flat against his head, was totally white. Rose wondered if he bleached it. His eyes were very pale blue and watery-looking. Obscurely Rose thought that he looked a bit like an oversized albino rabbit in a city suit. A suit which was a good grand's worth, she reckoned. He also wore a ring on the little finger of his right hand with a diamond only slightly smaller than the knuckle of that finger.

The office, on the top floor of the converted warehouse, was as pale as Sharpe's complexion – white leather furniture, cream carpet, glass-topped desk – and as expensive-looking as his clothes. A picture window offered a stunning view over the Floating Harbour and across much of Bristol city centre.

Terry Sharpe leaned back in his big white leather chair, a small figure quite at home amid the blatant opulence of his own creation. And if he was in any way shocked or even disconcerted by the sudden appearance of his unannounced visitors, Sharpe gave no sign. Indeed he seemed every bit as smug and convinced of his own superiority as the impression Rose had retained of him over the years. Being chucked out of the force did not seem to have affected that one jot. Even before he spoke, Rose began to relish the prospect of being able to deal him an even more devastating blow, and also to realise that this was unlikely to come easy.

'I hardly knew Wayne Thompson,' Sharpe said languidly in answer to her first question. His voice was every bit as smug as the expression on his face. His whole philosophy of life seemed to be 'catch me if you can'. 'I've got a number of tenants. They pay me rent. They're not my friends.'

Rose waded straight in. 'And is that all they pay you?'

Sharpe's lips curled slightly and he raised one eyebrow quizzically. 'I really don't know what you mean, Detective Chief Inspector,' he said.

'I wondered if your tenants also gave you a share of their earnings, Mr Sharpe?'

Sharpe reached for a giant Monte Christo cigar from the box on his desk. He did not offer the box around. The thought flitted into Rose's head that he was in any case the kind of man who would automatically consider that neither a black man nor a woman were suitable recipients of such a gift.

'Now why on earth would they do that, Chief Inspector?' Sharpe asked.

'Perhaps because of your association with Avon Escorts?'

'A legitimate escort agency, I always understood. And what makes you think I have anything to do with it, anyway?'

'It won't be too difficult to find out . . .' Rose left the words hanging.

Sharpe shrugged. 'Please yourselves,' he said. The curl in his lips was almost a leer now.

He lit the cigar, puffing vigorously, and almost instantly filling the room with smoke. Rose struggled not to cough. She was aware of the man studying her closely.

'Don't I know you?' he asked eventually.

'We have met, yes,' she responded curtly.

The slightly puzzled look now evident in Sharpe's eyes cleared suddenly. His face cracked suddenly into a full-blown leering grin.

'I remember, little Rosie. A DCI now! Little Rosie Piper. Well, I never.'

Rose forced herself not to visibly react. She was aware of Mellor stiffening beside her. The sergeant knew her so well. Terry Sharpe had called her Rosie all those years ago and she did not hate it any less now than she had then. But she must not let him get to her.

Sharpe was going to be a tough nut to crack, no doubt about that. It also seemed that he had alibis for the times of the murders of Wayne Thompson and of Colin Parker. Sharpe was a man with a busy social calendar. He had been at a local Businessman of the Year awards dinner – and that was a laugh too, thought Rose – when Wayne was killed and in London at a black-tie boxing tournament at the Park Lane Hilton when Colin Parker was attacked. He couldn't remember what he had been doing when Marty Morris died, and there was nothing in his diary. But he must have been doing something, he always was, he announced.

'I'll think of it sooner or later, for sure,' he said, and he smiled the smug smile through a haze of cigar smoke.

Rose didn't doubt him, although as far as she was concerned having alibis did not in any case rule him out as a suspect. He was the sort of character who would more than likely pay someone else to do his dirty work, she thought. She disliked Terry Sharpe even more than her brief memory of him had suggested she would, and realised that nothing would please her more than to be able to prove his guilt.

# Fifteen

Constance sat very still. The *Sun* newspaper lay before her, flat on the kitchen table. Rent Boy Killer Strikes Again screamed the front-page banner headline. She had a copy of the *Express* on her lap. The lead story was the same, of course. It was the same in every paper.

Constance was surrounded by newspaper reports of the third murder. She read each one thoroughly and, when she had finished, folded the newspapers with care and piled them in one corner of the table. The Aga made the whole room glow with warmth, but Constance was barely aware of its comfort. The chill which engulfed her came from her own heart.

It was late afternoon on Saturday, 19th December, the day after Wayne Thompson's body had been discovered in Bristol and around the same time that Rose Piper was setting off to meet Terry Sharpe. There had been quite a heavy fall of snow earlier on in Chalmpton Peverill, but Constance had not even noticed. Her eyes were red-rimmed. She had been unable to stop herself crying all day. She had, after all, done quite a lot of it lately. Although after the funeral things had seemed to settle down a bit for a few days. She had shut what she knew must be the truth out of her mind, and, for the sake of what remained of her family, had tried to force herself to behave as normally as possible.

Even William had encouraged that – at least when it came to any kind of public appearance. It was William who had made her pull herself together, and forced her to dress and behave the way she had for the funeral. She had known he was right and she had tried to keep that up, she really had. It was all a pretence of course. All a mere façade. But that was all there was left, really. And there wasn't just William to consider. She also had two lovely daughters, one still at school who so needed the love and support of a calm, strong mother – although even before this latest horror Constance hadn't really thought she could ever be that again – and the other, a mother herself, who was so nice and kind and normal.

But now, surely Constance could not go on pretending. Could not kid herself that life could ever return to any kind of normality.

She wiped away a tear. She had been sitting at the table almost all day. For once in her life she really did not know what to do next. Losing Freddie was so terrible. Her grief would have been overwhelming under any circumstances. But with everything else that had happened it was unbearable. And her guilt too. They say you always feel guilt when someone close to you dies, however irrationally – but her guilt was not irrational. She knew she had caused Freddie's death. There was no alternative to believing that. But she had been trying to convince herself that at least it was all over now. That nothing more would happen. It wasn't over though. It was still going on. All of it. And so it would unless she did something about it. Only she could stop it.

Constance took a deep breath and grasped the edge of the table firmly as if to draw strength from it. She had more or less lost her grip over the past few weeks, nobody knew that better than Constance – unless, she reflected, with just a flash of the old wryly amused Constance, it was Marcia Spry – but she had to pull herself together. After all nobody except her could help her family, if not herself, get through it all.

But Constance did not know if she had the strength.

Josh lay heavily across his mistress's feet, his tail thumping occasionally on the tiled floor, glancing upwards adoringly at her every so often.

She ignored him, as she seemed to so much of the time nowadays. Gone were the days when at the very least she would habitually if absent-mindedly scratch the top of his head whenever he rubbed against her.

He continued to thump his tail on the ground, hoping for attention. His eyes were sad. Josh knew his mistress was deeply unhappy. That meant he was unhappy too.

The villagers were amazed by the way in which Constance seemed to fall apart so quickly. Although they would have expected her to be devastated by her husband's death they would also have expected her to cope. She was, after all, that sort of person.

Constance did not appear to be coping at all. And, as Constance herself had predicted, the villager best informed about all of that was Marcia Spry.

'She just mope about day in and day out,' Marcia related that afternoon in the village shop, her enjoyment of Constance's predicament only thinly disguised. 'You'd never 'ave thought 'er'd 'ave fallen apart like that, but then, of course, 'er didn't have the breeding. I always said 'er true side would show itself sooner or later . . .'

But Marcia had chosen a bad moment to revel in other people's misfortunes, let alone to indulge in character assassination.

'I'm sure you always did, Marcia Spry,' responded an angry female voice. And the redoubtable Iris Phillips, mother of Harley, her usually beaming features arranged into an expression of uncharacteristic indignation, emerged from behind the shelf of video tapes at the back of the shop.

'And you'm right too. Us 'ave seen the true side of Mrs Lange often enough in this village. 'Er saved my Harley's life, 'er did, and there's many others could tell 'ee what that woman's done for them. A saint she's been to this village, if you ask me.

'You should be ashamed of yourself, Marcia, you really should, talking like that about 'er. Mrs Lange needs some support from this village for once, and look what 'er's getting. You'm a mean-mouthed, wicked old woman, Marcia Spry, that's what you be.'

And with that Iris Phillips swept out of the shop calling behind her, 'I'll pay you tomorrow, Mrs Walters. I'd better go before I says more.'

But in the doorway, with half her body already out in the street, she turned to glower once more at an astonished-looking Marcia. And her final parting shot was beautifully delivered.

'As believe me I could – a great deal more,' she said menacingly.

'Well!' exclaimed Marcia, as soon as the shop door was firmly closed and Iris had retreated out of earshot. 'I've never been spoken to like that before, I must say.'

Mrs Walters eyed her customer quizzically. Marcia, accustomed as she was to using the village shop-keeper and post-mistress as a sounding board and a sorting house for all her most scurrilous gossip, would, if she had thought about it, have realised that Mrs Walters had never before passed any comment at all really. But this time Mrs Walters not only looked like a woman who had seen and heard it all before, but also as if she'd had enough of it.

'So perhaps it's not before time, then, Marcia,' she remarked conversationally.

Marcia could barely believe her ears.

'Well,' she said again, and, most unusually, she said nothing more as she paid for the packet of digestive biscuits which had been her excuse for going into the shop in the first place.

Hastily now, Marcia left the shop, her features pinched into offended disapproval. As she did so she almost bumped into William Lange, who seemed to be so preoccupied that he barely acknowledged her.

Nonetheless, Marcia had been impressed by William's behaviour recently, if a little surprised. The boy seemed to have really taken hold of the reins, it seemed to her. He had announced right after his father's death that he would be giving up his studies to run the farm, and he was making a fair stab of it too – the Lange's most senior farm worker, Iris Phillips's husband Norton, had told her that. Norton still liked a good gossip, even if his silly wife didn't, Marcia thought – not that she thought of herself as a gossip, of course, rather a concerned neighbour taking an interest in local affairs.

As she proceeded behind William, a little more circumspectly than him on a street still covered by an inch or two of snow, Marcia watched the young man stride briskly along, his heavy boots crunching the white powder as he walked. At the entrance of Chalmpton Peverill Farm, he paused briefly to speak to Norton who had just pulled up outside in the Land Rover.

William went on into the house and Norton began to unload some trays of eggs from the back of the vehicle.

Marcia waved a greeting to him, and in spite of already having been effectively rebuffed by Norton's wife, force of habit moved her to pass comment on her observations of the dramatic events which were dominating village life.

'Proper chip off the old block, that William's turning out to be, takes after his father, of course,' she said to Norton who nodded his agreement. Marcia's manner somehow inherently implied criticism of Constance, but if Norton noticed that, then unlike his wife, he chose not to comment. In any case, Marcia needed only a half-receptive audience to be quickly back into her normal stride.

'He's been a bit of a lad, there's no doubt, but he's coming good all right now.' She sniffed the cold fresh air as if it smelt of something nasty. And her voice was full of double meaning and innuendo when she continued to speak.

'Somebody had to . . .'

William walked into the house through the kitchen door as usual. It was about the only usual thing left at Chalmpton Village Farm. His mother, still sitting at the table, made no attempt to greet him as he removed his snow-covered boots carefully in the

246

porch. She watched in silence as he picked up the big stainless steel kettle simmering on the hob of the Aga and poured hot water over instant coffee in a mug. When he turned towards her, his eyes were as cold as the street outside. His mouth was set in a thin hard line. He did not speak. He ignored her. He almost always did nowadays.

Constance was not sure that she could stand it any more. The atmosphere in the house that had always been so happy, was now perpetually strained. The memories made it all the more painful.

She studied her only son. The tears pricked at the back of her eyes, and try as she might she could not entirely stop them beginning to flow again. Constance knew really that her relationship with William was beyond repair, but, almost involuntarily she tried one last time to get through to him.

Her voice was cracking with emotion as she tentatively broached the subject that had so far been forbidden between them.

'I know I'm to blame, what happened was just so . . . so awful,' she stammered. 'But, but I never, never meant . . .'

He simply turned his back on her, his manner leaving her in no doubt that the true cause of the breakdown of their previously close relationship remained something he was not prepared even to discuss.

She made a decision then – on the spur of the moment, but probably the thought had been lurking. Suddenly it seemed inevitable.

'I don't think I can bear being here any longer,' she said abruptly. 'I think it would be better if I moved out. This can't go on . . .'

247

He interrupted her then, still with his back to her.

'If that's what you want, fine. You can have the cottage over at Dingwell. It's been empty since old Percy died.'

He spoke so quickly, the solution so readily at hand. Constance had little doubt that the thought must already have been in his mind. She had no fight left. She simply nodded her head.

'I'll get it organised straight away. If you're going, then the sooner the better.'

To Constance, the words, which had been half-snarled at her, seemed like a slap across the face. Only much, much more painful.

William downed his coffee and left the kitchen without speaking again. As soon as he had gone from the room Constance slumped on to the table, buried her head in her hands and let the tears fall freely.

Her only son was revolted by her. It was virtually unendurable.


William moved fast. Dingwell was made ready within two days.

Harley Phillips – who, with his one good arm and the other continuing to heal well, could by now drive his van, an automatic – had been called in to help her move. His ribs were almost as good as new, and he was big enough and strong enough to be able to shift and carry with one hand more than a lot of men could manage with two.

In any case, Constance expressed no desire to take anything much with her – except her dog, of course. But nobody, not even William, would have expected her to leave Josh behind.

She was, she said, quite happy with the few bits of

old Percy's furniture which were still in the cottage. And most of what she was taking with her, including her clothes, were being moved simply because William had made it quite clear that he no longer wanted them in the house once she had gone.

Harley had been told simply that Constance had decided to give William his independence at the farm, and if he noticed the strain between mother and son, verging on open hostility on William's side, Harley gave no sign of it.

Charlotte, however, was not so easily sopped. Her mother had told her much the same story as she and William had told Harley, and added that she felt she could no longer live among all the memories at the farm.

'I'm perfectly content, dear, believe me,' said her mother in a tone of voice which indicated almost anything but contentment. 'I need to get away from the past. It's for the best, really.'

Charlotte was not convinced. She felt sure there was more to it than that, but when she confronted William she was met with the same intransigence.

'Mother has told you why she doesn't want to live in the farmhouse any more, I have told you too, why can't you leave it at that?' he asked her.

'Because I want to know what the bloody hell is going on between you two, William, and it's time one of you told me, it really is.'

Charlotte was very upset, more upset than she had been since the night she learned the news of her father's death.

William regarded her coolly. It was, of course, a strained time for all of them, but Charlotte had noticed her brother hardly ever smiled nowadays.

That was understandable, of course. Following the death of their father and the stress they were all under. But it was more than that. Charlotte was sure of it. Every bit of William's old warmth and humour had left him.

'Nothing is going on, Charlotte, stop being ridiculous.'

William's voice was flat and expressionless, and his manner left his sister in no doubt that she was going to get nothing more from him.

Charlotte felt very alone and very afraid. Her wonderful family was falling apart all around her. Her mother seemed to have turned into some kind of zombie and her brother had become a stranger to her.

How she longed for her father. How she longed for things to be the way they had been before.

In the small front bedroom of Dingwell Cottage, Constance looked out through the window across acres of greenly rolling Somerset and began to think that it really was all for the best to be away from William. Every time she saw him, every time she was faced with his coldness towards her, it hurt desperately. She needed to think, and here at least, she reflected, she might be able to do that and even to find a little peace – if only for a short time.

But not yet, it seemed, she thought with a groan as she spotted Marcia Spry on her old black bicycle coasting down the hill towards the cottage. Not for the first time Constance, who had only just arrived at Dingwell, marvelled at the older woman's intelligence sources. Freddie had always said that if Marcia Spry had been employed as a spy during the Cold War the rest of MI5 would have become instantly redundant. In spite of everything, Constance smiled at the memory, then she hurried downstairs to deflect the old busybody. She really couldn't cope with Marcia on top of everything else.

Outside Josh was barking his head off – he'd never liked Marcia Spry either. Harley was still unloading his van – his name had not led him ever to share his father's enthusiasm for motorbikes – and as she opened the front door Constance heard the incorrigible Marcia remark with a certain relish to the rather bewildered-looking young man, ''Er's 'eading for a breakdown, 'er be, no doubt about it, mark my words . . .'

God, the woman really was impossible, Constance thought. Her cheek had to be admired though. Presumably hearing the door open, Marcia turned to see the subject of her latest diatribe approaching her and, barely pausing for breath, it seemed to Constance, continued to speak, her voice now full of false concern.

'Oh, Mrs Lange, there you be, I came over to see if 'ee could do with an 'and. Always that much work, moving 'ouse. I just came to 'elp.'

Constance looked her up and down. Harley had reddened slightly in embarrassment and was shifting awkwardly from foot to foot. Marcia Spry had probably never had the sensitivity to experience embarrassment in the whole of her life, Constance thought. She shivered as the chill of the day engulfed her. The snow from what had been the one brief fall of the winter so far had completely cleared, but there was an icy wind blowing in from the direction of Exmoor. Marcia Spry was muffled against the cold. Her slightly pointed nose protruded a vividly gleaming red from the depths of the woollen scarf wound around her head, and her unashamed eagerness to be involved, to learn all that she could about what was going on, shone almost as brightly.

'Miss Spry,' said Constance, who would normally have addressed the woman as Marcia, but was well aware of the impact of formal address on the right occasion. 'Miss Spry, knowing what I can hardly avoid knowing about your frequently expressed opinion of me, I would have thought I would be the last person in the world you would ever seek to help. So would you please go away and leave me alone. You are a malicious old woman and I really want nothing more to do with you.'

For the first time in months Constance felt quite pleased with herself. That had been a flash of the old Constance and she had almost enjoyed it. She had even managed to keep her voice firm and controlled. There were some advantages even in the depths of despair, even when you reach the lowest ebb of all, she realised. She had spoken sharply to Marcia Spry once or twice over the years, but never before had she felt able to tell her quite so bluntly exactly what she really thought of her. And to send her packing, too.

Marcia began to splutter some kind of outraged reply. Constance did not even bother to listen. She turned on her heel, a now growling Josh close behind her, and walked back into the cottage, vaguely aware that Harley had stopped blushing and was grinning broadly as he followed her carrying another load of bags and boxes.

Safely inside, she allowed herself a peep from the dining-room window and with some satisfaction saw Marcia wheeling her bike up the hill – in retreat, and obviously in high dudgeon, her head nodding up and down as if she were talking to herself. On the grounds that everyone else is sick of listening, thought Constance.

Harley was still grinning. 'Me mam gave the old bat a right telling off t'other day, too, Mrs Lange,' he remarked with obvious enjoyment.

'Did she really, Harley?' Constance responded with some surprise. Iris was known for her easy-going manner.

''Er takes some getting going, my mam,' continued Harley. 'But you'd be surprised what 'er can be like. Me dad and me, us knows better than to cross 'er, I can tell 'ee.' Harley shook his head at the thought.

'I can't bleddy stand that old cow Spry either,' he said later, before taking his leave. 'If 'er upsets 'ee again, Mrs Lange, you just let me know. All right?' And Harley drew himself up to his full towering height, throwing back his immensely powerful shoulders.

It was a spontaneous display of support. Constance knew that. Few understood the nuances of village life better than her, after all she had had to work at winning acceptance into it in the first place. Fleetingly she felt cheered.

But once Harley had gone any vestige of cheerfulness and normality left with him. Alone in the silence of Dingwell, except for faithful Josh, Constance could do nothing other than sink again into the nightmare her world had become. She wished she could go back in time, but she was honest enough to realise that she would in any case have to completely reinvent herself.

She told herself no one can be other than their true self, that she could not help being what she was, any more than her son, or any of her family could deny their own selves. But she did not really believe her own message, and certainly it brought her no comfort.

She still did not know where to go from here, but she was beginning to realise at last that doing nothing was no longer an option. If the nightmare was to grow no greater she had to act, she had to do something. She must take control.

There was no one else who could.

# Sixteen

Rose continued to build on an already perhaps unwisely close relationship with Charlie. That evening she met him again at the Portway Towers hotel. It was the second evening running. She had given up caring what Simon thought. She told herself that she needed to keep her best hope of any kind of witness in the case sweet. And Charlie was running scared.

'She's out there somewhere right now, looking for me, I'm damned sure of it,' he told Rose over a third Campari and orange.

'But *who* is, Charlie?' asked Rose.

'Mrs Pattinson, of course.'

Rose sighed. 'We don't know that. We don't even know who she is.'

Charlie had lost much of his bouncy self-confidence and Rose was sorry to see that, although she didn't understand quite why she should be. He was still staying at his mother's house in St Paul's, still afraid to go home to his smart flat overlooking the Floating Harbour, and he confided to Rose that relations with his much loved mother were becoming strained.

'She knows something's up, you see,' he said. 'I mean, it's pretty obvious innit? It's been nearly two months now. That's a hell of a lot of rewiring. I just don't know what I'll do if she finds out . . .'

On occasions Rose thought that Charlie seemed as scared of his mother learning the truth about the son she was so proud of as he was of being killed by the madwoman he remained convinced was hunting him down.

'Come on, Charlie, I'd better go home,' she said without a great deal of enthusiasm after another hour spent giving as much solace as she could manage.

Charlie's car was being serviced, so she dropped him off at his mother's house – well, just around the corner, actually, as a precaution, although she was of course driving her own car, a seriously unofficial-looking silver Scimitar and even Charlie, obsessed with his own problems as he was, had remarked more than once how little like a police officer she appeared. Which remained all for the best in St Paul's.

Not for the first time he pecked her on the cheek as he said goodbye. It was a familiarity that had some-how seemed quite natural from the first time he did it and Rose had not pulled him up on it, although she knew she should have done.

She watched him walk away from her down the street. His stride was still quite jaunty in spite of everything. Fleetingly she wondered whether Charlie Collins might have by now attempted something a little more serious than a peck on the cheek were he not staying with his mother. A blush touched her cheeks, even within the privacy of her own car. The boy's a male hooker and you're a married woman, she told herself sternly.

But perversely the thought made her smile.

Rose had been lying awake at night for weeks trying to work it all out. There was nothing else to keep her awake nowadays, that was for certain, Simon hadn't wanted to touch her in ages.

During the day she worked ceaselessly. She had been at her desk by 7.30 a.m., often earlier, ever since the case began. Weekends did not exist. The murder of Wayne Thompson had increased the pressure. On the Sunday after his death she was in her office at Staple Hill as usual, going over and over in her mind everything that had happened and the progress that had been made so far, such as it was.

The DCI wanted desperately to find Mrs Pattinson, although, in a curious way that she couldn't fully explain to herself, she didn't actually want Mrs Pattinson to prove to be guilty. She continued to resent the simplistic attitude of most of her colleagues which seemed to be that any woman bizarre enough to pay young men for sex was therefore pretty damn sure to be a serial killer as well.

Rose did believe that she now had a fairly clear impression of Mrs Pattinson. Her conversations with Charlie made her feel that she may not know who Mrs P was, but she did know a little bit about what she was. Certainly there was now a definite visual image – of a strong-looking, well-preserved woman in her forties, tall, good body, slim but shapely, good skin, startling deep-green eyes, blonde hair shaped in a long glossy bob – and, thanks both to Charlie and Janet the receptionist at the Crescent Hotel, a computer picture had even been put together. This had been published in newspapers and shown on television, and an appeal made for anyone who recognised the woman to contact the police. There had been a number of responses. Several had turned out to be little more than mischief-making and none provided a helpful lead. One was from a fourteen-year-old boy who said he was sure it had been Mrs Pattinson who some months previously had kicked a football back into his local playing field from the road alongside. The woman had made quite an impression, apparently. The playing field was in the Clifton area of Bristol not far from the Crescent Hotel and the date and timing of the incident checked out with the little that was known of Mrs Pattinson's movements. It had added somewhat to Rose's conception of Mrs Pattinson's personality; as a self-confident woman, charismatic, physically agile, athletic even, someone who appeared to enjoy life to the full – or at least had done until recently, thought Rose wryly. However the schoolboy footballer had not actually seen the woman park or leave a motor car, and his information in no way assisted the search to find the real Mrs P.

Rose had not been as disappointed as she might have been. For a start it seemed likely that Mrs Pattinson had made at least some attempt to disguise her appearance. Charlie admitted that he always reckoned the blonde hair was a wig, and that he had never seen Mrs Pattinson's real hair. And when confronted with the possibility Janet had said she'd never thought about it, but now she did, yes, perhaps that sleek blonde bob was just too perfect to be Mrs Pattinson's own hair.

'It was always exactly the same length, too,' Janet had remarked in a wondering kind of voice, almost as if she were a member of some weird religious sect who had just seen the light. 'I mean, I saw Mrs Pattinson virtually every month for the three years I've been at the Crescent. I suppose you might have expected her hair to have varied occasionally in all that time, mightn't you?'

Rose sighed, going over all the conversations, all the different lines of enquiry, seeking to weave the threads together into something constructive. Every statement taken by her team was on the HOLMES system. Sometimes there seemed to be almost too much information, too much to take in.

She wandered out of her office in the direction of the coffee machine across the yard in the main body of the police station. She wasn't alone in the investigation centre, of course, even though it was a Sunday. This was a major crime and a number of officers were at work, but Staple Hill was quieter than on a weekday. Rose wasn't sure whether that helped or hindered the remains of her thought processes.

Not without difficulty she persuaded the machine to part with a polystyrene cup containing a lukewarm khaki-coloured liquid masquerading as coffee. Back in her office one sip of it was enough. She pushed the cup to one side, grimacing in distaste.

For the umpteenth time she tried to put herself inside Mrs Pattinson's head. Was sex really all there was to it, was that Mrs P's only driving force, or was there something more?

Rose attempted to imagine the kind of life the woman led when she wasn't cavorting with the boys from Avon. She must have money – the Avon boys didn't come cheap and neither did the Crescent Hotel, and both Charlie and Janet talked about how beautifully she dressed in expensive designer suits. Presumably she either lived somewhere within easy reach of Bristol, or travelled regularly to the city, perhaps on business. What *was* her home life like, Rose pondered. Did she have a husband and a family? And if so, how did she explain her absences? There were so many unanswered questions.

The only evidence against Mrs Pattinson continued to be circumstantial. But Rose just wished there were not quite so much of it. She also wished fervently that she could find more to incriminate Terry Sharpe.

By the following morning Rose had her wish. Painstaking inquiries into the life and times of Sharpe conducted over the weekend had gradually compiled some very helpful material. Paolo eventually admitted that Terry Sharpe was his 'sleeping partner' – an appropriate choice of phrasing for an escort agency, Rose thought.

Meticulous checking of records also revealed that, in addition to all his other dubious activities, Terry Sharpe was also a part owner of the Crescent Hotel. To Rose this indicated at once that the hotel was probably not quite as respectable as it had at first seemed to be, its façade of exclusivity perhaps a front for all kinds of activities. Indeed she had half suspected from the beginning that might prove to be the case – but she had been honest enough with herself to be aware that her hunch was based more on her instinctive dislike of the hotel manager, Henry Bannerman, rather than anything more substantive. The Terry Sharpe connection firmly established a link between the Crescent Hotel and Avon Escorts – a link which before Sharpe came on to the scene, her team had not been able to prove.

There was more too. Telephone records showed that Sharpe and Henry Bannerman kept almost constantly in touch. Bannerman, it seemed, received a regular bi-monthly payment from Sharpe, paid directly into his bank account. Terry Sharpe was actually a director of the Crescent Hotel's holding company. In addition he was not only Wayne Thompson's landlord but also provided accommodation for several other young men and women on the books of Avon Escorts. And it seemed it was Sharpe who had put Avon Escorts together – a modern escort agency functioning within a shaky semblance of respectability – and then left Paolo and his people in charge of the everyday operations while he took a hefty slice of the profits.

The name of Terry Sharpe kept reappearing, and Rose actively wanted to believe that he was responsible for the murders. Perhaps the whole Mrs Pattinson scenario was just a remarkable red herring? She pondered that question, not for the first time, as she and Peter Mellor breakfasted on rather good scrambled egg in her favourite Staple Hill cafe.

'It doesn't really hang together, boss, that red herring thing, you know that, don't you?' mumbled the sergeant through a mouthful of buttery eggs.

Rose nodded. 'All the same, I think we've got enough new information to have another go at Sharpe. What do you reckon?'

Mellor shrugged. It was less than forty-eight hours since the first thoroughly unsatisfactory session. The sergeant's lack of enthusiasm was patently obvious.

'If you want the truth, boss, I don't believe it'll get us very far. He's tough as old boots. But, by God, I'd like to get the bastard!'

In an unusual display of emotion, his second in a surprisingly short period of time, Mellor thumped the table so hard with his clenched fist that tea slopped from both their cups.

Rose grinned, 'I wish you'd stop messing about and say what you mean, Peter,' she remarked drily.

This time Rose gave instructions that Terry Sharpe be brought to Staple Hill. Many suspects are completely intimidated by being taken to a police station, and are inclined to roll over once they find themselves shut in a formal interview room with two officers and a tape recorder. Terry Sharpe, Rose had realised before even starting this line of attack, was highly unlikely, with his police background and dodgy track record, to fall into that category. But it had been worth a try. And she certainly had not expected him to remain quite as smug as he did.

A very public pick-up at his office, a high-speed race to the station, and as much of a mauling as she and Peter Mellor dared hand out failed to shift his cool one jot.

'I'm a businessman, darlin',' he said, his pale face giving nothing away. 'I have fingers in a lot of pies . . .'

'Everything you do is centred around the vice trade,' said Rose, ignoring, although with some difficulty, his use of the term 'darling' because she knew it had been his deliberate intention to rile her. 'Vice is the basis of your entire so-called "business".'

Terry Sharpe's features hardened. The ever-lurking smirk merely twitched around the corners of his mouth.

'Prove it,' he said.

'I intend to,' replied Rose.

*

Linking Sharpe with the vice trade was one thing. Seriously linking him with murder was another.

Rose was eating again. Alone this time, she had nipped out of her office for a curry. The last thing she needed after that big breakfast earlier, she knew only too well. She suspected she was finally putting on weight although she hadn't dared go near the scales. There might have been a couple of supperless nights at home with Simon but once at work she seemed to snack and munch all day. Comfort eating, she supposed dolefully. She couldn't quite understand herself. One minute she was bristling with excitement, adrenaline pumping, because she was heading a major murder enquiry, and the next minute she was slumped into deep depression convinced that nothing was ever going to be solved and that she would merely leave a string of dead bodies in her troubled wake.

She piled some more mango chutney on to her already loaded plate. Damn Terry Sharpe, she thought. Even the circumstantial evidence was totally unhelpful. The barman at the Portway Towers had passed on a message to Colin Parker from a woman – and he was quite certain it had been a woman's voice on the phone – calling Colin into the car park where he met his death minutes later.

And Paolo remained adamant that it *was* Mrs Pattinson who called him asking for Charlie on the night Marty was murdered at the Crescent Hotel.

'No it wasn't just a woman saying she was Mrs Pattinson,' he had told Rose yet again when she had telephoned him a few minutes earlier. 'It was Mrs Pattinson. I've heard her voice on the phone enough, haven't I?

'And I hope to God I never hear from her again.'

Rose finished every mouthful of her curry. It didn't give her much comfort though. She felt bloated and even more depressed than before she had started on the meal.

That afternoon provided only hours more of plodding police work and certainly no miracle solutions. The evening which followed was a total disaster.

Rose hadn't wanted to go to Bill Jamieson's farewell party in the first place, and didn't know why she hadn't stopped Simon from accompanying her, the way things were between them. She supposed it was habit really. Simon had always come to these dos in the past, and Bill, her first station sergeant when she had joined the Avon and Somerset Constabulary all those years ago, was one of the few policemen her husband really liked. They shared a love of jazz for one thing, and indeed Bill would probably have made a better teacher than he had ever made copper, she thought disloyally. He had been lucky to be promoted to sergeant, they always said. The older man had never had the push and shove you needed to get on in the force nowadays, and was probably all the nicer for it. Both Rose and Simon were fond of him.

However, within minutes of arriving at the Compton Arms, Rose realised that the whole thing was going to be a big mistake.

She was aware of a few leers, a certain muttering, and a lot of laughter as soon as she and Simon entered the bar. Rose knew that she had been the subject of a joke or two around the station lately because of the time she was spending with Charlie Collins, but normally nobody would dare make any comment in front of her – let alone in front of her husband. Alcohol changed all that, and several of her colleagues were already fairly drunk. She reckoned that some of them must have been on the booze for most of the afternoon to get into that state already and half wished she had had the time to do the same.

She steered Simon into as quiet and safe a corner as she could find and ordered them both a drink. The corner turned out not to be safe enough.

'She's left the toyboy tart at home tonight then . . .' she heard one detective – not on her team but she made a mental vow to get him all the same – to another.

'Worn out probably,' muttered the other to an outbreak of only vaguely subdued laughter.

The men, well oiled as they were, thought of course, that their voices were low and did not realise that Rose and Simon were standing right behind them. They did not really mean to be overheard, Rose realised that, but you did not need her exceptionally acute hearing in order to do so. In their drunkenness they had lost all sense of sound level as well as all other kind of sense. And in any case the damage was done.

Rose felt Simon freeze beside her and she was aware of him glaring at her throughout the rest of the evening. He did not speak to her again while they were in the pub. She had, of course, wanted to leave as soon as the incident happened – but she decided that she wouldn't give her blabbing colleagues the satisfaction. That might indeed have made matters even worse. Instead she did not suggest to Simon that they leave until what she considered to be the first respectable moment – after the farewell speeches were over – and he silently complied.

The taxi ride home was also conducted in stony silence, while Rose reflected that she could have saved the fare by driving herself as her mood had been such that she had barely drunk anything at all. Simon, however, had done his best to drown his sorrows. In little more than an hour and a half he had downed several pints of beer and a couple of large whisky chasers. Gloomily Rose reflected on how that wasn't going to help either, and she was right.

Once inside the bungalow, and indeed more than a little drunk, Simon let rip.

'You cow!' he screamed at his wife. 'You thought-less bloody cow. What kind of a fucking fool do you take me for?'

At first she tried reason, then she joined in the slanging match. She really had had enough. It became the worst row they had ever had. Afterwards Rose remembered vividly her own stupid hurtfulness as much as she remembered his.

'And if I am screwing him, what's it to do with you?' she yelled. 'At least he's interested. What do you care?'

There were even one or two moments when she had thought he was going to hit her, something he had never done. But it was she who ultimately lost control, picked up a vase off the table in the hall – which was as far into the bungalow as they got before the fight started – and threw it against the wall where it smashed to smithereens.

Then she stormed out of the house, with Simon's parting shot ringing in her ears.

'Have a good time with your rent boy, you slut! I'd make sure he wears something though . . .'

Rose began to cry as she climbed into her car –

thankful only that the car keys were still in the handbag she was carrying and that she was quite sober enough to drive.

With tears streaming down her cheeks she swung the car out of the driveway and headed back into Bristol city centre. She had absolutely no intention of going anywhere near Charlie Collins, but she certainly wasn't going to tell Simon that.

In fact she drove straight to Jury's Hotel, which was both big enough and anonymous enough to suit her purposes and not as expensive as the ludicrously overpriced Portway Towers, and checked in for the night. More than anything else she longed for at least a few hours peace and quiet.

Yet again, though, as she desperately sought sleep which continued to elude her in spite of her emotional and physical exhaustion, it was not anxieties about her troubled marriage that plagued her. Instead her last conscious thoughts were once more of Mrs Pattinson.

She thought that the next day she would ask for the computer pictures of the elusive woman to be reissued, this time doctored with a selection of different hairstyles and colours.

As it turned out, she did not need to bother.

# Seventeen

It was the next morning, Tuesday, December 22nd, just three days before Christmas, when she arrived at Staple Hill Police Station. She was tall, elegant, beautifully dressed, and gave the impression of being quite composed and in charge of herself. But she was wearing dark glasses, which she removed when she spoke to the desk clerk to reveal tired red-rimmed eyes. And when you looked at her closely there were lines of strain around her mouth. This was obviously a woman under great stress. Her voice, however, was calm and she spoke clearly and unemotionally.

'My name is Constance Lange,' she said. 'I am also known as Mrs Pattinson. I would like to confess to murder.'

Almost everyone in Bristol, probably everyone in the UK, knew who Mrs Pattinson was – or certainly who she was supposed to be. The desk clerk, an experienced former police officer now re-employed as a civilian, tried not to gulp. He instructed his younger assistant to contact DCI Rose Piper at once. He did not intend to take his eyes off this Constance Lange until she was safely passed on to far more senior hands than his. The chances were she was no more Mrs Blessed Pattinson than his missus, but in his job you didn't take chances. And there was something about this woman which set his teeth on edge.

In fact, the clerk on duty at Staple Hill that

morning would imminently have preferred a return to the policing of another age. He would certainly rather have liked to handcuff the woman to the chair he had bidden her sit in – just to make sure.

Fortunately both Rose Piper and Peter Mellor were at their desks when the call came through to the porta-cabin incident room.

They dashed across the yard to the main station building, trying to suppress their excitement. It was a bitterly cold day and neither had bothered to put coat or jacket on, yet they felt no pain.

'Probably just another nutter, boss,' said Mellor.

Rose knew he didn't really mean it. The pair of them already had a gut feeling that this was the real thing, she was sure of that. There had been quite enough approaches from members of the public who had caused a lot of work and so far no progress by claiming that they knew Mrs Pattinson – but this was the first time anyone had claimed to actually be her.

Constance stood up as the inspector and the sergeant approached her. Rose appraised her quickly, searching for some quick visual confirmation that this really was Mrs Pattinson.

At a glance the woman more or less matched the physical description that had been compiled. Most importantly she was definitely about the right height, build, and age. Her hair was different, but Rose had expected that. She tried to imagine the face before her framed in Mrs Pattinson's glossy blonde bob, and she could certainly see nothing which precluded Constance Lange from being Mrs P – except maybe the colour of her eyes, which were light hazel rather than deep green.

Rather to Rose's surprise, Constance Lange stretched out a hand in greeting and Rose found herself taking it. The woman was behaving more as if she were the vicar's wife on house calls rather than a murderer who had walked into a police station to confess, Rose thought.

'Good morning,' said the woman, in rather nicely modulated tones.

Rose coughed, clearing her throat. The handshake had been firm but courteously brief. The other woman's flesh warm and compliant. Any kind of physical contact with an allegedly violent criminal was always an unnerving experience. But Rose knew better than to allow herself to make assumptions. She locked into professional mode, briskly introducing herself and Sergeant Mellor.

'I understand you wish to make a statement, Mrs Lange,' she said crisply.

Constance Lange merely nodded her assent. Like the front officer clerk Rose took in all the obvious signs of strain. But, nonetheless, Mrs Lange seemed quite self-assured, at peace with herself almost. She gave no indication of any nervousness or uncertainty at all about what she intended to do.

They took her to an interview room where she turned down an offer of tea or coffee, making it quite obvious that she wanted only to get on with the business in hand. Peter Mellor turned on and checked the tape recorder. For the purposes of security two tapes were always used. He and Rose sat across a simple wooden table from Constance.

It was a small airless room, but if Constance Lange was in any way daunted she gave no hint of it. And when she began to speak she did so with great deliberation and a kind of studied calm. She did not look at either police officer sitting opposite her. Instead she kept her eyes cast down towards her hands clasped on the table before her. They were strong capable hands, Rose noticed, hands that were definitely used to physical work, yet well cared for. The nails were without varnish but manicured. She studied the long elegant fingers, wound lightly together. The hands rested easily, perfectly still. There was not the slightest hint of any tremor. And neither was there any tremor in her voice, which remained clear and expressionless.

Firstly she explained who she was, the widow of a respected Somerset farmer, a mother and a grandmother, even giving a brief résumé of her background. She was a girl who had come from nowhere to become a wealthy middle-class woman with a lovely family. Someone to be envied. She spoke almost as if she were making a speech that she had rehearsed.

'But you see, for many years now I have lived a double life,' she revealed. 'Mrs Pattinson was the other me. The person I could never quite shut out. When I was Mrs Pattinson I could do things I could never do as Mrs Lange. Being Mrs Lange was not quite enough for me . . .'

Her voice trailed away a little there, as if she could not really quite believe what she was saying, Rose thought.

'I thought I could get away with it,' Constance continued. 'And I did for a long time. My excuse was an elderly aunt with Alzheimer's whom I used to visit in Bristol, and after she died I just pretended she was still alive. It was so easy. Once a month I would hide behind the identity of Mrs Pattinson and it almost became a routine part of my life. It even seemed quite safe, really, trouble free. That might sound crazy now, but I did what I did because it was a way of getting what I wanted with very limited danger. I thought it was less dangerous than a series of affairs.'

Constance paused, shut her eyes tightly for a few seconds and then opened them again. Rose could detect no sign of any weakness, but was aware, perhaps, of the first flicker of pain. The woman's voice had just the slightest shake to it when she continued.

'You see, I have always had certain needs. Certain fantasies I could never quite get out of my head. Fantasies that would lie dormant for a time, but never leave me completely alone. None of it has ever had anything to do with my family . . .' This time her voice definitely faltered. 'I don't suppose you'd understand.'

Rose could not take her eyes off the woman. She did understand, as it happened – up to a point, anyway. For Rose, keeping her own sex life under control had always been a bit like riding a bicycle – OK as long as you didn't lose your balance. Rose had so far kept her balance, just about, but was all too aware of how easy it would be to fall off.

The more Constance Lange talked about her sexual desires and how she had arranged a double life in order to satisfy them, how she had seemed almost to have no choice, the more Rose found herself sympathising, in fact almost bonding with her.

But this case was not about the mere realisation of allegedly harmless sexual fantasy. Constance Lange was in the process of confessing to murder – and that was something else. Rose Piper could never sympathise with a killer.

'I killed Marty Morris because he was blackmailing me,' said Constance, once again in the same matter-of-fact tone. 'Apparently he followed me home to Chalmpton one day. He threatened to tell my husband about my secret sex life if I did not pay him an extremely large sum of money. I paid up. But the demands continued. In the end I became quite desperate.'

'But you asked for Charlie Collins the night Marty was murdered,' said Rose. 'It always seemed likeliest to us that Marty Morris was killed by mistake.'

Constance shook her head. 'I'd planned to tell Charlie what Marty was doing, to call in his help. I'd been . . .' she hesitated as if searching for the right word, then continued, '. . . using Charlie for some time. I don't know why I thought he would help me, but I did.

'Then Marty turned up instead, and it seemed like fate. I couldn't stop myself when I saw him coming through the garden, I saw a chance to get rid of this evil thing that was threatening my life.'

She looked quite intense. The words seemed almost to be choking her, while at the same time Rose sensed that the woman was also relieved, every bit as if she were getting something terrible off her chest. There were flaws in her story, anomalies which would have to be cleared up before Constance Lange's statement could be accepted, but this was not unusual. The DCI just wanted to make quite sure that nothing was overlooked.

'Why would Marty have agreed to offer his services to you that night when he was already blackmailing you?' enquired Rose stonily.

273

'I asked myself that,' Constance responded coolly. 'I assumed that either he wasn't actually told he was going to see Mrs Pattinson – I am sure you have gathered already that I was not the only woman who sought to be entertained by Avon Escorts at the Crescent – or that he thought he would use the opportunity to further threaten me. I don't suppose he saw *me* as a threat for one minute.'

'But Mrs Lange, what were you doing lurking in the hotel gardens if you were waiting just to talk to Charlie Collins? And what on earth were you doing carrying a weapon capable of killing a man?'

The questions did not seem even to make Constance Lange pause to draw breath. She answered at once. 'I didn't book into the hotel because I didn't want to make my situation even worse. I only wanted to talk to Charlie so I hid and waited for him outside. I had been shopping in Bristol earlier – I had to go home with shopping like I always did, or it would have looked suspicious – and I'd bought a new carving knife, a good one, a butcher's knife. I had it in my bag.'

Peter Mellor butted in, making his contempt for the woman sitting opposite him quite clear.

'You didn't mean to kill, and yet you happened to have a lethal knife in your bag? Don't you think that is something of a coincidence, Mrs Lange?'

Constance seemed almost to smile. 'It may be, sergeant, but I think you will find that whole nations have fallen because of unfortunate coincidences before, let alone one confused and frightened woman.'

Peter Mellor raised his eyebrows. The corners of his mouth were turned firmly downwards. Rose knew he would have found Constance's remark patronising, particularly as the woman was a murder suspect. She did not think Constance Lange had intended that for one second, but her sergeant could sometimes still be overtly sensitive in the company of the well-off white middle-class.

'So what "unfortunate coincidence" exactly led you to kill Colin Parker?' he asked archly.

'None at all, sergeant,' replied Constance. 'I planned the murder of Colin Parker quite carefully. I had to kill him, you see, because, after Marty Morris died, Parker continued in his place. He carried on with the blackmail demands. I assumed they must have been in it together from the beginning.

'He was either a very brave or foolhardy young man, don't you think, sergeant, to carry on after I had murdered Marty? But I can assure you that he did. I suppose he thought that as long as he kept away from Mrs Pattinson he would be safe. He had no idea that the client he agreed to meet at the Portway Towers was Mrs Pattinson under another name. The thought obviously never occurred to him.'

'I don't think high intelligence is a criteria much sought after by escort agencies, Mrs Lange,' commented Mellor, who seemed to be allowing himself to become rather more riled than Rose would have liked.

'Oh, you'd be surprised, sergeant, you'd be surprised,' responded Constance Lange, and again there was a quickness and a certain edge of wry amusement in the way that she spoke which gave Rose the merest glimpse of the kind of woman she might have been before all this had begun. Nonetheless the DCI reckoned it was definitely time for her to step in again.

'OK, Mrs Lange, that's enough of that,' she said sharply. 'Let's move on to the third murder. Are you going to tell us that Wayne Thompson was also blackmailing you?'

'No, Chief Inspector. I killed Wayne Thompson for revenge, I suppose. Or maybe because I couldn't stop . . . That's why I'm here today. Because I want it to stop. It has to stop.'

At last she raised her gaze from the table before her and met Rose Piper's gaze full on. Her eyes were not just red-rimmed, they were also bloodshot. There were signs of broken blood vessels. This was a woman who had done a great deal of crying recently, Rose thought. And now she could see the pain for sure. The look in Constance Lange's eyes was beyond pain. She was a woman in torment. Rose had no doubt about that.

'I killed Marty Morris and Colin Parker to stop my husband finding out about me – and then he found out anyway,' she said simply.

And she related how Freddie had discovered her double life when Helen had suddenly been taken ill. How he had found that there had been no aged aunt for Constance to visit in Bristol every month, that there was some other hidden reason for her days away from home. A reason which destroyed the whole fabric of his existence.

'When I got back that night Freddie was sitting looking at two phone numbers which he had scribbled on a scrap of paper,' said Constance. 'One was the number of Aunt Ada's nursing home and the other was for Avon Escorts.

'After finding out that Aunt Ada had died three years previously he started checking out the numbers

I had programmed into my mobile phone. There were only about a dozen of them, Avon was number nine. Odd to think that if I had not forgotten my mobile phone that day Freddie might still be alive, isn't it?'

She paused again. Rose thought she might be about to break down, but she didn't. Not quite.

'There was nothing I could say to Freddie, really,' Constance went on. 'Avon Escorts had had enough publicity. He couldn't possibly have any doubts about what the outfit was, and there was no other reason for me to have the number except to make use of their services.

'I didn't tell him everything, of course. I tried to protect him, as much as I could. But it all fitted together for him, suddenly, you see. The whole sorry scenario. Once Freddie's suspicions were aroused it wasn't too difficult for him to fill in the gaps. He'd pretty well done it before I even arrived home that night.'

There was another brief silence, so intense that Rose could even hear the faint whirr of the tape recorder.

'Do you think your husband actually suspected you of murder, Mrs Lange?' she asked quietly.

Constance shrugged. 'I don't really know,' she said. 'I suppose he must have done, I was so obviously Mrs Pattinson. He didn't say so directly. But after that dreadful night he barely spoke to me again. And it was only two days later that he . . . that he . . . died.'

She told the story of Freddie's mysterious car crash.

'Freddie was the most careful of drivers, and he was extra careful when he was in that beloved MG of

277

his. He knew the road too. It couldn't have been an accident, smashing straight into a wall like he did . . .'

'So you believe your husband committed suicide, is that it, Mrs Lange?' Rose asked bluntly.

Constance nodded. 'Freddie couldn't live with the shame, with the grief,' she said. 'You have to remember that we had a wonderful marriage. I suppose that sounds strange . . . but we did have a wonderful marriage.

'I have no doubt that Freddie took his own life – after all, he reckoned it was over anyway. He would rather be dead than live with what he knew. And that was the ultimate terrible blow. I will carry the guilt always.'

Rose stared at her, trying to see inside her head.

'I still don't understand why you then killed Wayne Thompson,' she said.

'Neither do I, not entirely,' replied Constance. 'I told you, that's partly why I'm here. Sometimes I think I've gone mad. After Freddie died I just wanted to hit out. I'd been with Wayne Thompson as well, of course, and I found myself blaming him and the other boys. It was them who had destroyed my life, not me. Suddenly all I wanted to do was to destroy them, all of them. I barely remember killing Wayne Thompson. I was in a kind of trance. Only when I came out of it did I start to realise the full horror of all that I had done. I still cannot believe what I have been capable of. I have frightened myself.

'The Avon boys didn't destroy me. I destroyed myself, and my Freddie, my entire family. I want to be punished for the evil I have done. And I want to be stopped from hurting anyone else. I have to be stopped.'

278

Rose had one final question for that first session, to which she suspected she already knew the answer.

'Mrs Lange, we have more than one description of Mrs Pattinson as a woman with reddish blonde hair shaped in a bob and deep green eyes. You do not answer that description at all. Can you explain that to me please?'

Wordlessly Constance delved into the big handbag she had brought with her and on the table before her she placed a blonde wig and a small box containing a pair of green-tinted contact lenses.

Charlie was interviewed formally again at Staple Hill. He vehemently denied knowing anything about blackmail. 'I've told you, no way,' he said.

If there had been a blackmail scam and if Mrs Pattinson had got to him that night, yes, he'd have helped her sort it, no doubt about it.

The next morning his picture, snatched on the station steps, was on the front page of two national newspapers. Both described him as 'the male prostitute at the centre of the Bristol rent boy murders,' and also as 'the one who got away.'

Rose felt for him but realistically had been surprised that the Charlie Collins connection had not already surfaced in the press. It was a good juicy angle and one that could have been leaked much earlier from numerous sources both on the street and, she had to admit, within the force. And the press were still free to print more or less anything they liked concerning the murders because nobody had yet been charged and so the case was not yet sub judice.

However that might all change pretty soon, Rose thought. And all the papers indeed reported that ambiguous line into which so much can be read: 'A woman was last night helping police with their enquiries.'

Charlie Collins was woken that morning by his mother slamming open his bedroom door. She threw a copy of the *Daily Mirror* on to the bed. His own picture, beneath a particularly lurid headline, confronted him.

He was streetwise, wasn't he? He must have known something like this would happen sooner or later. And he had been half-aware of a cameraman outside Staple Hill. But he had put that out of his mind along with all the rest of it and carried on kidding himself that nothing would happen. That things would get back to normal sooner or later and he could carry on with his life just the way he had before.

He rubbed his eyes. Sadly the images before him stayed exactly the same. His mother looked as if she had already been crying.

'Look, it's not the way it seems, ma, honest,' he began.

Miriam Collins interrupted him.

'Answer me just one thing, Charlie,' she said grimly. 'Have you been sleeping with women for money? Is that what's bought that fancy flat and that smart car of yours? Is that what you do?'

'Look, ma,' Charlie tried again. 'I never wanted you to find out. It's not the way you think, you see . . .'

'Just answer the question, Charlie. Do you sleep with women for money?' Miriam Collins' gaze did not waver. There was ice in her voice.

'Well yeah, ma, but . . .'

Again Mrs Collins did not give her son a chance to finish. 'That's all I want to know,' she said. 'Now, get out of my house.'

Constance Lange was formally arrested on suspicion of murder and over the next thirty-six hours – the maximum time the police are allowed to keep a suspect in custody without bringing charges – Rose Piper and Peter Mellor interviewed her several more times, questioning the woman ferociously.

Constance was now accompanied at the interview sessions by a solicitor, provided by the police as the law requires, even though she had refused the opportunity to contact a lawyer herself and showed no interest at all in legal representation.

'What have you done with the murder weapon?' Rose demanded to know.

'After killing Wayne Thompson I was so horrified by what I had done that I drove out to the cliffs beyond Porlock Weir and threw it as far as I could out to sea.'

'Mrs Lange, we found the prints of size ten Timberland boots at the scene of the murders of both Marty Morris and Wayne Thompson. Those are clearly men's boots.'

'I knew there would be footprints – I thought they would put you off the track, make you think maybe the killer was a man.'

'But you said that the murder of Marty Morris was not premeditated,' Sergeant Mellor interrupted aggressively. 'You said you killed him on the spur of the moment, that you merely "happened" to have a lethal knife on your person. Did you also merely "happen" to be wearing a pair of man-size boots? Just in case, was it?'

'Not exactly, sergeant.' Constance replied without hesitation, apparently quite unruffled by the policeman's manner. 'I had bought the boots for my husband, as a present. When I realised how muddy the hotel gardens were that night I put them on before I went to wait for Charlie Collins so that I wouldn't spoil my good city shoes.'

Well, that made a kind of sense, anyway, thought Rose Piper, obliquely remembering her own orange suede heels which had been ruined at the Marty Morris murder scene. She said nothing, knowing she didn't need to. Peter Mellor was in full flight.

'Simply another coincidence, was it then, madam?' the policeman asked, his voice heavy with sarcasm.

'Yes sergeant, I suppose it was,' responded Constance Lange in level tones.

The sergeant grunted his derision. 'And where are these boots now?'

'I threw them into the sea too.'


The daily grind of police work on a major case continued.

Police divers were immediately despatched to the area of the Bristol Channel by Porlock which Constance Lange described. This was procedural. But as one of the divers remarked before the search operation even began, compared with trying to find a knife and a pair of boots at depth in an unspecific expanse of moving sea bed, looking for a needle in a haystack was a doddle.

Rose also sent a team of two, a woman detective sergeant and a male DC to Chalmpton Peverill to inform the Lange family of what was happening and to question them. As a matter of courtesy, and also in order to check details of Freddie Lange's accident, Inspector Barton at Taunton was also informed. He drove straight to Chalmpton Village Farm and arrived there just before the Bristol team.

It was Inspector Barton who broke the news to Charlotte. He didn't mean to – it was just how things turned out. She had been in the farmhouse, she said, trying to find out what had happened to her mother whom no one had seen since early that morning, when she spotted the inspector sitting in his car outside. He had not intended to approach the family until the murder team arrived, but this was not to be.

It quickly became apparent that Constance had told nobody of her intentions, and neither had she left word – except a note on the kitchen table at Dingwell asking Charlotte to take care of Josh. Just that. No explanation of any kind.

Constance had, apparently, just walked away. Even though she had moved into the Dingwell cottage the day before, her absence was quickly missed. And so, as soon as Charlotte saw Inspector Barton, her immediate first thoughts were that there had been another accident – this time involving her mother.

She immediately rushed outside to him. And, confronted by her obviously extreme anxiety, the inspector felt he had to take responsibility – even though he confidently expected to get a roasting for it later.

He allowed Charlotte to lead him into the farm kitchen where he could not help remembering having broken the news of her husband's death to Constance Lange just a couple of weeks earlier. He was now faced with an even more harrowing task.

First he made Charlotte sit. There was not, he thought, any easy way of doing this.

'Your mother has confessed to a very serious crime,' the inspector began. 'She is being questioned as we speak in Bristol.'

Charlotte looked at him in amazement. As soon as she had seen him he knew she had prepared herself for a shock, for bad news – but he was aware that what he was telling her would not only be devastating but also quite beyond her comprehension.

'What crime?' she interrupted, her voice incredulous. 'What on earth are you talking about, inspector?'

He told her then. All that he felt she should know.

'Murder!' Charlotte screamed the word. She was suddenly hysterical. 'Serial killings! The rent boy killings! My God! Are you mad, inspector?'

To his relief, Inspector Barton could see the patrol car which he knew would be carrying the Bristol murder enquiry team draw up outside. Almost simultaneously the kitchen door burst open, and in strode William Lange, obviously alerted by the commotion.

'What the hell's going on?' William demanded. And as he took in the scene before him, his tearful sister and the uniformed police inspector standing stiffly by her side, alarm spread across his handsome features.

Charlotte ran to her brother, threw her arms around him and half-buried her head in his neck so that the inspector could no longer see the younger man's face.

'William, William, they say mother's confessed to murder . . . tell them they're mad . . . tell them . . . for God's sake . . .'

From Charlotte, the words came tumbling out. But William said nothing.

Back in Bristol, whatever Rose and Mellor threw at her, Constance Lange stuck rigidly to her story. Both police officers wanted to be sure the case against Constance would stand up in court. It was vital to ascertain that her confession was watertight, although there was absolutely nothing to suggest that she might have any reason for making a false statement.

'I'm surprised you could even walk in those size ten boots,' Rose said. 'You can't take more than a seven . . .'

'I never had to walk far. I laced them as tightly as I could around the ankles and after the first time I wore a couple of pairs of thick socks. It wasn't too difficult, Chief Inspector.'

Constance Lange was curiously relaxed in her responses. She was also chillingly convincing – her knowledge of events surrounding the murders formidable. One way and another her questioning was fast becoming merely a procedural formality. She had an answer to every point. And when Constance spoke about her hidden sex life and how it had come about, her frankness was starkly apparent – and to Peter Mellor quite sickening, Rose had no doubt.

Constance talked quite freely. It was, in fact, rather as if when she started to reveal her secrets she didn't know how to stop.

'When the children were young this other side of me was in check, most of the time,' she related, her voice sometimes sounding as if it came from a very long way away. 'I was very busy, and fulfilled, I suppose. It was still there, though. Every once in a while,

285

even then, I went to London or Bristol, big cities where you can be anonymous, where you can hide away, and allowed myself to be picked up in hotel bars. It all sounds so sordid, doesn't it? But when I am doing these things all I feel is excitement, nothing else at all. It's only afterwards that I feel anything else . . .'

Her voice drifted away and Rose imagined that she was conjuring up half-buried memories of times she would rather forget, of urgent afternoons in forgotten hotel rooms, then dressing hastily and hurrying away down door-lined corridors.

'Then I would feel guilt, and fear too, I suppose. Anyway, I strayed only a handful of times until about four years ago. My eldest children were more or less grown up, and Helen was away at boarding-school. I had time on my hands. Time to think. Time to fantasise. At first I just tried to make myself busier at home – that's when I began to take on so many commitments in the village. But nothing worked. I couldn't ignore my . . . my . . .' She paused once more, seeking the right word. 'My needs. I really couldn't. I went on one or two more excursions to hotel bars in order to get picked up. The last man I went with thought I was a hooker, ironic really, and wanted me to do all kinds of things even I wouldn't do.'

She paused, allowing herself a small, humourless, self-admonishing smile. 'I left, but as I was going he got very angry and I thought he was going to attack me. It scared me a lot and I vowed I wouldn't put myself at risk again.

'Then I read a newspaper article about the growth of male escort agencies for women in London. I still remember the headline. "Safe sex adventures for

286

middle aged matrons." That wasn't quite how I saw myself . . .' Constance Lange managed a hollow chuckle. Even now, under such extraordinary circumstances, and with all that she was revealing about herself, with the terrible crimes she was confessing to, there was this lurking warmth and humour about her. The woman was one hell of a paradox, that was for sure, Rose thought, as Constance began to speak again.

'Then I was in Bristol, genuinely shopping one day, and I thought I'd try to find out if there was anything like that there. I went into a phone box and had a look in the Yellow Pages. There was nothing. Avon Escorts are in the phone book now, but they weren't then. However, one of their cards was stuck to the wall of the box. I called to ask if they provided men as well as women. The rest is history.'

She sighed, gazing into the distance, looking as if she would like to rewrite her entire life story.

'It was, I thought, the ideal solution. And it always seemed so safe, that is the real irony. It was even Avon who suggested the Crescent when I said I would need to find a discreet room somewhere. It was all so well worked out. Then my aunt died and I simply didn't tell Freddie. They had never been close, he was always quite happy for me to visit her but certainly never expressed any wish to come with me. In any case I told him she probably wouldn't even recognise him, which may well have been true when she *was* still alive. I then had a ready-made alibi for regular absences from home.'

Constance wrapped her arms around her own body, almost hugging herself, reliving the past, a whole double life, a second existence.

'Avon provided everything that I wanted, everything I dreamed of, all that I fantasised about. Wonderful raunchy exciting imaginative sex with no strings, no price to pay except money. It went smoothly for years, don't forget. The boys were actually nicer than I had expected – or I thought they were. I told myself that it was fun, and as long as I didn't hurt anyone it was all OK. In the end I even conquered the guilt. I learned to live, almost without thinking about it any more, with having two distinct sides to my life. And I convinced myself I could keep the two apart.'

Rose listened to Constance Lange for hours and could have gone on listening for hours more. She thought she was one of the most intriguing women she had ever met. So much of what she said made a deep impression on Rose. She wondered how many people, men and women, had not occasionally worried that they might become unable to control their own fantasies. Constance Lange had thought she had found a way to live with hers – perhaps there was no such way. Rose didn't know.

She did know that she had to charge Constance Lange with murder and she could not quite explain why she had even a niggle of uneasiness about it. There was more behind her almost didactic cross-examining of the woman than merely a desire to be sure of a smooth ride in court.

Her senior officers became impatient.

'Just get on with it, for Christ's sake,' instructed Chief Superintendent Titmuss, as the thirty-six-hour custody limit approached. 'You've got an open-and-shut case for once, just get on with it . . .'

An identity parade was staged and both Charlie

Collins and the Crescent Hotel receptionist, Janet, picked out Constance at once as being the fictional Mrs Pattinson – and that was without either the blonde wig or the contact lenses. However there was still no real evidence that Constance Lange was a murderer other than her own confession, as Rose somewhat fruitlessly told Superintendent Titmuss.

'Then bloody well find some if you really think you need it,' responded Titmuss, who was actually quite certain that a confession alone would, in this case, be sufficient to secure a conviction. Rose was well aware that to him as to so many of her colleagues it was simply a logical progression that a woman of Constance's bizarre sexual obsession – and being a man he naturally regarded it as quite unnatural for a woman to have those kind of fantasies – would become a murderer.

In Rose's mind there was no logic to that at all. But then, she felt that she understood so much of what made Constance Lange tick. Nonetheless the views of one woman detective Chief Inspector – Senior Investigating Officer or not – were unlikely to sway the might of the Avon and Somerset Constabulary, even had Rose herself considered that she had any rational cause to formally express them.

On the afternoon of Christmas Eve, 1999, it was arranged that Constance Lange would be formally charged with the murders of Marty Morris, Colin Parker and Wayne Thompson at Staple Hill Magistrate's Court.

# Eighteen

'I always knew 'er was a wrong 'un,' said Marcia Spry in the village shop the next day. Mrs Walters sighed extravagantly, but this time made no further comment.

Peter Mellor regarded the women curiously. They, in turn, had earlier eyed him up and down as if he came from Mars. Well, being black amounted to much the same thing really in a place like Chalmpton Peverill, he thought wryly.

It was the morning of Christmas Eve, just a few hours before Constance was due to appear in court in Bristol to be charged with three murders. The sergeant's mission was to attempt to get a picture of Constance Lange, and to talk to as many people who knew her as possible, as well as to her immediate family. Before his foray into the shop, he had spoken to the vicar, the headmistress of the primary school, the Langes' dairyman and a smattering of other villagers including a young man with a name like a motorbike who seemed to regard Constance as some kind of goddess.

Marcia Spry was the first person with anything but good to say about the woman who had pronounced herself a serial killer.

'As a matter of fact, sergeant, I pride myself on being a fine judge of character, many's the time I've said, haven't I, Mrs Walters, you mark my words I've said, 'er's a bad penny that one . . .'

And so the old woman continued her diatribe, apparently blissfully unaware of Mrs Walters' ill-concealed disapproval.

Peter Mellor was by now only half-listening. Marcia Spry left him in no doubt of at least two things – village life would never be for him, however idyllic it might seem on the surface; and Marcia's opinion of Mrs Constance Lange counted for little because he'd stake a month's salary the old biddy never had a good word to say about anyone.

His attention drifted to the scene he could see through the shop's plate-glass window. The vultures have landed all right, he thought to himself.

A small crowd of press, photographers and reporters were gathered outside Chalmpton Village Farm. Mellor recognised one or two he knew from the Bristol pack. Others would have been dispatched from their main offices in London, he supposed.

Peter Mellor didn't like this case, he didn't like anyone involved in it. He just wanted it over. He didn't like the victims, the witnesses, or the prime suspect. His opinion that Marty Morris and Charlie Collins had degraded themselves and let down their race extended now to everyone involved in the case. He thought the whole damn lot of them had let down the entire human race as it happened. He was particularly contemptuous of, even revolted by, Constance Lange. She was rich, middle-class and privileged. It made Peter Mellor's blood boil. He had had about as bad a start as you could possibly get, and he had single-mindedly worked towards carving a decent life for himself and his family. It hadn't been easy. It still wasn't easy. Being a bright black man in the police force remained a tough ride, and he sometimes wished he had chosen an easier route, if such a thing existed. He had learned that Constance Lange had also not been born into privilege, but that didn't impress him either. The woman had never had to work for what she had – she had married into it. And she had destroyed her husband, who, as far as Mellor could gather, had been a thoroughly good man.

Even thinking about Constance Lange sent a shiver down Peter Mellor's spine. She was depraved, totally depraved, in his opinion. It had been her bizarre sexual desires which had turned her into a serial killer and he had to admit that he was disconcerted by his senior officer's approach to the woman. Rose Piper was showing a great deal too much sympathy, if you asked him.

That aside, he did have some feelings for Constance Lange's family. And in any case Peter Mellor remained a by-the-book police officer, who would always meticulously carry out what he regarded to be his duty whatever the circumstances. So when, through the window, he saw that one snapper had climbed on top of the wall opposite the farm and had set up his camera on a monopod with a 400mm lens aimed at the Langes' kitchen window, Mellor made a mental note to have a word as soon as he'd finished in the shop. British law might allow anyone to take a photograph of anyone else in a public place and then publish it without permission, but aiming a Long Tom through someone's kitchen window breached the privacy laws in Mellor's opinion.

He wondered how on earth Constance's children were going to be able to cope with their lives after all this. Mellor was terribly sorry for the seventeen-year-old in particular. The poor kid didn't know what had hit her. Her brother was a real stiff-upper-lip Englishman, Mellor reckoned, who would never let on to an outsider what he was really thinking. And the elder daughter, Charlotte, merely kept protesting that her mother was innocent, that it all must be a mistake, and he supposed he could understand that. She just didn't want to face the truth.

What a mess, Mellor thought. Three young men – although it was true he didn't consider any one of them to be much of a loss – murdered, one thoroughly decent citizen dead, and his whole family wrecked. All down to a sex-mad old tart. The woman should swing, in his opinion. Peter Mellor was pro hanging. For some reason people always seemed surprised that a black man should hold such a view as strongly as he did. Peter Mellor couldn't understand why. He had no time at all for soft justice. He had clearly defined ideas about right and wrong. He did not see any conflict at all between capital punishment and his strongly held Christian convictions. Wrongdoers should be properly punished, he believed.

That afternoon Charlotte travelled to Bristol to visit her mother in jail. She would have gone before if her husband had not joined her brother in trying to dissuade her. She could do more good at home in Chalmpton Peverill, they both told her. Helen was confused and frightened and badly needed her big sister to comfort her. And in any case it was better for the whole family to keep their heads down, to wait and see what happened, they said.

Well, they had seen all right, hadn't they, thought Charlotte as she drove considerably faster than she knew she should down the village street – causing at least one cameraman to have to leap out of the way, which even in her present distraught state of mind did give her some brief satisfaction.

Her mother was about to be charged with murder, they had been told by that black policeman. Three murders to be precise. Charlotte was going to her, whatever anybody said. Nothing made sense. She had to find out what was going on. And she was fed up with hiding away from the world.

Her wonderful family life had fallen apart with a vengeance, into a nightmare beyond her comprehension, but Charlotte was darned if she was going to hang her head. That was not how she had been brought up. She had done nothing to be ashamed of, and she still could not really believe that her mother had, either.

William, however, was behaving like a complete bastard in Charlotte's opinion. She could not understand him at all. Of course the whole family was in shock, but William was being so bloody tight-lipped. Pompous, priggish – and ostrich-like as well, Charlotte reckoned. William had told his sister quite categorically that he wanted nothing to do with his mother ever again, and that all he desired in the world was to preserve Chalmpton Village Farm for future generations and restore normality to his family life.

Charlotte knew that in the village they all thought William was behaving wonderfully well. Even the dreadful Marcia Spry had remarked that morning – when she had just happened to be passing Charlotte's cottage as the younger woman left, lurking there for hours on the off chance more likely, Charlotte reckoned – on William's new-found maturity and sense of responsibility.

Charlotte did not see it quite like that. That lunchtime, just after learning the latest terrible news from DS Mellor, Charlotte had clashed angrily with her brother.

'It's obvious, Mother has had a complete breakdown because of father's death,' she told him, angrily. 'None of these things can possibly be true of her. How can you stop believing in her the way you have?'

Her brother had not even bothered to answer.

Constance sat on the narrow bunk in her cell in the custody unit of Staple Hill Police Station. The solicitor whose services she had so reluctantly accepted had told her not to expect bail. Constance, after all, was to be charged with three murders. It was a foregone conclusion that she would be remanded in custody until her trial which would probably begin in around six months' time. There was no women's prison in Bristol so she could expect to be transferred to the Eastwood Park Remand Centre, twenty miles or so away, immediately after her court appearance.

Constance didn't mind. It was strange that. She quite liked the seclusion of the small bare room in which she was currently confined. She had been shocked at first by the starkness of it, by the crudity of the lavatory without a seat in the corner and by the sight of the bars on the tiny window in one wall, too high even to see out of, by the severity of the narrow iron shelf, firmly attached to both floor and wall, which, covered only with a thin plastic mattress, served as her bed. Her initial reaction had been pretty much what you would expect from someone used to the creature comforts of life, who had never been in a police cell before. But almost from the moment the door was closed with a heavy clunk behind her and the metal viewing panel clamped shut, she felt more relief than anything else.

She had found her examination by the prison doctor humiliating, of course, when samples of her hair and body tissue had been removed for forensic investigation. She knew about DNA – deoxyribonucleic acid, the substance in the chromosomes of most organisms which stores genetic information. Didn't everybody? But she doubted that much would be deduced from it in this case. There had been next to no body contact at all. She was as sure as she could possibly be. She'd told them about the boots and the gloves and, in any case, she doubted they would ever be found, after all she had thrown them into the sea along with the murder weapon. No, without her confession they would have nothing. But she had wanted to confess. And she did not regret it for an instant.

The routine of her life in custody already seemed almost comforting to her. The regular times for exercise, the carbolic soap in the wash room, the provision of dull, sometimes unidentifiable, food at regular intervals. At no stage was she required to think for herself. Except when she was being interviewed. And that would stop soon too, she had been told. Once she was charged the police would no longer have the right to question her so intensely whenever they felt like it. She relished that. She particularly didn't want to have to talk to that woman detective inspector any more. That one asked the kind of questions which could get Constance tied up in knots if she wasn't very careful. She didn't want to have to be careful. She didn't want to have to think about anything. After all, nothing mattered to her any more. It was a curious feeling. There was a vacuum inside her head. Her life was over, and that was about the only thought she had.

So when the custody officer – a tall thin-faced sergeant who gave the impression that he had seen it all before and was pretty damned bored with it too – came to tell her that her daughter had arrived to visit her, Constance had some difficulty even taking it in. In her own mind she had dismissed her family. She had decided that she should have nothing more to do with them, that they would be better off without her. That had been a major part of the reasoning behind her confession.

She refused to see Charlotte.

'I don't want any visitors,' she told the sergeant. 'I don't want any contact with the outside world. That's all over for me, now.'

Charlotte, who had only got as far as the police station's front office, at first did not quite understand what the tall sergeant was saying to her.

'It is your mother's right, I'm afraid, Mrs Lawson. She does not have to see visitors unless she wishes too.'

'But I have to see her. I have to know.' Charlotte knew that she was shouting. She couldn't help it.

'I'm afraid there is nothing I can do, Mrs Lawson.' The sergeant spoke patiently, but he sounded weary.

Charlotte began to plead. 'Can't you at least ask her again, tell her I must see her, tell her . . .' Charlotte's voice trailed away. A small woman wearing a smart blue trouser suit, her fluffy blonde hair forming a halo around a sharply intelligent face, had suddenly appeared between her and the sergeant, behaving almost as if she had not even noticed that Charlotte was standing there.

'We need to see Constance Lange one more time before she goes to court, George,' said the small blonde woman.

Before the policeman could respond Charlotte heard her own voice. The words came out in a kind of childish wail.

'I'm her daughter, why should anyone else see her? I want my mother . . .'

The blonde woman turned to face her then, her eyes appraising.

'You must be Charlotte,' she said quietly. It was a statement, not a question. 'I'm DCI Rose Piper.' She held out her hand in greeting. Charlotte ignored it.

'I don't understand what is happening,' she said. 'Why is my mother being charged with these terrible crimes? Why? It's just crazy.'

Rose Piper continued to study her carefully.

'Your mother has confessed to murder . . .'

Charlotte interrupted her. 'My mother shouldn't be here, she shouldn't be locked up with criminals . . .' She was almost screaming now.

Rose Piper's voice remained quiet and well-modulated when she spoke again.

'Your mother has confessed to murder, Charlotte. We have no choice but to charge her. There can be no alternative.'

'Why won't she see me?'

The detective Chief Inspector placed one hand lightly on Charlotte's arm.

'I'm sure she will soon,' she said, and her voice really was surprisingly gentle. 'Give her time. And give yourself time. Go home. Get some rest. Take it day by day.'

Charlotte felt herself calming, just a little. The policewoman sounded genuinely concerned and reassuring.

'But there's so much I want to know . . .'

The detective inspector smiled slightly. 'There's so much I want to know too,' she said. 'And some of it you may be able to help me with. But not now. I have to see your mother first.'

Charlotte could feel the tears pricking at the back of her eyes. She didn't want to break down in front of these people. She was still a Lange after all.

'Will you . . . will you give mother my love?' she asked in a more normal tone of voice.

'Of course I will.' The detective inspector sounded gentler than ever now.

'And will you give her this?'

Charlotte held out the framed picture she had so carefully carried with her, glancing down at it as she did so. It was a photograph of the entire family, taken in the garden of Chalmpton Village Farm on the day of the christening of Charlotte's baby son, Alex. Even Josh was there. And they all looked so happy. The perfect family.

The DCI took the picture from her. 'Of course,' she said again.

Charlotte raised her eyes and stepped back. She just wanted to get out of the place now. Her legs carried her automatically through the big double doors and on to the pavement outside, but she was not even aware that she was walking.

Somehow she found her way to her car and there was something comforting about the mechanical familiarity of starting the engine, changing gear and threading her way through the city traffic.

It was not until she reached the M5 and turned west towards the home which had always previously given her so much joy that she began to cry. Trying desperately to concentrate through the tears she could no longer control, Charlotte began to realise how much she had been relying on this visit.

Her mother refusing to see her was the final blow. Constance had never before turned away from any of her children. And Charlotte realised that she had all along been harbouring the belief that once she had seen her mother everything would start to be all right again, that Constance would take her into her arms and tell her it was all a dreadful mistake. Constance had always been there for reassurance after all. And her daughter had even somewhat fancifully imagined herself leading a fight to clear her mother's good name.

It was not yet four o'clock but already almost dark. The traffic was heavy, people rushing home to be with their families for Christmas Day, Charlotte assumed, for the kind of celebrations the Lange family certainly would not be enjoying that year. She peered through the gloom, not sure if it were the glare of the headlights or her own tears which were blinding her. She knew that for safety's sake she should find somewhere to stop and to try to gather her composure – the remains of her family did not need another tragedy – but she was in too much of a hurry. If she couldn't hold her mother close then at least she could go back to the sanctuary of her cottage and seek what comfort she could from her husband and little son.

Peter Mellor was quite right, of course. Charlotte had been resolutely refusing to face up to grim reality. She felt certain still that her mother would never be able to look her daughter in the eye and lie to her. And so Constance's denial of her daughter led to all kinds of ominous interpretations. For the first time, Charlotte began to accept that it might all be true – that her mother really could be a murderer, and a lot more besides.

Constance heard, without interest and indeed with some irritation, the sound of the lock in her cell door being turned yet again. She was sitting on her bed and did not stand when Rose Piper, accompanied by a young detective constable, and, yet again, the solicitor she had no interest in, walked into the grim little room.

Then, just for a moment, her feelings got the better of her. The extraordinary calm which had quite genuinely been with her ever since she had decided to confess, momentarily departed.

'I wish you'd all leave me alone. I've told you that I did it, all of it, I just want to be locked up, and the key thrown away, that's what I deserve,' she shouted at Rose in an outburst of raw emotion.

It was the first time she had felt anything, really, since she had decided to confess. She hadn't been sure if she was even capable of feelings any more.

The Detective Chief Inspector listened patiently, as if trying to understand Constance, which Constance thought was a pretty impossible task as she didn't entirely understand herself.

'You'll get your wish soon enough, unless you show some inclination to help yourself,' said the DCI.

Constance could not quite work this Rose Piper out. The younger woman disconcerted her, made her not quite so sure of herself. She couldn't imagine why a senior police officer should have any sympathy or concern for her, not after all that she had told Rose Piper of what she had done, and yet each time she talked to the inspector she was aware of a certain empathy.

The detective constable certainly did not seem likely to confuse the issue with a display of sensitivity. He was already setting up a tape recorder.

'We have some more questions for you, Mrs Lange,' he said, as if her little outburst had never happened.

When Rose Piper spoke again, her words were unexpected.

'Your daughter sends her love.'

Constance was taken by surprise. She struggled not to react.

'Why wouldn't you see her?'

Constance shrugged. 'There was no point. I have nothing to say to her.'

'You have a younger daughter too, only seventeen. She still needs you. Charlotte wants to help you. Why don't you let her visit at least once?'

'No,' responded Constance, and only she knew how deeply the denial hurt. 'They will both be better off if they never have anything to do with me again. I can only give them pain now. They will forget me, in time. I don't want them near me. Never again.'

'You don't want this then.'

The policewoman held out Constance's favourite

framed photograph of her family which she had always kept by her bedside at Chalmpton Farm.

There is a limit to denial. Constance could not stop herself taking the picture. She hugged it close to her, unable to let go of it, reluctant to look at it. Suddenly she felt as if it were her own flesh into which that vicious butcher's knife had been plunged.

# Nineteen

Rose had never before seen Constance Lange display any emotion at all. She hoped that perhaps the other woman might be a little more vulnerable for once. She studied Constance carefully, unsure of what she wanted from her, but still convinced somehow that what she had so far was not entirely satisfactory.

There was no relevant DNA evidence. The killer of Marty Morris and Colin Parker, forensic had confirmed, had worn gloves and had, in any case, barely touched his or her victims, so adroitly had the crimes been carried out. Rose was sure it would prove to be the same with Wayne Thompson when she finally received the full forensic report on him in about a week's time.

'I want the gloves that you used, Constance,' she said.

Constance, as if with a huge effort of will, put the family photograph down on the bed beside her, and almost leaned away from it, as if rejecting even that.

'I threw the gloves in the sea with the boots and the knife,' she said.

About all that the SOCOs had found worth mentioning at any of the crime scenes were the footprints in the mud at the Crescent Hotel where Marty Morris had been killed and by the side of the Feeder where Wayne Thompson died.

Both were indeed from the same Timberland

boots, an immensely popular and widely available brand, and size ten was a common enough size. Without Constance's help Rose did not think it would even be possible to ascertain where they had been bought. And predictably, Constance was not helping.

As soon as the questioning began again in earnest, she seemed, to Rose's disappointment, to swiftly regain control of her emotions.

'I can't remember where I bought them, not a clue,' she said. 'And I'm afraid I paid in cash.'

'Why in cash, Constance?' asked Rose. 'They're over a hundred quid a pair. That's a lot of cash to be carrying around spare, even for a woman like you.'

Constance shrugged. 'If I hadn't paid cash for the boots I would certainly never have used them again after the first time, just in case they could be traced back to me in some way,' she replied. 'I read Patricia Cornwell, Detective Chief Inspector. I may have acted like a fool in more ways than one, but I am not an unintelligent woman.'

And that, Rose had thought, was part of the problem she had about the whole scenario. Constance Lange certainly was not unintelligent. There was so much that did not add up.

On Colin Parker's suit jacket, made of the kind of wool and polyester mix to which tiny fragments of material are inclined to adhere, forensic had found traces of wool fluff which might have come from the gloves of the murderer. But without the gloves themselves that was no help. Constance said that she had banked on the tide taking care of everything when she had thrown all that might incriminate her into the sea, and more than likely she would prove to be right. It was all so plausible and yet almost too neat for Rose's liking. Her mind just would not stop racing.

Yet again questioning Constance Lange took the case no further. Her story never varied. She never added anything to it either.

Her appearance and charging at the magistrates' court – the last case of the day before proceedings were shut down for Christmas – was a brief formality. Rose drove her own car to the court, and, with Constance charged and on her way to Eastwood, the policewoman was able to go off duty at last. But she realised that she could not stop. Not yet.

Behind the wheel of the Scimitar she made a quick decision and headed out of the city towards the M5. She couldn't wait any longer before visiting Chalmpton Peverill and seeing the rest of the Lange family for herself.

Peter Mellor had been one of the team who had already made enquiries there, and had reported back to her fully. Somehow it made no difference. She knew she had two big faults, as her senior officer, Detective Chief Superintendent Titmuss, had told her often enough – she was reluctant to delegate and she had a disconcerting tendency to go off on her own, to be a maverick.

Off she was going again, she thought to herself, an hour or so later as she pulled her car to a halt outside the Lange family farm. She opened the car door. There seemed to be no press around. It was dark, perhaps they had got all they wanted during the daylight hours. Perhaps they had simply gone home to celebrate Christmas. She presumed that even hacks and snappers did that.

The church bells were sounding. She was in the

middle of a sleepy Somerset village on Christmas Eve. Yet what secrets did this place hold?

William Lange, a bucket in each hand, emerged from one of the loose boxes in the stable yard next to the house as she stepped out of the motor. She could hear the sounds of horses contentedly munching behind him. Presumably he had been giving the animals their evening feed. It was now almost 6.30 p.m. and growing very cold. The yard was brightly lit. William was wearing a heavy quilted jacket over corduroy trousers tucked into workmanlike boots. A layer of thick sock showed at their tops.

She thought how boyishly good-looking he was. And there was something about his face which indicated that once upon a time he had laughed a lot. Not any more, she reckoned.

He greeted Rose without much interest or concern, but with a slight air of impatience, more as if she were a commercial traveller about to try to sell him something he didn't want than a senior police officer investigating a series of murders to which his mother had recently confessed.

'You'd best come into the house,' he said without enthusiasm.

He did not offer her tea or coffee. His manner made it clear that he was busy, that he was fed up with being interrupted. And she found that talking to him was a bit like talking to a stuffed dummy. His face was set. His responses were automatic and inhuman, almost as if he had programmed himself to behave and react in a certain way. It seemed that he was simply refusing to have anything to do with what was going on, as if he were pretending, almost, that it wasn't really happening. Rose already knew from Peter

307

Mellor how resolutely William was carrying on with his day-to-day life regardless of all that was unfolding around him. She recognised that he was probably in deep shock – nonetheless she found his behaviour disconcerting.

'I'd like to talk to you about your mother,' Rose began.

'I have no mother,' he told her coldly.

It was not an easy interview, and it occurred to Rose how alike mother and son were, not so much in appearance but in every other way. Their eyes had the same shutters on them, she thought obscurely.

The village, which she found even more uncomfortable and claustrophobic than she might have expected, was every bit the hotbed of gossip which Peter Mellor had described to her. And the welcome she was given at Church Cottage was very different to that which she received at the farm. Marcia Spry was not so much warm as downright eager.

''Course us knew there was summat wrong with 'er, knowed that for years,' said the old woman.

She was yet again keen to detail the doubts she said she had always had about Constance, but praised William, whom she described, with considerable edge, as 'a true Lange'.

'He took it all so calmly, 'is own mother arrested for murder and all,' Maria said. 'He must have been shocked to bits, but 'e never showed it. Just got on with running that farm, 'e 'as . . .'

But it was when Marcia touched upon the relationship between William and his mother that Rose decided it might be worth interviewing the young man once more before leaving the village that night.

'They was always thick as thieves them two. Not

lately though, he's 'ad no time for her lately, and seems he was a good judge too . . .' rambled the old lady.

Rose was thoughtful as she strolled slowly back to Chalmpton Village Farm. She was not in a hurry to get away. Christmas this year filled her with little more enthusiasm than she imagined it did any of the Langes.

Rose had not gone back to Simon after walking out on him three days earlier and neither had he asked her to. They had met only once – when she returned briefly to the bungalow to pick up some things – and he had been frosty and uncommunicative. She had moved into a police section house until she had the time to sort out something more permanent – or even time to think about what she really wanted. The next day, Christmas Day, she planned to spend the morning at Staple Hill – work on this one wasn't going to stop for Christmas, not as far as she was concerned – and was then due to have Christmas dinner with her sister and her family in Weston-super-Mare, where they had recently returned to run a guest house. Her mother would be there too, which filled Rose with dread. The Christmas Day arrangement had been made some time ago, and had, of course, included Simon. Rose had somehow not got around to contacting her family to tell them that Simon would not be with her. Let alone why. She had already contemplated calling her sister and backing out of the whole thing, using the murder investigation as an excuse. In the long term, though, she reckoned that would cause her more bother than simply turning up Simon-less tomorrow and facing up to the inevitable barrage of questions. Particularly from her mother.

The prospect of being with her mother filled Rose with misgivings at the best of times. Neither mother nor daughter had changed much with the years. Rose still thought her mother was a shallow, priggish human being, and had little real love for her. All the same she felt guilty. She had never made much effort, after all. She should at least go through the motions of seeing her mother more frequently. Nonetheless, again rather like Constance and the way in which she had come to regard her cell as a sanctuary, Rose would just as soon stay all alone in her soulless little room at the section house.

When she arrived at the farm she was still thinking about Christmas and reflected how there were no signs of any festivities – no tree, no holly, no coloured lights. Well, there wouldn't be, would there? No sign at all of the kind of Christmases she felt sure had been celebrated here in lavish style in the past – before this apparently nice, ordinary, rather up-market family had become embroiled in a particularly sordid series of murders.

William Lange greeted her, only after she had knocked on the front door of the house this time, with even less enthusiasm than before. He was wearing a dark suit now, a striped tie around his neck but not yet knotted.

'I'm going to church,' he muttered irritably. She raised her eyebrows. 'It's Christmas Eve, there's a special service, it's expected,' he continued. 'Life goes on, you know.'

'I see,' she said. She thought he was extraordinary. She studied him carefully. She had just one more rather important question, something that had occurred to her while she was talking to Marcia Spry.

'Mr Lange, did you have any idea that your mother was Mrs Pattinson before she gave herself up?' she asked.

William – who had been busily continuing to get himself ready to go out, putting on his shoes, tying laces, checking the change in his trouser pockets – faced her directly for the first time during this second, so far brief conversation.

The hooded eyes stared at her intently. 'Why, did she say that I had?' he asked sharply.

Rose told him truthfully that Constance had not.

'I should hope not,' said William. 'Wouldn't that make me an accessory to murder or something?'

Rose didn't know what to think. William Lange obviously had no time for his mother any more, but, regardless of all the strain and bitterness, the Langes were a close-knit lot steeped in their own family history. There were nuances there that were beyond Rose.

Would William have shopped his mother if he had found out about her double life, if he had suspected that she was a murderess? Or would he have publicly protected her, even if privately he made her life a misery?

Rose wasn't sure. And she didn't even know if it was relevant anyway. She had to accept that her visit to Chalmpton Peverill had been a bit of a waste of time, really. But at least she had done it now.

She settled into the passenger seat of the Scimitar for the drive back to Bristol. Some Christmas this was going to be. She actually wished she was working all through Christmas Day, to tell the truth. Her mother's inquisitive concern, for appearances more than anything else if she ran true to form, as Rose was sure she would, might not be the worst of it, either. The jollities of her little niece and nephew, much as she loved them, would probably make her feel even less festive than she did at the moment, she suspected. And then it hit her. She hadn't even bought any presents. It was gone eight on Christmas Eve. Desperately she tried to think of a shop, any shop, that might still be open.

Somehow or other she got through it all. An off-licence had provided champagne and malt whisky for her sister and brother-in-law, a bottle of some disgustingly elaborate liqueur for her mother, some halfway decent plonk as her contribution to the Christmas dinner, and a couple of decorative net stockings packed with assorted sweets for her niece and nephew – which she supplemented by pinning a twenty-pound note to each, thanking God that children were always such mercenary little beasts.

She fielded her mother's questioning with more ease than she had anticipated, largely thanks to a succession of well-timed interventions from her ever tactful sister and a merciful excess of alcohol which effectively numbed both her senses and her sensitivity. This also forced her to spend the night on the sofa as she didn't dare drive back to Bristol. However she fled early in the morning before having to face her mother in a condition of grim and rather painful sobriety.

Work again provided a welcome excuse, although it was the day after Boxing Day before the incident room returned to being anything like fully operational.

Rose was coming under more and more pressure to

make some kind of melodramatic gesture concerning Avon Escorts, whose activities, now so publicly revealed, seemed to have caused far more public outrage in Bristol than a few killings – after all, murder was everyday stuff.

It was about ten days after Christmas when she realised she could no longer resist the demands of her superiors that Paolo be charged with living off immoral earnings – however inconsequential she still considered this to be – but it did at least also give her an opportunity to get the odious Terry Sharpe for something.

Constance's confession had put the former vice cop in the clear as far as the big one was concerned, much to Rose's chagrin. But the murder investigation had produced evidence which should finally nail him for vice crimes. Rose believed she had a good enough case to charge him, as well as Paolo, and Sharpe was duly arrested along with the younger man.

It was Terry Sharpe's complacency, his way of always giving the impression that he knew things you didn't, which annoyed Rose most about the man. And this time when she turned up at his plush converted warehouse office – accompanied by Peter Mellor and two uniformed officers, all making as much commotion as possible – Rose found that she thoroughly enjoyed seeing the habitual smug expression wiped from Sharpe's face for once.

But the arrest of Terry Sharpe was about the only thing in her whole life giving Rose even the remotest sense of satisfaction.

The weeks passed in a haze of hard work. The momentum of the investigation did not lessen as the police continued to strive to ensure that the case against Constance was flawless. You couldn't rely entirely on a confession any more, not since the Guildford Four, in fact. Every police officer knew that – even Chief Superintendent Titmuss when he was thinking about anything other than politics and social climbing.

There was, however, plenty of circumstantial evidence. Even the efficiency of the stabbings could be construed as further pointing the finger at Constance. After all, she had trained as a nurse. She would know well enough where the blade of a knife would do the most damage.

Rose had every reason to be quite confident, and still could not really explain why she wasn't. Yet as the day of the trial approached, she became almost as unhappy at work as she was in her private life.

She insisted that each statement Constance Lange made, every possible weak link in her story, be checked and double-checked. Superintendent Titmuss accused Rose of doing the job for the defence much more thoroughly than the defence itself seemed inclined to do. Constance, it seemed, continued to show no inclination whatsoever to help formulate any defence at all. And indeed, at one stage, Rose had even found herself actively trying to establish an alibi for a woman who had already confessed to the crimes in question.

Constance had been a busy woman, involved in so many aspects of village life, but an early check of her diary had revealed conspicuous blank spaces at the time of all three murders. Close questioning of family, friends and neighbours produced nobody who could definitely claim to have seen Constance, either in the village or anywhere else at the appropriate times.

Charlotte at one stage began to insist, after already having been questioned more than once, that her mother had visited her at the time of at least two of the three murders. But Rose found her unconvincing. The young woman somehow contrived to look as if she didn't even believe herself, and Constance, when told by her solicitor what her daughter had said, apparently merely shook her head.

'She's trying to protect me,' she had said tiredly. 'That's typical of Charlotte. She's always been a very loyal girl.'

Rose continued to be unable to sleep at night and during the day she drove herself mercilessly. Three months had passed since she had walked out on Simon, and she was still living in the police section house. She had had neither time nor inclination to make other arrangements. Sometimes she would have dearly liked to go back to her husband, but she didn't have the energy to cope with him or anyone else at the moment. The section house provided a welcome limbo. Simon had called a couple of times and once suggested a drink 'to sort things out a bit'. She had said no, and afterwards wished she had said yes. He didn't call again. The strain of the break-up and her compulsive preoccupation with the Constance Lange case had become so overwhelming that there were days when Rose feared she was heading for a break-down.

Certainly she was aware that she was becoming dangerously obsessed with the case. It was on her mind all the time. One night, during a rare couple of hours of fitful sleep, she even dreamt that she was Mrs

Pattinson. She woke in a trembling sweat from a numbing nightmare of convolutedly thrashing naked limbs and the flashing of lethal knives.

As she jerked into consciousness she could still see dead faces, and for a few awful seconds she thought that her own sweat was blood.

Still Rose drove herself relentlessly onwards. She did not believe she knew the whole truth and she was determined to find it. Still she harboured the notion that Charlie, perhaps unwittingly, held the key.

Alone one night – and, not for the first time in her dealings with Charlie, totally against procedure – Rose visited him in his dock-side flat. With the Rent Boy Killer allegedly behind bars, and in any case proclaiming that she had never been seeking to harm Charlie in the first place, there was no longer any reason for Charlie to stay away from home. Additionally, although she had not discussed this with Charlie, Rose assumed that his mother must know all too well by now exactly how her beloved son had acquired his beautiful apartment and funded his extravagant lifestyle. The publicity had stopped, of course, with a suspect charged and the sub judice laws in operation, but Charlie had hit so many headlines at one stage they had been almost impossible to avoid.

Charlie looked positively pleased to see her. Rose supposed that his life was not quite as full as it had been. He offered her a glass of wine. She accepted and, yet again, asked him to go over everything he could possibly tell her about Mrs Pattinson.

Charlie sighed. 'How many times, Rose?' he asked.

She couldn't remember at which point he had started calling her by her Christian name. Somewhere along the line. It seemed quite normal now.

'You're intruding on private grief here, you know,' he went on. 'My life's in tatters now thanks to that bloody woman. What else can I tell you?'

'I don't know.' Rose's head was throbbing dully. She had been fighting a nagging headache for several hours. And that wasn't unusual nowadays. 'It's just, and I can't quite explain it, something isn't right here, I feel sure of that,' she went on haltingly. 'Perhaps there is something we've overlooked, you and me – something that will straighten things out. Will you give it a try? One last time.'

Charlie nodded, as if resigned, and started to talk. He told her all of it all over again – the visits to the hotel, the sex games, how convinced he had been at the time that Marty Morris had died instead of him – racking his brains, he said, for anything extra, anything he had previously left out.

After an hour of this, and with the wine bottle almost empty – it had been too sweet for Rose's taste, really, but she had drunk her share nonetheless – Charlie paused.

Rose could feel him studying her carefully.

'You look a bit how I feel,' he remarked bluntly. 'Bloody dreadful.'

Rose managed a small dry laugh. 'Thanks a bunch,' she said.

He smiled back. 'Sorry. You do look stressed out though, tired too.'

'I am,' she said. 'All of that.'

'Fancy a spliff?' he asked.

In spite of herself she burst out laughing. 'You've got a bloody cheek, Charlie Collins,' she said. 'I'm a cop, remember.'

317

He grinned the disarming grin. 'Yeah, I know. So, fancy a spliff or what? Do you the world of good.'

She gave in, remembering the pleasantly soothing numbness induced a long time ago during her few early experiments of smoking marijuana.

He rolled one swiftly and expertly, lit up and passed it to her.

The first draw felt wonderful. Her head started to spin at once – she didn't even smoke tobacco, after all – but the dull ache evaporated. The sense of ease and well being, the relaxation after so much tension, was quite overwhelming.

'Umm,' she murmured.

She was sitting on one end of the black leather sofa and Charlie was in the armchair opposite. Still looking at her he walked across the room and sat down next to her. He took one of her hands and held it lightly.

'You know, if you like I could make you forget your troubles altogether for a bit,' he said casually. 'I'd do an even better job than a spliff. I'm quite good at making women forget their troubles.'

He flashed a dazzling and wonderfully provocative grin.

Rose could not stop herself thinking how inviting he looked. Young. Fit. Virile. Surprisingly nice to be with.

He took the spliff from her and dragged on it, long and deep. Then he leaned close to her and just brushed his lips against hers. His mouth was warm and he tasted sweetly masculine.

She had not had sex since about three weeks before the big row with Simon – that was nearly four months ago. And, it occurred to her obscurely, that was the longest period of sexual abstinence she had endured since she lost her virginity at the age of seventeen.

Rather to her surprise she found herself greatly tempted to take up Charlie's invitation. Apart from anything else, she thought him so genuinely likeable. Fleetingly she imagined his arms around her, his hands caressing her, and she couldn't help wondering what it would be like to sleep with someone with so much experience. With a professional. With a man accustomed to being paid to give pleasure. The idea excited her. Just the way it must have excited Constance, she thought. And it was ultimately that thought which brought her to her sense.

'I don't think so, Charlie,' she said at last, trying to make her voice sound normal.

'No one need ever know.' He moved his head slightly and began to kiss her neck just below her left ear, his lips tickling her in a place where he surely could not have known she had always been particularly sensitive.

Her body was responding of its own accord, and she didn't want it to. She really didn't. She had forgotten how dope enhances the senses, indeed how thoroughly randy it had always made her when she had tried it before.

'We'd know,' she said eventually.

'Wouldn't we just,' he replied, and very gently he bit the soft flesh of her neck.

With a huge effort of will she shook herself free. 'No, Charlie,' she said more firmly now.

He grinned again. 'As you wish,' he said. 'I reckon it's a shame though.'

She could not help smiling back. 'You're probably right – but it's still no.'

She had left right away then, not trusting herself to stay. Certainly not daring to smoke any more.

The fresh air hit her when she stepped outside and she knew she had better not drive for a bit. The wine and the dope had proved a powerful cocktail – in more ways than one.

She tipped back the driver's seat in her car and crashed out for a couple of hours, eventually returning to the section house just before one in the morning. And it was not until then, her dull throbbing headache firmly reinstated, that she realised just how big a mistake she had nearly made – both professionally and personally.

She warmed herself a glass of milk, spooned some comforting honey into it, and headed for bed with a couple of aspirin, wondering, only half-joking to herself, whether she shouldn't have a cold bath.

Even before the temptations of this evening with Charlie Collins, Rose, perhaps partly because of her four months' abstinence, had been indulging in some strange sexual fantasising. And she worried about herself sometimes, wondered quite what she would be capable of, given the opportunity. Dreaming that she was Mrs Pattinson was only part of it. She daydreamed too. Found herself imagining being in bed with two young men, young men paid to please her. Tonight she had had a narrow escape, she thought. And lying alone in her single bed with her hot milk and her headache she could not believe that she had very nearly gone to bed with a male prostitute – and a witness in a murder case at that.

Still, she hadn't done it, had she? In the end something had stopped her. She supposed that for her, ultimately, fantasy was fantasy and no more or less than that, as it was for most people, men and women. Constance Lange was the exception who had taken her fantasies and turned them into some kind of bizarre reality. Constance had turned herself into Mrs Pattinson, one day a month, every month. She had lived out her fantasies.

But Rose Piper couldn't do that. She could never be a Mrs Pattinson – although sometimes she half-wished she could be.

# Twenty

Charlie woke up the morning after his near liaison with Rose Piper feeling very alone. The truth was that sleeping with Rose would have provided him with just as much comfort as it might have given her. And, of course, to a young man with his track record, sex with a senior police officer investigating a murder case in which he was a prospective witness had not seemed that crazy at all. In fact he had not even considered that side of it.

He pottered to the bathroom. Italian tiles provided by the Merry Widow, bath suite from funds out of Miscellaneous, and a state-of-the-art American power shower courtesy of the Aged Water-Babe – a customer in her early sixties capable of exhibiting the sexual energy of a twenty-year-old who always liked to start her sex sessions with Charlie in the shower.

Charlie looked around him without feeling any of the satisfaction usually instigated by his beautiful home.

Avon Escorts had gone – for ever, more than likely, Charlie moodily reflected. His entire world was in disarray. He honestly believed that he had only narrowly escaped violent death. But being alive was suddenly not nearly as good as it used to be. The publicity he attracted before Constance was charged had horrified Charlie. He had always managed to kid himself that what he was doing was perfectly straightforward business. But when you saw the headlines in the *Sun* and the *News of the World* it all looked so sordid. And Charlie had never considered that he did anything sordid. There were the practicalities too. He had no work and the contents of those carefully labelled drawers in his wall safe were beginning to run low. He had tried, discreetly, to contact some of his regular customers directly. They had not wanted to know, and, under the circumstances, you couldn't blame them, Charlie thought. Nonetheless he was still trying to fund an expensive lifestyle and he would not be able to do so for much longer unless his fortunes changed dramatically, he knew that well enough. He might even have to consider that offer from the *News of the World* for a big buy-up piece about his exploits with Mrs Pattinson to run at the end of the trial. He shuddered at the thought. Charlie was used to being admired and envied by his friends and family. He didn't like his new image at all. In fact his standing was in any case so low that a full and frank *News of the World* exposé probably wouldn't make much difference.

For several weeks he had been trying to call his younger sister Daisy in London where she lived with her new husband, Jarvis, the up-and-coming solicitor. Charlie had not spoken to her since the truth about him had become public knowledge. Or rather she had not spoken to him, he feared. He had left several messages on her answering machine but she had not responded.

He looked at his watch. It was not yet 8.00 a.m. He decided to go for it. This early would be a good time to catch her. Surely she would answer the phone. She did. And more than anything else she sounded embarrassed.

'Hi, Charlie, I've been meaning to call you,' she said, her manner indicating that she had had no such intention.

'I just wanted to talk to you, explain a few things, you know . . .' he began.

'Yes but I can't, not now, uh . . . I have to go out . . .'

It was abundantly clear to Charlie how ill at ease his sister was. There seemed little doubt that he was the last person in the world she wanted to hear from. That hurt. That hurt a lot. Charlie had always adored Daisy, and until these last few months had been quite confident that she felt the same way about him.

He didn't know what to say. She saved him the bother. He could hear the sharp intake of her breath down the line. After just a brief pause she began to speak again.

'Look I'm sorry, Charlie, you may as well have the truth.' Her voice was quite firm now. She still sounded embarrassed though. 'I know Jarvis would rather you didn't call here again. It's his job, you see. We can't afford to be associated with you.'

Stunned, he heard himself mutter something half-apologetic. He rang off straight away. And that was his beloved kid sister for whom he would walk over broken glass. What chance did he have? The wedding, when he had been so pleased to make his family happy, to give them things they couldn't give themselves, had been only five months ago. It seemed like something out of a different world now.

Worst of all, of course, was having so dreadfully disappointed his mother. He had not seen her since the day that the news had broken and she had asked him to leave her home. She had been so angry, angrier than he had ever seen her in his life.

'I will not have a prostitute in this house, male or female,' she had said, the hurt shining out of her. 'You are no son of mine.'

It wasn't the anger that got to him though. It was her pain that he could not bear to see. He had not known what to say or do, so he had simply packed his bags and left, staying in a hotel until after Mrs Pattinson was found and he had felt it safe to return to his flat.

He had called his mother several times since and she had been every bit as reluctant as his sister to speak to him, he knew that. But she had not told him not to call again. She *had* told him she did not want to see him, although when he had asked starkly, 'Not ever?', she had replied: 'Not yet, certainly not yet.'

Perhaps he should take that as encouragement, he thought, and on this particularly grim and lonely morning he decided to take the chance, to turn up unannounced at his mother's house.

The BMW purred into powerful action at once, but not even the car could give him any joy as he ploughed through the city traffic into St Paul's and up the Ashley Road.

His mother was cleaning the house when he arrived. He thought that it looked even more sparkling than usual. Perhaps she was using housework as a kind of therapy.

She led him into the front room wordlessly and he saw that she was not angry any more. There was something about her that was beyond that. He would definitely have preferred anger. He stepped forward,

325

wanting to hug her, but she moved away from him and he could see the tears forming in her eyes.

'I'm sorry Ma, I never wanted you to know . . .' he began.

'You've said that before,' she responded curtly.

He merely bowed his head.

'So if you hadn't been found out it would be all right, Charlie, would it?' she asked, her voice brittle. 'Is that the way I brought you up?'

'No ma, it's not,' he replied.

What else could he say? But the truth was that he still was not ashamed of anything he had done. He hadn't hurt anyone, after all – well not until now, and never intentionally. His mother was actually quite right, as it happened - he had thought it was all quite all right as long as nobody, or certainly nobody in his family, found out.

His mother sat down heavily on the velveteen covered sofa, dark green, matching the carpet and her dress, he noticed obscurely.

'Charlie how could you?' she asked, and this time her voice was almost a wail of anguish.

Now Charlie really didn't know what to say. Maybe this visit was a mistake. He seemed to be hurting her more than ever by being there, and it really broke his heart to be rejected by his mother.

He wanted to tell her again that it wasn't the way it seemed, it really wasn't. He had just been trying to make the best of what he was, he had only given pleasure. What was so wrong with that? He wanted desperately to make her understand. There were worse ways of making a living, surely? But to her he knew there probably weren't. And he just didn't have the words to explain.

In the end he left almost at once. He could hear her crying as he shut the front door behind him. Elderly Mr Martin, his mother's next door neighbour, whom Charlie had always considered to be a rather unpleasant old busybody, came out of his house at the same time and burst into snide laughter at the sight of Charlie.

'Hi, Charlie boy, got any leftovers for an old man?' he asked.

Charlie had had enough.

'Fuck off,' he said, even though it was quite out of character for him to speak to an older person like that and, indeed, to use such a phrase in the first place.

He got into his car, pushed the gear shift into drive and roared away. Once safely into anonymous territory he found a lay-by and pulled to a halt. He slumped back in the driver's seat and closed his eyes. He felt as if he had nowhere to go and no one to turn to. His near-perfect world had collapsed around him every bit as devastatingly as had Constance Lange's.

Rose Piper was not the only one who had become obsessed with the Lange case. After all, one way and another, that was the source of all that had happened to him, of all that was still happening. The only difference was that to Charlie, Constance remained Mrs Pattinson, and always would. And Mrs Pattinson was constantly on his mind nowadays. There really was little else.

He went over again in his head, for what felt like the millionth time, the details of his dealings with Mrs Pattinson, all that he had told Rose Piper last night and on so many other occasions. Like her, he had always reckoned that something somewhere did not quite add up. He could not believe that the woman he knew as Mrs Pattinson would want to harm him or any of the boys who had given her pleasure. Apparently she had said she hadn't sought to harm him – but that call to the Crescent Hotel still looked like a set-up to him, and it was, after all, him who had been set up. Rose Piper had told him the story about Mrs P waiting in the bushes to talk to him, about her having the knife on her by accident, and he didn't buy it any more than, he suspected, did the detective.

He still didn't really believe that Marty Morris or Colin Parker had been blackmailing her – they had both considered themselves to be professionals like him. If the truth be told, Charlie reckoned Marty wouldn't have been bright enough for such a thought ever to have occurred to him, and Colin would have been too bright to do such a thing even if the idea had crossed his mind.

So much of it didn't make sense to Charlie when he really thought about it. One simple answer was that the woman was mad. Stark staring bonkers. Off her trolley. Out of control. But Mrs P had never seemed mad to him. Nor out of control either – except occasionally in bed. She had always seemed quite normal and rather nice to Charlie – just unusually highly sexed. And Charlie, unlike so many in a world steeped in double standards, saw no particular conflict there.

Suddenly Charlie made a snap decision. On an impulse he decided to drive to Chalmpton Peverill, to see for himself the sort of place Constance Lange came from.

Once he had turned off the M5 on to the succession of country lanes that would eventually lead him to the village, even town-boy Charlie could not help being bowled over by the beauty of the countryside. It was the end of March and a particularly good year for daffodils. It seemed that every hedgerow and every field was full of them. A smattering of early bluebells – a warm sunny March following a wet February, had provided perfect conditions for spring flowers were already in bloom. The Somerset countryside was a picture.

So was the village of Chalmpton Peverill. Charlie drove right through the village at first, taking in the pretty thatched cottages, the shop, the green, the farm he suspected must be the Lange family home, and the neat row of council houses – as well cared for as any of the other properties – on the edge of the village. Everything was immaculate. Some of the lawns had obviously been given their first cut of the season already. The trees and bushes were just bursting into life and several of the village gardens boasted tubs of winter pansies and heathers, as well as vibrant spring flowers. At the top of the village Charlie turned his car around and motored slowly back down, parking in a lay-by he had noticed on his way in.

He locked the BMW and started to stroll up the main street, past the farm which he was fairly sure he recognised from pictures in the newspapers published before Constance had been charged. It was a strange sensation. Charlie wondered fleetingly if he was being over-sensitive but he felt that he could hear the whispers coming out of the hedgerows and seeping through the tiniest of cracks in the garden walls. Since he had gained notoriety Charlie was getting used to being conspicuous – to being pointed out by some and equally pointedly ignored by others – around where he lived. But this was something else. He didn't think the whispering he could feel in the very fabric of Chalmpton Peverill had anything to do with who he was and what he was involved in – not quite yet anyway, and not before he had closer contact than he had had with anyone so far. He was just a stranger, and, of course, a black stranger at that.

Brought up in St Paul's, and still living in a highly cosmopolitan city with a large black community, Charlie was unprepared for the reaction caused by his sudden appearance in the village. Rural Somerset remains almost one hundred per cent white Anglo Saxon. Chalmpton Peverill was not on the tourist track and had few visitors and certainly no black ones – ever.

Charlie did not know that the villages were still recovering from being interrogated by a black policeman, nor, of course, that quite a few of them had not been happy about that at all, as it happened.

He kept his stride steady as he walked past Constance Lange's home – Mrs Pattinson's home, as he thought of it – peering sideways, not feeling able to stand and stare as he would have liked.

At a glance he took in the quiet splendour of the place, the beautiful well-proportioned old farmhouse, its large perfectly tended gardens with manicured lawns, the impeccable stable block, and the stunning views across acres of open countryside that you could just glimpse beyond. For the first time Charlie found himself wondering why all that hadn't been enough for Mrs Pattinson. Charlie liked his creature comforts, appreciated beauty, and relished the lovely things that money can buy. He reckoned he could quite happily give up sex for ever to live in a place like

Chalmpton Village Farm – as long as you could transpose it into a decent-sized city, of course.

A little further up the street the curtains in the front-room window of Church Cottage twitched as he passed. He noticed the material moving, almost as if it were being blown about by a draught. Marcia Spry missed nothing that moved in Chalmpton Peverill, but that was something else Charlie didn't know about.

The weather had changed dramatically in the last few minutes. Typical March, he supposed, although the climate seemed so much more important to him in this picture-book village than it ever did in Bristol. You don't notice the weather nearly as much in cities, he thought. A few spots of rain were just beginning to fall as he approached the Dog and Duck, and a look inside the pub suddenly seemed like an exceptionally good idea. However the reactions of a closed community to an alien-looking stranger became no longer a mere feeling in the air. In the public bar of the Dog and Duck a group of working men were enjoying a lunch-time pint, and every head turned at once towards Charlie Collins as he entered. He could sense the wheels of half a dozen or so brains creaking into action. There was a busy flurry of nodding and muttering.

Charlie ordered a pint of Guinness. The publican served him silently, and Charlie suspected that the small assembled throng were beginning to guess exactly who he was – there had been enough publicity after all.

The man on Charlie's left somewhat deliberately turned his back on him. Charlie was by now pretty sure that his suspicions were right and wondered whether it was worth even trying to get into conversation with anyone. He supposed that was what he had been intending when he entered the pub, but he was no longer entirely sure.

While he was still contemplating what to do next the door opened and a tall young man wearing a cloth cap and a Barbour jacket with the collar turned up took a step into the bar. Charlie thought he looked familiar even before he removed his cap. The young man stopped suddenly in his tracks, stood hatless in the doorway for just a few seconds, then swung around and walked smartly out again.

'Young William don't like the company, and neither do us much,' commented the man on Charlie's left in a conversational manner. He still kept his back to Charlie.

Charlie downed the rest of his pint in one and also left the pub. He didn't want trouble – and, more importantly, he was quite sure he had met the young man with the Barbour and the cap once before.

He remembered from newspaper reports and from conversations with Rose Piper that William was the name of Constance Lange's son, and Charlie was deep in thought as he strode quickly back through the village to his parked car. The rain was falling quite heavily now and he had left his leather jacket in the BMW. He was getting soaked and he was in a hurry for that reason as well as all sorts of others. The curtains of Church Cottage twitched again as he hurried past. This time he caught a glimpse of an elderly woman with a rather mean-looking mouth peering through the window at him. The Lange farm was still and silent, almost unnaturally so.

Charlie realised that even if the sun had been still

shining he would no longer want to hang around. Chalmpton Peverill was just too uncomfortable for him. He could feel the hostility now almost as clearly as if he could reach out and touch it. And in any case he now believed that the truth was at last within his grasp.

All the way home Charlie concentrated hard on his brief encounter with William Lange. He was becoming increasingly more certain that he had not been mistaken. And suddenly the whole terrible affair made devastating sense.

He called Rose Piper from his mobile phone while he was coasting down the Portway. She was not in her office. He left a message on her voice mail saying he needed to speak to her urgently. Charlie was born into the computer age, into the era of the Internet and automatic answering services. Nonetheless he hated voice mail. He muttered to himself under his breath. This was important. But he wasn't kept waiting long enough, in spite of his impatience and his anxiety, to start fretting about what to do next if he couldn't raise Rose.

His mobile rang just as he was pulling into the car park beneath his apartment block. It was DS Mellor who had picked up the message Charlie had left for Rose. The DCI was in court, explained Mellor. Charlie remembered then – the immoral earnings case against Paolo and Terry Sharpe had started in the Crown Court. Damn! He really needed Rose.

'Can I help?' he heard Mellor ask in a tone of voice which indicated that he would actually like to do anything but.

Charlie had never had any doubts about the

sergeant's opinion of him from the first time he had met him. He had felt not only the superiority but the anger in Mellor who had made his distaste for Charlie and everything that he stood for abundantly clear. But Charlie wasn't really any more put off by Mellor than he would have been by anyone except Rose Piper. It was only Rose that Charlie wanted, only Rose that he trusted.

'No, you can't help,' he said bluntly, his voice much louder and more highly pitched than usual, he realised. 'I need to see Rose. Just get to her. Tell her it's important. Urgent. I know she'll come.'

Peter Mellor noted the use of his superior's Christian name. Charlie sounded nervous and over-excited, but Mellor thought that the boy was right about one thing – Rose Piper would go to him sure enough, even if it meant walking out of court he wouldn't wonder. He sighed to himself. He didn't know what was going on, but he knew he didn't like it.

He contacted the Crown Court – even Rose Piper with, in Sergeant Mellor's opinion, her quite cavalier disregard for procedure and regulations, would not dare leave her mobile switched on there – and asked for an urgent message to be delivered to the Detective Chief Inspector. A response came back within minutes. DCI Piper was about to give evidence but a note had been passed to her. She had indicated that she would go to Charlie Collins as soon as her evidence had been completed – which the court official who called Sergeant Mellor reckoned would be in no more than forty-five minutes.

Mellor made no comment beyond thanking the official for dealing with his request so promptly.

When the phone call was over he sniffed his disapproval to himself, but, scrupulous as ever, considered only the close proximity of the court house to Charlie's home down by the Floating Harbour before calling the boy back. However, when Charlie picked up the phone, Mellor could no longer disguise his dislike of the entire proceedings, and neither did he make any attempt to do so.

'She'll be with you within the hour,' he said frostily and hung up without giving Charlie a chance to reply.

The doorbell rang less than forty-five minutes later. It had seemed much longer to Charlie. Thank God, he thought. He couldn't believe that he would ever be quite so pleased to see a police officer.

He flung open the door without thinking, without attempting to check who was there.

His assailant pushed Charlie back into the room with the violent thrust of one hand and brought the heavy lump hammer carried in the other hand crashing down on to Charlie's head.

There followed a torrent of blows, but most of them were quite unnecessary.

Charlie's skull had been crushed by the first one and he died almost at once.

# Twenty-One

Rose Piper arrived at Charlie's apartment block little more than ten minutes after his murderer had left. But she didn't know that. Neither did she know that the murderer, ironically, had used the same method of entering the block as she was about to.

As she stood on the pavement outside Spike Island Court she was momentarily surprised, but not really alarmed, to get no reply when she pushed the intercom button for flat thirty-six. Fortunately a resident appeared with a key, and by virtue of an apologetic smile and a mumbled excuse, Rose managed to gain entry without having to play the warrant-card trick.

She took the lift to the third floor where she found that the door to Charlie's flat was slightly ajar. This did alarm her somewhat. Rose called his name, got no response and then tried to push the door open. It stuck after just a few inches. She leaned against it, pushing it as far as she could and then squeezed her way in around the edge.

Charlie's body was blocking the way.

Rose uttered a small involuntary cry and dropped to her knees by his side. He had fallen on his back and his bloodied and broken face stared unseeingly up at her. Charlie Collins was only barely recognisable. His nose and cheek bones had been smashed to pieces. There was more than one concave recession in his head and his hair was matted with blood and tangled with small pieces of bone. His torso had not escaped attention either. One arm was lying at an impossible angle, indicating that it was fractured. Charlie had patently been the victim of a quite frenzied attack. Rose hardly needed to check his pulse to know that he was dead, but she did so anyway.

For just a few seconds she felt as if she were frozen with shock. Then her training took over. She operated on auto-pilot. Swiftly she used her police radio to contact her own HQ to report the crime and to call an ambulance, although she was quite sure that would prove to be a waste of time.

Leaning against the wall in the hallway for support, she felt as if her legs could barely hold her upright. But she was functioning – just about. And a frightening thought crossed her mind. Charlie's wrist had felt warm when she had checked his pulse. It was possible that his murderer was still in the apartment. The doors to the bedroom and the kitchen were both closed. She craned her neck to peer through the open door into the living-room. She could see no sign of life and neither could she hear any sound.

She resisted the urge to search the flat properly. At worst she could end up being attacked herself and at best she would get a rollicking from the SOCOs for messing up evidence. Instead she left the apartment, this time being careful to touch as little as possible, and waited outside in the corridor.

Back-up was with her within minutes, but even the short wait on her own had been long enough for the grim reality of what she had walked into to overwhelm her. Rose never failed to be affected by the sight of a dead body, but this was only the second time she had ever actually discovered one. Also, it was the first time she had ever seen a dead person that she had known – and, she had long ago admitted to herself, in spite of everything and her better judgement, a person she had grown fond of.

She felt much worse even than she usually did. Poor Charlie looked so awful too – she had never seen a corpse that had been so badly beaten. She knew she was shaking and was only just in control of the waves of nausea which were spasmodically rising from the depths of her belly, causing her to gag.

It was a relief to hand the situation over. Peter Mellor turned up within minutes and, even in her shock and distress, it gave Rose some fleeting sense of satisfaction to note that the expression of stiff distaste he had always worn when dealing with the living Charlie Collins had departed swiftly with the young man's death.

In fact Mellor looked uncharacteristically flustered, and Rose guessed that he was wondering if he would have dealt with Charlie Collins's call for help any differently had he not disapproved so strongly of the boy. Rose, still a professional in spite of feeling so wretched, did not see how he could have done but neither did she think it would do her sergeant any harm at all to experience self-doubt for once.

Detective Chief Superintendent Titmuss also made an extremely rare scene-of-the-crime appearance, but then this one undoubtedly held far-reaching repercussions. Doctor Carmen Brown, Rose was told, was on her way.

And if anyone noticed the state the DCI was in, they were tactful enough not to mention it.

Rose suddenly couldn't take any more of it. She did not want for the moment to have to look again at

Charlie Collins's battered face and broken body and she knew exactly what she did want to do. In fact she couldn't wait.

'I'll be back,' she announced briefly, and left a rather surprised-looking Peter Mellor to it.

Outside she battled for control. Charlie Collins's ruined face was right inside her head. The handsome young man lying obscene in death in his own home. The nausea was suddenly too much for her to fight. She reached her car but could go no further. Holding on to the door handle for support she started to retch and had little choice except to bend over and be heartily sick on the tarmac, splashing the wheels of the vehicle. It was a relief to vomit, and she actually felt very slightly better as she straightened up – only vaguely aware of a typical Spike Island yuppie type hurrying past and resolutely pretending that he hadn't noticed what she was doing.

Rose couldn't care less. The enormity of the murder of Charlie Collins and all that it might signify was everything to her. She mopped herself up as best she could, using the box of paper tissues she always kept in her car. Then she started the engine, manoeuvred her way carefully out of the car park, aware that her hands were still trembling slightly, and set off purposefully in the direction of the A38 heading north towards Gloucester.

She was going to Eastwood Park to see Constance Lange.

Rose saw Constance glance at her in some surprise when she was taken to her cell by a prison officer. She supposed she looked a mess. She certainly felt it.

Constance, by comparison, contrived to look

elegant even in these surroundings. She was wearing an unmistakeably cashmere sweater over a straight calf-length skirt. As a prisoner on remand she was allowed to wear her own clothes and, although she continued to refuse to see any of her family, she had accepted readily enough the clothing which her elder daughter Charlotte, resigned to not being a welcome visitor, had in any case sent to the prison.

It occurred to Rose obscurely that Constance Lange would probably contrive still to look elegant even if she had to wear prison garb. And there remained an eerie calm about her. Rose wondered if the news she was about to break might shake that at last.

Technically Rose should not have been there at all now that Constance was awaiting trial. Certainly she could not demand to see Constance, and it had been a relief when she arrived at Eastwood Park and the accused woman had agreed to see her.

Quite bluntly she told Constance about Charlie's death and the manner of it. There was just the briefest flicker of response. Rose could only imagine what was going on inside the other woman's head. Constance, sitting on her bunk bed, merely stared silently at her family photograph, almost as if nothing that she had heard had anything remotely to do with her.

'Constance, Charlie's death is just too much of a coincidence not to be connected to the other murders,' Rose told her. 'He was trying to get hold of me when he died. I reckon he had something important to tell me. And I can't help thinking that Charlie might well have been killed by the same person who murdered the others. Now that could not be you.'

Constance still didn't speak. Rose sighed and continued.

'I believe you know the truth. Please will you tell me? We must put a stop to these killings.'

Constance raised her eyes at last from the photograph and met Rose's earnest gaze. She looked haunted. It occurred to Rose that she might genuinely have been driven quite out of her mind. Constance had been interviewed by police psychiatrists already, of course, who had pronounced her quite sane. Suddenly Rose was no longer sure of that.

She carefully studied the woman sitting before her on her little bunk bed. Certainly nothing much seemed to register properly with Constance Lange any more.

Rose had one more go. She reached out and touched the other woman's arm. Constance flinched but did not draw away.

'You're not a killer, Constance, are you?' asked Rose, and the tone of her voice made it apparent the question was quite rhetorical. 'You shouldn't be here, should you?'

At last the imprisoned woman's composure seemed to drop. And eventually she spoke. She sounded faraway, as if she had shut her mind off from all reality.

'I can't be let out,' she said. 'I mustn't be set free, it's all my fault.'

Rose had to give up in the end. Constance appeared to have nothing more to say. She answered all subsequent questions with silence. Rose watched her as she picked up the family photograph and hugged it close to her. It was extraordinary to think how perfect Constance Lange's life had once been and that this one picture was all she had left of it.

Rose sighed. Beaten for the moment. But starkly aware that the mystery was even greater now.

The next morning Rose had the first of a series of new rows with Chief Superintendent Titmuss.

'You had absolutely no right to visit Constance Lange,' he told her angrily. 'You could jeopardise the entire case stepping out of line like that.'

'I interviewed Mrs Lange informally concerning a new crime, the murder of Charlie Collins, sir, and she willingly agreed to see me,' responded Rose with a confidence she did not feel. Privately she suspected that Titmuss was quite right and that she had indeed contravened PACE, the Police and Criminal Evidence Act. 'And with this fresh development, I also believe it would now be quite wrong to allow her prosecution for the three earlier murders to go ahead, sir,' she continued, taking a deep breath.

Titmuss exploded. 'You're getting above yourself, Detective Chief Inspector,' he stormed. 'The woman has confessed – and you will just get on with the job you are paid to do. Which is to keep murderers behind bars where they belong.'

Rose tried to speak. He silenced her abruptly with a raised hand.

'There is absolutely nothing to suggest that the murder of Charlie Collins is connected with the other killings,' the chief superintendent continued, sounding more dogged than angry now. 'I've talked to Doctor Brown already as I'm sure you have. The method used was completely different for a start – not that you need to be a pathologist to see that!'

Rose continued to stand her ground.

'We should at least double-check everything with forensic,' she said. 'Maybe there'll be some DNA this time. Something we can compare with the earlier murders.'

The Superintendent's voice began to rise dangerously again. His impatience with her was quite obvious.

'There was no struggle, Rose. This Charlie Collins died from the first blow more than likely, according to Dr Brown. As for forensic – if they come up with anything to indicate a connection with the previous murders, then we'll think again. Meanwhile Constance Lange stays exactly where she is. There is no question of dropping charges.

'And forensic aren't going to come up with anything, by the way. They can't - because we already have the person responsible for the first three killings banged up.'

Rose could not hide her frustration. 'That's catch-22, sir,' she said.

Her boss looked really irritated now. 'Rose, I'm beginning to think you're getting too close to this case,' he said.

Oh, Jesus, not that old chestnut, thought Rose. She forced herself to sound reasonable when she replied, keeping her voice level only with a great effort.

'Not at all, sir.'

Her senior officer merely grunted. 'I want you to lead the Charlie Collins case because of how well you knew the lad and all the knowledge that you already have which may be relevant to his murder. That should give you a head start - as long as you didn't know him too bloody well, of course, Rosie.'

Chief Superintendent Titmuss smiled when he made the last remark but it didn't in any way lessen the message. And Rose could not believe he didn't know how much she hated being called Rosie, either. She stared at him in amazement.

'I'm sorry, sir?' she said, turning the sentence into a question.

'You heard me, Detective Chief Inspector. Do you think I go around this nick with a blindfold on and cotton wool in my ears?' He shook his bespectacled head almost sorrowfully. And when he spoke again his voice was just a little gentler. 'Look Rose, if I believed any of that crap you wouldn't be on the case at all, OK? But you have to understand that this is a new murder enquiry, you said so yourself, and that's the way I want it treated. You've got a budget to deal with as well as everything else and I don't want you going over it because you're desperate for some obscure reason of your own to get a case dropped against a woman everyone else reckons is as guilty as hell. Do I make myself clear?'

'Yes, sir.'

He made himself clear all right. Rose knew only too well that the Avon and Somerset, like all British police forces, had to pay forensic laboratories for work carried out on their instructions. Superintendent Titmuss certainly didn't want a big bill brought about by one of his staff attempting to mess up what seemed to be a rather nicely solved case.

Boiling over with resentment, Rose quickly left her superior's office. Sometimes, if you want to hang on to your job, you have to keep your mouth shut. Even Rose Piper understood that. Nonetheless she didn't trust herself to stay in the room with the bloody man a second longer than she absolutely had to.

Rose was having an extremely bad day. There was something else happening to add to her misery. The trial of Terry Sharpe and Paolo Constantino, accused of living off immoral earnings, was due to be wound up that afternoon – and it looked very much as if Sharpe was going to get away with it.

In spite of the murder of Charlie Collins, Rose had heard enough of the evidence to be thoroughly sickened. And watching Sharpe himself in the witness box had been a truly nauseating experience.

No, he'd had no idea that Avon Escorts was being run as anything other than a reputable escort agency, that had always been his intention as one of the founders of the business. He had been very disappointed to learn anything other.

And as for the Crescent Hotel, well, didn't all hotel rooms get used for various kinds of illicit purposes occasionally? He really didn't know what the manager was supposed to do about it, let alone a director like him who was not even involved in the day-to-day running of the place.

Surely he couldn't be held responsible for the activities of the young men and women to whom he let his assorted properties in absolute good faith. He was only their landlord, after all.

Sharpe was good in the witness box. He always had been, Rose had been warned, and he was a plausible character too, when he wanted to be. The case against him fell like a pack of cards. And as she watched, Rose realised she had probably been too preoccupied with other things and had not given the

345

weaknesses of the prosecution nearly enough attention. She felt she carried considerable blame for what she had realised – well before the jury was asked to deliver its verdict – was fast becoming the inevitable result.

Annoyingly Paolo, who as the front man for Avon Escorts actually sent boys and girls out to clients, did not have the same ability to wriggle. His lawyer protested valiantly that Paolo was not responsible for what his escorts got up to beyond the call of duty – that was their affair. But the jury obviously did not believe a word of it. They were however quite taken in by the obsequious Terry Sharpe.

Paolo was found guilty and went down for twelve months. Sharpe was cleared.

Outside the court, and already smarting, Rose had to endure a confrontation with the former policeman. Sharpe looked smugger than ever.

'Next time pick on someone your own size, Rosie darlin',' he leered at her.

Rose supposed that slapping his face would not help her position in life a great deal, but wondered fleetingly if it wouldn't be worth it.

Summoning the last vestiges of her self-control she walked away in what she hoped was dignified silence – and without resorting to violence. But for the first time in her working life Rose began to wonder if her future really lay with the police force.

She made a conscious decision that she was going to do everything in her power to unearth the truth about the rent boy murders, even if it meant bending the rules, and whoever she might upset – including Superintendent Titmuss.

The opportunity came more quickly than she

might reasonably have expected.

The next day Constance Lange tried to kill herself by making a noose from her bedclothes which she suspended from the light fitting in her cell. Predictably the make-shift arrangement collapsed when Constance kicked away the chair on which she had precariously balanced. Her weight at once pulled the light fitting from the ceiling and she fell heavily on to the tiled floor. She was bruised and shaken but remained very much alive – her greatest injury a badly sprained ankle.

And she had asked to see DCI Rose Piper.

Rose arrived at Eastwood Park late that afternoon accompanied by Peter Mellor. She thought that for the first time during their association Constance looked really vulnerable – as if the act were finally over and she knew it. She had a nasty black bruise on her forehead and her eyes were dark with pain. Mental pain. Rose was pretty sure she would barely be aware of any physical pain.

The inspector again felt a bond with the woman lying helplessly before her. This time she sensed it more strongly than ever before, and there was something in the way Constance was looking at her that made her suspect, also for the first time, that Constance might feel it too.

'I'm glad you're still with us, Constance,' she said quietly.

The other woman smiled wanly. 'I'm not, I'm really not,' she said.

'Why did you want to see me?'

Constance looked uncertain. 'I'm not sure,' she murmured eventually. 'There are things I could tell you, but I don't know . . .'

Rose was aware of Sergeant Mellor by her side shifting impatiently in his seat.

'We should be formally re-interviewing the bloody woman in a tape room with her brief there, or not at all, boss,' he had said quite correctly during the drive from Bristol.

'I don't know if she's ready for that,' said Rose. 'She just asked for a visit, that's all . . .'

Peter Mellor had mumbled something about how murderers should be given not what they asked for but what was good for the rest of society and, in his opinion, life would be a lot less troublesome if Constance Lange had succeeded in killing herself.

Mellor continued to believe in Constance's guilt as much as did everyone else, Rose knew, and he didn't really want to waste any more time on the deaths of a few male hookers, either. She had overheard him grumbling to that effect on the telephone only the previous day – having quickly recovered, it seemed, from any lurking guilt he might have felt following the murder of Charlie Collins. Mellor was fed up with his boss's obsession with raking over old ground, and he had made that quite clear to Rose, who had only brought him with her to Eastwood because she so wanted to have him on her side. The man could be infuriating, but she had great respect for him – and liking too, although at that moment she did not like him as much as she usually did. She had rather hoped that this bedside visit might throw up something to shake her sergeant's certainty – but to begin with, at any rate, it did not seem that that was going to happen.

'Don't you think it would help if you told me the truth?' prompted Rose.

Constance had resignation written all over her.

'It won't help me,' she murmured.

'It might help someone, though, mightn't it, Constance? I still think you're the only person who can stop all this. Isn't that why you asked to see me?'

Constance half-nodded.

Rose, ignoring Mellor's fidgeting, was gently persistent. Eventually Constance eased her bruised body in her bed. She looked as if she had just made a decision.

'Can I talk to you alone?' she asked the Chief Inspector.

Rose agreed at once, aware instantly of the further disapproval of her sergeant whose body language was more articulate than that of anyone else she knew, she thought. Nonetheless she waved him out of the room.

Afterwards back in Bristol she went straight to see Superintendent Titmuss.

'Constance Lange wishes to be formally re-interviewed, sir,' she told him.

'Rose, what did I tell you?' Titmuss demanded of her angrily.

'Prisoner's rights, sir,' responded Rose. 'I'm just the messenger. Oh, and it won't cost anything sir, will it?'

Rose knew she was pushing her luck but she was past caring. At least he wasn't likely to be calling her Rosie for a bit.

Superintendent Titmuss left her in little doubt that he would deal with her insubordination later, but agreed for arrangements to be made for a new interview. He had no choice and Rose had known that.

All she cared about was that Constance Lange's

new statement be put on the record as soon as possible. Rose only had the merest outline of it so far. But she had learned enough to realise that the story Constance had to tell would shock even the most case-hardened copper.

Alone in her hospital bed, Constance pondered her decision. It was the hardest she had made so far – much harder than deciding to confess to murder. She was about to completely break her own heart, to cause herself even greater agony than she had so far suffered, she knew that. But once again she was quite sure of herself. Again she was certain she was doing the right thing.

Nothing could end her own torment, not even death. All that was left in the world for her was pain – but she could not let this go on. She was actually glad that her pathetic attempt at suicide had failed. Perhaps she had not really wanted it to succeed. She had one final task, and it was a vital one. She could not be responsible for any more deaths, and she was becoming increasingly certain that there would be more. She hadn't believed that at first – but now she believed it absolutely.

# Twenty-Two

Constance Lange looked pale and ill.

'There was a game I liked to play . . .' she began.

Her voice was very quiet. Rose had to remind her that the interview was being recorded.

'I'm going to have to ask you to speak up, Constance,' she prompted her gently.

Constance carried on as if she had not been interrupted, but she raised her voice very slightly.

'When I confessed I thought that would be the end of it all. I thought it would be over. I never dreamed there would be another murder. Charlie should not have died.'

Constance stopped abruptly then, as if she did not know what to say next. Her solicitor was with her in the interview room at Eastwood Park. He seemed content to let his client have her say, at least at this stage.

Rose prompted her again. 'Just start at the beginning,' she instructed.

Constance sighed. 'There were a lot of games I liked to play. And there was one in particular. My favourite, I suppose. It was all about having sex with a stranger. Usually Charlie was involved. I specially liked Charlie, you see . . .'

She paused, staring straight ahead of her at the blank wall, perhaps remembering Charlie, perhaps seeing something the others with her there in the room could not. This time Rose let her take her own time. She did not think Constance would stop now, not when she had got this far.

'First I would have sex with Charlie,' Constance continued almost expressionlessly. 'Then he would leave and I would remain lying on the bed, face down, the room lit only by candles. A second man – the stranger – would then enter the room. I was always . . .' She paused again. '. . . ready. The stranger would start to have intercourse with me at once. I would not even turn to look at him. He would not see my face, nor me his – that was the most important rule of the game. There would be no foreplay – and no dialogue until after it was over.'

Constance's eyes were quite blank, her words curiously precise. She could have been reciting from the telephone directory.

'I used to find it very exciting,' she said, and with a dry humourless laugh added, 'So did they, I think.'

Rose could imagine it so vividly. Constance lying there naked in the dimly lit room, with the blonde hair of her wig spread out, her face buried in the pillow. Wanting sex at its most basic. Excited. Expectant. The young men eager, aroused by something different, relishing the game nearly as much as she did.

Constance's voice came to the Detective Chief Inspector from the distance when she continued to talk, jerking Rose out of her brief reverie, back to the present. Back to the truth behind it all at last.

'The last time, the very last time I hired Charlie, it went horribly wrong. In fact . . . in fact, it turned into an unbelievable nightmare. The stranger Charlie brought with him was good, very good, perhaps particularly good. I can still remember the pleasure, in spite of everything, and that makes it even more awful. I can remember, too, being aware of just how much he had seemed to be enjoying himself, even though he was being paid for it. When it was over and we were both fighting to get our breath, he spoke for the first time. I shall never forget what he said.' She paused. '"God, that was amazing."'

Constance gripped the edge of the table in front of her. She almost spat out the last four words.

'"God, that was amazing,"' she repeated, her voice cracking this time. 'And I shall never quite be able to explain how I felt when I heard his voice. I was over-come by horror, no, more than that, by fear. I had to turn around and look at him. But I didn't want to, because I knew what I was going to see. Knew, with-out doubt. My . . . the . . .'

Constance seemed to be physically gritting her teeth now. Rose noticed that she had closed her eyes, seeing it all again, reliving it, the policewoman realised.

'The young man was grinning broadly, pleased with himself, I suppose. But when he saw my face, when he recognised me, the grin seemed to freeze.'

Constance looked around the room, almost as if she were seeing Rose, DS Mellor and her own solici-tor for the first time, and was challenging them to react.

'I had just had sex with my son,' she said.

She sounded quite detached, as if she were telling a story about somebody else.

She stopped then, for a while. The enormity of what she had revealed was just too much.

'Could I have some coffee?' she asked, and she attacked it thirstily, drinking deeply from the steaming liquid as if it contained some magic elixir which might revive her.

Rose did not push her, instead waiting for Constance to speak in her own time. Sergeant Mellor cleared his throat and the silence was such in the room that the rasping sound he made seemed very loud and was somehow almost as shocking as the story Constance Lange was telling.

Rose glanced at him. Mellor was virtually open-mouthed with amazement. She noticed that he even appeared to have forgotten to arrange his stunned features into the expression of disdain which seemed to have become customary for him when confronted with behaviour of which he disapproved.

Then Constance began to speak again, and instantly nobody in the interview room had eyes or ears for anyone but her. She was a naturally articulate woman and now, telling the whole truth at last, her words came fluently, almost pouring from her.

'I tried to explain to William. But how could I explain? What could I say? That I liked sex, raunchy illicit sex? That I had never wanted to hurt anybody – least of all him? That it had all been a ghastly accident, a shocking coincidence, that we should both forget about it and carry on being a normal caring mother and son? That it didn't matter? There was nothing I could say.

'William screamed. It was a terrible haunting anguished cry. He rushed into the bathroom and turned on the shower full pelt. Then he dressed, pulling on his clothes. He was weeping and shaking uncontrollably, yet I could not comfort him because

354

he would not let me near him. He would not look at me. He would not talk to me. And afterwards he totally refused to discuss the incident with me. He would never talk about it. Not when the murders started. Not when Freddie died. He just shut me and all of it out.'

Constance picked up her coffee mug and drained it.

'Could I have some more?' she asked.

Rose gestured to Mellor who left the room briefly and returned with a refill. Only then did the interview continue. Rose stared at Constance.

'And you, how did you feel?'

Constance shook her head. 'I didn't matter, did I? I already didn't matter.'

'But how did you feel, Constance?' Rose persisted.

The other woman seemed to crumple in her chair.

'I suppose I went into total shock. I stayed at the Crescent much later than I usually did. I know that I began to cry, and once I had started I couldn't stop. I was physically sick, then and later. It took me several hours to completely stop crying, to clean myself up, to regain any kind of self-control. I made up a story about breaking down on the motorway and having flat batteries in my mobile phone. It didn't sound very believable to me, but I think Freddie believed it then. He trusted me, you see.'

Her voice cracked again. Her eyes were full of tears now, Rose noticed. The policewoman forced herself to be businesslike, to be professional.

'What was William's motivation for getting involved with Avon Escorts?' Rose asked. 'Presumably he didn't need the money.'

'No,' agreed Constance. 'His father provided him

with more than enough. I could only assume that he found that kind of sex exciting – as I did, that he too had liked the idea of games.'

She held her head in her hands. 'Well, I know he liked the game I enjoyed most, don't I? And that, liking it, me knowing that, made the whole sordid thing worse for him.'

'Do you want to talk about the murders, Constance?' asked Peter Mellor.

Rose guessed that Mellor couldn't cope with much more discussion about sex games and was not surprised by the interruption which, in any case, came at an opportune moment.

'Why don't you tell us the truth about them, too, Constance?' she joined in.

Constance nodded and half shook herself as if returning reluctantly to reality. Her eyes lost the faraway look and at last she focused on the Detective Chief Inspector who was continuing to stare at her earnestly.

'You've known, you've always known, haven't you?' she murmured. 'I don't know how, but you have.'

Rose shrugged. 'I was never totally convinced that your confession was a true one,' she agreed. 'I'm not sure about knowing exactly. I'd like to hear the truth from you.'

Constance nodded again. 'I'm no murderer. I'm innocent of that at least. I've never killed anybody. I didn't kill Marty, or Colin, or Wayne. I had no reason to, either. There was no blackmail, and I wasn't angry with them. Only ever with myself.

'My confession was entirely false. You were right, Chief Inspector Piper. I was trying, you see, to cover up . . .' she hesitated again, '. . . to cover up what I believed to be the truth.'

'Come on, Constance, what is the truth?'

Constance began to tremble. The last vestiges of elegant sophistication crumbled.

'You know, you know . . .' she said.

'You have to tell us, Constance, on the record you have to tell us.' Rose leaned forward across the table, willing the other woman to go on, to put an end to it once and for all.

It was as if a dam had broken. The tears began to pour down Constance Lange's face. She made several attempts to speak again before eventually seeming to force the words out, looking almost as if it caused her physical pain to do so.

'My son did it. William killed them. All of them. I'm sure of it.'

Constance's sobbing became louder and more uncontrolled. Rose was aware of Peter Mellor tensing beside her. Even Constance's solicitor could not stop himself giving a small involuntary gasp.

She didn't lose eye contact with Constance, she didn't dare.

'How do you know that, Constance?'

Rose saw Constance battle to gain control of herself again. Eventually the sobbing eased and she managed to speak once more.

'As soon as Marty Morris was murdered and the Mrs Pattinson connection was all over the papers I began to wonder about William. I didn't know right away, I didn't want to believe it anyway. But I did wonder. You see William has always been impulsive, a bit wild, but so aware of his family, so proud of his ancestry, so proud of his mother.'

357

She seemed to choke on the last words. Her lips were trembling quite violently. She took several deep breaths before she continued.

'He'd always been stubborn too, liked to get his own way, a bit spoilt really. I was the one who spoiled him most, actually. I could believe him becoming obsessed with revenge. He wanted revenge against me and he wanted revenge against the boys I went with. I'd been degraded, you see, that was how he saw it, I know.

'Then when the other two were killed I was quite sure, really. It all pointed to William if you knew what I knew. And the second time, the night that Colin Parker was murdered – well, I'd gone to see William, to confront him, to see if there was any hope for us – still kidding myself about all that had happened, I suppose. I couldn't find him. He wasn't at his digs. Nobody knew where he was.

'I waited and waited. Freddie was away at an NFU conference. I waited until the early hours. I saw William return, eventually, but I didn't approach him. He got out of his car carrying a bundle which he put in the boot. He looked so strange. There was something about him – I didn't dare go near him. Then when I got home . . . well, the next day I learned about Colin Parker's murder.' She broke down again.

'Go on, don't stop now,' prompted Rose quite softly.

Curiously, Constance managed a weak smile through her tears.

'The most frightening thing of all was that William always seemed so cool, so calm and in control,' she continued as instructed. 'Yet, who else would have pretended to be Mrs Pattinson? Who else would have hand-picked the victims? It had to be William. I kept telling myself it couldn't be him, I kept kidding myself, I suppose, and yet I also kept looking for clues.'

There was another period of silence, this time broken by Peter Mellor.

'And did you find any clues?' he asked, ever the complete policeman, already thinking ahead to the need for hard evidence. 'Did you find any proof to back up your suspicion?'

Constance nodded, but did not answer directly.

'I looked in William's room at the farm,' Constance continued, once more in a voice so small that Rose had to gently prompt her to speak up again. 'I looked in the office, in the milking shed, in the stables. I didn't know what I was looking for and I certainly didn't want to find anything. But I kept looking.

'On the Sunday after Wayne Thompson died William left his car keys on the kitchen table, and I searched his car. I looked in the boot and couldn't see anything at first. Then I found it all stowed away in the spare wheel compartment.'

She stopped then as if she meant it. As if she had no more to say. But Rose knew that she had not finished, that she could not let her finish.

'Found what?' Rose demanded.

Constance sucked in a huge breath of air. She closed her eyes as if trying to shut out the dreadful reality now surrounding her. But when she spoke again this time her voice was quite clear and somehow completely resigned.

'His Timberland boots, a raincoat, a pair of gloves and . . . and . . . a butcher's knife. All wrapped up in a bundle. There were some stains, blood stains, I thought, on the coat and the boots. One thing I told you was true – I drove out to the cliffs by Porlock and threw them all in the sea. I still wanted to protect him, you see.'

'Did he know, did he know you'd taken the stuff?' Mellor again, always checking, always one to look for the facts of a case.

Constance shrugged. 'I suppose he must have done. He didn't say, but then he never said anything. It was like he was leading two lives, and he'd shut one out of his head.'

She gave a little strangled laugh, even more humourless than before. 'I should know about that, shouldn't I?'

'Did you ever feel in danger from him?' Rose asked. 'You were living with someone you believed to be a murderer, someone who gave every indication that he hated you? Weren't you frightened?'

Constance looked surprised, as if she'd never thought of that. 'No,' she said. 'I never even considered that he might hurt me physically.'

'And the confession, that was just to protect William?'

'I wanted to save him. Yes. I thought I could do it. And I wanted to put a stop to it all. I thought I would do that by confessing. I suppose I thought, in a way, it would satisfy him. It would give him his revenge on me. I didn't even mind very much. It was all my fault after all. My life was over, anyway. And I thought there would be no more deaths, I really did . . .'

'But Paolo was so certain that it was Mrs Pattinson who phoned on the night of the first murder,' Peter Mellor interrupted, sounding puzzled, and it was typical of the man's attention to detail that he had so quickly picked up on that, Rose thought. 'Paolo was quite sure he had recognised Mrs Pattinson's voice.'

'Yes,' responded Constance quietly. 'That was one of the things that first made me think of William. You see, he was always a good mimic. And he had my voice off perfectly. He could even fool his father on the telephone.'

# Twenty-Three

Less than an hour later Rose Piper and her team drove to Chalmpton Peverill to arrest William Lange on suspicion of murder.

The weather was cold for the time of year but thankfully dry and clear. It was only the day before that Constance had asked for Rose to visit her at Eastwood. A lot had happened since then. The formal interview with Constance had taken most of that morning. It was just after three o'clock in the afternoon when the police team knocked on the front door of Chalmpton Village Farm. Nobody responded. The door proved to be unlocked so they walked straight in.

William was sitting at his desk in the farm office, and Rose was the first person to enter the ordinary little room with its state-of-the-art computer system, a big copying machine and two telephones, one a fax, piles of paper everywhere, and an NFU calendar on the wall.

She found herself looking straight down the barrels of a twelve-bore shotgun. William Lange was cradling the gun in his arms as if it were something very precious.

'I've been expecting you, Detective Chief Inspector,' he remarked in a quite casual fashion.

Rose did not think he was actually aiming the twelve-bore at her, but that was the way it seemed.

She gestured to the rest of the team to keep back and was vaguely aware of Peter Mellor using his radio to call in an armed unit, which she knew perfectly well he had thought she should summon in the first place.

Rose struggled to keep her voice calm – no easy task when you are confronted by a man with a gun whom you believe to have already murdered four people.

'OK William, why don't you put the gun down, and let's talk, shall we? I really think we need to talk.'

William's response was merely to grasp the gun in a more businesslike fashion. He shifted his right hand slightly so that the forefinger now rested lightly on the trigger. Rose was not a firearms' specialist but she had undergone basic weapons training. She could certainly see that the twelve-bore was cocked and ready to fire, and she could also see from the way William handled the shotgun that, as you would expect from a farmer, he knew what he was doing.

She swallowed hard.

'Don't make things worse for yourself, William,' she said. And as she spoke the thought rather absurdly occurred to her that she sounded like a supporting player in a bad B-movie.

'I think that would be hard to do, don't you, Chief Inspector?' replied the young man.

Rose had never met with a situation like this before. In spite of how it might sometimes seem to the public, it remains mercifully rare for a British police officer to have to face up to a loaded gun. Her heart was racing. Mellor had been dead right, of course. She should have predicted this and used an armed unit to check out the farm and make the first approach. She had been in too much of a hurry as usual. Now she might have put more lives at risk – not just her own, but those of her team too.

Suddenly, with a quick movement of his wrist, William swung the shotgun around, resting the butt on the floor between his feet so that the business end of the weapon now pointed towards his own head. His finger was still on the trigger. He bent slightly forwards and put his mouth over the end of the barrel.

Rose stood very still.

'Why don't you give me the gun, William?' she repeated. Lame she thought, but she didn't know what else to say.

There followed a few seconds of complete inaction. Nobody moved. The room was absolutely silent. William Lange's eyes were closed. Rose was sure she could see his trigger finger twitching. The whole thing lasted only a few seconds – it felt like several days.

Then as suddenly as he had taken the gun into his mouth in the first place, William straightened up in his chair and tossed the shotgun to the ground.

Rose dived for it, yelling 'Get him!' over her shoulder to Peter Mellor and a uniformed constable who were already rushing at the young farmer. William did not attempt to move, allowing them each to grasp an arm and slam him, chair and all, on to the ground.

Rose was breathing fast. She noticed at once that the safety switch was back on the shotgun. Extraordinary, he must have done that automatically once he decided not to use the gun, she supposed. She stood up and looked at the man who was almost certainly a serial killer.

His eyes were quite blank. The handsome face expressionless.

'I don't have the courage to hurt myself,' he remarked almost conversationally as Mellor and the constable dragged him to his feet, pulled his arms behind his back and secured them there with hand-cuffs. And it was the only regret of any kind that he was to show.

'It's all right,' he said, addressing Sergeant Mellor now. 'I know it's all over.'

Rose had just about got control of her breathing now and even managed to speak without her voice having too much of a tremor in it.

'William Lange, I am arresting you on suspicion of murder,' she began the formal caution. She wanted him back at Staple Hill fast, before he had time to start thinking.

There were several police vehicles outside the farm by the time they brought William out and, as they bundled him into the back seat of one of them, Rose saw Charlotte Lange running almost flat-out down the village street towards them. She sent a woman detective constable to intercept her and to explain as best she could what was happening. Rose had considerable sympathy for Charlotte, who seemed to her to be a straightforward and kindly young woman, but she didn't have the time to deal with her right now.

She also became aware of a small crowd of villagers gathered already outside the farm. The bush tele-graph works fast here, she thought. Marcia Spry, the biggest busybody of the lot, Rose had previously worked out, was craning her neck, mouth hanging open, jaw slack with excitement, determined to miss nothing. Obscurely Rose reflected fleetingly both on how she could certainly never cope with the claustrophobia of small town or village life again, however idyllic it might seem on the surface, and on what fun Marcia would be sure to have with the latest news.

William was ready to tell the truth at last even before he was informed that his mother had told the whole story of both their dealings with Avon Escorts and the sordid sex scene which had led to the killings.

Handsome, educated, eminently middle-class, still managing to retain much of his natural self-assurance, he seemed completely out of place sitting in the interview room in his white paper suit. Rose didn't know quite what a serial killer was supposed to look like, but there was no doubt that the casual observer would deem William Lange to be the un-likeliest of murderers.

It was only when he spoke, his voice cold and matter-of-fact, that you got an idea of the monster shock and bitterness had turned Lange into. It appeared that he did indeed see himself as some kind of avenger.

'I suppose I knew I wasn't going to get away with it any more after I killed Charlie Collins,' he said. 'Actually I knew that before I killed him, I knew that as soon as I made the decision to kill him. But by that time I was past caring. Charlie had seen me in the pub, and I was pretty sure that he had recognised me as Sandy – a carefree young student making a few bob selling himself for sex. What a laugh!'

William had the same dry humourless laugh as his mother.

'I drove straight to Bristol to kill Charlie. Another death didn't seem to make much difference by that stage. I didn't have the knife any more, though. I'd kept it and the rest of my gear in the boot of my car. I knew it had all gone missing, of course. I guessed that Mother had dumped the stuff. I suppose I hoped she had. I didn't know for certain. I just shut it out of my mind.

'I needed a new weapon, so I grabbed a lump hammer from the workshop. I told myself that this one last murder would cover my tracks once and for all and, after that, life would return to normal. But I was only pretending. I didn't really believe that. It was much more than that. As soon as I saw Charlie Collins I wanted him dead.'

William's voice faltered for the first time. 'He'd been with my mother more than any of them. It was Charlie who set me up with her.'

The eyes were harder than ever. Rose began to find it quite easy, after all, to imagine him thrusting a knife into another man's back, battering another human being to death.

'And the earlier killings? Your mother thinks you were motivated by revenge. Was that really it?'

William nodded. 'Yes. Revenge on all of them, all the little bastards. And revenge on Mrs Pattinson.' He spat the words out. 'It was Mrs Pattinson I hated more than anyone. I was glad when she confessed. I was actually happy.'

'You could have killed her too?'

William looked surprised. 'If I'd ever seen her again I would have done, gladly.'

'But Mrs Pattinson was your mother, William, you saw her virtually every day of your life.'

For a moment William seemed bewildered. The façade of self-assurance deserted him. He seemed dazed. The granite eyes clouded over. Then, abruptly, the mists cleared.

'I have no mother,' he said.

The eyes were bright again, and there was ice in them.

Sergeant Mellor, who could never quite stop his disgust at it all from showing, had had enough once more.

'Why did you get mixed up with an outfit like Avon Escorts in the first place? You had every advantage in life, looks, money, education, everything,' he snapped. 'Why did you need it?'

William shrugged. 'For kicks, I guess. Bravado, too. Loads of the lads did it. Sex with some grateful old tart who'd let you do anything and you got paid for it . . .' His voice overflowed with bitterness.

'Your mother did it for kicks too, is that so different?' interrupted Rose Piper.

'I told you before, I have no mother. Not any more.'

'Your mother was prepared to go to jail for crimes which you committed – terrible violent crimes,' said Rose. She could not believe that this young man could still manage to sound self-righteous.

'She's a whore.' William spoke through clenched teeth, hatred pouring from him.

'No, that was you,' said Rose Piper.

But William Lange just looked at her as if she was mad.

They found his bloodstained clothes, the lump hammer and the rubber kitchen gloves he had used for the killing of Charlie Collins buried beneath the compost heap at the bottom of the kitchen garden, just as he

368

had told them they would.

William Lange had left no DNA evidence on Charlie Collins or in his apartment. That killing like all the others he had been responsible for had been brutally efficient.

'I've studied human as well as animal biology. I'm a farmer, I know how to kill efficiently. They even gave elementary butchery training as part of the course at agricultural college, so that we'd understand the entire food producing process,' he explained cursorily, and with the now familiar dry humourless laugh.

'And I know how to avoid leaving forensic evidence, I know about DNA, doesn't everybody?' he asked, adding, almost in echo of his mother, 'I read a lot of detective books.'

However, the evidence William Lange had carried away on his person was another matter. And once the police had been led to Lange and found the clothing and weapons he had used for the final murder, the situation changed dramatically. While he was being battered to death, Charlie Collins had deposited much of his life's blood on William Lange's person, drenching the young farmer. There was sure to be plenty of forensic and DNA evidence on his clothing. It would be elementary to prove that the lump hammer William had buried was the murder weapon. And a search of William Lange's car, particularly the boot area where he had kept the butcher's knife he had used for the previous murders, revealed a number of tiny older blood-spots which Rose and her team were confident would prove to have come from either Marty Morris, Colin Parker, Wayne Thompson, or all three.

William made a full and detailed statement.

Everything added up. And his mother's statement further incriminated him.

'That's it then,' said DS Mellor at the end of what he thought had been a pretty good couple of days' work. 'Getting the case against Constance Lange dismissed should just be a formality now, eh boss?'

Rose Piper merely nodded curtly, as if her mind were somewhere else.

'She'll be a free woman again,' Peter Mellor continued. 'Can't say I envy her though . . .'

Sergeant Mellor was feeling pleased with life for the first time in a long while. He was owed a few days' leave which he planned to take now, and he looked forward to being able to be with his family. It was always a good moment when you knew a case was solved, and Mellor was truly glad to see the back of this one. He hadn't enjoyed it. He didn't like to witness human beings degrade themselves, and this case had left a nasty taste in his mouth. Also, some of it had been a little too close to home for his liking. Still, it was over now. Done and dusted.

'Fancy a celebration pint, boss?' he asked cheerily.

Rose frowned, as if he had irritated her. She stood up, turned away from him and headed for the door of the incident room.

'What the hell is there to celebrate, Mellor?' she demanded brusquely over her shoulder.

The sergeant regarded her retreating back curiously. 'A result, guv, we got a result, didn't we?' he murmured almost to himself.

The only response he got was the slam of the door. Sergeant Mellor shook his head sorrowfully. The memory of the moment when his DCI had nearly got half their heads blown off was still vivid. He wondered sometimes why he still maintained respect for her, let alone affection. He did – although he was unsure how long he was prepared to go on working for her.

'What a difficult bloody woman!' he said, rather louder this time.

Constance Lange sat alone in her cell, overcome by the enormity of it all. For hours on end she stared at the blank wall facing her bunk bed. She knew that it was now just a matter of time before the case against her would be dismissed. But that made little difference to her either way.

Sometimes her mind drifted back to the good days. There had been so many of them. It was spring, the time of rebirth, every country-person's favourite season. Through the small square of her barred window she could see a patch of bright blue sky.

Sometimes she imagined herself walking over the hills around Chalmpton Peverill, Josh running before her, the warm welcoming kitchen of the farmhouse and her equally warm and welcoming family awaiting her. Sometimes she could not really believe it was all over, or that it had ended in the way that it had.

She was glad only that she had finally told the truth. She knew she had done the right thing. And she trusted Rose Piper. Rose had been right. Constance felt the bond too.

Back in Chalmpton Peverill in the front bedroom of Honeysuckle Cottage, Charlotte and Michael sat up in bed that night and talked into the early hours. By the morning they had made a decision.

Charlotte, fighting to remain sane only because of her family, sat a now eternally tearful Helen down at the kitchen table. Josh lay how he always did nowadays – facing the door, his eyes sad, his tail flat on the floor – waiting patiently for his mistress to return.

Charlotte regarded him sorrowfully. Even though it seemed likely that her mother would be released, the dog's devotion would never be rewarded by his mistress coming home. She knew that with absolute certainty. She sat down opposite her sister and began to talk.

'We are our entire family now, Helen darling, you, me, Michael, and little Alex. I don't know how we're going to survive, but we will, somehow. And this is what Michael and I want to do . . .'

Two days later, early in the morning, Constance Lange was found dead in her cell at Eastwood Park. She had taken a massive overdose of Valium. An enquiry was immediately launched to discover how she had got hold of the drug, but the investigating officer was not confident of a conclusive result. You rarely could be in prisons. They remain the ultimate mystery.

That same day Charlotte, Michael, Helen and Alex drove to Heathrow airport to catch a flight to New Zealand. There was Lange family land over there, currently farmed by a distant cousin, and a home, at least of sorts, awaited them. Josh was going too. Both Charlotte and Helen considered the dog to be all that was left of their mother as they liked to remember her. Before the nightmare had begun.

372

Honeysuckle Cottage was on the market already. Charlotte had said she could not wait until the future of the farm was sorted out. It was all over. She just wanted a new life now.

'Shall we stay a little longer?' Michael asked Charlotte when the prison called to break the news of her mother's death.

'No,' said Charlotte bluntly.

'It's all right to still love her, you know,' said Michael, who was becoming more and more of a rock as every day passed.

Charlotte looked at him almost in surprise. 'I know that,' she said. 'I'll never stop loving her. She'll always be my mother.'

'So don't you at least want to go to her funeral?'

'No,' said Charlotte. 'She wouldn't have wanted that. Not now. I don't even want to know where she will be buried.'

'Are you sure?'

Charlotte nodded her head quite vigorously. 'Absolutely sure. My mother died for us all the day we learned that she was Mrs Pattinson . . .'

Later that day, on the night of Constance's death, Rose Piper was feeling particularly low. And when her husband called her just after she arrived back at the section house prepared for an uncomfortable night alone, she was almost pathetically pleased to hear his voice. For a moment all she could remember was how much she had once loved him and how much she needed comfort.

'I heard on the news,' Simon said. 'I knew you'd be upset.'

For the first time in so long she agreed to meet him.

She accepted almost eagerly his invitation to go round to the bungalow for supper.

'I'll be there in an hour, and this time I won't be late,' she said.

He laughed then, and she remembered, too, how much she had always liked his laugh.

When she saw him and he smiled, she also remembered the effect that smile was inclined to have on her.

Supper went well. Simon had cooked his special pasta dish, and remarked very lightly that he hoped it would be better received than the last time. It was. Much better received. The pasta was good and washed down with plenty of excellent red wine. What happened afterwards was good too, and somehow inevitable.

It was also passionate. Fine earthy sex. How Rose had missed it. They hardly slept all night. It was as if they had both been waiting for this moment, saving themselves for the time when they would be together again. Certainly, in spite of the fantasies that had so disturbed her, she had not had sex with anyone else since their parting. And during their long and inventive session of lovemaking Rose found that the demons which had been plaguing her for months seemed to disappear as if by magic.

Sex with Simon was real, warm and caring. It always had been. It meant something. Almost as soon as they began to make love she felt that this was where she belonged, in his arms, and she started to come to terms with herself again, to accept herself for what she was and to stop punishing herself so much for being what she could only be.

Suddenly with devastating clarity she knew that she

wanted Simon back. And she told him so. In fact she screamed the words at him at the moment of orgasm, so that he held her tighter and tighter and pushed himself into her more deeply, more desperately, than ever before.

The morning after was warm and companionable. Rose and Simon might have been apart for some months, but they had been together for nine years before that. It was only natural that they should start, over breakfast, to talk about their lives, to talk about their work. After all, they always had done.

'Do you really think the Constance Lange case is over now?' Simon asked her.

'Yes, thank God, I really do,' she responded.

'I'm glad,' he said. 'You did get obsessed, you know.'

'I do know.' She reached out and touched his hand. The hand that had given her so much pleasure.

'My boss told me the same thing. I suspect you're both right. I'll try to do better in future.'

He grinned, that heart-melting grin which had quite literally turned her legs to jelly all those years ago.

'In that case, Mrs Piper, everything will no doubt be just fine,' he said.

He poured her more coffee, leaning forward and kissing her lightly as he did so.

'I have to say though, I'm just amazed that the woman could get hold of all that Valium the way she did inside a prison. I mean, don't they have any bloody security or what?'

He was munching toast. It was just a casual remark. Rose knew that. Nonetheless, she couldn't meet his eye. She turned away and did not answer.

'What's the matter, Rose?'

He stared at her. The bloody man could always read her mind, and she was pretty sure he wasn't going to like what he saw there.

She was right.

He thumped the table with the clenched fist of his right hand and cried out as if he had suddenly experienced a flash of intuition. Then he became deathly calm.

'I don't believe it, it was you, you gave her the pills,' he said quietly.

Again she did not reply. She didn't need to. She saw the dark cloud of anger descend over him. His mood changes were always so dramatic, had been for years now. That, of course, had been part of their problem, part of what had led to their parting, part of all the torment and tension which she had over the last twelve hours or so banished from her mind.

He was no longer the gentle funny man she had spent the night with. No longer the passionate lover or the affectionate husband. He was absolutely furious. Plain hopping mad.

'You played God with that woman!' he screamed at her.

He changed so fast, and that was not all of it. There was no tenderness in him now, none at all.

She realised there was little point in trying to explain, but she so wanted him to understand. He never did understand, of course, but after their wonderful night together she could not just give up without trying.

'Constance Lange wanted to die, she could not live with what she felt she had been responsible for,' Rose began, the tiredness of her sleepless night suddenly overwhelming her as much as the hopelessness of trying to talk to Simon when he switched into this kind of mood.

'She did a deal with me. She would tell the truth, in as much as she knew it, if I would help her die with dignity. She had never wanted to hurt anyone, you know. She was no murderer, for Christ's sake, just a woman who liked sex too much and let it get the better of her. She did not want to leave prison. Her only wish was to be able to end it all before having to face the outside world again. She at least deserved that. I kept to the bargain, that was all.'

'You're a monster.' Simon was still screaming at her. 'You made a deal to kill in order to get a result. How far will you go, Rose, for your damned career? Is there any limit?'

'It wasn't like that,' replied Rose in a very small voice. The louder Simon shouted, the more quietly she had started to speak.

'It fucking well is for me, darling,' he shouted at her. 'I can't live with you, you may as well know that now. How could I live with you? How could anyone live with you?'

She cringed, cowering away from him, completely beaten, and yet a part of her was so terribly angry that anyone could do this to her, reduce her to this. He hadn't even finished. His anger rose to a near hysterical crescendo.

'Forget last night – that was just a stupid mistake, a one-off fuck! OK? I still want a divorce – fast!'

Rose walked out into the cool morning air. The sun was rising above the city below. Her husband's words tore at the core of her. '. . . a stupid mistake, a one-off fuck . . .'

377

Her heart ached. Her head ached. Yet her body still glowed from last night. That already seemed like a lie, or at the very least a bad joke.

She passed a newspaper stand then, its billboards advertising reports of Constance Lange's suicide. The slogans were predictably lurid.

Rose shuddered involuntarily. She was clutching an envelope in her hand. It contained her resignation from the police force, written the previous day before she had spent the night with Simon, before they had made such wonderful love, before everything had been destroyed when they had yet again quarrelled so viciously.

She hurried past the news-stand, then paused by the post box. Yesterday she had been so sure of herself. Now she did not know whether she wanted to post her letter or not. Her face was wet with tears. And she had no idea whether she was crying for herself, or for Simon, or for Constance Lange – or even for Charlie.

In the hold of a 747 jet somewhere over the Indian Ocean a black Labrador cowered trembling inside a wooden crate.

Josh was not afraid, not of flying, which he did not understand, nor of being in the crate, which was actually quite cosy. He had been treated kindly. He had been fed and watered. He assumed that he would continue to be treated well. After all, he had never been mistreated. But although Josh had no conception of travelling across half the world, he somehow knew that he was leaving everything he loved behind. For months the dog had existed merely in the hope that his mistress would return. Every day he had watched and waited for her. Now he finally understood that he would never see her again.

Josh did not know that his mistress was dead – only that she had gone away for ever. He threw back his fine black head with the sad brown eyes and howled.

*Also by Hiliary Bonner*

# A FANCY TO KILL FOR

Richard Corrington is rich, handsome and a household name, but is he sane?

A journalist is murdered only a few miles away from Richard's west country home. Richard's wife suspects he has been having an affair with the journalist and forensics implicate him in the killing.

But Inspector Todd Mallett believes that the murder is part of something much more sinister and complex. There have been other deaths; the senseless killing of a young woman on a glorious Cornish beach, another in a grim London subway . . .

And somewhere on the Exmoor hills a killer waits. Stalking his prey. Ready to strike again.

**Read on for an extract from *A Fancy to Kill For*.**

In a little terraced house in Fulham Joyce Carter, Fleet Street's latest killer interviewer, was stretched on the sofa in front of her gas fuelled imitation coal fire carefully sifting through copies of several years of newspaper and magazine stories on Richard Corrington.

Britain's most successful television actor was about to become her latest interview subject, or victim might be more accurate. In showbusiness circles it was known as being 'Cartered'. Yet she still got the interviews. Sometimes she wondered why, but she knew really. In the first place she worked for the *Dispatch*, the last of the great establishment broadsheet newspapers. And people approached by the *Dispatch*, particularly actors, were inclined to roll over belly up – so flattered were they to feature in such an illustrious paper. Most of them had apparently failed to notice the not so subtle changes in the *Dispatch* over the years.

Secondly, people in the public eye, particularly actors and other showbusiness personalities, were inclined to be incorrigibly vain. They almost all believed that they would be the one about whom Joyce Carter would eulogise. The one she would find irresistibly funny, charming, clever etc. etc.

The thought always made Joyce giggle. Didn't they understand that she was paid not to like them? Would it never occur to them that she earned probably the top non-executive salary in the Street of Shame specifically to execute hatchet jobs which varied only in their degree of viciousness?

Obviously not, she thought to herself for the umpteenth time. And be thankful Joycie, she said out loud.

The doorbell rang, and she consulted her watch. Early tonight. Well, the randy little devil would just have to wait while she finished reading the cuts.

Preparation was the trick of her trade. The interview was scheduled for Saturday, tomorrow she had another job, and for once she was trying to get ahead of the game. Work still ranked ahead of sex. Just. Although since young Jacky Starr had come into her life it was touch and go. Joyce liked sex. She liked it a lot. And at the moment it was about as good as it had ever been . . .

Not all that reluctantly she put down the file of cuttings and went to open the front door. Jacky was twenty-two years old and twenty years her junior. He worked as a stage hand at the National Theatre. He was crude, vulgar, scruffy, smug, streetwise and full of himself. He also had the most perfect body she had ever had the luck to experience. And he couldn't get enough of her.

'I've got a present for you,' he said, as she opened the door. He grasped her wrist and pulled her hand to his crutch. She could feel the bulge there.

His eyes were very dark. She could smell his sweat and there were small beads of it trickling down his forehead. He looked as if he had been running.

'I started to think about it on the tube,' he muttered. 'I ran all the way from the station . . .'

He pulled her tight against him. He was wearing Levi 501s. The buttoned fly stretched tight over his erection and pushed hard and rough into her through the softness of her own clothing. It felt wonderful. He began to simulate intercourse with her through their clothes. Then he walked her backwards, still pressed tightly against him, until they reached the staircase. He pushed her down so that she was sitting on the third stair and knelt across her. His hands began their exploration of her. Everything that he did always seemed so natural and so effortless – even in this awkward location there was a smooth fluency to his lovemaking and his body promised as always to cause her no discomfort whatsoever, merely to give unimaginable pleasure.

There was only one thing to do. She reached for him and unbuttoned his flies.

It seemed that any further study of Richard Corrington would be postponed until the next day after all.

In the stinking darkness of the Waterloo underpass Ruth Macintosh wished she had dodged the traffic at ground level – anything would be better than this. She thought she heard a footstep close behind her and turned to see a rat scurrying into the gloom. She shuddered.

Cardboard city surrounded her. Ruth had known it was there, of course, but had forgotten all about it. She still could not associate this dismal half-underground shanty town with London – the great city she had loved from the moment she landed there from the Scottish highlands almost twenty-five years earlier, just eighteen years old and bursting with enthusiasm and excitement.

Until recently London had only rarely disappointed her. She still believed that the sentiments of Samuel Johnson were every bit as appropriate at the end of the twentieth century as they had been when he first expressed them during the eighteenth century. 'When a man is tired of London he is tired of life. For there is in London all that life can afford.'

She had spent her youth, during the heady seventies, working and living in the heart of London.

Marriage and the birth of two sons interrupted a high-flying secretarial career, but now that her boys were aged thirteen and fourteen, and no longer needed her constant attention, she had returned to a part-time job as a legal secretary in an office in Lincoln's Inn just off Fleet Street.

That night she had stayed much later than usual grappling with a tricky problem. The senior partner had insisted on buying her a glass of champagne in El Vinos, still used by the lawyers but long abandoned by the journalists – now isolated in their ghettos in Wapping and even further east at Canary Wharf – who used to frequent it. She had been fairly easily persuaded as she still thoroughly enjoyed the camaraderie of drinking after work with colleagues. And she retained a lurking affection for the now fairly soulless El Vinos, where she had met her journalist husband, another Scot, all those years ago.

It was well gone eight, a March evening and already dark, when she stepped outside on to the pavement to hail a taxi to Waterloo Station. She rooted around in her handbag for her wallet, which also contained a cash purse. After a minute or two she was forced to accept that it wasn't there. Damn. Had she left it in El Vinos? She remembered with some amusement the days when the place had not allowed women to buy drinks. It now invited women to spend as freely as they wished, but that night her boss had insisted on doing the buying. She had not taken her money out once.

She recalled that as she left the bar a man wearing a dark raincoat had brushed rather heavily against her. And the zip was broken on her bag – she had been meaning to replace it for days. Had the man perhaps taken her wallet? She sighed. More than likely not, she was eternally careless, the wallet was probably sitting on her office desk – and the office was locked now.

She checked the little buttoned pocket at the front of the bag where she always kept her rail tickets. Fortunately her return ticket to Kingston was at least safely where it should be.

She debated what to do next. Her drinking companions had already departed and the doors of El Vinos, which closed at eight, were being locked behind her. There was a public telephone kiosk at the street corner and she wondered if she should call home – but what for? She could hardly ask her husband to drive all the way into central London to pick her up. There was nothing for it, she would have to leg it to Waterloo and serve her right for being so stupid.

Resolved, she strode purposefully along Fleet Street, past the Aldwych, and then turned smartly left on to Waterloo Bridge across the Thames. Once or twice she glanced briefly backwards. She had occasionally over the last week or two had the feeling that someone was following her. There was hardly a soul on the bridge at this hour, and certainly nobody anywhere near her. Of course there wasn't. She was being silly. She began to look around her at the river views she always appreciated – St Paul's over her left shoulder, parliament and Big Ben over her right shoulder, and the South Bank straight ahead; all conspiring as ever to look so much more glamorous and exciting after dark. Actually, now that she had settled into her stride, it was not too bad at all. The evening was mild enough and as she made her way over the bridge she could see the illuminated city reflected diamond bright in the mirror surface of a still river – picture postcard London. She had, in fact, half begun to enjoy the walk until she found herself in the underpass.

Rows of ill-clad feet emerged from cardboard boxes. The stench of urine was overpowering. Somebody was using a broken luggage trolley as a bed. There were signs of considerable initiative – post office sacks apparently made excellent bedding. None the less, the scene was a shocking one to her, and the extreme youth of some of the faces she glimpsed through the increasing gloom added to her sense of sudden despair. Stark, desperate faces. She could not believe that the capital city had come to this. Always in life there are going to be drop-outs, people who cannot cope, men and women at the bottom of the pile – even when she first came to London there were those who slept rough, but nothing like this. The scale of homelessness in the modern capital was suddenly very clear to her and it was utterly shocking. In America, she knew, they had a name for them – the Underclass.

Ruth was quite warm from her brisk walk. None the less she found herself shivering.

As she turned right in the open central section of the underpass below the big roundabout at the south side of Waterloo Bridge her attention was attracted to a young man leaning against the wall at the entrance to the alleyway. His sleeve was rolled up above the elbow of his left arm and he was in the process of injecting something into his body. As he did so his head jerked back against the wall.

Ruth kept walking quickly but found her gaze drawn to the youth. She must have led a sheltered life, she thought to herself. She had never seen anyone shooting up before. She knew all the terminology, didn't everybody? She read newspapers – her husband filled the house with them every day – watched television. But seeing with your own eyes is something else. With a little of the righteous revolutionary fervour of her youth Ruth found herself cursing the Tory government and resolving she would be more active in her local Labour party to get the bastards out at the next election. Surely something could be done, and destroying the last vestiges of Thatcherism had to be a start.

The young drug addict disappeared into the distant gloom as Ruth swung further left into the tunnel leading towards the station. She was surrounded by smelly murkiness. Something moved behind an upturned iron bedstead obscurely tipped on end against the side of the tunnel. Ruth looked across, unable to see properly. The lights were on, but not all of them were working, and some parts of the tunnel seemed quite dark. Then close behind her she heard a sound. She turned quickly, swinging on her heels, alarmed. But as she did so, peering intently through the gloom, her fearful expression faded. Her lips parted in a tentative smile.

Ten seconds later Ruth Macintosh was dead.

# THE CRUELTY OF MORNING

A twenty-five-year-old murder

A missing girl

And fatal attraction in a small seaside town . . .

On a sunny Sunday in 1970, in the Devon resort of Pelham Bay, teenager Jennifer Stone discovers the corpse of a woman in the sparkling summer sea. It is an event that is to shape her destiny and that of Mark Piddle, the young reporter called to the scene, for the next twenty-five years, until the intense tragedy is resolved and a long-buried mystery comes to light.

*The Cruelty of Morning* is a tale of dangerous obsessions, small-town secrets and a destructive, mesmerising love affair.

# ROAD RAGE

## Ruth Rendell

A by-pass is planned in Kingsmarkham that will destroy its peace and natural habitat for ever. Dora Wexford joins the protest, but the Chief Inspector must be more circumspect: trouble is expected.

As the protestors begin to make their presence felt, a young woman's badly decomposed body is unearthed. Burden believes he knows the murderer's identity but Wexford is not convinced. Furthermore, having just become a grandfather, he is struggling to put aside his familial responsibilities and emotions in order to do his job.

The case progresses, the protest escalates. And alarmingly, a number of people begin to disappear, including Dora Wexford . . .

'*Road Rage* has everything a Rendell addict treasures'
*Sunday Telegraph*

# THE RELUCTANT INVESTIGATOR

Frank Lean

*Shortlisted for the CWA Gold Dagger Award*

The discovery had been accidental. A property repairer, working on the Fallowfield house where Billy Fox rents an attic flat, decides to cut a few corners. While looking for a way to get out onto the rafters he finds the key to a locked cupboard – a cupboard where Billy keeps his collection of severed heads.

Billy Fox has disposed of fourteen women, and, with this gruesome evidence, it's an open-and-shut case. But when David Cunane, private investigator, is employed to research Billy's 'true life' story, he quickly concludes that nothing is as it seems.

Somebody is adding to Billy's total. Is it a new killer? Or have the Manchester police got the wrong man?

'In the running for the best crime book of the year . . . shines with a rare brilliance' *Yorkshire Post*

# ALSO AVAILABLE IN PAPERBACK